LOBSTERS ON THE AGENDA

by

NAOMI MITCHISON

with an introduction by
ISOBEL MURRAY

To the memory of
JACK REID OF KINLOCHLEVEN,
one time aluminium worker, trade unionist, County
Councillor of Argyll and Convenor of the Housing
Committee, who will be remembered in the West, with
admiration even from his enemies and with love and
bitter sorrow from his friends, of whom I was one.

British Cataloguing in Publication Data
A catalogue record for this book is available from the British Library

The Publishers acknowledge subsidy from the Scottish Arts Council
towards the publication of this volume

ISBN 1 899863 20 6

First published 1952
First paperback edition by House of Lochar 1997

Printed in Great Britain by SRP Ltd, Exeter
for House of Lochar, Isle of Colonsay, Argyll PA61 7YR

INTRODUCTION

NAOMI MITCHISON has always been best known for her historical novels, and the meticulous research she puts into them. But it is a very different story, when it comes to her fine contemporary novel, *Lobsters on the Agenda*, published in 1952. Here there is little need for research; she writes compellingly of Scottish local government, with unique experience. It is a novel of the Scottish Highlands. In her *Saltire Self-Portrait* she describes the stages of her 'approach to Scotland': a holiday at Craignish Castle, two summers on the western edge of North Uist, and 'Then came Carradale'. Carradale, she writes, 'strengthened my growing feeling of being a Scot and a Haldane at that'. The Mitchisons bought the Big House and the remains of the Carradale Estate in 1937 as a holiday home, but in 1939 it became the permanent family home. For many years she worked the land, found in poor condition, with less than up-to-the-minute equipment:

> I had to start the hard way. We got a light horse who worked in a pair with one of the garrons. During the next years I harrowed and mowed with them. I worked summer and winter, spreading dung with a dung fork, sowing oats or grass seed equally by hand, crawling on the ground singling turnips, snedding in the December cold. Because of all this and because it is now decent farm land, I feel it is mine in a way that is far from unreal legalities.

This thorough acquaintance with the realities (and pests) of Highland life is fed into the very first chapter of *Lobsters*, where the protagonist Kate is milking the cows on her helper's day off:

> She passed her arm across her face again; she was sweating now, between the two cows. 'Stand over, Rosebud!' she said and dug her elbow into her. But Rosebud didn't budge. The midges were on her damp wrists now and getting up under her skirt. She sat back for a moment, stretching her fingers; Wallflower's teats were getting like leather.

The experience of many years is fed into *Lobsters*. Mitchison was always political: one of the first things she did at Carradale was to start a Labour Party branch. She also believed in Scottish Self-Government, and as early as 1942 she contributed a chapter called 'Rural Reconstruction' to a book called *The New Scotland*, published by the

London Scots Self-Government Committee. Her paper was for the Highlands generally, but she made a point of basing it on Carradale, which was in many ways typical, and which she knew well by this time. She called for new houses, sanitation, electricity, and improved transport – she described the loss of a ferry, the remoteness of the railway to Carradale's needs, the scarcity of buses outside the summer visitor season, the bad roads and the need for a new safe harbour. She underlined the need for social services, water supplies, better schools, and even rubbish collection. Virtually all these topics feature to some extent at least in *Lobsters*. And already she had a special mission, to recreate community life in the Highlands, and a tool, the provision of village halls. She was ultimately concerned with creating a new, positive sense of community, which might prevent young people haemorrhaging away to the lights of the towns or the hope of employment.

> Life is dull… There is little alternative employment for young men; those who are ambitious, especially if they are mechanically minded, go to the towns, where they are not necessarily happy. Whereas dullness drives young people away, it drives some of the older ones to drink. And it drives the girls and women into endless, pointless, gossip and quarrelling, family feuds, church feuds, feuds between the 'Rural' and the Gaelic Choir, one vast series of mole-hills talked into mountains! The discontent produced by dullness is very painful.

The practical antidote to dullness Mitchison proposes in 1942 is the village hall, and characteristically she uses Carradale as exemplar:

> It is always a help if there is a central place where people can meet and where some at least of the activities can be carried out… Our own hall is constantly let for dances, concerts, sales of work and so on; it pays its way largely because it is a very attractive building to start with… Here we have games in afternoons or evenings or both; carpet bowls, table tennis, billiards, etc., and sometimes badminton. We have a cinema once a week… Our reading room must probably wait until after the war. We have a Games Committee, Social Committee, Cinema Committee, and so on; so far, a few people do most of the work – but the younger generation will grow up to an increasing sense of responsibility.

This is the idea that is troubling the fictional little town of Port Sonas throughout *Lobsters*. The forward-looking want a hall, and are prepared to work for it. The various churches tend to disapprove or oppose. Individuals may oppose in their own financial interest. But by the time

Mitchison wrote *Lobsters* she had acquired a great deal more direct political experience of the problems of the Highlands, and of local government. In 1945 she was elected to the Argyll County Council for Kintyre East, and began to understand what she calls 'the game of you vote for my harbour and I'll vote for your road'. She was very upset to lose the seat again in 1948, when the fishermen, a substantial part of her support, did not get back in time to vote. To some extent her feeling of local ingratitude precipitated the writing of *Lobsters*, although it remains as she describes it, 'a Highland comedy', and the exasperated criticisms of Highland characters and ways, comic or serious, are usually to an extent affectionate. She was re-elected subsequently, and served on the County Council until 1965.

Not only that. She had refused nomination to the Westminster Parliament in 1945, throwing herself instead into her husband Dick's successful campaign, but in 1947 she was invited to join the Highland Panel as one of two people chosen from Argyll. She and John MacNaughton were both socialists:

> Mostly we talked about local problems, the needs of the Highlands and how to stop further depopulation, what more could be done in the way of employment. Suddenly we turned to one another and I'm still not sure which of us spoke to the other first, saying we mustn't think only of Argyll, but of the whole of the Highlands and even perhaps of all Scotland.

The Highland Panel, she writes, was 'the thing which mattered most and which brought me closest to Scotland.' She served for twenty years, although some of her initial excitement was tempered by the experience, and she had to forge her own weapons:

> We would be able to do so much for the people of the Highlands. But now I find myself wondering whether the Panel was designed by the politicians of the time – the Labour Government – ably assisted by their civil servants, as something which would look as though it was a big step towards helping the Highlands. However as it would have no power and no money it would be totally unable to achieve anything and so would not in the end bother anybody. But yet this was not exactly what happened. The Panel did manage to get a few things done which would probably not have been done otherwise, and also to drag quite a lot into the light so that sooner or later whatever it was simply had to be dealt with. I was one of the people who dragged things into the light and nagged people right up to the topmost layers of St Andrew's House. In fact I managed to cry over Woodburn who was then in charge and this always made

him so uncomfortable… But I never went into tears twice on the same floor of the Scottish Office. That would have been counter-productive.

So the author of this 'Highland comedy' was a working farmer, was expert in fishing and knowledgeable about forestry, had served on years' worth of committees and coped with years of bureaucracy – and was also a very fine writer. This is *not* a tract or a political mission-statement: it is a very strongly imagined, intricate, many charactered novel.

She writes of a week in the life of an imaginary Highland village. Her heroine Kate is a qualified doctor, a widow in her late forties with a daughter away at school. She is tied to Port Sonas by her responsibility for her elderly father and his collection of china teapots. Several other women in the novel are similarly tied, or deprived of education, and patriarchal society and its gender assumptions are frequently highlighted in the novel. Kate has more education and personal resources than most, and has become a District Councillor. As the Contents page indicates, this week is crowded with meetings, formal and informal. As we discover, the official and unofficial agendas are not always identical.

A first reaction to the novel might be that nothing happens; as perhaps we might expect of a week in a small Highland village. But closer atten-tion reveals that the agenda is a very long one, and some of the items are resolved or disposed of, while others are not: this adds to the feeling of authenticity. The various items of 'business' illustrate important themes, such as community, factionalism between old and young, between the Established Church, the Wee Frees and the Free Presbyterians; sexism in churches and in society generally, the nature of democracy with its penitential committee meetings and the preservation of the Highland way of life – to name but a few.

But they come up through small, everyday matters, on the whole. Here are some of the items that get resolved in the course of the supposed week. First, the title points to lobsters. In the end, it is arguable that they are the least important item on the agenda. We hear early that Matta, a lobster fisherman, had collected a big box of lobsters under water, moored well out, but when he went back for them they had been stolen. A great deal of distress is caused by this, especially as circumstances dictate that 'it must ha' been one of oursel's'. This generates painful general suspicion. In particular, a respectable, church-going, 'good' man, takes it into his head to suspect the harbourmaster, whom he only half-consciously dislikes, and he becomes obsessed with proving the man's guilt, to the point where he doesn't want to know the culprit if it isn't this man. But in the end the culprit owns up to Kate: it had been a young men's prank only, and Matta is reimbursed by anonymous letter.

Second, the nice but slightly timid young schoolmaster David is living in mortal fear of strict and holy Miss Gillies, his 'assistant', who bullies both him and the children unmercifully. By the end Miss Gillies comes down inexplicably with measles (possibly the result of magic by one of the Village Hall committee), and it is reported in the final chapter that she has said 'she was going to ask for a transfer to a more godly place'.

What else is on the agenda?

Two apparently minor matters relate to the primary school picnic, but neither turns out to be trivial in its outcome. First, a mother who knows her children have measles nonetheless allows them to go to the picnic, something dangerous both to the infected children and to all the others who may be infected. By the end, we are still waiting for the epidemic: no one but Miss Gillies has gone down so far, and she has gone down inexplicably early – but sadly by then one of the invalid Mackinnons has died and another is in danger.

The other picnic story concerns one of the boarded out children from Glasgow. Here one trivial incident comes to stand for a lot of exploitation. Little Greta from Glasgow had been given a new dress by a friendly village woman, but 'here Snash and his wife had taken it away and given it to Peigi' (their own daughter). David, the weakish schoolmaster, blames himself for not confronting Snash, and when he eventually does, it is no good – well coached, wee Greta says she *gave* the dress to Peigi, and David is routed. The general exploitation of the Glasgow children is really serious:

'The poor wee souls made to howk the tatties all along the glen and the worse the crofts the more bairns they take!'

'The inspectors should see to it.'

'Ach, they know fine when the inspectors are coming, and everything couthy and trim and the wee books for the inspector to sign, and oh, the great love they have for the bairns!'

Most people are afraid to snitch on Snash, because everyone has something to hide from the various inspectors, and they fear Snash's retaliation. In due course Kate writes to Glasgow about the boarded-out children.

But more significant is the case of old Norman MacDonald, an Elder in the Wee Frees. Norman is an interesting example of Mitchison's ability to present people who almost simultaneously exhibit attractive and unattractive qualities. At one moment he is very perceptive and very kind to Kate, understanding without being told how trying her father is. A minute later, Kate, Norman and Janet are discussing the sins of Snash:

all agree until Janet asks a question, supported by Kate, and Norman changes:

> 'But you can't just leave it that way!' said Janet, 'what for is the Kirk Session if it's not to deal with the like of Snash?'
>
> 'Yes' said Kate, 'can't the Elders deal with him?'
>
> Norman said nothing for a moment. Then he drew himself up. 'It's not for the women to say what we should do'. He turned from Janet to Kate: 'For neither of the two of you: go you home now and be not presumptuous'.
>
> He was staring at Kate, and now, she thought, he is no more kind nor wise; he is only jealous in case he is proved to have less power than he wants to have.

At a stroke, kindly, wise old Norman becomes sexism incarnate. These qualities war in him again when he wrestles in prayer for a long, long time, while his elderly sister works her hands to the bone, and neither sees any problem about *that*. But his prayer convinces him that he must speak up for the unfortunate Glasgow children – and he does, at whatever risk of Snash's vengeance.

Roddy the Forester has a difficult week. Bureaucrats turn down his promising scheme for a local sawmill. He is fed up and lonely with the dullness of the place, ordered about as he is by his Wee Free landlady, who also drives him to church, since it runs in the family. He is an ardent campaigner for a village hall. He wants to marry a nice girl, but hasn't met one! Instead he gets a letter from the legal representative of a girl called Kenny's Chrissie. Chrissie has apparently had so many men that she probably does not know the father of the child she is expecting, but Roddy is rumoured to have savings. He knows he cannot be the child's father, and seeks Kate's advice. Meanwhile Donnie, an apparently godly young man with a motor bike and a bad reputation among the girls, goes off to Glasgow and gets engaged to a very godly cousin. He stands up in the FP kirk, relieved:

> He thought of his own wickedness, his deceitful heart, and groaned slightly. And this offer that is made to me, thought Donnie, this offer of atonement. Christ's blood offered gratis; deal generously with your soul while the low prices last, it will repay you, oh in eternal life! He would turn from wickedness, he would sell his motor bike, he would cease altogether from carnality. He groaned again as the leaven worked in him like a terrible great godly dose of castor oil.

But whether or not by the same kind of magic that may have given Miss Gillies measles, sprained a preacher's ankle, and made a woman teacher vomit pins, Donnie has a slight accident on the motor bike, before reliable witnesses, with Kenny's Chrissie on the pillion. Roddy is off the hook, but his landlady throws him out anyway, which is all to the good. By the end of the 'week' Roddy is seeing Kate's young friend Janet home – a much better prospect!

If we look at all the subplots like this, the impression that nothing at all happens is overturned. Given too that in the course of the week the Village Hall committee is established, broken by church pressure and self-interested parties, and re-established on a better, more hopeful basis, *and* that the same week includes an important visit from the Highland Panel, including a woman from Carradale called Mrs Mitchison – 'They say she writes books' – we could argue that a sight too much happens for credibility. But all this realism is a kind of qualified realism, and I think here a helpful comparison can be made with George Mackay Brown's much later novel *Greenvoe*. That novel too apparently is built round a single week, but clearly not literally so: maybe it is one particular week when the stranger comes to Greenvoe to take notes, as in *Lobsters on the Agenda* it is the week of the visit of the Highland Panel, but in some sense it is also in both cases every week, giving an impression of the relatively smooth tenor of very many days. A synthesis of time and timelessness seems present in both books, and a strictly literal, linear week is not what is intended.

Further, although so much *is* resolved in *Lobsters*, many things, small or large, are *not* resolved. Ella the school cleaner, for example, has resigned, and all the male local councillors think Kate should be able to find a replacement: but local women find other jobs are more rewarding and congenial, and many people see the new welfare state as a good reason for not working at all: at the end of the novel, a new cleaner still has not been found. And no one has seen to the business of the book box at Kilmolue, kept locked by the teacher 'in case the people of Kilmolue would get reading profane books!' Kate worries throughout the book about Dr Mackillop's inertia, for example in the matter of quarantining measles victims, and inoculation. As only an occasional locum, she cannot do anything, and there's no sign of anyone else even noticing.

All the major works required as long ago as Mitchison's 'Rural Reconstruction' chapter have been raised – and that is all. There is still a hole in the harbour wall. No one has even attempted to solve the question of whether to replace the ferry with a bridge, which would unite a currently divided community, if only because this would not be in the personal interest of a hotel owner who is also a County Councillor. A crazy edict has come at last, allowing work on a new road – to a dying community already almost deserted – but the other roads which desperately need repair get none.

By the end, only a small step has been taken toward the goal of having a village hall. At the start a Committee is set up, by no means whole-heartedly. The publican-cum-local politician, as usual, has his own interests at heart, and the churches on the whole oppose. In the course of the 'week', the committee disintegrates, for these reasons. Mrs Mitchison, the woman from the Highland Panel, encourages Kate and her friends to persevere, and helps them to analyse the situation so far, and in the end there is a new, more promising committee – but any hall is years off still.

So many themes have been treated. Janet is usually bitterly aware of sexism, taken as normal by the men:

> She'd not need to do out the earth closet today, that was one thing. It was her worst job and every other woman would say the same. If once they could get the water in! But none of the men would bother terrible much about that, unless it would be young Hamish MacRae. There were certain things always left to the women.

There is a lot about committees as the necessary but infuriating and inef-fective tools of democracy. There is a lot about religion. It is clear that the narrator is critical of most of the Ministers and church goers. So is the woman from Carradale, the mischievous Mrs Mitchison, who is delighted at reports that Fred MacFie has been practising magic on Free Presbyterians, but Kate is firmly opposed to any credulity about magic, and we have more reasons to trust Kate whom we know than the Mrs Mitchison whom we do not know. Kate is both inside and outside the community, and we have learned to trust her opinions and her maturity. The third person narrator is something else – or some*one* else? The narrator is noncommittal about magic, but usually hostile to religion or amused by its adherents. Here is part of a Free Presbyterian Prayer meeting, mediated through the unimpressed narrator:

> Mr Munro was mainly troubled in the Lord over two things. One was the Roman Catholic Church, forever assailing the realm of Scotland, and the other was the Port Sonas Village Hall. After much wrestling and speaking on the telephone with a brother in the Lord in the town of Halbost, he had come to the conclusion that Village Halls were part of a Papist plot... Horror was on them and all to think that the Hall was a trap laid by the Romish power before their innocent feet. That Thursday night, strong things were spoken there in Port Sonas against Rome, the mother of harlots and the abomi-nation of the whole earth. Well were the godly warned that the time-serving politicians, yea, even their own Member of Parliament, had

been duped by the snarling Pope into defending the Vatican against Communism.

So – *is* it the case that the dice are too loaded against the believers? After all, all three of these voices, the narrator, Kate and Mrs Mitchison are against religious extremism and see it as destructive (in a rather post modern sort of way…). But at least one important character gets a chance to put it another way; the Continuing Free minister Mr Stewart, who serves with Kate on the District Council. The book becomes an examination of the Highland way of life, what sustains or sustained it, and what *might* restore or improve it. *Lobsters* is about a community divided over bridge or ferry, over rival churches, over rival hamlets, and here is Kate's answer:

> Well, the Village Halls might be the thing we need, the kind of magic thing to keep people together, to make them able to stand up against the cities and all they've got there. Some place where people would come together naturally in friendship, for a common purpose.

But Mr Stewart questions the simplicity of the 'neutral' approach:

> 'Now I've a question for you. This Highland way of life, and I think we know it when we see it, both the two of us: it's in the old folk, isn't it?'
>
> She nodded, thinking of Norman and a half dozen more whom she knew…
>
> 'And aren't they all strict church-goers and in your own words getting something out of it?'
>
> 'I think I would agree,' she said.
>
> 'They are not even in the Established Church, most of them. It's scarcely strict enough for the finest… You will find most of your best Highlanders of the old school in the narrowest churches… They have values that are away stronger than the money one. So that they are not tempted by money.'
>
> 'And when the Church goes, that goes. And how can a Church stay alive when it's based on fear and hell-fire?'

Kate's answer has not refuted his point: it only stresses the gulf between them, and the unresolved questions in the book. Like many of the smallest details of the plot, the deepest theme or problem of the book is expressed and teased out, but not resolved. Restoration of a good Highland way of life is a goal further off even than building the hall. But by the end the new committee is united and ready to work, undeterred.

ISOBEL MURRAY

ABOUT THE AUTHOR

NAOMI MITCHISON (née Haldane) was born in Edinburgh in 1897, and brought up in Oxford by parents of distinguished Scottish ancestry. Her father and brother, J.S. Haldane and J.B.S. Haldane ('Jack') were both distinguished scientists. Young Naomi was allowed to go to the Dragon School at Oxford – a boy's school – but removed at puberty, when her mother began the hopeless task of trying to mould her into a proper young lady of her time.

The Great War was the first momentous event in her life, and in 1916 she became engaged and then married to Dick Mitchison, a close friend of her brother Jack. Dick was subsequently wounded in France, and the dauntless young Naomi went out to nurse him there. The war over, she and Dick, a rising barrister, lived in London, and although still very privileged, she began to develop socialist and feminist ideas which never left her. She published *The Conquered*, the first in a famous series of historical fictions, in 1923, to great acclaim. He became a Labour candidate for Parliament.

Naomi and Dick and their five surviving children settled in Scotland, at Carradale in Kintyre, by 1939, and it was here that Naomi spent most of the war. She became a distinguished diarist for Mass Observation. The Second World War caused a hiatus in publishing, and led to the long gestation of the great Scottish novel many consider her best, *The Bull Calves*, an account of her own Haldane ancestors immediately after the Forty-Five. In 1945 Dick was returned to Parliament, while Naomi, having now great experience of farming and fishing, became a County Councillor, and a member of the Highland Panel, and all of this unique experience of Highland local government went into *Lobsters on the Agenda*, published in 1952.

Her career continued to change and prosper, taking an African turn when she became mother of a tribe in Botswana; moving into science fiction as she began to be aware of environmental and genetic engineering problems some twenty years ahead of the general public. She has written a great deal for children, and volumes of short stories, and of autobiography, venturing also into philosophy, politics and poetry. But it is as a fine novelist and story teller, whose extraordinary and prolific career spans some 55 years, that she will surely be remembered and celebrated.

CONTENTS

CHAPTER I

SATURDAY: DISTRICT COUNCILLOR

IF ISA WAS TO see her boy who was working at Lochaber with the aluminium, and they were engaged and all now, so she would be wanting to surely, she would need to get the Friday afternoon bus into Kinlochbannag, through Glenlurg to Halbost and on to Fort William with the late lorry, and even so she would scarcely get there till the small hours. But his mother would know and would be sitting up for her. At least she should be doing just that if Isa had remembered to send a card and if the card had got the post, but the mail van had been on time three days that week, which was a thing no one expected, and so most of the letters were missing the post. Anyway it was no use worrying about Isa: she'd fend for herself. Kate Snow tugged the strings of her milking overall through the slots, tied it behind her, and picked up the pails from the scullery.

It was early yet. The golden azaleas along the path between Tigh na Bheach and the road, were honey smelling and brushing cold with dew. There was a wild din from the birds everywhere. The starlings were nesting in the rhones again. I'll need to take a pole to them, she thought, walking along the short stretch of road down to the byre. The way across the low park was still deep in mud at the gate.

When Isa was away, Kate did the hens and the milking. Sometimes her father helped with the hens, but it always meant a fuss; it was less bother doing them herself. When they first came to Tigh na Bheach they had of course kept bees, but they had stung him several times every summer, and, even during the war when you were extra glad of the honey, it wasn't worth while. The hives were empty now, but in Port Sonas most people just spoke of Kate's place as the Bee House, though the ones up the glen and at Osnish who were mostly Gaelic speaking, stuck to the old name.

She washed Rosebud's teats and drew in the stool. Rosebud

9

was going back now, she would calve in summer. But Wallflower was in full milk. The fifteen acres of the wee property just did nicely for the two cows and follower, and the poultry, and Isa was the great one at getting a bit extra corn from one or other of the farms. Kate's father, Mr MacFarlan, was a retired land agent and it was just grand for him to have a bit of property to fuss over. It was less fun for Kate to have him fussing, but at least it was a change from his collections. And he was tolerably happy.

At least she supposed so. For, if he wasn't, thought Kate, what was the use of my coming back here? After mother died he seemed to be lost, and I was lost myself then, and I thought if once I could come back to Port Sonas, things would be kindly and slow and happy again. No, not happy exactly, but healing. But welcoming. I remember saying that. I wonder what I'd say about it now. The oddest thing is that there are times I'd say the same thing. Not often. One doesn't begin to know a place till one has lived there a good few years. I don't know it, not even with me being District Councillor and all. Not even with this get together about the Village Hall. Or is it just me getting older and taking things harder?

In the old days, when Kate MacFarlan had come to Port Sonas in the vacations—a young medical student she was then —staying with her mother's elder brother, Thomas Revie the curer, the place had seemed gay and friendly as a summer day opening out into sparkle after storm. And she would be practising her Gaelic and going out with the fishing boats and laughing away with everyone, and most of all with her first cousin Andrew, twelve years older than herself and as tough as a rock, who could say things that would leave even a Glasgow medical gaping. There had been walking and swimming and the sun hot on sweet turf under one's hand. It was the memory of all that which had decided her to come back after Harry was killed. She did not want to go into practice again; it had been difficult enough being in partnership with Harry, at any rate after Alice was born. She was so tired. So very tired. She had hoped Port Sonas had forgotten she was a doctor, but soon enough Dr MacKillop was calling on her to do a locum for him. And indeed she had done an odd fortnight in a dozen places round the County; she had begun to read up some of the Journals again. Well, if it hadn't been for that job, she would never have run across the Laird and him with his own trout fly hooked into his eyelid. Ach, Sandy, standing there, on the top of the stone steps with the rod in his hand and the thin streak of blood on his cheek!

Someone bicycled past the door of the byre, whistling loud, one of the Forestry boys coming in to work from the crofts, then a group of three. The bicycles made all the difference; they could stay at home now and go out three or four miles to their work and no bother at all. It was full light now, and the midges dancing in through the open door to the warmth of the byre. Kate rubbed the sleeve of her overall over her face to get the midges off, and hooked the full pail on to the weighing machine and noted the weight with Isa's pencil stub. Two pounds under Rosebud's morning average. Oh well, she's holding back on me, always does. Or did Isa say you had to allow something with the dial showing wrong? I wonder, she thought to herself, if there is such a thing as a Highland weighing machine that shows the weight right.

She turned to Wallflower to wash her. Was Isa remembering not to mix the udder cloths? Probably not. And probably it wouldn't matter. But Wallflower had had a touch of mastitis in her left fore-quarter; she had been all right this lactation, but you never knew, though Isa laughed at the bare idea—dear Isa, forever laughing at things, and mostly she was right! Before Isa took over, Kate had tried all kinds of fancy hens out of books that never somehow laid as they should, and fancy crops too, un-Highland things such as sunflowers, artichokes and lupins. The County Agricultural Adviser from the College was always hopeful and as surprised as herself when they failed. Port Sonas leaned over the fence and watched her working, quite sympa- thetically. It was grand altogether to see her at it so hard, the woman. Then Isa turned up and laughed and there were no more fancy crops, but the hens started laying as though their lives depended on it—as indeed they did—and the milk yield went up and Kate at last had time and energy over to deal with the weeds in the garden and to repaper all the rooms in the Bee House, to read a good deal of serious literature and even to take an oc- casional day on the river with the Laird.

Another boy went by. No, it was one of the girls going down to the Forestry nursery. Kenny's Chrissie, late as usual. And then she could hear the lambs in the high park. She settled herself down on the stool with her head into Wallflower's flank and

11

pulled at the teats, squirting the first milk on to the floor of the byre. She got the pail between her knees and talked to Wallflower who fidgeted at an unaccustomed milker. As usual Kate thought Wallflower was a most inappropriate name, when she always came regularly for the bull. But her father had been Wotan the shorthorn bull that the Laird had bought in just before the war, thinking everyone would make use of him. But it was an unlucky name perhaps, too German; and all five of the farms going in for Ayrshires, though she thought herself, and so did Isa, that the shorthorn cross was better tempered and needed less pampering. And they had a Highlander from the Board at the township, though why the Board wanted to send a Highlander at all——!

She passed her arm across her face again; she was sweating now, between the two cows. "Stand over, Rosebud!" she said and dug her elbow into her. But Rosebud didn't budge. The midges were on her damp wrists now and getting up under her skirt. She sat back for a moment, stretching her fingers; Wallflower's teats were getting like leather. And there was Chuckie standing in the byre door with a kind of halo of midges all round him. He would be on his way over from the village to Balnafearchar to help out while Donnie was in Glasgow. She buried her face in Wallflower's side again and spoke past the wet hiss of the milk, "What's the news, Chuckie?"

Chuckie took off his cap and scratched his head, "Oh well, well" he said "there's not much news, Mistress Snow, no, not much at all. The Dorchus had a good shot last night we were hearing, fifty cran she had."

"Where did she land them?"

"At Mallaig. If once we had our bridge now, and the new road, the boats would be back landing here——"

"Yes, but it's not a District Council thing. It's no good talking to me, it's Mr Thompson you should be at!"

"Och him! There'll be no bridge out o' him while he has the licence at Kinlochbannag, and indeed we all know that well! Will the gentlemen that are coming to the meeting no' help us?"

"Which meeting, Chuckie?"

"Ach, well, they are some o' the head yins from Edinburgh. The Highland Panel it is. Someone would be telling you surely, Mistress Snow?" He took a step nearer. She changed hands on the warm, throbbing teats.

"I expect they told Mr Thompson. How did you hear?"

"Well now, it was the Fishery Officer at Mallaig was speaking to the boats, and Johnnie Beg was speaking to his mother on the telephone."

"The Fishery Officer—is it about the hole in the sea wall?"

"It could be that, but if there was head yins coming, someone should speak about the ferry."

"Well, I'll see. You'll be coming to the meeting tonight, Chuckie?" She was stripping now and the spurt of the milk came unevenly through the talk.

"Me, is it? I'm too old to be bothering my head about Village Halls. We'll just leave it to the young fellows."

"Oh Chuckie! You know fine what it is, they'll not come, they'll leave it to the ones that are used to meetings, and this Hall is to be for everyone, not just the young ones. We must get a real good meeting with everyone in it if we're to get the money out of the Home Department, and there's some that will be against us."

"Aye, aye" said Chuckie noncommittally "there will be that." He half turned to go and scrubbed at the midges on his face. "It was a terrible thing altogether about the lobsters, Mistress Snow."

"What lobsters?" said Kate, tugging at a teat, "No, you must tell me now."

"Well, well" said Chuckie, pleased, "so you hadna heard! Well now, it was Matta and his brother were out all week and they had their box full of lobsters and they were sending them off yesterday, and the box moored well out by Eileann Everoch, and here, when they went to it there weren't half the lobsters, no, not a quarter. And there had been one lobster, oh, a great fellow, four pounds he was, or maybe five. And he was gone too."

"Had they not fastened the box?"

"Ach, it wasna that! The box was fastened good-o. No, if it had been that——"

"Do you mean someone took them?"

"Someone took them that knew where they were. It must ha' been one of oursel's. A terrible nasty thing when a man canna trust his friends."

"Rotten! I'll need to start locking up my own door next." She stood up with the pail, wiping her wet hands on her overall. "Have you any idea who it could be?"

Chuckie lighted his pipe. "Well" he said, "I wouldna like to be casting the blame where it shouldna rightly be. But yon lobsters must ha' gone by lorry or else by boat."

"Or by bus."

"I wouldna say the bus would be taking stolen lobsters. No, no. That is not the way of the bus."

"Perhaps they didn't know."

"Ach, how wouldn't they know! And there is more than one in Port Sonas that knows, I'm telling you, Mistress Snow. Och there was a great striley on and Matta coming back without his lobsters! Well, well, I must be getting on, or they'll be asking themselves at Balnafearchar where at all I am."

"Well, do remember the meeting" said Kate, hooking the pail on to weigh.

"Aye, aye" said Chuckie, going, with a slow look back in case he would be missing anything. But she knew he meant no! Did they or didn't they want a Village Hall? Oh, the devil of a crowd they were! And the Highland Panel meeting, shouldn't the District Councillor have had word? Did St Andrew's House know there was such a thing as District Councils? It had been great altogether for old Chuckie, her not knowing! Herself angry and uneased, she unhooked the chains from the eased cows, who turned slowly and ambled out, each with her own cloud of midges. And it would be worse they'd get as the summer went on. But the clegs were hardly in it yet.

She filled the zinc pail at the tap and swashed water hard over the concrete floor. The pale stain of the spilt milk dribbled away, stuck among straws at the grating; she poked the grating angrily with the prongs of the byre graip. God, what a place, Port Sonas —them and their lobsters now! What a lot there was to be said for the English virtues, honesty, truthfulness, punctuality. And then her facial muscles tightened round eyes and mouth as she thought of Dr Harry Snow. If her husband had been less faithful and less punctual, he would not have been down at the surgery when it was hit—if he had been even five minutes late——

Alice was like her father, even though she had picked up a Port Sonas accent at the village school. Horrid now she was away in the south. Horrid when the holidays ended. Melting away like a lump of fat in the pan, as Isa said last week!

She picked up the two pails; there were midges floating in

them already. Then she remembered she hadn't shut the gate of the low park behind the cows, went down and did it and, coming back, saw small William, the Tirnafeidh ploughman's boy, throwing a stone accurately into the milk. She caught him and gave him one good skelp, having long ago given up as hopeless the attempt to talk reasonably to any of the children. They weren't used to it, and if she told his mother, she would either fly up in a rage to defend him, or else give him a wicked slashing. If only William had thrown nothing worse than a stone into the milk pail!

The sun was well up now, warm in the long drifts of light between the shadows of tree or wall. The early midges had settled. She picked up the two heavy pails and saw Janet MacKinnon coming round past the Drum with a big shopping basket over her arm. As Janet came nearer through the cross dazzle of sun and shadow, Kate saw she had one of her father's sheepdog puppies in the basket. "Where are you taking the wee fellow, Janet?" she said as she came abreast.

"Down to my Auntie's at the harbour. Ach, you know, Katie, the old sweetie shop."

"Now isn't that the queerest thing! I never knew she was any relation to you, Janet."

"Well, that's true enough too. She's my mother's elder brother's widow, and we bairns never liked to be calling her Auntie. But mother just said we must."

"She's a bit of a muddle head."

"Ach, yes, and a blether at that. But she was forever at father for a dog and so we're just giving her this one."

"You're early over, Janet."

"It was such a terrible bonny morning, and I just left one thing by another up at the croft and my dishes not washed even, and came a race over. I'll get my messages at the shop while I'm down."

"You'll be for the meeting, Janet?" Kate asked anxiously.

"This evening? Ach, yes. I'll pick up my bike this time; Lachie's Minnie had it while her own was mending and I'll give them a bit stir at the crofts on my way over. But I'm just not sure how it will go, Katie dear; folks here are funny. Ach, you'll be the first to know that! But there might not be a great number at the meeting, not near what there should be. There'll be plenty that will be speaking of it, but not ettling to be seen going over to the meeting."

"But if they *want* the Hall——?"

"Ach, they're just a set of clowns and you know it! You shouldna distress yourself for the likes of them. Do you mind of the time there was a meeting for the District Nurse and only five folk came forby yourself, the way every one of them was afraid in case they would be put on a committee and find their-selves with a bit work to do? But they don't know what's good for them and maybe none of us do. And they're wanting the new Hall and yet kind of not wanting it, the way they're afraid of any kind of new thing and what others will be saying. Ach, they've no kind of education."

"Would you say there will be anyone from Kilmolue?"

"You know just as well as me they're mostly all Free Presbyterians up there, except for the Balana crowd."

"And all smelling hellfire in a Village Hall!"

"Aye, and the Wee Frees not much better, and maybe not wanting to be thought less religious than the F.P.'s!"

"If only we could see the young ones any better. Do you think they are, Janet?"

Janet laughed a little and stroked the puppy, and a glow seemed to come off her: the black, bright hair and the high colour with it and the white teeth like curd. "I'll be over at the school treat in the afternoon" she said "and I'll see! Will you be there, Katie?"

"Is Mr MacTavish taking it?"

"No. Miss Gillies. So we'll not be seeing you, Katie, I'm thinking!"

"I can't stand the woman! I don't believe you can either."

"I can so! She's just a wee bit over religious."

"Call her a devil-worshipper and be done with it! A great pity that Semple lassie went and got herself married—she had the wee ones fair worshipping her!"

"Aye, and the boys just the same! This one'll not get married in a hurry, and she has the ears scared off poor David MacTavish with her lecturing; but I can manage her fine. Ach, I wish I could be teaching myself."

"I wish you could, Janet. Yes, that would have been fine."

"I would have done it fast enough but for the croft and my

brothers going off to the University; and then Mairi getting married. One of us had to stay with father and him the age he is."

"It's always the woman!"

"Aye, I was downhearted leaving school and me thinking I would sit my Highers! But there it is. The two pails are heavy: give me the one. No, why wouldn't I have the time? I'll see you to the house. Is Isa off with her boy? Aye, aye, a decent lassie. Wallflower's calving at the back end? Aye, that's the best if you can work it."

They walked on together, Janet easily, balancing the puppy against the milk pail, smiling at the weather. But Kate no longer ever felt herself part of the Spring. Her hair was wispy in the breeze above weathered cheeks and brows, fair, bleaching to grey; only her eyes were still sharply blue. But she walked with a certain vigour for all that, beginning to think that breakfast was the greatest meal of the day and she would fry herself a duck egg and read one of the Library books with it, for her father wouldn't be down for another hour . . . with any luck.

"Did you hear about the lobsters?" she asked. Janet shook her head and Kate told her.

"Well, well" said Janet "we'll all be needing to lock our doors now! And it was Chuckie told you. Do you think now he could have had a hand in it himself?"

"What, old Chuckie! Are you thinking he might? Ach, surely not, Janet."

"I'm not saying he did. But you can scarcely trust your own brother these days."

"I trust you, Janet."

"And how wouldn't you?" She laid the pail down on the path up to Tigh na Bheach and leant over to smell the honey azaleas. Kate broke a couple of sprigs and put them into the basket. "Is your father keeping well?" Janet asked. Kate nodded. "And how are his collections doing?"

Kate broke another sprig. "There isn't a shelf in the house that's free of them, Janet!" she said. "And if one tries to dust them——! I keep getting nightmares about them. I wonder why men have to go in for these idiotic things."

"Well, well," said Janet, "it's better the collections than the drink." And then suddenly she looked down and coloured, for had she not said a rudeness to her dear Katie, mentioning the stuff, because of the Laird—and if the Laird and herself——

But Kate Snow had not noticed. She was thinking about her father and about the Village Hall meeting and about the Ministers and would any of them come? And would her cousin Andrew Revie come? He had been cross and difficult when she had talked to him about it. He had aged a good bit during the war. When once a man started ageing, he was apt to go quick. That type anyway.

And then she thought about breakfast again and she would not fry her egg, no, she would bake it with a drop cream and her own butter—she would have two eggs—— But Janet suddenly put an arm through Kate's and gave her a quick squeeze: "Ach, never mind, Katie, it'll all come right!"

CHAPTER II

SATURDAY EVENING: VILLAGE MEETING

THE MEETING WAS CALLED for seven o'clock at the school, and the schoolmaster himself was the first there, ten minutes before the hour. But he had been so terrible upset and affronted that he could scarcely take his tea; the good kipper was choking him and he couldn't get down a mouthful of his sister's home-made cake hardly, for thinking of what he should have done. If once he could have got round to using his authority on Miss Gillies, instead of her on him! He ought to have sent Peigi Snash straight home—if it was true. He ought to have known whether it was true or not. And if Peigi had done what they said—or not herself, but her folk, and old Snash was a right devil—— He looked round the big class room, the benches and desks, the blackboard, still with money sums chalked up on it, the maps, the jam jars full of flowers; and his own desk a perfect clown of a desk from where he sat now at the corner of the front row. He stuck his fingers through his hair, a thing his sister was always speaking to him about; he had red, wavy hair and a pale, freckled face: narrow, rather strong hands. Sometimes for months on end he managed not to bite his nails, but now he took a nibble at one. It was still light, but they would want the Tilleys lit before the meeting was finished.

The Forester came in, his friend, quick stepping, black haired, with bright dark eyes, in Forestry coat and breeches and one hand bandaged. "What's the matter, Davie?" asked the forester, "take a reef in yourself, man. Yon Gillies hasna given you the strap, surely?"

"Ach, it's not just her" said the schoolmaster, "it's—ach, I don't know; but if it's what I think it is, it's something that shouldna be."

"What is it?"

The schoolmaster looked round and spoke in a low voice, "You know Snash?"

"Aye, the dirty old devil, fine I ken Snash; I've had more trouble over the head o' Snash than ten o' the young fellows. Has he been at you, Davie?"

"Well, it was this way, Roddy. We had the school picnic in the old place at the back of the Drum. Plenty of room for games and all. I wouldn't have minded taking it, oh no, but——"

"Herself took it."

"Miss Gillies has taken it two years now and it's just beyond me to stop her."

"You could just try telling her you would do it."

"Ach, Roddy, it's no' that easy! And I was never perfect at discipline. But anyway I thought I would take a race over and see how were they doing. When I got there they were running races. I wanted to be sure the Glasgow children were doing all right and playing themselves with the rest."

"Aye, the rest can be gey sore on the boarded-out children, poor wee souls. And all this blether about the goodness of the crofters to them. I could tell you a thing or two, Davie."

"Maybe I know. Well, there was Doreen and Moira and the three wee boys and the two Carters, and Johnnie with the squint—he gets on well enough with the rest—and then there was wee Greta Cullen that stays with Snash and she looked terribly down, poor kiddie. I could see she had been crying, but she wouldn't speak. And then the big Carter lassie began on a long story of how Greta had been given a dress for Sunday school by Florag at the boarding house and wanted to wear it for the picnic, but here Snash and his wife had taken it away and given it to Peigi and she was wearing it now."

Two of the young fishermen had come in and were sitting at the far side whispering and smoking. If there was a packet of fags going in Port Sonas, the fishermen were sure to get them. David MacTavish went on in a low voice. "There was Peigi Snash, sure enough in a new dress, and I was for going straight to her, but Miss Gillies came up and I spoke to her——"

"And she told you to mind your own business——"

"Well, it was the picnic and Peigi would have denied it and it would have been the crofts against the boarded-out kiddies once more. She said I should see Snash himself and not make a row then. But it was sore on me. The Glasgow kiddies were looking to me to help them."

"And you never did it, Davie! You'll need a tin of spinach at your elbow whenever you speak to yon one. The poor wee souls made to howk the tatties all along the glen and the worse the crofts the more bairns they take!"

"The inspectors should see to it."

"Ach, they know fine at the crofts when the inspectors are coming, and everything couthy and trim and the whitewashing done and the wee booky for the inspector to sign, and oh, the great love they have for the bairns! No wonder they go back to Glasgow at the end of their time. See, there's Florag coming—go you and ask her about the dress."

"Maybe I should do it after the meeting."

"Go now, man, and get it over, she'll not bite you." The forester gave him a wee shove and watched him go over and speak to Florag, a plump, handsome girl with a fur collar to her coat. Four lads from the glen crofts had come in. Now the forester looked at them and suddenly found the spark of fury burning in him. When he came to Port Sonas, his first post as a Forester, he meant to start a Boy Scout Troop and maybe teach them plenty that would do them good if they came on into the Forestry. He would have given his own time, aye, he had spent plenty Saturdays trying to gather them. They would come for a game of football, aye, but try to get them to learn first-aid or woodcraft! He had given it up a year ago now, but it still hurt him to be baffled by that lot.

The schoolmaster came back. "Aye, it's true enough, she gave the dress to wee Greta and it with a pink collar the same as the one Peigi was wearing."

"Well, you're for it, Davie" said the forester, and then "Were you hearing about the lobsters?"

"I was so. Oh, here's Mistress Snow and her father."

"Is it him was brother to Andrew Revie's father?"

"No, no, Roddy, not at all, it was her mother was a Miss Revie from Peterhead, and auntie to Andrew Revie. A well-doing family, all of them——Ah, here's the Laird now and not often he comes to a meeting!"

"Mistress Snow will have the hames on him," said the forester, "Or so they're saying." And then, lower, "He has a shoogly look, has he not?"

"Ach yes, he's at it altogether too much now," said the

schoolmaster. "Ach, I wish we could export all the stuff and have done with it!"

"You shouldna go too far, Davie" said the forester, "what would we do for our New Year?"

Kate and her father came over and sat beside them. She helped him off with his coat and then helped him on with it again, since it was not as warm as he had supposed it might be going to be. He had a little neat white beard, and indeed the children of Port Sonas had acquired the habit of bleating when he went by. But he was rather deaf and would in any case never have dreamt of such an occurrence, and, oddly enough, it had been kept from Kate.

The Laird nodded to Kate and she shook hands. "I never thought you'd come, Sandy" she said, "Now, you've got to move the vote of thanks to Councillor Thompson. No, you must!" He grinned and sat down at the further side. He was a good bit older than Kate and six inches taller. His knees were bony under the kilt, and so were his hands, clasped over his stick.

Mr MacFarlan looked round at him, tightening his mouth and frowning. He had never liked the Laird. The Laird had never asked *him* to fish. Which he should have done. Not that he himself liked fishing, he would sooner potter about his property —but it would have been the right thing. Yes, the right thing. If people neglected to do the right thing, it undermined the fabric of society. And the Laird never did the right thing. Enough to make anyone a socialist, the way the Laird behaved!

"Do you think we'll have a good meeting tonight?" said Kate to the schoolmaster, and looked round anxiously. A few more boys and two of the girls who worked at the Hotel in summer had come in. "I had another complaint about the school lavatories, David" said Kate.

"I'll speak to Ella again" he answered, "these cleaners are all the same! But I've got my new stove in at last in the other room."

"Miss Gillies will have to think of something else now!" said Kate.

A few more people came in. Red Dougie from Molachy and his young wife; Mr MacMillan from the Hotel with the moulting flies forever in his hat; Krooger the ferryman and his brother; Postie who came and sat behind the Laird so as to get the smell

22

of the stuff off him; big Minnie from the East boarding house and her chum, Mrs MacLean the chairman of the W.R.I.; Andy Smith the caretaker of the Mission Hall; two of the weavers; Hughie from the hotel garage and his cousin Hughie the drainer. Not a bad meeting really, but still nothing to be proud of out of a population of three hundred and twenty in the village and around, and more if you counted Osnish and all up the glen.

"Mr Thompson's late" said Kate, glancing at the clock and then round at the school room. A few more dribbled in, young ones, giggling together at the door, then hushed.

"Oh, him!" said the forester "he never likes a Saturday meeting, that's their best day up at the Hotel. But he'll be over, sure."

"The doctor said he'd manage."

"He's no' back yet from old Mistress MacDougal" said Postie, leaning forward. "I saw his car going up the way and they say she was taken worse the day."

"What's the matter with her?" Kate asked. "Ach, well, she was after having injections in the brain" said Postie "and the lassie was saying it had brought on a kinna kittly feel on the liver; and you'll mind how her sister went, Mistress Snow——"

"Well, I do hope she doesn't keep Dr McKillop all night."

"Ach, she'll do that sure enough" said Postie, "she's kinna droll now."

Janet came in with two other lassies from the glen crofts, pink faced from bicycling. She made as if to come over, but one of the lassies pulled her back and she sat down at the far side.

"I hope Mr Thompson's car hasn't broken down again" said Kate, frowning.

The Laird leant over towards her: "Don't fuss, Kate! He probably didn't look at the clock till seven and you know it's eight miles and a bit to Kinlochbannag and the road in the condition it is."

"His self-starter was out of order" said Hughie-the-garage "and she's kind of heavy to swing. It would have taken him a wee while to get her started. If he had brought her over early I could have fixed her, but they aye think they can manage at Kinlochbannag." He snorted.

23

"If you could fix my lights——" said the forester.

"I'm just waiting on the spares, Roddy, they shouldna be long now. Maybe they'll come with the Monday steamer."

Three more of the W.R.I. came in and sat beside their secretary, leaning over and talking in whispers; it was still the same trouble about judging the jam.

Old George the keeper, who had been a power in the 'twenties, came in and touched his cap to the Laird, who acknowledged it with a jerky movement of his own hand. Two of the skippers came in, Pate of the Silver Bird and Ian Ciotach of the Cluaran, and a few more of the fishermen with them. The schoolmaster thought worriedly of the dottles of their pipes ground into his schoolroom floor. The clock said half past seven.

A big fair man with khaki trousers, the half buttoned top of a battle-dress and a heavy leather belt, came in: young Fred from Balana on the Kilmolue road. He sat away from all the others. There was not a soul from Kilmolue itself.

"C'aite bheil am ministear?" Roddy whispered to Davie, who shook his head. He had scarcely been hopeful enough to expect any clerical approval. Kate, overhearing, answered "Mr Fergusson doesn't disapprove, but he doesn't exactly feel he wants to be at the meeting."

"Aye, aye, they were the same kind at Laodicea!" said the forester. "And my own Minister puts on yon dour look and turns his eyes up the like of a hen in a storm if the Hall is as much as thought of in front of him!"

"And the other?" asked Kate.

"He would no more come here" said David suddenly and bitterly, "than be seen without his trousers on the Sabbath, if you'll excuse me, Mrs Snow."

"Ach, we all know what the Free Presbyterians are like, David" said Kate "and you with your own thorn in the flesh!"

"She even gets censoring the pictures for the Infant room" said David, "but there's another thing I wanted to speak to you about. You know the boarded out children——"

But there was a stir at the door. Councillor Thompson came in, a big man in a big coat, and three others with him, one of whom had a bottle showing out of his pocket. Once one of the young fishermen had seen it the whisper went round and for a moment everyone's eyes were on it. Councillor Thompson went straight up to the table and slapped down his gloves and beamed round, "You'll take the chair for me, Mrs Snow?"

"Yes, certainly" said Kate and came over in a business-like way.

"Not as many as we might have" he said with a touch of accusation, looking round.

"I don't think it's bad" she said "for a Saturday night. Some are—elsewhere."

"And I don't blame them" said the County Councillor heartily "it's a fine evening for a crack with old friends over a dram." There was general laughter from everyone except Kate. "But Saturday it must be to suit my friends the fishermen." The two skippers and some of the men growled and shuffled their feet amiably in reply.

"Well, shall we begin?" said Kate.

"Is this all that are coming?"

"There may be a few more coming, but the meeting was billed for seven."

"Well, well, it would be a queer meeting that started to time" said Councillor Thompson and laughed richly, "but I'll just do as you say. The ladies are always right!"

Kate took the chairman's place without answering. If you were a woman and stood for a Highland District Council, you brought it on yourself. She apologised for lateness in starting, congratulated those who had come on their public spirit, and introduced Councillor Thompson, who, as she said, needed no introduction. While she was speaking, a few more came in, including, she was glad to see, her cousin Andrew Revie and, just after him his friend, old Norman MacDonald. They were both Elders, one in the Established Church and one in the Wee Frees, and might have some influence with the Ministers.

Councillor Thompson launched himself comfortably, and the audience sat back. Most of them liked it to be lengthy. If they were to spend their evening at a meeting, there should be a smooth sea of speech from one able and willing to speak, islanded with an occasional story about a wedding or a funeral or a man seeking for a dram. Councillor Thompson provided it. There was also talk of money to be had from the head ones in Edinburgh, towards a Village Hall. This would be money for nothing, at least for no tangible object such as fish or cattle or cloth, but only for effort which, because it cannot be measured, is not valuable.

Three members of the audience had their eyes steadily on the money sums on the blackboard. One of them was Ian Ciotach; he was dead keen on the fishing and dead keen on money. As there were no herring here to think about, he did the money sums over and over, especially the big addition one, savouring it like a psalm tune. He heard the speaker's voice also speaking of money to come into the community. For every pound they raised themselves, the Government would give five pounds. Thus they would be doing the Government, setting their fleet of nets for the money to come swimming by, and hauling it in.

Mrs MacLean of the W.R.I. went through the sums too, kind of hoping to catch out Mr MacTavish. She had a feud with him dating from the time he had not let off her niece from the school to help in the family shop, as they had a right to expect, and the lassie big for her age and could have saved them ten shillings a week of wages. All this schooling might be good and well for the ones with a right head-piece who could do well for themselves and their families out in the world. But for a strong lassie that would only have from her school leaving to her wedding to do good to her family, it was just nonsense. But unfortunately there was nothing wrong with the sums. If they got this Hall, the W.R.I. would need to get it for the evenings on special terms. It would be great to have somewhere you could play whist, for cards were not allowed in the Mission Hall and every time they had an evening at the school there was trouble with that Ella; maybe Mr MacTavish set her against them!

The third one who looked at the sums was Eilidh Macrae from Osnish, who had never understood from the beginning how to do money sums. How could you carry the penny line? She had a kind of grasp of the way you carried the tens, but these wild pennies were in twelves, anyway in a real shilling. Ach, what was the use! If you had the money you could just put it by in a cup and you would soon know if there was enough for a thing you wanted. And there would be the great dancing in this Hall, maybe many, many times in the year and the boys seeing her home to Osnish. Oh, the boys, the boys, and the life and wickedness that

26

was in them! Eilidh and her cousin Jessie Bheag and her cousin Mairi had all three the same thought as Mr Thompson spoke in a pleasant leering way of the dancing there would be and they clasped one another's hands and dropped their heads to stop the giggles from coming out until after the meeting.

"And if we are all resolved on the need of a Village Hall at Port Sonas" said Councillor Thompson, "it will be necessary to elect a committee and to fill in some documents. There's no getting anything these days without we fill in a form!" (Laughter.) "Well, then, there's this matter of a form to fill in. A form—oh, aye, here is my good friend Mrs Snow with the right form—trust the ladies to keep us straight! Aye, aye, here we are. Forms V.H. 3 and 4, and I am sure Mistress Snow and your good selves will have no difficulty at all in filling them up. And then we can trust ourselves to the good offices of the Council—aye, the Council for Social Service: and they'll help us to get the best of the Government!" (Laughter and cheers.) "Well, now, I'm thinking some of you will have some questions to ask before we put it to the vote and maybe our good friend Mr MacTavish will give us a bit light on the proceedings."

He sat down and David MacTavish jumped up and began to prime the Tilleys. There was whispering all over the room. Councillor Thompson beamed on them full of success. Kate asked for questions. Compared with him her voice was dry and without richness and half foreign.

At last, one of the fishermen, nudged by his friends, asked: "Will the Hall have a licence?" The response to this varied from laughter to shocked giggles.

"No, no" said Councillor Thompson, "but there will be the chance of a cup tea!" (A little clapping from the W.R.I.)

Mr MacMillan from the hotel got to his feet. "It's all very well talking about cups of tea and Village Halls" he said, "but are we any further on with our water supply?"

"The scheme is before the County Council, Mr MacMillan, and we are just waiting for the Department to make up its mind."

Mr MacMillan snorted, "Why are we paying an Engineer to the tune of a thousand a year and never getting our water? You know the position well enough, Mr Thompson, and if there was no water in Kinlochbannag you would be shouting about it yourself. And here we are with no more than a trickle off the peat, I have my sample with me——"

This was a turn the audience knew by heart, but unexpectedly Red Dougie interrupted, "Ach, to Hell! You and your sample! Are we not after seeing it a hundred times already? I'm needing to get every drop from the spring and me with cows, and if I can get by, so can you! We're here to get a Village Hall!" (Some clapping.)

The forester got to his feet. "Can we get a Hall big enough for badminton?"

"That will depend on yourselves" said Councillor Thompson "you will need to discuss that in the committee."

"Will the W.R.I. be able to get the Hall?" asked Mrs MacLean. Kate pointed out something in a leaflet to Councillor Thompson; he beamed and explained that all bodies of an educational and recreational nature in the community would be represented on the management committee of the Hall.

"Will we get to practise the choir?" asked Jessie from the tearoom, bobbing up and down in one breath.

"Certainly, certainly" said Councillor Thompson. David MacTavish gave the Tilleys a good pumping and hung them up. In the hard light Kate looked older and tired. She ought to be using make-up, thought Sandy, but she'd make a mess of it if she did. He sighed and crossed his legs once more and his hands shifted from his stick to his grey drooping moustache, and back. A tedious way of spending an evening: but Katie had asked him to come. He looked round the schoolroom and engaged his fancy lightly in shooting the audience, beginning with Mr MacFarlan. He had his old revolver somewhere, the police had never bothered with it. It would be a pleasure to shoot Councillor Thompson. How it would worry Katie! But the man who really shot Councillor Thompson would equally be able to comfort Katie Snow. He crossed his legs again, half shut his eyes and sat back.

Mr MacFarlan took a notebook out of his pocket and glanced at it. No, it was the wrong one; it was Unusual Mineral Specimens. He put it back carefully and found the right one. Was it seventy-two or seventy-three teapots? (Counting, of course, the Staffordshire, which might have served another purpose.) There was a letter from Inverness that afternoon about a teapot

28

from a farm sale, one of the clocking hen type, fine primitive colouring, scarcely chipped; he felt in his other pocket to be sure the letter was still there.

A white-haired man stood up at the back, old Norman Mac-Donald, one of the few who still worked with a real hand loom. "While we have our Councillor here" he said, "we will all be wanting to ask is there anything more about the bridge?"

Councillor Thompson shook his head and smiled.

"Well, well, we have been expecting it for the last fifty years. The Governments come and the Governments go and still there is no bridge. But it is something indeed if we are to get a Village Hall and I am the thankful one that I have been spared to attend this meeting and to hear the eloquent speaking of our good friend. I am hoping that the Hall will be conducted in such a way that no harm will come to the spiritual wellbeing of the young people of Port Sonas."

"That's just the question we are needing to ask ourselves" said another big bearded man, Cameron, the farmer from Balnafearchar. "In my young days" he said "we would come together to hear an edifying discourse and there would be singing of our grand old Scottish psalms. Are we certain that we are not stepping aside from the straight path?"

"Dancing and card playing!" said a sharp woman's voice: Bella Smith, wife of the caretaker at the Mission Hall. Old Andy was a douce wee man himself; it was Bella the Steamroller that would see to it that all was seemly and quiet within, and that nobody visiting the Mission Hall should seem to be partaking of over much worldly enjoyment.

Out of the row of fishermen someone dropped a remark in Gaelic to be followed by male titters. Kate pushed back a hairpin into the double plaits that went round her head and thought it was as well she didn't know the language thoroughly.

Councillor Thompson said, "Well, my friends, you all know there is nobody likes the thought of the good old days better than myself. But times have changed, aye, times have changed. And maybe not so much for the worse as we might be thinking, as the old wife said at her man's funeral." (Laughter.) "A quiet game of whist has never hurt anyone yet, and there are worse things than dancing that the young ones can be at. How and ever, it will be for you on the committee to draw up the

29

regulations and there will be the time to discuss these matters. I think we should put it to the vote now" he whispered to Kate.

"Well, if you think—" But the schoolroom door banged open and in with a certain amount of stumbling came eight big men, including the Whale, skipper of the Righin Og, and most of his crew. They stood and blinked under the lights and David MacTavish jumped up and went over, whispering that there was room down at the side. The Whale looked doubtfully at the benches and desks; some of the grown-ups had squeezed themselves in and others were sitting on the tops of the desks. But neither prospect appealed.

"I canna sit on they bloody wee bits o' things" said the Whale rather loud, "they're no' made for the like o' me" and to the meeting at large, "Carry on, boys, carry on, we're wi' ye!" He stood and swayed, smiling and powerful. Most of the others looked friendly enough too; only the Beisd scowled, with the drink getting him the wrong way as usual.

Kate glanced at her watch. They must have come away before closing time, which argued—didn't it?—a certain amount of public spirit. If once they would sit down! While they were standing you never knew which way their feet might not carry them.

"What were you after saying, Jock my boy?" said the Whale to Councillor Thompson, who bristled. He never liked to be called Jock, which was not his name anyway and he had meant to get the meeting finished and himself and his friends back to Kinlochbannag before the Saturday night was over.

"I was about to put to the vote" he said "that this meeting is in principle in favour of a Village Hall at Port Sonas."

"Aye, aye, a great idea altogether, and ye'll tak' a wee refreshment, Jock, the way ye'll manage to put it to the meeting a bittie stronger." He produced a bottle out of his pocket and looked at it earnestly, "She's full to the shoulder almost."

"And you're the same, ye daft old devil" said one of the Kinlochbannag men, "sit you down quietly now and let Mr Thompson be getting on with his meeting."

He gave the Whale a push, which luckily brought him down on to a desk, his bottle clutched. But the Beisd was holding on to the table, "So you wouldna tak' a refreshment wi' my chum! You ca' yoursel' a man, Jockie Thompson——"

Kate hurriedly got to her feet: "Will someone from the body of the hall propose that this meeting is in favour of a Village Hall at Port Sonas?"

"Yes, I propose that" said the forester. The Beisd, deserted, looked round.

"A seconder!" said Kate. The schoolmaster hesitated and caught her eye; she signalled with a movement to wait, and looked to the back of the room.

Norman MacDonald got up and said he had great pleasure in seconding the motion, hoping that it would work out for the good of Port Sonas.

"All those in favour, please signify."

There was clapping and stamping and whistling; the Whale and his men going on for longer than any. One of the younger men had hold of the Beisd now and had taken him off to the door where he stood glowering.

"I thought it had better be put from the meeting" said Kate, low, to Councillor Thompson, who had, in fact, meant to do it himself. He nodded.

"Is anyone against?"

There was a small silence, then Bella the Steamroller put up her hand, followed after a pause by that of her husband, and finally, Cameron of Balnafearchar.

"A large majority of this representative meeting being in favour of a Village Hall, we should go on to form a committee, but first I must thank Councillor Thompson——"

She went on with the thing until the butter had entered into his soul. Everyone applauded again with thunders from the bar contingent. Now she asked for nominations for an *ad hoc* committee from the body of the meeting.

The forester and Norman MacDonald were proposed and seconded and accepted, though Norman protested a little that he was too old. Then came the schoolmaster and Mrs MacLean and herself. Red Dougie was proposed, but would not serve, saying there was too much to do on the farm—"Another time, maybe." One of the young fishermen was proposed, but refused.

"We must have a fisherman" said Kate.

"Aye, you're right there, my lassie" said the Whale "ye canna do wi'out us! Here's to ye!" and he tilted the bottle.

Pate Morrison of the Silver Bird was proposed and after some fuss, accepted. Kate knew very little about him, not even which church he went to. Was he the father, or maybe the uncle of the wee Morrison with the red hair? She could not just be sure.

Mr MacMillan from the hotel was of course put on. Did he even want a Village Hall? Then, in case the boarding houses were left out, not Florag, who might have been interested in music and dancing, but Florag's auntie, Mrs McKeith, was proposed; she was said to have a grand business head. Andrew Revie was proposed; Kate signalled to him to accept, but he refused abruptly.

"I think" said Kate "that we should maybe have one or two representatives of the youth of the community." If only someone would propose Janet! "What about the crofts?" Silence. "We ought to have someone from the glen and someone else from Osnish."

At last someone proposed Willie MacLean, Jessie Bheag's father, who wasn't there. Would he want to serve on the committee? Nobody knew. Should she rule that he couldn't be put on, not being there, or might that be missing a chance of getting someone fresh? She decided against him and asked for further nominations. She realised that none of Councillor Thompson's friends had been put on and said pointedly that the Village Hall was to serve all parts of the peninsula, including Kinlochbannag. Someone thereupon nominated Mr James Morrison MacLean. "And I think" said Kate, "that in view of the great interest that Councillor Thompson has taken in our plans, we should ask him to be a member of our committee, even though in view of his many engagements, he may not always be able to attend."

Everyone clapped and she thought: I've done my duty; please God he won't attend very much.

For a time the meeting hung fire. Kate wondered which of the committee were under fifty, let alone under forty.

Krooger was proposed, but said he was too busy with the ferry.

"How?" said one of the fishermen, "and you always stopping it at five."

"You should know well enough that in summer when there's the demand, I carry on till dusk and no thought for myself."

"Aye, when the tourists are here and giving you half crowns for five minutes in the boat!"

"Order, order" said Kate, "can I have some more nominations?"

"I will nominate the name of the Lord" chanted the Whale in a loud and sudden voice, and leaned forward, tipping the desk, which was seized just in time from behind.

"You'll do no such a thing" said Ian Ciotach, shocked, "keep you quiet, man!"

The Beisd, who had been standing quietly by the door stampeded back, "You keep your bloody wee neb oot o't! Why canna we nominate just the same as the bloody Cluaran?"

"Be buggered to nominate!" said one of the others of the bar party.

"Order, order" said Kate.

The forester came to her rescue, saying they ought to have a representative from Kilmolue, but as none of them had come he proposed Fred Macfie from Balana, was he agreeable to stand? He scratched his head, "Well, I might or I might not."

"It wouldn't be necessary to attend every meeting" said Kate quickly, "you'll accept, Mr Macfie?"

"Well—aye."

"Any more nominations?"

None, and one or two preparing to slip out. We could take power to co-opt further members, thought Kate. "Will all committee members please stay on after this meeting?"

"I'll need to go home and get the supper ready" said Mrs MacKeith, "you can manage fine without me."

"And we must be making our way back to Kinlochbannag" said Councillor Thompson, "you'll not need Mr MacLean for the first meeting."

"Well, just before you go——" said Kate, and signalled to the Laird, who half woke, got to his feet, and proposed a hearty vote of thanks to Councillor Thompson. By the time the Whale and his crowd had got themselves safely and vocally through the door, but before everyone else was quite away, Roddy had proposed another vote of thanks to the chairman. But she was over at the far side of the room by then, talking hard to Janet. After a minute or two she looked round for the schoolmaster, who was coming over. "Listen to this, David" she said, "there's trouble."

"Is that about what happened at the school treat? I'm afraid I know about it."

"But to let them come with the thing on them!" said Kate, "they may have infected the whole school; it's incredible that even here people should be so—so wickedly stupid!"

"I—I'm not sure if we're just speaking of the same thing" said David.

"It's the wee MacKinnons from Osnish, Mr MacTavish" said Janet, "did you not know they came to the treat with the measles on them?"

"No" said David heavily, "that was one thing I didn't know. I don't think I remember seeing them, even."

"It wasn't till we started on the tea I noticed them mysel." said Janet, "when they were drinking any amount of tea and lemonade, but never eating a spark of food. I thought they were just hot with running, but when I went to look, there was the rash out on them. I took them straight back myself and made Mrs MacKinnon, my cousin, put them to bed. There's the way I was late for the meeting myself, and the other two would never have come without me!"

"What excuse did Mrs MacKinnon have?" said Kate.

"Ach, she just said they had it light and it would have been sore on them missing the treat!"

"You know" said David, "I think Highland people are kind of droll about illnesses. They think it is kind of unlucky to admit you have a real illness."

"That may be" said Kate, "but it is doing a wrong to the whole community. You'll have to look out for an epidemic, David. It's a ten days' incubation period and I doubt if many of your children will have been exposed before. However we'll need to start the committee meeting now."

"Aye" he said, and then, "was there anything else you noticed at the school treat, Janet?"

"Just Miss Gillies!" she said, "why?"

"Well, maybe you'll hear. I wish I had thought to propose you on to this committee!"

"I wish you had" said Kate. "I couldn't very well do it from the chair."

34

"Ach, never mind" said Janet, "nobody thinks a woman's anything till she marries—I mean—ach, they'd not think anything I said worth listening to. You know fine how it is yourself, Katie dear. But if there's anything I can do, well then, I'll just do it." She slipped out, tying the scarf over her head, and Kate heard her calling to the other two.

The new committee waited and looked at one another.

CHAPTER III

SATURDAY EVENING:
VILLAGE HALL COMMITTEE MEETING

Roddy was watching Kate and David coming over and asked himself, had they been speaking about Peigi Snash and the boarded out bairn. Poor Kate, in thon old dress he had seen her in at every kind of meeting and sale of work, a nice enough dress if one hadn't seen it so often: clear green, the colour of the underside of a Silver almost. And she with her man killed down south in the war. What did she do with herself evenings? Her father could be no company for her at all, him and his teapots. And as for the Laird, there was no saying. Well, at least there was no crofter on this committee!

Mr MacMillan of the hotel said impatiently that they must elect officers and get it over: chairman—he turned to Kate. She shook her head and said, "No, no, Mr MacMillan, that should be yourself."

"I second that" said Pate Morrison, determined to show that a fisherman could speak with the rest.

"Well" said Mr MacMillan, "seeing I've the biggest business in the place, maybe it's just as well."

For a moment the anger blazed in Roddy, when he thought of the Forestry Commission with its forty men and girls on the plantings and nurseries, against his miserable hotel; and the electric light engine going wrong mostly every month! Some day he'd make the old bugger sing a different tune!

The Tilleys were dying down a little, so David gave them a pump up. Mr MacMillan sat himself down at the table and the others sat on the desks. "We'll need a secretary and treasurer" said Kate.

"I think Mistress MacKeith should be the treasurer, seeing she has such a good business head."

"Good enough not to be here" said Roddy. But that was carried unanimously.

"The secretary will need to tell her" said Mr MacMillan, "we'll need a secretary now?"

"I move Mr MacTavish" said Roddy.

"I second that" said Pate.

"I move Mistress Snow" said Mrs MacLean.

"I second that" said Pate.

"You canna second both, Pate" said Mr MacMillan.

"What for no'?" said Pate, "they would both be good, both the two of them."

"What about it, David?" said Kate, "if you could manage——?"

"But you will have written up for all the forms and that, and they'll know your name in Edinburgh. I'll come over and give you a hand with the writing any time, but I would sooner it was you."

"All right" said Kate, "I'd better start keeping minutes. Give me a jotter, will you?" He took one out of the cupboard and handed it over.

"Well, what will we need to do?" said Mr MacMillan.

"Perhaps you should read the leaflet and the form we have to fill in."

"I hanna got my specs."

"Well, there are some questions that they ask us, and we'll need to think about a site and tell the Planning Officer, and we'll need to raise funds."

"We should have a sale" said Mrs MacLean. "If we all sent some baking——"

"There's only the one site for a Hall" said Roddy, "along by the Post Office. The wee park there is level and we would get the water from the spring up on Tomnaturk and the drains would catch on to the Hotel drain."

"The only site, is it?" said Mrs MacLean "are you saying that, and you almost a stranger in Port Sonas!"

"It doesna take three years to see all round Port Sonas, aye, and *through* it!"

"Now, now, now" said Mr MacMillan, "there's no question of a site yet—no, not for years maybe. Why, we're still no' just sure that the bulk of the people here are in favour. There are plenty that havena said. And we must go cannily." Kate and David exchanged looks: had it been a mistake having him as chairman?

"Aye, aye" said Norman, "we will need to study it out right. We will need to see that nothing is done to harm our grand old Highland ways."

"Well, shall we just look at the forms?" said Kate. She spread them out and put on her reading spectacles, then began on the questions. David MacTavish looked over her shoulder, the rest sat round listening and occasionally commenting. Only young Fred from Balana said absolutely nothing: there was a strong farm smell off him and the heat of the Tilley lamps seemed to bring it out.

The first questions were easy enough to answer. The rateable value could be got. Chief occupations: fishing, crofting and farming, weaving; summer visitors perhaps. The Mission Hall does not meet village requirements, as dancing, cards and ordinary games are forbidden there.

"Will there be nothing at all forbidden in the new Hall?" asked Norman with some anxiety, "that cannot be right, surely?"

"There will be no disorderly conduct" said Roddy, and the old man nodded, more satisfied.

"Are we thinking of having a playing field by the Hall?" There was a pause.

"We could do with a nice wee golf course" said Mr MacMillan, "but I doubt we'd no' get that nearer than the machair at Osnish. It would be a great attraction for the visitors."

The schoolmaster said: "We should be thinking of our own young people primarily. And it's kind of stupid that we've none of them with us. But they never seem to be at a loss for some field for a game. Still, we should look to the future."

"I was forever playing shinty when I was a young fellow" said old Norman, with a sudden delightful smile and a flash of very blue eyes.

"It would be grand if we could start that," said David. "My cousin at Ballachulish says they have a great shinty team there and go into Oban for the big matches and all. And it is our old Scottish game. But with the newspapers and wireless they are mostly all thinking about football."

"And not always playing it, even!" said Roddy. "If you knew the amount of money out of my pay packets that goes into the pools! And once we get this television, they'll just sit on their backsides watching the big matches and betting on them. You'll be thinking to have a set at the hotel most like?''

"Aye, well—no' just now, Roddy. You've no idea of the price——''

"Well, we can put in that meanwhile we are not thinking of a playing field" said Kate. "Now about Part Two, that's for the County Council, and we'll need to write formally to Councillor Thompson and to the County Clerk, who will hand it on to the Director of Education. And now, the next thing is the site."

Roddy and Mrs MacLean glared at one another. David said quickly, "We could look into the site question before the next metting and see could we maybe come to some agreement."

"Anyone with a spark of sense would know . . ." began Mrs MacLean.

But Norman said, "Well, now, if each one of us were just to think of the good in some other body's ideas, we could manage fine and it would be nearer the way we should all try to be."

"Aye, aye" said Pate.

"Well, now, the size——" said Kate.

"I'll find out the size of a badminton court!" said Roddy.

"We could have a wee kind of reading room" said the schoolmaster, "and the County book box coming there instead of to the school. I could go on looking after it just the same, but maybe people would come more. And we could have Youth Club meetings there and debates maybe——"

"It's hopeful you are, Davie!" said Roddy.

"A wee reading room with flowers" said Mrs MacLean, "and books about foreign parts!" And it was clear the thing had suddenly come to her as a picture. Then she turned round to Fred. "Is it true about the book box at Kilmolue?"

"Aye" said Fred without moving.

"What's that?" said Kate.

Fred did not speak. But Mrs MacLean said "Ach, it's just Miss MacIntosh, the teacher at Kilmolue. Whenever the book box from the County comes into the school, she keeps it locked up in case the people of Kilmolue would get reading profane books! These F.P.'s!" she snorted, herself being a member of the Established Church.

"Did you know, David?" said Kate fiercely.

"Aye, well, I had heard—unofficially."

"It's a matter for the Education Committee. I'd better write to Councillor Thompson. Even he—he'd *have* to take notice."

"Mr Facing-both-ways Jock Thompson!" said Roddy. "He wouldna want to get himself into trouble with the F.P.'s. It's yourself will need to speak to the School Inspector, Davie."

"You're right enough about Councillor Thompson!" said Kate. "The best thing will be to let the Director know—poor man! He's got plenty on his shoulders with this County. Is that why we get no support from Kilmolue, Fred?" He nodded. "It's a Missionary they have there, isn't it? Is he—actively against the Hall?"

"He preached against it" said Fred. "Me, I'm from Balana, I wasna heeding. But the rest were."

"That's terrible" said Mrs MacLean. "I wonder will they be the same here?" She glanced at Norman, then at Pate Morrison; there was no Free Presbyterian on this committee, but the Wee Frees were the next thing. Norman, though, was lighting his pipe, and Pate and Mr MacMillan were whispering to one another in the Gaelic. About the lobsters sure enough—she caught the word giomach. Anyway, religion sat lightly on the fishermen at Port Sonas, excepting at the time of the Communion, or maybe a revival, when they would all be saved for a time and the Mission Hall full and folk only going to the bar by the back way.

"Well, then," said Kate, "we'll need to think of trustees and a Management Committee. We haven't many organisations here, excepting, of course, the W.R.I. and the Fishermen's Association. And the Kirk Sessions. Oh yes, and May's Choir. Is there a branch of the British Legion?" Roddy said there was and he himself the Treasurer. She bit her pencil: "I wonder, have the weavers an association?"

"Ach, aye" said Roddy, "address: care of the Black Market!" Norman looked up and shook his fist, smiling all the same at Roddy. "Ach, I didn't mean yourself" said Roddy, "and you with yon great old loom. But it's these young ones with the Hattersleys, getting the yarn on commission from the factories and getting their own two yards in the piece out of weaving loose!"

Again Kate thought she must intervene. She liked the forester, but she began to be afraid he might be a wee bit difficult on the committee. "Wasn't there a branch of An Commun?" she asked.

There was a silence you could hear ticking. Then David said, very formally, looking at his toes: "Do you not mind, Mistress Snow, of the—the wee unfortunate occurrence——"

"Oh lord, yes" said Kate, "the Treasurer drew out all the balance and went for a blind to Fort William! That was it, wasn't it?"

"He has been intending to pay it back" said David anxiously—he had been the secretary—"there was no actual dishonesty meant."

"Just the way the months slip by," murmured Kate solemnly. The schoolmaster looked away, he was terribly afraid she might break into an unseemly joke and the treasurer had been a cousin of Pate Morrison's.

Indeed Pate was making a tack over, coming to his rescue; you could see his mind changing course. "It was only the pure Gaelic songs he was singing in Fort William" he said, "there was that to it at least, poor Donul! He aye kept the one flag flying until he went under."

"But it'll maybe start again" said David.

"Well, let's hope so," said Kate. "Meantime we can be thinking about what organisations there are, and decide on a letter to send them at the next meeting. But we'll also need to think about the raising of funds."

"Aye" said Mr MacMillan, "the way I see it we'll need to raise a sixth of the money ourselves, but if other places can do it, why not Port Sonas?"

"I second that" said Pate.

"Now, ladies and gentlemen" said Mr MacMillan "will we decide now on a house to house collection and a sale and raffle in the summer when the visitors are here?" Everyone agreed. "And for the collection we should have a list of names and get two or three good subscriptions at the head—Maybe the Laird would help us? And we should surely get a hearing from Miss Campbell of Kinlochbannag—and that way we would be encouraging the rest. I am mostly sure the farming community will put their hands in their pockets if the sales are good. Now, how about the fishermen?"

"We might put a levy on the boats sure enough" said Pate, "maybe a ha'penny a basket—or a penny itself for the season. That wouldna hurt."

"You'd not feel it" said Mr MacMillan with conviction. "So you'll bring it up at the Branch meeting, Pate? Now, ladies and gentlemen, was there anything else?"

"Excepting" said Norman "we are needing to ask ourselves is it certain that this is the will of the community? I can see plenty folks that are not at the meeting. We will need to search our hearts, forby our pockets."

"There's always some will be against anything at all, Norman" said David anxiously and gently. "It's just part of the way things are in the Highlands, but maybe we shouldna take overmuch heed to them. This is a kind of divided community here and we all know that; and we're not the only Highland place to be afflicted the same way. We're divided over the question of a bridge or a ferry, and there's some for the drink and some against, and there are Established and Wee Frees and Free Presbyterians, and on top of that, the Episcopalians at Kinlochbannag. And the Glen will fight with Osnish and both the two of them with the village, and there's one thing and another and all of us pulling every which way. But surely we can all agree on this new thing! Surely we can all be for the Village Hall and—and make it the kind of place where folk can get together and agree."

"Aye, well said, mo bhallaich" said Pate, and indeed he liked nothing better than to hear a well said piece.

"Well," said Mr MacMillan, "we canna do better than find out the way the wind is blowing and meet again, and we might have a good idea of the best site by then. Will we meet Saturday first?"

"Aye."

"At seven o'clock?"

"About that."

"You will let Councillor Thompson know, Mistress Snow? Oh, aye, and Mrs MacKeith to be Treasurer."

"Should we take power to co-opt other members, Mr MacMillan?"

"Just as you say, Mistress Snow. Well, good night all." "Oidhche mhath." "Cheerio!" "Oidhche mhath leibh!"

Mr MacMillan went out with Mrs MacLean, Norman and Pate. Fred got up. "You don't think anyone will come in from Kilmolue?" said Kate.

Fred shook his head. "He has them gripped" he said. And then "There was a wee fellow, a piper, kind of cheery he was, and music in him well. But it was the same with him. He brought his pipes over to me to keep, the way he might be moved to destroy them. He is gripped the now." And Fred moved to the door and they heard him get on his bicycle and go.

"It's a pity, yes, it's a great pity about Kilmolue" said Kate, "but still it was a good meeting I think. What do you feel about it yourself, Roddy?"

"I wonder, will we get the Hall?" said Roddy, and he looked suddenly grim.

"Of course we will, if we all put our backs into it. Do you know this, I've been round to half the houses in the place, talking to them about it, this last six months. If everyone did the same——"

"I know that's what you did, Kate," said David, "and more honour to you. But do you know always what they said when you had gone out the house? They're gey ill to move, these ones, and Krooger's crowd is more or less against you."

"It's pure nonsense, that! The Hall is nothing to do with the ferry!"

"Nonsense, is it? Look, Katie, it's known that you are keen on the bridge and keen on the Hall and the two are put together, and it will give them more pleasure to be stopping you getting your wish than to be getting the Hall themselves. That's true enough, isn't it, Roddy?"

"Aye, true as you're there! And fine for the likes of them to think they can hurt you, and you a kind of high-up one. And if you'll take it from me, Mrs Snow, the best way is not to let them see you're hurt."

"Damn it all, Roddy, I'm not a child!" said Kate. Why should he suppose she was hurt? She began to pencil an elaborate pattern on the cover of her Minute book jotter and looked at it critically, feeling them look at her. And they're quite right, she thought, it does hurt. She looked up and said: "There was a time once when folk in a village could get together for a thing that was for the good of all."

"There was a time, right enough," said the schoolmaster, "in the old days when it was the only way to do. When folk are desperate poor and having nothing to lose, they'll get together. But Port Sonas is too prosperous for that these days. They got together in the old Free Church days to help the

43

People's Church against the Lairds, but there's none of that now."
He shook his head gloomily.

The forester went on. "Nobody is being bad to us, Mrs Snow,
not right bad. And we're none of us believing in anything hard
enough."

"We did during the war."

"Maybe. But that's over. And even so, it was never some way
tight on us here, the way it was in the south. You would know
that. Aye, you would know it. But in the old days Highland
people would come together for work, to build a house it might
be, or to cut peats, and they would come together at nights for a
ceilidh. But now it's all past, is it no', Davie?"

"Aye, aye. If folk got together to work the way they used,
who's to pay the insurance stamps? And the ceilidhs went out
with the wireless. When a man can hear all the top singers, he
doesn't have much notion for his neighbour's singing, or his own.
But it's a lonely thing, the wireless. You can feel kind of cold and
sad listening to it. You know you could take ill and die in your
own chair, at your own fireside, and yon wee unfriendly box
laughing away to itself and never heeding."

"The cinemas in the town are the same" said Kate. "You
just sit back in your seat and watch, and you're not helping to
make it happen, the way you were a wee bit, even, when you
were part of a theatre audience. Odd, isn't it? These things which
have come in our own time: the cinema and the wireless, and
both breaking up the community! And when there is television,
we won't need to go out of our own lonely room. There was a
story by E. M. Forster——" She broke off—neither of them
would have read it.

"And there are the scientists inventing away and never
thinking what they are at," said David.

But Roddy had followed another tack. "If we do get this
Hall, we could have a cinema, one of these sixteen millimetre
projectors, the same as the Forestry Commission has. It would be
great to have films."

"And sit alone watching the strangers on the screen in front
of you?" said Kate, smiling at him a little, him and his
enthusiasm.

"There wouldna be much sitting alone for Roddy!" said David,
"and maybe we could get educational films. It would pay its

way and cut out all this going into Halbost for the films, and nothing much when you get there."

"You think we'll get the Hall anyway, David? You're not as gloomy as Roddy here?"

"Well, I wouldn't say it was certain, Katie. There are some ugly, thrawn folk here. Not that it's much different from other wee places."

"And most of them no doubt able to get together to dislike somebody—me, for instance!" She laughed, but somehow it didn't sound quite right.

"Ach, they've not got enough to think about, so they're jealous of you that have. They may like you fine, half of them, but still and all they'll be wanting to thwart you. If they think they can do that, then they'll feel terribly strong and powerful like one of the old Kings of Israel."

"Well, it's nice to know that, Davie! I suppose Solomon would be the favourite?"

"I doubt they'd be no great hand with yon burden of wisdom——"

"Oh, it was the wives I was thinking about! But if we'd the Hall and everyone taking their part in running it, maybe they'd not feel so weak in the ordinary way and then they'd not have the same need on them to be powerful. Do you not think, David?"

"I do indeed. That's how we are wanting the Hall so much."

"And the dullness here!" said Roddy, "you'd not know which way to turn for a wee bit life."

"Aye," said David, "there's just the prayer meetings and that."

"Ach yes, and the Bible study and folks only going there the way there's nothing else for them."

"The choir's something," said Kate, "though I'm not that keen on cousin May's choice of songs."

"It's the way they've got to be half religious in this kind of place," said Roddy. "The Ministers would be stopping it if they were a bit lively. But that's just a dozen folk. And the same with the Rural. Mrs McCulloch that I lodge with, she'll not go near the Rural, it's not holy! I wished she would, then I'd have peace from her one evening." He stopped abruptly; maybe he'd said too much; it was not as though he knew Mistress Snow that well. And you'd not know how the gentry would be thinking. And she was gentry right enough, for all she was cousin to Andrew Revie that had lived here all his life. She had the education and the manners. And there were those that said she could be going to the Castle if she played her cards right.

"Aye, it can be dull right enough," said David, "even if you like a good read at a book, the same as myself. And queer the way you can move amongst folks and not know them."

"We'll alter all that yet," said Kate. Her pattern on the jotter had developed an important-looking tail. Or was it an eye?

But the other two were glancing at one another. "I wonder, Roddy," said David, "should I tell her about what happened at the school treat?"

"You should, so" said Roddy.

"But I know" she said, "the measles——"

"It's more than that. Ach, maybe I shouldn't worry you with it. It's part of this mix-up, making people behave like they know they shouldn't. Tell me, how's Alice doing at her boarding school?"

"Oh well, she's getting on with her French and Latin. I miss her."

"And I miss teaching her, though she'd got beyond me at the school. There aren't many bright ones. And these poor wee Glasgow kiddies. That was what I was wanting—ach, no: I'll not worry you."

"I'm here to be worried" said Kate, "I'm your District Councillor after all." And she turned back and sat down again at a desk and listened gravely while David told her about Peigi Snash and wee Greta from Glasgow.

CHAPTER IV

SUNDAY: MORNING SERVICE

Roddy wriggled round in bed and stretched and
scratched himself in the gap between the top and bottom of his
pyjamas and wished he was married. Good and well going with a
lassie in the evening, but it left you worse in the morning, and
one of these days he would find himself engaged. But some way he
didn't care so much for any of the lassies he was going with,
and least of all maybe for Kenny's Chrissie that he had met on
the road back from the school. Maybe it was as well the boys
had come by when they did, or he might have gone too far, and
he wouldn't like to find himself taggled up with Chrissie, not
in the daylight. He had half meant to walk back to the Bee
House with poor Kate, instead of letting her go back on her lone,
but there, he was not just sure how she would take it; he wouldn't
want to be putting himself forward and he wouldn't know how the
gentry might feel over such things. But it was kind of sore on
him to see her going off into the dark with nothing but her wee
torch, never a man's arm to go round her. Maybe she was not
wanting such things. He could not know at all when the womenfolk stopped wanting them. It must be eight years since her man
was killed. The lassie would be eleven years old now.

Mrs McCulloch called up to him, "Your bath is ready, Mr
MacRimmon." The old bitch was always terrible keen to get
him up on a Sunday morning. He wished he could have got
other lodgings, but there were not many would take him, the
way they made more out of the summer letting, and the visitors
paying anything you cared to ask them.

He rolled over at last: he didn't like to miss his bath. You
needed to take a bath once a week. He looked out clean things;
his working clothes and his dirty vest and pants and the dirty
bandage off his hand were kicked about the room. Let her gather
them up, the old bitch!

The bath was hot and he began to sing in it, but he wasn't

half way through Faililoiriag when Mrs McCulloch knocked with her broom on the ceiling below. It was always that way if he started on a good-going song on a Sunday morning, even with the windows shut and no one to hear! He came down to his fried eggs and tea. When he was halfway through, Mrs McCulloch came in and sat down opposite him. He knew well the look on her! "What is all this about a Village Hall?" she said.

"Well, we're going to have a Village Hall here" he said, as amiably as he could.

"You seem very sure of yourself, Mr MacRimmon" she said, "but there are two opinions on that."

"The meeting passed it with—with acclamation." He was pleased he had found the word. "A pity you werena there yourself."

"Meetings!" she said, "you'll not get decent godly folks going to your meetings. And I can tell you this, Mr MacRimmon, no lassie of mine will go to any Village Hall. Aye, I would sooner see my Jamesina and my Euphemia dead at my feet, than be falling into temptation in your dances and wickedness that you want to bring into our village."

"There's nothing wrong with Village Halls" he said, trying to keep his temper, "they have the approval of the Department of Education in Edinburgh."

"They may have the approval of Satan" she said, "and most like they have. You are not eating your good egg, Mr MacRimmon."

"I'm not hungry" he said, getting up.

"I will see you at the Church" she said grimly.

He went up to his room, not trusting himself to answer. Looking out of the window he saw Baldy the baker, Hughie the digger and Sandy the Coileach, engineer of the Silver Bird, decent lads all of them, but stiff in their Sunday suits, dark in the sunshine on the green grass, gangling there, not knowing what to do. They would be sure to be speaking of the Hall and all for it if once they dared to say so! Mrs McCulloch and her lassies and their temptations! He had kept off walking back with Jamesina on the dark evenings round New Year—she worked in the Post Office—but it was not she was the unwilling one! See her dead, would she? H'm. The old bitches and their lassies. He looked in his pocket book, behind the ten shilling note and the insurance card and sweetie points for what he knew was there. And a good make. But not with any of his own Forestry lassies.

He took his hat and set out, dodging Mrs McCulloch. Almost immediately he saw poor Kate in her decent blue coat and hat, not dressed up to kill like some of them.

"A fine morning, Mistress Snow" he said, falling in step beside her. "You're for the Church?"

"Yes" she said, "if I go once a month I can just about stand it!" She laughed, "You'll not tell?"

"Me, is it? I'm quiet as the grave. I'd not go myself if I didn't get chased out. Anyway I'd never go to the Wee Frees. But my folks were that way and once Mrs McCulloch got to hear of it, that was me finished. How did you like the meeting, Mistress Snow?"

"Well, you and David were a bit gloomy, weren't you? I wrote to the Director of Education this morning, he'll keep us straight. At least if I go to Church I don't go on writing letters all day!"

"I find the Sunday gey handy for doing my returns" he said, "but is it sure the Education ones will help? I mean—with this not being just pure education."

"Of course they'll help" she said. "You know, Roddy, these halls are terribly important from the educational point of view. Because all you said about the break-up of the community is true enough. Our old Highland way of life isn't standing against the films and the wireless and that, yes, and the general better standard of living that gives people more leisure and more choice. And we've somehow got to find some other way of holding together, or—or we're clean done. Do you see, Roddy?"

"Aye, I see fine."

"Well, the Village Halls might be the thing we need, the kind of magic thing to keep people together, to make them able to stand up against the cities and all they've got there. Some place where people would come together naturally in friendship, for a common purpose."

Roddy looked along the road, half shutting his dark eyes. There were single people and couples walking along all bent in the one direction to do the one thing, though when they drew near the quay head they would divide up, some to the Parish

Church and some to the Wee Frees and some to the Free Presbyterians. He looked round at Kate and said low, "Isn't that what we're all supposed to be doing now? And do you wonder that the ministers and their crowd are jealous at the thought of a Village Hall?"

"Yes" she said, "I see that. But I don't think Mr Fergusson objects. He more or less said so to me."

"Aye, more or less, so long as you keep it the way he wants. But if it ever got—ach, well, alive—ach, I don't know right how to say it: but if the young fellows got on to it and made it go their way instead of it being the respectable ones, the womenfolk and the Elders, what I mean is, that was the way of the old ceilidhs and now you canna have a right ceilidh, the way you must be picking your songs and stories to suit the good-living ones that are maybe no better than the rest of us—ach, maybe I shouldna be saying this, Mistress Snow."

"No, that's all right, only it's difficult to know what to do. I mean, here am I, one of your respectable womenfolk, and you elected me to the District Council after Mr Crawford had his stroke, and not one of the young ones wanting to stand! And do you know this, Roddy? There's many a Highland place with no one at all willing to take on the local government jobs!"

"Ach, I know, and Port Sonas can think itself lucky. It's maybe only an idea of mine, and you've the education. Well, we'll see how it goes." For a couple of women had come level with them and were obviously wanting to speak to Kate; he dropped back, letting on he had to tie his shoe, and so got level himself with Malcie the joiner and wee Shillings. They were talking about America where Shillings had a brother and about the cost of living there. "And would they have Village Halls in America, now?" said Malcie.

"Not at all" said Shillings, "they hanna got villages."

The two women wanted to talk to Kate about the school lavatories. "Once we get the new water supply——" she said, with her mind back on Roddy and what he had said about the oligarchy of respectable women. "I'll see what I can do, Mrs Campbell. Yes, I'll see about the paper; you know sometimes the wee ones play with it. But it's fine to think we may be going to get our Hall, isn't it?"

A quiver went through the two women. Mrs Campbell drew

herself up. "I would not say that, Mrs Snow. We have done very well in Port Sonas without such things."

Oh Lord, thought Kate, glancing at them, they must be Free Presbyterians. She answered, very gently, "Other communities have Village Halls, Mrs Campbell, and make good use of them."

Again Mrs Campbell drew herself back. "Well, Mrs Snow, they say there is a terrible carry-on at the Village Hall in Glenrig."

"That is certainly not the case" said Kate, "they have to be properly conducted." But of course they weren't convinced. Mrs Campbell gave her a hard look, muttered something and moved to the far side of the road. They wanted to believe evil. They were brought up to think in terms of sin. They would have liked to have sinned themselves, to have some pleasant memories to brood over—as most of the men had. But when you think of sin in terms of sex and when birth control is ill understood, women can't afford to sin. So the women, thought Kate, are just that much worse than the men.

One of the Forestry workers came down the path from the houses at the back of the Post Office. A decent lad, one of the ones Roddy could trust to do a job without needing to be on his top all the time. He seemed to want to speak, so Roddy dropped behind. The Church bell was beginning to jang and nag at them now. "What's at you, Alasdair?" he said.

"I'm just browned off and that's the truth, Roddy" he answered, in a voice with a touch of the army accent, southern English or American, "I passed my exam and I've been through Benmore and here am I still burning brushwood."

"We all needed to wait a good wee while" said Roddy.

"Aye, but I served my time in Africa, and plenty promises made, and here am I, getting a farm servant's wage and not even a farm servant's free milk and tatties. I thought when I signed on with the Commission that I would get a chance of promotion."

"You're learning your job, Alasdair."

"Cleaning and draining! I could do it on my head."

"There's more to it than you maybe think, Alasdair. But the Commission is a wee bit slow at promotion. Still and all you're working at home among your own folks, no need to pay for lodgings and that."

"That's all very well, Roddy, but there's nothing to do at home. You canna get to dance nor nothing. Is this true that we're to get a Village Hall?"

"Yes" said Roddy, "you should have went to the meeting."

"Ach, meetings! But will we get to dances?"

"You'll get any kind of thing, Alasdair, if you take the trouble to ask for it. Have you any notion for badminton?"

"Ach, aye, anything to pass the time."

"Once we get this Hall we'll need to get a Games Committee and we'll have you on it, and you'll not need to mump about it, Alasdair, for it's you lads with drive that we'll need to keep this Hall going. You'll need to keep on asking for it or yon old sheep's noses will stop us getting it." He slid his head round towards an elderly group. He knew some way it must be the Hall they were speaking of!

It was possible on the whole to tell the Established from the Wee Frees and the F.P.'s. There was more latitude in the dress, especially of the ladies of the congregation. The Free Presbyterians were mostly all in their blacks and a few older ones still wore the long black mantles and black bonnets on their heads. Like black beetles, Roddy thought, and wished he could take paraffin and a match to the lot of them.

It was a two or three mile walk from the crofts at Osnish or up the Glen, but it was further still from Larach, an old crofting and fishing township up the coast a bit to the north-west, and the only way to it a rough road from behind Osnish where the roads were bad enough in all conscience, and round the towering dark screes of T'each Mor and along the cliffs. They were mostly old people there, indeed there was only one child of school age, who had a walking allowance, for there was no possibility of fetching him to school by car. They were all Free Presbyterians. None of them had come to the Saturday evening meeting, nor were they expected. None of them would have used a Hall. The end crofts were untenanted already and most of the young people had left. When you saw the Larach folk in a crowd they seemed some way a wee bit different from the rest. They walked in slowly in their blacks, making a day of it with both services, and taking their Sunday dinner with relations in the village. Everyone walked from the Glen crofts, but Red Dougie and his wife and mother came in his wee Ford. There was no car at Balnafearchar; it was a motor bike that the son Donnie had.

Janet came in with her father, walking the two and a half miles, pleasant enough on a spring day. They had left the collie shut up and howling at home. She was wearing the dark brown coat and skirt that she had got by mail order and it had never some way been as nice as she had hoped. All the way she kept a wee kind of half-look-out for a new hat or coat or shoes on any of her friends. Mostly at Port Sonas new clothes were bought for a wedding or that, but the next best was the road to Church on a Sabbath. She suddenly found herself wondering—supposing they got the new Hall, would that be the place where one would take one's new dress? She wished she could be going to the Established Church with Kate, but her father had belonged to the Wee Frees all his days and there was no choice about it for her. If he had known the thoughts she was having now, he would have taken his stick to her! Still and on, he was nice over the new Hall, had not said a word against her going off to the meeting and had asked her how it had gone. When she told him Norman was on the committee, he had seemed kind of happy; he had lighted his pipe and puffed away and then he had said it would be something for the boys to do when they came home. After that, while she mended his socks, he had taken out their letters and read them through again as he mostly did on a Saturday evening.

She saw Roddy and Alasdair ahead and dropped her eyes to the psalm book in her gloved hands. Her father went ahead steadily, saying a text over to himself, half aloud, as though he were out on the hills. They drew level with the other two and he greeted them in Gaelic. They answered, and the old man began to tease Roddy on his Skye accent. Janet said nothing. It was not for an unmarried woman to be speaking with the young men on a Sabbath morning.

One of her friends, young Mrs MacCrae from the back croft, came up next to her on the far side. Her husband was one of the ex-Servicemen who had put his gratuity into a Hattersley loom. He worked at it most of the time and she looked after the croft. They had been married a year and no wee ones; the old folk were kind of worried and thinking maybe it was due to himself sitting in at the weaving all day. But Janet, who knew them better, had an idea it was not that at all.

53

"Were you over at the meeting, Janet?" she asked, "will we get this Hall?"

"If once we get together and ask for it" said Janet, "it will be just the thing for you and your man."

"Aye, but the old folks is against us. It was wild the carry-on we had last night. Hamish and me, we were just dressing to go over to the meeting and here, didn't they come in, and oh, the row they made over the head of us going! So in the end we just left it."

"Well, one needs to look to the old folk" said Janet low, glancing round at her father, "but still and all, they should not be allowed to break our own lives."

"No" said her friend, "but it's kind of difficult all the same."

There was a moment when the Sabbath stream broke up into three, on a note of social embarrassment. Kate's two constituents left the road to take the path up, at the back of the bar and the old sweetie shop to the corrugated iron church of the Free Presbyterians.

"Do you know this, Seonaid," said one, "maybe we should not have been speaking to her at all!"

"After yon carry-on at the school?" said her friend, "aye, but mark you, Jean, it'll come to nothing. And indeed I was not meaning to speak to her at all the day, but it just came on my tongue seeing her."

"We could better have spoken to Miss Gillies." For there she was entering into the tabernacle a hundred yards ahead of them.

"Aye, and maybe—ach, maybe it was not seemly to speak on—on yon things at the back of the school—on the Sabbath." They shook their heads and hurried on.

"Well, Balnafearchar" said one of the other farmers; old Jackson from Achnahabhainn, the farm between the ferry and the Forestry Commission plantings along the side of Lochbannag. They nodded to one another unsmiling. "You havena the family with you" said Jackson, making a slight statement. For only the youngest boy was with his father, silent and uncomfortable looking.

"Donnie is with my brother in Glasgow" said old Cameron, "they are a godly household; they worship with Mr Reid in North Street."

"Aye, aye" said the other. Then slanting his head towards the door, "I wonder what will the text be the day?"

"He will be speaking about sin."

"Aye, aye. And about this Hall."

"There will be no Hall" said Cameron of Balnafearchar.

Kate hurried a little. It was not that she was late, indeed she was early, but she didn't want to be caught nor have to speak in her official capacity to any other person. It was her Sunday too: day for a change of focus, day to get strength and help and a steady heart. It should be a day of fellowship, of the Kingdom; and who at all could she be in fellowship with? Not the regular church-goers, who used it, at best, as a comforting habit, at worst as a show-off. Those who went reluctantly, driven by public opinion? Roddy? But he never expected the heavens to open! It was time she stopped doing it herself. Her father never went now; he pretended that he might have gone to the Episcopalian church at Kinlochbannag if the road had been better. But that was really a gibe at her, since he did not particularly approve of her becoming the District Councillor. If any member of the family was to take it on, it should have been himself. And little enough she could do about that road anyway! The District Council rates would not even patch it.

He seemed to be nagging worse now than in the first years. About everything. Or was she imagining it? Or was it that she had been so deadened at first that she could not feel any pain except the one big one. Or was it just that she was being less nice to him, that her patience was giving out? Probably. It was time she got away. Here, for instance, was this measles case. In an unprotected Highland population. She had sent round a tactful note to Dr MacKillop, asking if he were going to immunise the younger school-children, and, if so, would he be sure to call on her if he needed any help. But would he actually do anything about it? Wouldn't he just let things take their course? There were other places which could make use of her! If once she felt she could leave her father. And all the rest that had her tangled in Port Sonas. She'd have to see this Village Hall through, anyway. She walked faster again.

And the Laird? Once in a way he came to the Parish Church and sat alone in the Castle pew. But, whatever motive Sandy might have for doing this, it was clear enough to Kate that the last thing he was looking for was fellowship. If he ever felt the need for that, it was not when he was at the church. She had never known him to look colder and more remote than he did at these times, and different altogether from himself with a fishing rod or a glass.

She caught up with her cousin Andrew and tapped him on the shoulder. He winced away from her, growling. "How are the rheumatics, Andy?" she asked. It was this, she was sure, which had aged him, this group of symptoms which was the curse of the west coat, rheumatism cutting into folk's lives with pain and disablement and sleeplessness, a constant drag, hardest, often, on the strong.

"No' too good, Katie," he said, "it's at my neck all the while, the same as an otter biting."

"You should make up your mind to try some deep treatment one day soon," she said.

"Ach, Dr MacKillop gied me some wee pills. Kind of aspirins. I didnie bother wi' them."

"That's not what I had in mind at all. I'd like to get you to a specialist, Andy——"

"Trust yin o' ye to send me to anither!"

"Aye, but ye'd no' have to pay, Andy, it would be under the National Health!" She had dropped into his way of speech. And I'll make him go, she said to herself, as they came to the door of the Parish Church, where the rest of the Elders, Mr MacMillan, Ian Ciotach, Jock from the Store, Baldy and Johnnie Beg were standing round about, watching the folk coming in. I must be extra polite to this lot, she thought, one never knows. It might make them better pleased with the Hall! But what do they think of me behind my back? As she went in, Ian complained, "I canna hardly make out what she says with yon Englishy voice she has!"

"Ach, well" said one of the others, "maybe she canna change it." •

But she did not hear, for now she was inside, had slipped into her place and bowed her head in her hands. For a moment her mind became quiet and ordered, streaming in the one direction. Then suddenly she caught herself wondering if she had scalded the milk pails thoroughly enough that morning. Perhaps if she had taken them right up into the kitchen, instead of bringing the kettle down—— Mrs MacLean began on her harmonium

56

Voluntary. Was there a note sticking? Was there? Was there? There was.

The Wee Free Elders were gathered too. Pate and the Whale were in their dark suits; they did not speak of fishing; they scarcely thought of it. The Whale was seeing that his crew were all there, in good order, excepting for the Beisd who was Established, if anything. Nobody spoke of the Hall.

Krooger and his crowd went in, the ones from the ferry house and the two or three crofts that stood at all angles round it. Krooger's army, the rest called them. And that dated back from the days of the first Krooger, this one's father. None of the young ones knew what the name meant, even, but they were so well-used to it that they never asked, though there was a good enough story to it, which the older fishermen knew. Mrs MacCulloch in black, with Jamesina and Euphemia in dark navy, stalked Roddy and Alasdair into the Church. At the door she stopped to speak to Mrs Mackintosh, the Minister's thin little wife, about the sale. By now it was part of the Port Sonas calendar that the Wee Free sale was in the spring and the Free Presbyterian one in the autumn, while the Parish church had the best time of all, just before Christmas. The Lifeboat and the District Nurse had theirs in summer when the visitors were there. But those two non-religious sales were general, open sales, without the warm, close, jealous arrangements of the others, the whispered conversations in bus or post office, with one eye on the enemy who might overhear, and the final boastings about the takings there had been.

Most of the crofters were Wee Frees and Mr Mackintosh himself was a crofter's son. By and large, you could tell the crofters by their boots, but the girls were just the same as the girls at the hotel or anywhere else. Two or three of the boarded-out children came with them. However, each church had its Sunday school as well. The little Carters came sidling up to Janet at the church door; she was their teacher. The Sunday schools had, of course, their male principal—it was Norman for the Wee Frees—who looked after the theology. But Norman, who had never been married, was not quite at home with the young lassies, most of all the Glasgow ones; he couldn't hear right what they said, and his answers might be altogether at cross purposes. But Janet would tell them Bible stories great, and go on from that to tell them about the old, old days in Scotland, the Cameronians and all, battles and blood, like in the boys' papers from the paper shop. Mary Carter began to whisper to Janet, who bent down to listen. Snash had gone in just ahead of them, his wife in her blacks following a yard or two behind.

While the services went on, Port Sonas lay shut and quiet; the dead houses in a half-circle round the bright ripple of the bay. The old stone jetty without a soul on it. The wee bare Curing Island, with the ruins of the old curing station and the old wooden landing jetties. And beyond, to the south-west, guarding against storms, Eilean Everoch and its tail of rocks where the young seals lay and flapped, and back of them the rough height of Eilean Garbh. Due south was Torskadale, the far side of the ferry. On a fine summer evening, when the sun was well back into the north-west, you would see the glitter from the windows of the Torskadale crofts and the track that went round the end of the mountains by Torskadale Point and beyond to the main Glenlurg road to Halbost. As things were, the Torskadale crofts might have been in another country almost. The Torskadale folk couldn't come over to Port Sonas for a meeting or a dance, because the ferry didn't run in the evenings. The children went to school in Kinlochbannag; the big brake from the Kinlochbannag hotel, owned by Councillor Thompson, picked them up and drove them in by the bad but passable road along the east side of Lochbannag and charged the County a shilling a mile for it. And it was at Kinlochbannag that the mothers did most of the shopping and the fathers most of their drinking. Councillor Thompson naturally had his cronies amongst them.

But all that would be different if once there was a bridge across the Kyles at the mouth of Lochbannag. A steel bridge could be flung across in a single span, with the peacock coloured tides tearing away below it. Then the main road from Port Sonas to Halbost would cross the bridge and go south along the Torskadale track that followed easy contours and could be made into a Class II road anyway. And so twenty miles would be saved as well as the bad, twisty Meall Dubh pass two miles out from Kinlochbannag, where after a storm you might find rocks down in the middle of the road. Once the bridge was there, the Torskadale children would walk in to school at Port Sonas and there would be coming and going and friendliness. But

Kinlochbannag would be by-passed and the custom at the hotel would drop by half.

Meanwhile, there was no steel and no money in Great Britain to spare for the Lochbannag bridge, so Councillor Thompson was not bothering himself.

The churches muttered or hummed. The seagulls floated and swooped. The youngest MacMillan boy from the hotel ran across the street to the sea wall and was almost over it when his mother made a scandalised dash and got him. She was seeing to the joint and the vegetables, would go to evening service later. They had only a couple staying at the hotel just now, but they were well booked up for the summer months. Behind the shut door of the garage, Hughie was doing a secret and well paid electrical repair. The Doctor was still asleep. He had come back late and nobody was going to chisel him about going to church. His housekeeper shared his immunity, but she had tuned in the wireless to a service while she was slowly polishing the ashtrays and the presentation cigarette box in the consulting room, and now and then glancing out of the window to the blue, empty Sound of Torskadale. There was a wee note lying on the table; that would be from Mistress Snow, now. Forever bothering the Doctor. But as like as not he'd pay no heed to it. Ah, men!

The churches began to skail. Mothers of families hurried off to do the dinner; fathers lingered, smelling the air and the sunshine, some way relieved. Pipes were lighted here and there, though the Free Presbyterians on the whole did not countenance smoking on the Sabbath. The Established was out first, but the slower walkers would find the first ranks of the Wee Free crossing over on to the main road. Kate had hung behind the rest, dropping her gloves once or twice, buttoning her coat high, then undoing it again. She did not want to go home. She did not want to hear complaints about the size of the Sunday joint, nor to have to go over the rationing again. Above all, she did not want to spend the afternoon looking at teapots. She could get to the milking early; she could look for an outlying layer among the hens; she could sterilise every pail and strainer that was in it; she could even go over to the Castle and see what kind of temper Sandy was in. But if only, just for once, the Heavens would open!

David MacTavish and his sister were ahead. They stopped to speak to Jameus of the Glen store, who went to the Wee Free

59

Church where most of his customers went, but always scuttled out after the service like a cork out of a bottle. When Kate was over at the store getting a new mantle for a lamp, he had told her he was for the Hall; but he hadn't come to the meeting. Why?

Then Norman and one of the old crofters came over together. They spoke of the beauty of the day and of the goodness of its Creator. Their speech was of the same kind as that of the psalms which were in their minds. But Kate was not responding. "How is your father keeping?" said Norman.

"Oh, all right" said Kate, flatly, and suddenly to her own great surprise, choked.

"My lassie, my lassie" murmured Norman, and the softness of his voice broke something in Kate.

"You know well enough, Norman" she said, "it's not always very cheery."

He nodded. His friend the crofter, who knew her less well, had drifted away, tactfully as a summer cloud. "Direach sin," said Norman, "aye, aye, just so. It's a hard row you have, lassie, and you doing so much for other folks."

She looked up, comforted a little. If some of them thought even that——! "I'm very glad you're on the Hall Committee, Norman," she said.

"Aye, well, we will all do our best, under the Lord's guidance" said Norman. "Your father was with you at the meeting, Mistress Kate. But I doubt he did not have so deep an interest as yourself. That's easy seen."

"He only came so as to tell me afterwards just what nonense it was!" said Kate suddenly. Already it was a comfort to have said it, to have got it off her chest. There was nobody she could say that to, not even Sandy, she always pretended to him that there was nothing wrong. And she had kept her temper last night. If that did any good.

"He should not have done that on you," said Norman, shaking his head. "But still and on, he is your father."

"And I'm nearly fifty! But there's nothing to be done." She was feeling better. She took a deep breath. But she would say one thing more. "And his collections. His tea-pots. They're beginning to get me down."

"Aye, they would so, my lassie" said Norman. He nodded his

head, comfortingly, wisely. He had seen such things before. He knew them for inessential. "It is hard enough to see a folly when it is one of ourselves" he said, "but it is away worse for the like of you, that have education. Yet he is a good man at heart, Mr MacFarlan, and if once he would seek the aid and comfort of the Lord God, all could yet be well, for him and yourself. And maybe it will be yet. Aye, maybe it will."

"I sometimes wonder if he cares for anything at all but his collections," said Kate, "It's—oh, it's not like a grown man."

"Aye, aye, he has not put away childish things. But he is mild with it all. You should not be too angry at him, my lassie."

"I'm not really angry, Norman. I just want something else to happen!" She was almost smiling now, and then over Norman's shoulder she saw Janet shake herself loose from the rest of the girls from the Glen crofts. She was older than most of them; had refused more than one offer. Now, in anger, her black brows gathered together, she looked her age. "What is it?" said Kate.

"Listen" said Janet, "and listen, you, Norman! Did you ever hear the like of this—and yon Snash sitting so snog there in the body of the kirk——"

"Oh, *that*" said Kate, "yes."

Norman listened and nodded and clicked his tongue.

"You ought to take the skin off him" said Janet, "The wicked old—old——"

"Do you not file your tongue over the like of him, lassie" Norman said. "The Lord will judge him."

"But you can't just leave it that way!" said Janet, "what for is the Kirk Session if it's not to deal with the like of Snash?"

"Yes" said Kate "can't the Elders deal with him?"

Norman said nothing for a moment. Then he drew himself up. "It's not for the women to say what we should do." He turned from Janet to Kate: "For neither of the two of you: go you home now and be not presumptuous."

He was staring at Kate, and now, she thought, he is no more kind nor wise; he is only jealous in case he is proved to have less power than he wants to have. Better if neither of us answer. "Come, Janet" she said and took her by the sleeve and turned away and began to walk up the road towards the Glen. After a minute she noticed that her own hand was trembling. "Probably better to leave this to the secular arm!" she said, not so much to Janet as to reassure herself, to assert intellectual superiority.

Janet did not notice: she said, low, "I hate men, I hate men." She was thinking in a confused, flashing, jerking way of several men at the once, but mostly of her father, whom she was bound to love, but who had taken her away from school just when everything was opening out; and her brothers who had taken it for granted that they were to go on; and Duncan Macrae, that had seen her back from the meeting of praise one time, and she had thought he was a decent lad, but when she said no, he had said—ach, she could never forget it!

Kate was speaking again, saying, was it? that she would write to the Inspector. But Kate was only a woman like herself. And there had been Matta and Baldy and Hugh, each of them at her to marry him, to belong to him, all wanting to take her away to use for himself, the same as her father had taken her from school! And not one of them the kind of man she would want to marry. And that man maybe not at Port Sonas at all. If only she could get away. Away from her father. And now she found herself looking away out, with the wind soft on her wet eyes and the flush going out of her cheeks, up the road and beyond, and there was T'each Mor, so quiet, so quiet the great hill: not troubling itself, not troubling her, reaching into the sky, and the line of it never changing. I to the hills will lift mine eyes. And the hills will neither want me nor fail me.

CHAPTER V

SUNDAY EVENING: SERVICE OF PRAISE

AT THE TURN OF the century the Revie's had come from
Peterhead to Port Sonas on the West coast. Andrew Revie's
father had started a curing station there, one of half a dozen for a
time in the best years of it, when the harbour was full of herring
boats coming in and carriers going out, then one of two, and last
the only one left. Andrew had been a lad with a quick tongue in
those days, good with his hands, good at a bargain, a great one for
the lasses and soon enough, but not before time, married on the
bonniest of the three bonny MacKeith sisters, cousins to Florag's
father. A great wedding they had, with the whisky flowing like
lemonade and the dancing going on until far into the night, and
wee Katie MacFarlan in pink muslin with blue bows and her hair
down her back, allowed up to midnight and wild to be dancing
reels. There was a matter of four sons and two daughters within
ten years after that, for the Revies, but their mother died when
they were all young. Andrew Revie brought up the older boys to
be curers, but by the time they had learnt their trade well, the
bottom was going out of the curing, no more barrels shipped to
the Baltic markets nor likely to be for long enough, the American
market small and tricky, the home market poor; and the best
thing for a young fellow with knowledge of coopering was to sit
his exam for Fishery Officer. So here were two of the boys in the
Fishery Service and one a teacher back on the east coast near
Aberdeen, and one in New Zealand and doing well. The younger
daughter was married down in England, but May, the elder one,
who had never cared much for the boys, was still keeping house
for her father and mostly always walking with him over to the
church for the evening Service of Praise. May Revie was in the
first line of contraltos in the choir and a great one for the old
psalms, but she liked the Scottish songs and could read and play
from staff as well as sol-fa. She had thought to take her exams in
music and maybe teach a wee bit, but some way she had never

got round to it. But she was the conductor of the Port Sonas ladies' choir.

Andrew was speaking to Sandy the Coileach and a friend of his, another of the crew of the Silver Bird, Donald MacDonald who was mostly called Coories. They were discussing the lobsters, trying to narrow it down. "It would never be one of the fleet" said Sandy.

"Are ye sure o' that?" said Andrew Revie, and his voice still had something of the quickness and decision of the east coast, though he had been so long over on the west. "It cud ha' been true enough in the old days, but there's young fellows now wud sell their mither's petticoats off her while she slept. And look at the wild bing o' stuff there is to tempt folks to come by the money ony which way, and the women folk at them a' the while to buy!"

"Don't you be blaming the women folk, Father!" said May. "It's you with your great pipes, smoking away a pound's worth of this tobacco before you know and nothing to show for it in the end!"

"Well, I believe I'm a bittie to blame there," said Andrew. "But the way I'm looking at it is this." He frowned and screwed his face, grey bristle up to the cheek bones, trying to get it right. "We old yins wudna ha' been dirty to one another—no' thon way. We cud ha' cheated them fairly, the same way as they cud ha' got the better of us. But—but yon lobsters o' Matta's—och, it was plain dirty stealing!"

"True enough," said Coories, "and whoever it was must ha' kent what Matta had in the box."

"That wud be easy," said Andrew, "and him bragging himself at the Bar!"

"I doubt it wouldna be shore folk," said Coories, "they wouldna risk taking a boat at night."

"There's some o' the forestry crowd can manage a boat as well as oursel's. There's young Charlie and the Kettle. They're forever off fishing in the summer in yon old punt that belongs to Charlie's uncle."

"You wouldna say it was them, surely? The Kettle's a decent boy——"

"Ach, no, I wasna saying it. But it could be."

"Easy" said Sandy.

64

"It micht be easier sayin' who it wasna," said Andrew meditatively. "And it wasna mysel' nor yet Norman, for I was ower at his house for a crack and gey late we were, aye and wearied, two old bodachs as we are!"

"And it wasna me no' yon night!" said Sandy.

"Not wi' the Silver Bird fishing."

"Aye, but she wasna fishing! Was Pate no' telling you? We were mending the net all Thursday forenoon. We got a terrible tearing early on, a bit up from Duisker—ach well, there wasna much doing, so we thought we'd just come back." He was laughing away now, but inwardly, without noise because it was the Sabbath. And so was Coories laughing.

Andrew looked at them. At last he said: "Well, if it wasna the lobsters, what kinna ploy did ye have, boys?"

"If you can be speaking of it before me!" said May. Though it was the queerest thing: May Revie was the kind a man could speak away with and say every kind of thing that came into his head and never feel affronted, and that although she had never been married nor ever going with a lad even, for there was a sincerity and understanding about her that is a great thing in man or woman.

Coories and Sandy gave each other a look. "Ach well," said Coories. "I was wearyin' for a wee taste o' salmon and my chum here wearyin' to try out a wee net that came his way a whilie back."

"Well, well" said Andrew, "I heard they were running. It will be an early season. But you shouldna be too hard on the Laird."

"Na, na" said Sandy "we'll no' spoil the river on him. No' like some. Yon Torskadale crowd! They're up and down wi' the tide still and we took no more than would make us our tea. Could you do wi' a cut, Andrew?"

"You should be asking me have I the heart to cook a stolen fish!" said May. "Aye, stolen, Sandy!"

"Ach, May, it's only kind of half stolen," said Sandy.

"Then I'll only kind of half cook it! What weight of fish was it?"

"It was all of fifteen pounds. Oh a bonny one! I'll bring you your cut over after the service. And a two-three sea trout. It was great ploy we had and the wee net fishing grand."

"Did George not see you at it?"

"Oh poor George! No, no, he's no' that active these days and he didna know there was any o' the boats in. He isna watching right except on a Saturday night. There was more sport wi' him in the old days when he had his two legs and another watcher along wi' him."

"Aye, that's so," said Coories, "but isn't it a shame to be suspecting the poor fishermen! And yon forestry lads as bad as the worst of oursel's. But he aye casts the blame on us wi' the Laird. And here, there was more shore folk than fishermen on yon ploy!"

"Who all was there?" asked Andrew, "was it Jameus?"

"Och aye, and wee Chuckie and Hughie. There's fine ploy wi' yon boys." His eyes softened, thinking back to Thursday night and the thing arranged in whispers and low laughter. Secrets and devilment! Aye, and better than with a lassie, for there is less risk of it turning out badly in the end. And the sack with the net, a dark easy burden under the stars, and the great beauty of the night with the land breath of budding flowers and brairding corn, and the sea breath cool and salt. Sandy was speaking of it now to Andrew with May letting on she was not listening; but the Church was coming in sight.

They had rowed round from the back of Curing Island where Sandy had a wee punt, and up through the Kyles against the current, with an eye open for lights in the ferry house or the crofts. But all was dark and safe. And so, softly and cannily, in among the great rocks at the mouth of the river where it flows out into Lochbannag above the Kyles. There in the wee wood above the rocks the smell was sweetest, with seaboots heavy on the moss and the starlit faces of the primroses and the birken tassels brushing against the cheek of the one that waited on shore with the end of the rope gripped and the flutter like a bird in the throat in case the land shadows would move and pounce. For it might have been that old George could have been warned, it might have been that all was betrayed and the trap waiting! And indeed without that fear it all would have been too easy. And dark and wee the boat going off on her circle, and no sound from the canny oars and light as leaf fall the corks and leads on the muffling sack over the gunwhale, and the net sinking below the ripple and the rope going down into the dark water, and the one on the rock still and hunched as the rock itself, all his life in his holding hands, his eyes on the water and the top of the net going out on its circle, but his

66

ears straining back for a land sound, for the light crack of a twig underfoot. And back comes the boat taking the inner side of the curve of the net, with splash and patter to fright the fish into the mesh. And then the sudden living throb on the taut rope that comes when the great fish charges the net, and now he is ranging along it, the wise salmon, and if he can get over or under, then it's goodbye. But the rope throbs and tugs, as one's heart also, and the boat comes nearer, gathering in the circle. And they see him below, the sudden twist and gleam of breaking silver in the wet darkness and now quick, the flow of the net round him, men's clever hands against the struggle and strength of the salmon! And great for the one on the rock to leap aboard, one foot on the gunwale and a friend's hand in his own, and the sweet dangerous wood receding, the birk and hazel no longer a dark trap, but the boat full of pleasure and friendship and praise of each by all and the mastered salmon shining on the net!

All through the service the minds of the two fishermen were still rocking and luminous with thought of the Thursday night's ploy, with praise and delight. So longs my spirit, Lord, for Thee and Thy night full of sweet scents and the delicate curve of the net stretched in the water and Thy gifts and grace! Aye, aye, and there was Hughie, a fine lad altogether, and a great tenor, and I myself, thought Sandy, I have never heard me sing in better tune, and the great swelling and blending of the voices, as though they were a net for the catching of grace! There was only the one jag in all this, the thought of poor Matta and his lobsters. They had come to no conclusion.

From behind, May Revie was watching the men singing away there. Why did none of them see any harm in poaching? It was partly no doubt the way they said themselves, that they did not see that any man had the right to possession of the wild birds and beasts and fishes. But that was only what they said. In their inside minds they knew the salmon belonged to the Laird, but they themselves were the clever ones to outwit and cheat and steal and get by with it. And yet for all that they had no enmity against the Laird. And when he dies they will all be lamenting and speaking of his virtues!

But who had taken the lobsters? Aye, that was different altogether.

Andrew Revie was studying on that too. He had learnt not to

listen, especially to sermons, though he liked fine to be passing the time at an evening service. May would as soon have sat in listening to a service on the wireless, or for that matter a good concert. But that way you missed the walk. It would need to have been someone that was not feared to handle a boat. He thought back to Thursday night. There would have been a bit jabble beyond the harbour, not much surely, but enough to scare a right landsman. And it would need to be someone that knew just where the box was, for you couldna see it easy. And would there have been any punt lying in the harbour with oars and rowlocks in her? And then to get them away—you would scarcely market them in Halbost, no, it would need to be Fort William. Unless the cargo boat were to take them—and if so they would still be lying somewhere and would need to be put on tomorrow. Ach, nobody would dare! Unless yon wee devil Archie were in on it.

Archie! The thought stayed in his head, working its way round. Archie the harbour master who was so grand and eydent twice a week when the cargo-boat came in, set him up! He had been no friend of Andrew's since a matter of some herring barrels that had gone astray thirty years back. The devil of a row they'd had. Aye, aye. A muckle great splash Archie had made in the water! He'd liked a row fine in yon days, had gone out of his way to provoke them. And a wheen bonny nights at the poaching, the same as yon lads on the Thursday. But for all that he had got on fine with the Laird; many a crack they'd had together in the old days, after the first war, when the Laird had come back. And half the regiment killed. And the drink so handy. But Archie now— he wouldna have risked to do the thing himself and he with his reputation and his safe and steady job; but there was his nephew Jim . . . Maybe I should go down the morn's morn, he thought to himself, and take a wee look through the boxes that are to go on the steamer. Aye, if I could catch Archie . . .

But suddenly he began to attend to the sermon. Mr Fergusson had been daundering round his text and time for him to stop or he would be over his evening length. But all at once he was speaking about the Hall, saying that such places might prove a blessing, if rightly used, but if wrongly—och, och, he was much more eloquent over that! Andrew Revie began to growl perceptibly. May turned and patted his knee: "There, there, father, take no heed of the silly man!"

Mr Fergusson wound up. There was the final hymn and Andrew quietened down. May helped him on with his coat and he stumped over to the vestry. There seemed to be quite a few there as it was. Mr Fergusson often experienced a certain shrinking from his congregation, above all from the fishermen who were so much bulkier physically than himself. They would say things aside to one another in the Gaelic and his own was not up to following them, although he knew by heart a few prayers in the Gaelic. The other two churches, by a kind of unspoken understanding, had Gaelic evening services on alternate Sabbaths. Mr Mackintosh of the Wee Frees and Mr Munro of the Free Presbyterians, were both equally at home in either language, and it gave them an advantage which Mr Fergusson had to counter in some other way.

Meanwhile May waited for her father in the porch. She spoke a word or two to Mrs MacMillan from the hotel and Miss MacTavish, the schoolmaster's sister, a sensible decent soul, but not a note of music in her. The evening was coming softly with a sweetening of the air. Jessie from the tearoom had a bunch of primroses in her hand, wilting a little after the service, but they would freshen up yet. "We'll need to hold a wee meeting for the choir, Jessie," said May, "could we come over to the tearoom tomorrow evening?"

"Tomorrow Monday?" said Jessie, "Och aye. We can just have our meeting after the fishermen." For in winter and spring the tearoom was a kind of cheery place to meet, lighter a lot than the mission hall and less draughts. And the same to pay. But once the visitors began it was no good that way to the village.

"Will you tell Anna and Christine and the rest, Jessie?"

Jessie nodded. "I'll be seeing them, sure. And I'll send a message up the Glen by Angus. Och, there's nothing else on. Nothing else at all. You'd be wearying for something, whatever it could be. Do you think we'll get this Hall? There was some saying it would cost terrible. But could we no' get up a concert? And maybe tea. We could get thirty pounds easy."

"That's just what we could do" said May. "Will you be bringing it up at the committee?" She turned to Florag, who had joined them. "If we made a start now we could have a good-going concert by the time the visitors are here."

"Where would we get to practice?" said Florag. "You'll

69

not be able to let us in to the tearoom after next month, Jessie. What was your uncle saying about the Hall, anyway?" For Jessie's uncle Dugald, who was mostly called Bits, was the owner of the tearoom.

"He wasna speaking any to me," said Jessie doubtfully, then: "He's kind of droll. And if the Hall was to take custom away from the tearoom, well, he might be the same way he is over the Bar."

"The Bar, is it? But that's with him being Temperance, surely?" said May. She was on the whole against the Bar herself, and her father apt to get yon nasty turns on the liver nowadays if he indulged, and indeed, barring the rheumatism, it was the only thing that ever went wrong with him.

Jessie giggled and ducked her nose into the primrose bunch: "Are you saying that to me, and mother keeping house for him all these years! He aye sings the Band of Hope hymns best when he's had his parcel off the bus from Kinlochbannag!" She hummed a line of *My drink is water bright*. "Och aye, he puts the expression in great!"

"Well, well, are you saying that!" said May. "But I doubt there's hardly a man in it that's Temperance in his bones."

"Some of the young fellows that comes to the tearoom are that," said Jessie. "They say the stuff's too dear for them. And Mr Fergusson is strict temperance; he'll not take a glass of port even."

"Och well," said Florag, "The Ministers is different. They'd need to be strict with all the folk watching them. But if your uncle was against the Hall, we mightn't get to practise for a concert there. It'll be work enough to get the choir members from the other churches to come for any concert that's not just a holy concert. But that would never do for the visitors."

"No, indeed!" said Jessie, "we'll never get Maggie nor yet wee Lizzie. It'll be hard enough with the Wee Frees, but the F.P.'s'll just not come unless there's gunpowder under them! And there's two of our good sopranos out of it right away."

"I wonder is there no way round it?" said Florag.

"Not unless we stay Holy. Ach, it's not them so much, it's their folk. Why, they'll not like a psalm even, if it's not a Minor!"

"I'm asking myself," said May, "could we not get to practise at the Bee House. There's a bonny piano there and not getting enough use. It was there with the furniture when cousin Kate took over the house. But she's not one for the music."

"Aye," said Jessie, "it's in the room with all yon queer teapots! I was over last year about the raffle for the Nurse, and here didn't I get ten minutes looking at Mr MacFarlan's teapots. Do you know this, Florag, there's ones like wee houses and ones like hens and jucks and loaves of bread and all in the bonniest colours, and other ones with wee kind of flowers and ribbons all over, like—och, like a summer hat, only in china!—awful difficult to clean, only maybe they're never used——"

"Well," said May, "we'll just bring it up at the Committee. If we have a concert, you'll need to practise your duet with Ella."

"Sweet Afton, aye," said Jessie, "I like that awful much. Ella says she's after putting in her notice to the school."

"Is she now! I wonder who'll take it?"

"I couldn't say at all," said Jessie, "nobody's terrible keen on the school cleaning."

The Elders came out now, with Mr Fergusson, who walked away towards the Manse with his face pinched up, the way it went when he was displeased. Andrew Revie said to Ian Ciotach: "There he goes wanting to be holier than the other two!"

"Man, Andrew, isn't it great the sins the Ministers think on!" said Ian. "But I canna see the young ones getting so terrible much worse than they are now, over the head of this Hall."

"Och, it's no' that ava!" said Andrew impatiently, "It's just the way you'll never get a right Minister in these wee places. My son that's teachin' near Aberdeen was after tellin' me there's Ministers you'd not know from ordinar' decent folks. They'd go into the pubs and all and speak away there, let alone a Village Hall!"

"Are you telling me!" said Ian.

"I am, so," said Andrew, "but mind ye, Ian, there's no' that mony o' thon kind. I mind of a Minister in Peterhead—och, well, maybe this is no' exactly the day to be speakin' agin them." He nodded abruptly to Ian and went stumping on, then signalled with his head to May, who smiled at the others and followed after him.

There was no question by now about the Hall, for the Free Presbyterians, at least for those who went to the Tabernacle out of a sense of heaven and hell. The Elect would have nothing

71

to do with any Hall. Yet there are backsliders in every congregation and especially in large families. The knowledge that this must be so swept furiously across the rest, the followers of a jealous God. Nor had they, quoting from Exodus or Kings or Chronicles, aye, or good old Genesis itself, less than the grandest and savagest of words with which to lash themselves and others, and the Gaelic service working them up better even than the English! If there were doubters it was in silence that they doubted.

But the Wee Frees were more riven. It was almost certain about Mr Mackintosh himself. Yet he had not said in so many words that the thing was evil. Indeed he had worked round it like a cow eating round a clump of thistles. His eyes had encountered now Norman and now one or another of the crofters and fishermen; his purpose had wavered. It kept on coming through his mind—and was it temptation or was it a fact?— that compromise with the world was necessary in so far as the immortal soul is shaped into a body, some of whose needs at least cannot be gainsaid. Could it be that this Hall might be a lesser evil? Yet the lesser evil is also evil, and we must wrestle. He prayed mightily for deliverance from the lesser evils, without yet speaking of what they might be. Let those that had ears, hear!

There was an uneasiness in the congregation. It was somewhat different now from that of the morning. The older folks from the crofts would not always be wanting another four or five miles of a walk, though a few might have taken their Sunday dinner with friends. Janet and her father were not there; Janet would be milking and feeding the hens, and then she would come in and her father would read from the Book and she would listen or think her thoughts. From among the fisher folks it was mostly the women and some of the young ones that came. Yet it was few enough of the young fishermen that were religious. It had been different in the old days; when there was constant danger in the small sail boats and the first motor boats, then a man had need to lay hold on something stronger than the sea. But there had been no boat lost, nor any of a crew lost, for long enough now. And these bigger boats were going further afield, seeing other kinds of life, and the men believing in their good, complex, expensive diesel engines, and maybe speaking of radar and echo sounders and the like. And what was miracles compared with that?

And they had the Fishermen's Association. That had started by being religious and some of the older men forever saying that it was not like the Unions on the east coast that no religious man would join. But in itself the Association was something which put people in a fellowship which was not of the church. That was it, when it came to the bit. For those who thought themselves truly religious, most of all for the Free Presbyterians, any association that was not directly of the church was a distraction, was a temptation and a leading away from the true race and the only goal. Therefore all such things were evil, whatever good earthly intention they might have, aye all, Boy Scouts, political parties, the Women's Rural Institutes, the Farmer's Union, above all anything which in any way encouraged games, dancing, the heathen Highland pipes or any other thing to do with the body where Satan might enter to seize from there on the soul. And yet, knowing that, knowing the danger, men remained men and women—what was worse—women.

Norman was worrying himself terrible over Snash. There would need to be something done! Yet he could not do what the women said, not after them saying it! The worry of this was stopping him from thinking much about the Hall. At the door he laid a hand on the sleeve of his friend Alan, one of the other crofters from the Glen, a man with a son in the Forestry as well as the one that helped on the croft, and a daughter that worked in the East boarding-house in summer, so that he had money coming in and no need to take the Glasgow children. His croft was next to Snash's, but on higher land, and the house on a wee knoll, so that you could see out well. They stepped aside from the stream of folk a little. "Were you hearing about Snash, Alan?" he asked.

"Man, Norman," said Alan, "hearing, is it! I saw."

"How?"

"Well, there was I at my window watching the road and along came poor David MacTavish on his bike. Was he at the Church in the morning, do you know?"

"I doubt he wasna. Aye, Andrew was saying that. He will have been wrestling with the thing on his lone. Och, poor David, poor David! And was Snash seeing him?"

"Aye. And yon wife of his. And there was Peigi and Mairi and the wee boys and the Glasgow lassie with them. They were up in the bushes between his croft and my own. Well, David got off his bike and went toiling up the path and my lord not stirring to meet him, a Dhia, a Dhia! At last he came to the bit brae where Snash had his oats last year—you'll mind? And here Snash appeared at the head of the brae and stood like a rock, and poor David never got near with Snash letting out a great roar—for indeed I had come out the house and down to the wee shed where I could be observing. Och, poor David, the man! He was getting dog's abuse from Snash whenever he opened his mouth and at last Snash called for the bairns and they came up and Greta sniffling in the midst of them. And here Snash shouting at the poor wee lassock, did she or did she not lend yon dress to Peigi of her own free will. And, Aye, squeaked the poor wee soul with her hand up to her eyes and, Away you! says Snash, and turns on the schoolmaster again. Man, it was great the language he had! So after a while David turned tail from yon Goliath and went back the way, and Snash watching him and throwing a word or two he had spare after him! And do you know this, Norman, David got to the road and he was so shaken up he let his bike fall twice."

"A Dhia nan Gras, isn't that a black shame!" said Norman, "and the poor wee lassie not daring to speak the truth!"

"Aye, you're right there. It was later on a bit, my own Sheila saw her sitting her lone under a rock and greeting, so she went over and gave her a bit sweetie. But it's a wild thing to happen and Snash getting away with it."

"It's yourself knows the truth of it, Alan. Could you not be writing to Glasgow?"

"Ach no, I wouldna like. No, no, I could not be doing that. Not at all! He's a bad one, Snash, but he is my neighbour and I'd need to be living with him all my days."

"You would not need to say it was you writing."

"Aye, but it would get round. No, no, it would not be right for me to be doing anything and him and me neighbours so long."

"But something will need to be done. It would be terrible altogether if such badness were to go unpunished. There was no such badness in the old days."

"In the old days there were no Glasgow bairns in the crofts so it was not possible at all for folk to be bad to them."

"In the old days folk went in fear of Judgement."

"But there was aye a hard one here or there the like o' Snash that would not care."

"He could have been made to care. Maybe we are none of us believing deep enough. It is hell fire that is needed. When all believe, Alan, it is a strong net. But now it is broken. Maybe the fault lies in ourselves. Och, maybe we are all guilty for Snash!" He began to look more and more troubled and his voice went low into his beard. "Aye, maybe we are all backsliders. Maybe Snash was sent as a sign and a warning to the rest of us. We will need to examine our conscience and our actions."

A few of the young were going by now. Jamesina McCulloch and Eilidh and Mairi MacRae from Osnish, all doucely together in a row with their dark gloves and psalm books. But there was a row of boys following close behind, all in their dark suits and hard white collars, but speaking to one another in voices that would carry to the girls. And suddenly there was a high giggle from one of the row in front, abruptly cut off as she saw the two old men and ducked her head. Norman looked across at them and now there was a terrible frown on him. "Hell fire," he said, "hell fire! It is time yon crowd were to think on it, the way they look to be going! And our own fault if they do not. Hell fire. And myself going to meetings about Village Halls!"

CHAPTER VI

MONDAY: AT THE STEAMER

On a good day all those with time to spare would go down to watch the boat come in. And if you are working on your own and not for a boss, or even if the boss is another Highlander like yourself, you can surely spare the time and maybe put in a bit extra work some time else when you are in the mood for it. So there were plenty down at the quay, leaning against the wall, sitting on bollards or packing cases, feeling the spring sun in their faces. Miss Beaton, the District Nurse, was apt to see her patients near the harbour on a boat morning; her auto-cycle was leaning against the wall. The boat came twice a week, but it was best on a Monday for the fishermen would still be there, redding everything up, the cooks bringing down the week's rations, the nets brought in from the drying poles on a net barrow that was no one's and everyone's; barrels of diesel oil going aboard, water tanks filling up; the men all in their working clothes, jerseys and overalls, but still clean and shaved from Sunday, their cloaks and sea boots waiting for evening on the boats.

There were eight drift-net herring boats at Port Sonas, but two of them were old and smaller than the rest, with the Zulu sterns and small, cramped looking wheel houses, good sea boats in their way, but not near so fast as the new ones, for all that they were paying a good share-out just now. Among them these boats were employing between forty and fifty men and boys. Beside these drifters there were three lobster boats, fifteen and twenty footers, each with a crew of two or three, and a few small punts with hand lines that were mostly used in summer for visitors. There was a proud, bonny look to all of them, waiting to leave on a Monday, moving a little against the side of the quay, and the seagulls going back and forth between them and the sun, or lighting for a moment on a high masthead.

Pate and the Whale and Johnnie Beg had the harbour master by the shoulders and were rubbing into him that when these

Highland Panel folk came over, he was to speak of the hole in the sea wall. A storm twenty years back had loosed a block of concrete and since then it had been nobody's business to see to it and it was worse it had got and now it would take maybe two or three hundred pounds to sort it. There had been talk about it on the District Council, but it had seemed to be nobody's responsibility. Now it might be the money would be got from the Government with no trouble at all. And if there was cement coming to Port Sonas, there could well be a few bags over which would come in gey handy for a number of worthy objects. But that was not said, only understood.

Malcie, the joiner, was down, for he was expecting some wood. He had plenty of work ahead of him for the next year or two, with repairs and additions to houses and steadings, all under a thousand pounds and licensed by the Council. And forby that, there was the new dining-room and three bedrooms over it for the East boarding house, and that would cost into four figures well. And there were those who asked themselves how the licence had been got. Kate had been surprised to hear that it had been going on—Mr MacMillan from the hotel had come over to see her about it in a great state of indignation, and after that Mrs MacKeith from the other boarding house. She herself had been down a few days later and spoken to them about it, but Mrs Crawford of the East boarding house had answered her that everything was in order. There was some talk of second-hand materials, and Kate was never very good at doing sums quickly in her head, and she didn't just like to ask the Planning Officer at Halbost, whom she didn't know at all well, and who had a scratchy little beard that she always found rather putting-off since the day when at a meeting she had seen crumbs in it. Malcie at any rate had the contract as far as the woodwork was concerned; but first he would need to finish the wee job at the Achnahabhainn byre and the other on the sarking of the old roof at the side of the sweetie shop. There was slater's work to do there, but at a pinch he could do that as well as any slater from Halbost. Hughie-the-garage was down to see would he get the spares for Roddy's car lights.

Dugald Bits from the tearoom was down to see would his crate of utility cups and saucers come from Glasgow. He stopped to speak to Big Jock of the village store, who was standing outside his own door. The store was down on the quay, close to the landing place and it was easy for anyone that was waiting to go into the store and there they might think to buy themselves a pack of cigarettes when there were any, or a few kirbygrips or a jar of meat paste. But Big Jock, though he was aware of that, was more set on them just coming in and speaking; he didn't like it if he was not the first with any news. From time to time there would be a rumour, whether he himself started it or not, that he was selling out, either to the Loch Broom Trading Company, or else to the Co-op, and then everybody in Port Sonas would be in before long to find out was there anything in it.

"You werena at the meeting on Saturday" said Bits.

"I wasna" said Big Jock, "but here, I didna want to commit myself one way or the other. But I was hearing about it great."

"You're not the only one that's no' committing theirselves" said Bits, "I'm no' that keen mysel' and Krooger's crowd will scarcely come in. I canna hardly see what benefit it would be to the bulk of the community; the young ones are up to plenty as it is."

"Aye, aye" said Jock, and then dropped his voice, "Were you hearing what they were after saying about Kenny's Chrissie?"

Dugald listened and clucked with his tongue, "Well, well, well, and who would she have been going with? I mind now her being in the tearooms with the Kettle a whiley back. Aye, and there was Jim."

"And maybe a two-three from up the Glen."

"And do you mind she was seen one night with Donnie Cameron from Balnafearchar, and him with his motor-cycle?"

"Aye, these motor bykes is a great occasion for sin. Great altogether. But the boys was telling me they had seen her up at the back of the tree by the Post Office with Roddy."

"Roddy! He'll have something saved, will that same Roddy. Well, well, it's wonderful what will happen. Were you expecting anything on the steamer, Jock?"

"Aye, aye, Dugal. My jams and my minerals. And there should be bacon this week. Ach, it's terrible the bacon we're getting! When I think of the good bacon that was in it before this

78

Government had everything rationed. They'll be keeping it all for themselves down in London!"

"You can depend on that, Jock. Well, well, there's wee Malcie, I'll away over and see whether can he help me a bittie over my extension."

"Were you thinking ou an extension, Dugal?"

"Well, I was kind of half thinking. There will be more visitors in the summer and if I can get a wee tottie place it wouldna need heating and Jessie could manage surely. If she thought less about her choir—but they're all alike, the young ones." He made his way over to Malcie, nodding to some of the fishermen and to Archie and speaking a few words with Red Dougie, who was down with his horse and cart, ready for a ton of potato fertiliser that was to come off the boat. It was planting weather right enough and he had half his drills open and was just waiting on the manure to make a start.

Malcie was slowly cleaning his nails with a small screw-driver and feeling the sun. He looked up at Bits and smiled; he half knew what was coming.

"I am asking myself, Malcie" said Bits "how you are for timber, for I was thinking of building a wee kind of place——"

Malcie shook his head; "You'll need to get a building licence and the wood from Timber Control. Unless it's hard wood you're wanting, and that's devilish dear."

"Ach, but it wouldna hardly take any—you would do it with yon Celotex panels on a frame——"

"That's controlled just the same" said Malcie.

"Ach, well, maybe I could get a-hold of some if you could get the framing, three by two's, Malcie—you wouldn't notice it. And you wouldn't find it hard to make a price with me," he whispered.

"The Lord himself couldna make a timber allocation stretch beyond a certain point" said Malcie, "and it's long ago that I passed yon point. And I wouldn't want to be getting into trouble, Dugal."

"No one of us wouldn't want that for you, Malcie, but——"

"There's Angus now wi' the lorry" said Malcie, "I'll just need to see him a minute. I'll mind on what you said, Dugal." He moved off towards the lorry which Angus was turning and backing.

Angus was one of the ex-Service boys and had bought this lorry himself. Today he had brought down a calf from Balnafearchar, its body in a sack and its sad head sticking out and crying. He had a crate of empties from the Glen store, jam jars and minerals mostly, and a barrel returned from the hotel which was expecting another full one by the boat. Most of the agricultural and hotel stuff came by boat, but the yarn for the weavers came in by bus or lorry from the mill at Halbost, and the woven webs went in the same way, except for what might be sold locally. But in the season the main work of the lorry was on herring, and even so there would be mornings when they'd need to phone in to Halbost for a dozen more.

It was summer fishing in the Sound of Torskadale and in the old days the fishermen had worked their crofts in spring and fished in summer with a few days off for the harvest, and then in winter they had sat back and made and mended nets, or worked on boats and houses and lived poorly on meal and salt herring mostly. But now with the bigger boats and the money that was eating its head off in them and their gear, they needed to fish whole time; so they would be away the week, sometimes crossing the Minch or going away down to the Isle of Man. If they were there, they might stay away a month and then there was a kind of deadness about Port Sonas. Just now the fishing was beginning to move nearer home. They would be landing at Oban and Mallaig, and the shoals slowly making north. With this way of fishing there was not one of them now who worked a croft, though two or three had crofts in their names still, worked by relations or just neglected. For a de-rated croft house was still something; the old folks or the wife might potter about with hens; or the land might be worked by a neighbour for a rent—perhaps in kind— and who was to know? Well, maybe the Department kind of half knew, but nobody was going to draw the attention of the gentleman from the Department. Not unless there was a row. But it was in everyone's interest to keep the peace, at least on the surface and against strangers or the Department.

But there was a gap growing between the crofters and the farmers at the foot of the Glen, who had put land to land, and either owned it or were tenants paying rent to the Castle. In this district there were no Forestry Commission farm tenants, and just as well, thought Roddy, for he had come from an Argyll district where the Commission had more farmland than it wanted. Most of his plantings were on the north-west side of Loch Bannag, on sloping ground with rocky spurs, where he could get in a few Scotch to break the monotony of the lines of spruces. The only agricultural land was the nursery which lay just beyond Achnahabhainn, and a source of unease to old Jackson, who had the feeling constantly that it should be part of his farm. The Forestry Commission, he would say over and over, should never have been let buy that bit of land, it was their wickedness and the Laird's folly, selling it. Trees should be grown among trees. He said this to Roddy—or shouted it at him—every time he saw him. The worst of it was that Roddy was half inclined to agree with him. He had the feeling that seedlings could be grown in more natural conditions, in forest clearings, and then they would stand up to the life they were to lead. He had heard that was the way they did in foreign countries, and indeed there had been a piece about it in the last number of the Forestry Journal.

He was down now with his own lorry; he was expecting a consignment of spades, axe-heads and such. But the thing that was occupying his mind was the possibility of starting up a saw mill. The plantings were coming on well. He would need to make a start on thinning any time now. If they would give him a mill he knew the boys to put in charge, Alan's boy from the Glen and the Kettle—if someone could just come over and give them a start. Then Alasdair might be put in charge of the thinning; he would feel he had something to get his teeth into then. If only the District Officer would say definite that the mill was coming, then he would be able to make his plans. He backed his lorry in by the other and asked Angus whether he had got to the root of the trouble with his distributor.

"Ach, aye" said Angus, "it was new points she needed; Hughie and me fixed her on Saturday before the meeting."

"You didna get to the meeting, Angus" said Roddy.

"Ach, well, I'm no' very keen on meetings" said Angus, "and I would hear about it quick enough from Hughie. He's dead keen. He was saying to me there might be a wee cinema and he would get to work it. Ach, I'll come to the Hall right enough when it's going."

"We'll need to make a fight for it" said Roddy, "or the Ministers will have it stopped."

"Aye, aye" said Angus, who was Established, "but your crowd is worse than my one, and the F.P.'s worst of the lot. Did you hear about Kilmolue?"

"No, what was that?"

"Well, then" said Angus, "I was hearing it myself up the Glen. This missionary they have up there was on about the Hall and the wickedness of it and the wickedness forby of us Port Sonas folk thinking on such a thing. And ach, he was working them up and working them up, all yesterday he was at it, and a terrible conviction of sin all through Kilmolue, and the Sunday dinners not cooked nor eaten, the way folks were so set on holiness. And whenever two or three would meet, someone would start on a prayer, and hell fire licking at their tails! And the end of it was the wee piper took himself off to Balana, walked in when Fred was over at the byre, found his pipes, took them back with him to Kilmolue and burned them outside the tin Kirk with the missionary praying and every man and woman in the place running up with a peat for the burning and crying on the name of the Lord. Ach, a wild thing altogether."

"A Dhia!" said Roddy, "he'll have woken up with a sore head in the morning, the wee piper."

"Aye, aye. It is like the drink."

"It's worse it is. For the drink doesna go so deep mostly. I would sooner a drunk man than a holy one. He was a good wee piper. I mind of hearing him play *I got a kiss from the King's Hand*."

"I heard him play the *Lament for the Children*. It was a good set he had, his father's before him. They would be worth maybe fifty pounds."

"Plenty cause for a Lament! He will need to send the bill in to the missionary. Young Fred will have something to say."

"That's so" said Angus, "that's so indeed. And I wouldna like myself to get across the Balana crowd."

Roddy was twisting the knob on the end of his gear lever, frowning, then he looked up. "Why?" he said.

Angus said nothing for a moment, and when he answered it was kind of slow in coming. "Och, well, it's just a feeling I have. There's a kinna antrin look about Balana. I'm up there an odd time with seeds and manures and that. They aye ask me in. Och, extra decent folk in a way, and there's aye a wee dram and a bit cake and old Mistress Macfie real nice and homely. But there was a picture of a lassie in the kitchen."

Roddy laughed. "There's pictures of lassies in plenty kitchens! They're easier to come by than texts these days, you can aye cut a picture of a lassie out of Picture Post."

"This one wasna out of Picture Post" said Angus ruminatively; then, pointing out to the Sound, "See, there she comes now!" For the steamer was in sight beyond Eilann Garbh on her way in

Roddy looked at his watch. "No more than an hour late! Wonders'll never cease." And then, "Have you any notion now where would be the best place for the new Hall?"

"Well," said Angus, "it would need to be kind of flat and there's no' that many sites. There's yon wee square piece past the Wee Free manse, where Johnnie Crubach has his hens. But I'm asking myself how it would do so near the manse?"

"You'd not get the Wee Frees coming except at night!"

"Like that, are ye?"

"No' me—it's driven to church I am by yon old bitch I stay wi'."

"Ach, you canna resist the ladies, Roddy! Fine we ken that! But Johnnie Crubach would sell if he got his price. There's more eggs in it now. Why, at the end o' the war he was getting ten shillings a dozen; he'll no' get the half o' that now."

"The mean wee cratur, I've seen him often enough hirplin' round, him and his stick, but never-ever did I speak wi' him. Who is he at all?"

"He's brother to Mistress MacLean of the Women's Rural. His leg went thon way when he was a wee fellow."

"Well, well! But what about the bit ground behind the Post Office?"

"Aye, that might do; it's the Laird's land that, and he wouldna maybe be too hard over the price. Well, I'll need to go down to the boat."

"And me the same." Roddy got down from his lorry. "You'd not hear any word about poor Matta's lobsters, Angus?"

"How would I?" said Angus. "And it must ha' been someone wi' a boat that took them."

There was a general move towards the edge of the quay where the fishing boats had left a berth clear for the steamer. Archie's nephew, Jim, a tall, youngish-looking man with very black hair, went to stand by for the first rope. He had been expressing himself in favour of the Hall, and no wonder; it would give him the greatest opportunities. He was one that could dress up well, with a good suit and all, and in the summer season he would let on to the more easily taken in of the visitors that he was a Banker or an Officer or a Land Agent in the south and just helping for the fun of it. He could put on an English accent great and speak about folk that were mentioned in the newspapers just as though he knew them; and his friends would play up to him well, letting on he was different from themselves, and it was great ploy to see him do this on a summer visitor that was maybe a decent wee woman from Glasgow that had saved up for her summer holiday, and oh, the stories she would be telling herself and the long walks they would take in the evenings, and maybe he would get what he wanted or maybe he wouldna, but all the same he would be speaking of it great and what colour knickers she had on and how quick he had got them off her and with what words. For he was the great one at making up conversations and it would be a better yarn than the wee books about love in the paper shop, for they would stop at a certain place, but Jim in his yarns would go on well beyond. But he didna do so well with the locals and there was another yarn of Janet MacKinnon boxing his ears on him.

The boat was coming in grand, beginning to take the curve round, when those who were watching her heard voices raised in anger behind them. They all turned and there was Archie shaking his fist at Andrew Revie and shouting out that he would have the law on him, coming and disturbing his boxes and speaking about lobsters! "You and your dirty lobsters!" said Archie. "It's no' me that's needing to steal. And I wonder what the polisman will be saying at all——"

"Now, now" said Malcie, who had come scurrying up, "this isna a matter for the polis! No, no indeed! Andrew wasna accusing yourself, Archie——"

Everyone was joining in now, and not always to calm things down. For there are few people that have no relish for a right row if it's not themselves that are directly in it. And almost all had some reason for being either on Archie's side or else on Andrew's. And one or another would throw in a word in English or in

Gaelic to hot up the flames, and more than one spoke loud enough to be overheard about yon great row thirty years back, though it was so long now since there had been a herring barrel seen on the quay at Port Sonas. And all the while the cargo boat was curving in slowly and grandly with the sunlight showing up all the dirt on her. But the few womenfolk who were down let on they were looking at nothing but the boat. Janet's auntie from the old sweetie shop was kind of half expecting an allocation, but she had always been late sending off the coupons and now maybe they weren't paying as much attention to her as to some. The two girls who worked at the hotel were there with little excuse, but they worked hard and willingly during the summer season and Mrs MacMillan kept a light hand on them during the rest of the year. Now the cargo boat blew her whistle and the noise gave a jolt to the crowd, and as the rope slapped down on to the quay and Jim caught and made it fast, there was a general break-up. Archie came stalking down, only his face a bittie red, to shout up to the captain of the cargo boat.

"Isn't it as well the polis wasna there!" said Malcie. That some way was always the general thought in Port Sonas about Sinclair the policeman; a kindly decent man, but his job was against him.

The cargo boat would take a few passengers, though there was nothing great in the way of accommodation. But it was there and handy if you wanted to get to Oban, say. There was only one passenger this time, a crofter's boy back on leave. "Wait you," said Angus, "and I'll give you a lift back up the Glen." The boy put his kitbag in the back of the lorry and then helped Angus to load up Malcie's wood and a couple of cardboard boxes, packet puddings and cereals and the like, for the Glen store. "Did you hear" said Angus, "we're to get a Village Hall? Aye, it will be at the back of the Post Office most like; or so I was hearing."

Red Dougie was waving his invoice at the captain, "You hanna got my potato manure! And why in the devil's name hanna you got it? Here's me with my drills open and waiting a month on it, and here's your bloody invoice! Aye, you canna get by that!"

The captain said he had seen no manure in the warehouse.

"You!" said Dougie, "you couldna see a whale until it was

85

halfway into your mouth! And me coming all the way down from Molachy and a good morning wasted. Ach, isn't it terrible!" He turned to Roddy. "They're doing anything at all on us, this lot. Invoices! You canna believe a bloody word they say."

"You could lay a complaint" said Roddy.

"Me?" Ach, they wouldna care for me what I was saying."

"Well, then" said Roddy, "why wouldn't you and the rest start a branch of the National Farmers Union? Granted there's not terrible many of you, but who's to know? And they would be bound to listen then."

Dougie gathered his reins up. "The N.F.U.? Begod, I will!" And then he shouted at the captain, "Then you'll not get off so light. You and your invoices!"

The captain spat over the side and leant down to talk to Archie. Jim and the young soldier were putting the cases aboard. The barrel for the hotel was rolled down the gang plank and an occasion for merry sayings. The sweeties for Janet's auntie had not come, nor yet Dugal Bits' cups and he was blaming the Government for that, saying they were as bad as Macbrayne's. Hugh hadn't got the lighting spares, though he had a couple of new tyres. But Roddy had his stuff and got it on to the lorry and checked it up there and then, for it was no use making a complaint later.

Andrew Revie came over and spoke to him, "Did ye hear what yon bugger Archie was saying?" he asked, "Did ye ever hear the like? Here was me asking him as friendly about yon lobsters o' poor Matta's and here didn't he flare up as cross as a conger. Well, I'd my suspicions afore that, but now——"

"You'll take a lift over on my lorry, Mr Revie?" said Roddy, for he thought Andrew looked a bittie shaken. "He had no call to be shouting at you anyway. What does Matta think himself about the lobsters?"

"Och, Matta! He'd not need to think; he's no' the kind to use his head except it was to knock down a wall! He's kinna half forgotten it by now. It wud need to be the lave of us do his thinking for him." He got up into the cab of the lorry. "Och, you'll get to know Port Sonas great before you're done, Roddy MacRimmon! Aye, and the ones ye can trust and the ones ye canna. D'ye like the wee place?"

"Aye, mostly" said Roddy, putting the gears in.

"Dinna trust yon double-dealing Archie, nor yet Jim. If it wasna them took the lobsters they'll know something about it for sure! D'ye ken the ither coast?"

"I was in Fife once."

"Ach, Fife! A wheen miners. D'ye ken Aberdeen?" Roddy shook his head. And suddenly Andrew Revie felt terrible homesick for the east coast and the nipping cold winds that make you stand up straight and feel yourself a man again.

CHAPTER VII

MONDAY AFTERNOON:
FISHERMEN'S MEETING

THE FISHERMEN'S MEETING was supposed to be open
to all, but there were only about a dozen of the share fishermen
there, mostly older men, some of whom had been skippers or
acting skippers, and one younger man, Colin MacLean, who was
hoping to get a boat himself one day. His father had been a
skipper in the old days with a thirty-foot boat, but had lost her
and himself in a storm when Colin was still a wee fellow. Only
Colin had come to a certain determination then and had stuck
to it since. He was with the Cluaran now. Six of the skippers were
there out of eight possible from the drifters, and four men from
the lobster boats, including Matta and his brother. Pate Morrison
took the chair behind a small tea table with a bunch of daffodils
on it. It was a bit past the hour and they wouldn't need to be too
late because of getting a start and being out on the fishing grounds
before night. Coories and Sandy came in and sat down together,
not seeming to take much notice, with a poke of sweeties between
them. Pate adjusted the daffodils to the dead centre as though he
was steering on a compass, then he coughed importantly; "Hae
ye got the minute book, Calum?" he asked the Secretary,
Malcolm Macrae, a big, fair, slow-moving man, skipper of one
of the older boats.

"Aye," he said, "I've a grip of her." He fumbled in his pocket
for a huge pair of glasses and peered down into the book. The
rest settled themselves and coughed and whispered. Ian Ciotach
was doing a sum in his notebook. The older men spat on to the
floor of the tearoom and stamped it out with their boots. Colin
stared at the daffodils. Jessie looked in through the glass doors,
"No' terrible many" she said to her mother, who was weighing
out sugar, "you would think they would care more for their own
meeting."

"It's well known" said her mother, who was a fisherman's

widow herself, "that the fishermen of Port Sonas care only for the two things, fishing and women. And there's some that are no' that keen on the fishing."

Malcolm Macrae read the minutes, with pauses while he deciphered his own handwriting or went back again to the beginning of a sentence. They had been protesting to Edinburgh about the opening of a sea loch to the ring-net boats.

"What at all happened?" said Ian, "did we never-ever get any answer?"

"We didna get anything different" said Malcolm.

"They bloody ringers" said Ian, "aye getting the ear o' the Board; and them sweeping up the herring, all sizes, like a bloody vacuum-cleaner!"

"They've maybe got their living to make the same as ourselves," said Malcolm.

"Living—them!" said Ian, "they shouldna get to make a living, it's just the way they're favoured."

"Well" said Pate, "will I sign the minutes?"

There was a general murmur and he signed. "We'll need to agree what will we want from the Highland Panel—I've a letter here from the Fishery Officer and he was asking would some of us manage the meeting. Where are ye fishing, Johnnie?"

"It wouldna be terrible easy" said Johnnie Beg, "what for can they no' come on a Saturday?"

"Ach, well, they've more places than this to visit" said Pate: "I could maybe manage; Fergie could go in my place?" He nodded over to Fergie his cousin and senior member of his crew. "You all can manage?" he went on to the lobster men.

"I'll need to speak to them about where my lobsters went" said Matta.

"Aye, aye," said Pate sympathetically, "but they'll maybe not know. I'm thinking if one or two men could risk back for Thursday it wouldna hurt, for we canna let yon ringers, nor yet yon buggers o' seiners get the better of us." Nobody answered for a moment. "It could be a blank night," he said encouragingly.

"I'll wait in" said Colin, "I'm wanting to know right about the grant and loan. Maybe I'll get another two-three of the ex-Servicemen to stay."

"I might wait in myself" said one of the older men, "I've the rheumatism gey bad."

But none of the other skippers felt like waiting in and maybe missing a good shot. While they were speaking of it another man pushed open the door, looked round at the meeting, seemed to think ill of it and went out again.

"Well" said Pate, "so long as we give them some kind of a meeting. And wee Archie knows to speak about the hole in the sea wall; but I dinna think they'll do much, it's all alike, the head ones, plenty promises and there's the last you'll hear o' them."

"The Fishery Officer was saying" said Johnnie Beg, "that there was one of them a woman."

"God help us!" said Pate, startled, "what would a woman know about the fishing?"

"Just as much as a cow's arse!"

"What were they thinking to have a woman?"

"This one is from Carradale, the Fishery Officer was saying" Johnnie Beg said, "so she's bound to favour the ringers!" Pate spat largely, then, remembering where he was, rubbed it out with his boot. Johnnie went on "Mr Wood the Chief Officer will be there."

"Ach, well, he's a grand man. I mind of him being here in '25——"

"No, '26 it was" said the Whale.

"It was '25, because that was the year we were at Castle Bay."

"Well, if it was the year you had yon row wi' the wee priest, then it was '26 it was; because it was the same year Rob Mor sold the Sieradh."

"Aye, aye" said one of the others, " '26 it was. And he should be told about the seiners and the way they're spoiling us."

"Aye" said Ian, "they shouldna be let! East coast buggers all the lot o' them."

"Friends o' Andrew's!"

"He should be told" said the Whale "that the seiners is scaring all the herring clean away, aye, and the ringers killing off the small fish. It's worse than the trawlers they are."

"If it was damage by trawlers we are to speak on" said Ian, "you would need to say there was trawlers seen in the Sound."

"When?" said Coories, shifting the sweetie in his mouth.

"Ach, well, was it no' last year?" He looked around. "Or maybe two years back? Ony way they shouldna be let! If they werena here last year, it's all the more reason they would come this year."

"There's folks that'll see trawlers swimming in the water after they've pished," observed one of the older men. Ian glared at him.

"We'd need to think about a contribution to the Village Hall" said Pate, quickly.

"Is it sure we're to have it?" asked Colin.

"Amn't I on the committee" said Pate, "and Mr Thompson saying it was specially for the fishermen. 'My friends the fishermen' those were his very words, boys! So we'll need to give him a hand wi' it." He peered at the other fishermen from round both sides of the daffodils, then shoved them away.

"And for every pound of ours, there's five pounds from the Government" said Ian, "is that no' a fact?"

"Aye, true as you're there. Mr MacMillan was saying we might have it in mind to put a levy on the boats. A ha'penny a basket maybe."

"Him!" said one of the men, "a pure shore bastard, doesna know a herring from a tattie. What is the shore ones doing theirsel's?"

"There'll be another committee called on Saturday first, but Kate was saying we should give an example."

"She could give an example herself."

"And who's to say she'll no'? You canna say she's tight on the purse, poor Kate."

"We could give maybe five pounds from our own money that we have."

"Aye, but that was for widows and orphans."

"There's no' that many these days."

"Touch wood!"

"Aye, but it should go to the ex-Servicemen!" said Colin. He had been at the old ones already over that. Greedy old buggers.

"Five pounds isna much for a Hall" said Ian, scratching in his head, "the Government would only give us twenty-five pounds on that."

"Well, then, Ian, will we make it a levy? What do you say, boys?"

"I move we do" said Colin, "a ha'penny a basket for four weeks."

"Will I put it down in the book?" said Malcolm.

"Aye, just that, Calum, or was anyone against?"

After a moment, when it looked like all being agreed, someone spoke: "We hanna thought right about this Hall—how at all will it work out? We'll no' get to it except on Saturdays."

"We did well enough wi'out a Hall, we would need to stay in our homes on a Saturday."

"Aye, or go to the pictures at Halbost!"

"Or to the hotel at Kinlochbannag. Putting money in Mr Thompson's pocket! We should have a place o' our ain."

"There's the Mission Hall."

"Ach, to hell with the Mision Hall, nothing but buggerment there with old Andy and the Steamroller! We canna get to play cards even. We would need to get a Hall right enough, but what about the lobster crowd? How would they work in with the levy?"

"We canna give the same as the drifters" said Matta, "and look at the great loss I had——"

"Hae ye no kind o' notion where they went, a bhalaich?"

"Och, I don't know at all, at all! And me leaving them in the box year after year and never a whisker missing! And now I'm clean scared to leave them a minute. And wasn't Balnafearchar after telling me he had missed four of his hens. It would be the same one took the hens and they worth a pound each nearly. It wouldna be so bad in the summer with visitors and strangers and yon hikers and all manner o' queer folk, but now it must be one of oursel's."

"It's never one o' the fleet, Matta."

"I hope sure enough it wasna, but I canna put in the same as the rest."

"You would get more out o' the Hall than the rest of us."

"Maybe, but I mightna want. I'll put in a pound between myself and my brother." He pulled out a rather grubby Clydesdale banknote.

"That's the boy! What will we do with contributions?"

"Bessie MacKeith is treasurer, we'll just give it to Jessie to give to Florag at the choir meeting, and she will give it to her auntie."

"Will I put it in the minutes?" said Malcolm.

"Aye, aye, but we hanna exactly passed the motion. A ha'penny a basket, boys, will we vote on it?" Most of them put their hands up. "And is anyone against?" Two put their hands up. "Ach, well, that's kind of half unanimous. Could we no' get together right, boys?"

One of the dissentients put his hand down, "I'm no' caring if you boys are terrible keen."

"Aye, but I'm strong against" said the other, who was skipper of the Pride of Port Sonas, "we dinna want a Village Hall."

"We do so" said Pate.

"The young crowd are all wanting it" said Coories, "are they no', Colin?"

"Aye, that's right enough."

"The young crowd is aye hankering after vanities. Were none of you at the church, or were you sleeping through it?"

"Aye, well," said Pate, "but you canna be doing what the Ministers want all the time; it's late getting, surely you'll vote with the rest of the boys?"

"You'll no' get a ha'penny a basket off me for any godless Hall."

"Well, we'll need to leave it yon way," said Pate. "This is the end o' the meeting, boys, or we'll never see the tail of a herring the night!" He got up, so did the others, and made for the door. Young Colin was beginning to turn it over in his mind that the young ex-Service crowd would need to hold a meeting if they were ever to get their own back on the rest. There was a branch of the Legion sure enough at Port Sonas, but it had too many of the old crowd in it. Shooting out their mouths about *their* war! He pushed angrily through, into the road.

At the table, Malcolm bit the end of his pencil and went on writing the minutes. Sandy stopped beside him, "You'll be for the hall yourself, Calum?"

"Ach, aye, the boys would have liked it fine."

"Aye, so they would," said Sandy, "so they would." For Malcolm's two boys had both been lost on the Rawalpindi. They went out together and Malcolm gave the pound note to Jessie, who said she would see to it getting to Mrs MacKeith, then she went into the tearoom to clear up and get everything ready again for the choir meeting. After some thought she moved the daffodils on to the mantelpiece and brought her own primroses on to the table instead.

CHAPTER VIII

MONDAY EVENING: CHOIR MEETING

ONE MINUTE THE TEAROOM was empty, the next it was full of girls and all talking and titivating and munching and giggling, loosing their coats, untying their scarves, shaking out their kilts, settling the collars of their blouses. Nurse Beaton had a dark blue dress under her uniform coat and an official-looking case where the girls glimpsed nameless obstetric possibilities under the music books. She sat next to Sarah the Doctor's housekeeper and they appeared to have much to say to one another. The three from the Glen, Janet, Sheila and young Mrs Macrae, were trying over a port a beul, very lightly, a living breath of humming. Florag beside them took it up more emphatically, then Isa. Here and there a foot not yet tapping twitched towards it. May Revie slipped off her jacket; she wore a maroon rayon blouse with a suit of good tweed, rather badly cut. She looked up from the chairman's place and her pencil rapped the table. "Will you read the minutes, Jessie?" she said.

"The last was our own wee ceilidh" said Jessie, "and I just wrote that a very enjoyable time was had by all. And seven and ten on the teas. And here, I'm at the end of my book! But if I just turn it round and write on the blank pages it would last a good wee while."

"Well, I think you should do that" said May, "there's nothing ever gained by wastry."

Anna Morrison, Pate's daughter, came scurrying in, soft-lipped, her hair a dark fuzz under her crimson scarf, settled herself at the end of a line and whispered to Jamesina, her neighbour; she was engaged to Colin and she had been a race down to the boat before the meeting. Jamesina giggled and whispered to her sister, who giggled too.

"Order, order, ladies" said May, "we'll just start the proceedings with a nice psalm." There were several suggestions.

Finally they sang *The Lord's my Shepherd*, tune Orlington. Jessie slipped over into the alto line. May conducted. "You're going too hard at it, ladies" she said, 'be easy now, you should flow! We'll have the last verse again."

They practised several psalms after this and May slightly regrouped her sopranos. That always meant a fuss. Certain ones were used to looking over the same book. Neither Miss Beaton nor Sarah, who was getting on in years a bit, liked to be isolated among the young lassies. Ella complained that wee Lizzie had pinched her; Lizzie denied it. Florag was saying it was time they tried something new. She and May and Jessie began to look through the books; Mrs MacMillan from the hotel joined them, pointing to some songs in her own Mod books that she had with her. One of them would hum a thing, running her eyes along the sol-fa and then break off and try another. "Has Ellen got one of her colds again?" asked Isa.

"Aye, and Donaldina the same," said Anna, "there's a cold just raging round."

"And did you hear they had the measles at Osnish?"

"Now isn't that just like them! Is there many has it?"

"Well, it's the wee MacKinnons, they've got it real bad."

"Do you know this," said Janet, "they were at the school treat with the thing on them!"

"Were they now—well, well."

"I mind of me going to the school treat with the whooping cough" said Jessie, "and wasn't it the funniest thing—half the school was down before the end of the month."

"It's kind of silly all the same" said young Mrs Macrae, "folks should have more sense."

"Och, if you're going to catch them you're just going to, and that's all there is to it."

"It's kind of hard on poor David MacTavish" said Janet.

"Och, him" said Ella leaning across, "d'ye ken what the mannie said when I gave in my notice? He said 'Och, Ella,' he said, 'and me doing everything to make you happy'—you would think he was married on me, the man!"

A chorus of giggles: and Isa said "You should ha' tooken him at his word, Ella, and tellt him what more he should do to make ye happy!"

"Aye, but has he got it in him?"

"I wouldna wonder if it wasna somewhere in below!" said Isa, "where are you for, Ella? The Forestry?"

"Roddy says he'll start me next month at the nursery. That'll be fine for a while. Plenty company."

"Aye, if it was Roddy doing every kind of thing to mak' ye happy, Ella!"

"Roddy, is it! He knows plenty about that, does this same Roddy! Would you say it was sure enough him going with Kenny's Chrissie?"

"Not at all" said Janet, "He's a decent lad, Roddy, and she's a bad wee monkey and better if someone had had the skelping of her early on."

"But is it true what they are saying now?"

"Aye, it's true; and the bus was saying she was away over to Halbost to see the lawyer about her Ailment."

"Och, och, is it sure enough Ailment? And who at all will it be on? Will it be the Kettle? I hope it's no' and him going with Minnie this last month! He'll no' have much saved."

"If it's savings she's after——"

May looked up from the books and tapped on the table, "Now ladies, will we try *An Aitchairachd Ard*? There's a nice wee bit for the altos."

"Is it kind of quiet?" asked wee Lizzie, and the rest all knew why, for she was one of the Free Presbyterians and she had a bit bother with her conscience. A love song would not do for her at all, at all, not even where the loving two were to be parted forever.

"Ach, aye" said Jessie, "It's kind of half religious."

"Well——" said Lizzie. They tried it over, first the soprano part and then the alto, taking it through once or twice in sol-fa and then the first verse only of the words. There were enough Gaelic speakers to get the meaning, but May Revie, for all her mother had spoken plenty Gaelic, she'd somehow never bothered with it herself. There were phrases that came over and over in the songs or in conversation and you couldn't help but know them. But this song now; the words were maybe nothing great if you looked at it as a matter of sense; yet the music, aye, that was another thing. Sad it was, sure enough, and they tried it over and over again, steeping their voices in its rich sadness. Oh, a great feeling, and it took you out of yourself well!

96

"Well" said May at last, sitting down again at the table as the choir too sat down, "that's no' bad. Aye, we've made a beginning. But you'll maybe need a bit sorting out. I would like to see one or two of you a bittie stronger on the broad vowels." She tapped her pencil against her teeth, wondering could she get Miss Beaton into the back line and bring Anna forward. Anna's tone was coming on great; but if she was to shift Miss Beaton, Sarah would be affronted. Well, maybe one of them would get the cold and she could try it then. It would be worth waiting.

"It was a terrible nice song that" said Jessie contentedly, then she leant over, "Will we be speaking about a concert for the Hall?"

"That's just what we should do" said May. She gave a wee cough and began to speak about the Hall and the great use it would be to the choir and how they might think to hold a concert for it. She was watching the girls and sure enough Robina and wee Lizzie were glancing at one another and then Maggie leaned over from the back and whispered to them. Well, if the Free Presbyterians wouldn't come in on it, then the choir would just need to go on without them. She herself was as god-fearing as the next and she would stand no nonsense from that crowd. "Well, ladies, what do you say?" she asked. She picked out Florag with her eye.

"It's a great idea altogether" said Florag, "and the Hall is just what we need for our practices. Other places have Halls."

"Aye, it would be great" said Mrs MacMillan and added, not that everyone didn't know, "Mr MacMillan is at the head of the new Hall Committee."

"The Doctor was saying it would be good for the place" said Sarah.

"We could have Red Cross classes" said Miss Beaton, and then with a still brighter idea, "and I could maybe distribute my orange juice from there!"

Robina looked up in a sore worry, her lip caught on to her teeth. "I dinna think my folk would like it, not at all, at all, Miss Revie!"

"Nor mine" said Lizzie, "these Halls—och, we canna be doing what's no' right."

"But are ye sure, Lizzie? Could it no' be that it's a mistake of judgment over this?"

Lizzie and Robina looked at one another; "We were at the Kirk, all three of us, and Mr Munro didna leave ony room for doubt. So we're terribly sorry, Miss Revie, but we canna see our way to help over this."

"And I'm thinking" said Maggie, and there was a sob in her voice, "I'm thinking if it goes on we'll need to leave the choir, for we couldna give any kind of countenance to a body that was supporting this Hall."

"There would be nothing else for it," Robina said, "though we would be gey spited."

And then Euphemia McCulloch stood up, "I dinna think we should stay, Miss Revie, neither me nor my sister. My mother was saying—if there was any word of this Hall—Och, it's bound to be a sinful thing, and this concert not to be a holy concert, but the kind o' songs the visitors look for! So we'll just need to go, and Ellen will think the same as us when her cold is past!"

"I'm sorry you feel this way" said May, "for I think you are seeing the thing wrong, and it'll be the break up of our wee choir that we've all laboured for." It would be goodbye to the F.P.'s anyway and she saw that the others from the Wee Free congregation were whispering to one another. "You'll not see anything wrong in this, Janet?"

"Not at all" said Janet, "but we'll need to keep from giving offence where it need not be given. We should maybe start and finish our concert with a psalm."

"And just to have good songs" said Sheila, "the real Highland songs, none o' this American trash."

"I think that's just what we all want" said May.

"There's some real nice American songs" said Sarah, "there's yon one the Doctor is forever singing in his bath, *Come Along, Little Dogies*—ach, I can just see the wee doggies come rinnin' along and barkin', wee collie doggies maybe."

But now Jessie and Ella, who had gone out, came back with the big teapot, the cups and a jug of milk. The choir members had each brought a few sandwiches, buttered farls or a wrapped scone still hot from the girdle, and most of them a wee poke of sugar. The three Free Presbyterians and the McCulloch lassies were all feeling downhearted and the others were trying to cheer them up a bittie, speaking of this and that. "Were you speaking to Donnie lately?" Florag asked Robina, for she had an idea that

Robina had spoken with a certain kindness of Donnie Cameron once in a while.

"Donnie!" said Robina, "ach, Donnie and his motor-bike! You'll not get going with Donnie without you'll ride on yon thing. And my folk wouldna like me to be doing that."

"It's a surprise to me that Donnie's father let him have the bike, and he so godly," said Florag.

"Ach well, he was forever complaining, saying he was fed-up at Balnafearchar and thinking to go to the R.A.F. So maybe it was that way his father let him have the thing."

"Kenny's Chrissie was on the back o' yon same bike more than once," said Ella, "they say yon things joggles you up great."

"She disna need to be joggled, her!"

"I'd sooner a joggle in a boat!" said Anna Morrison, and giggled.

"Would you no' sooner a joggle wi' a certain lad, Anna?"

"I'm kinna partial to a joggle wi' a lad in a boat!" said Anna.

But Miss Beaton had overheard: "Think shame on yourselves with your joggles, lasses! Wait you——" And her look had in it a threat of the black bag.

Florag took the conversation back: "It's time Donnie was thinking to settle, anyway."

"His father will settle him, and no leave asked," said Ella. "Ach, Balnafearchar likes to put penny by penny. And there's no much sport to Donnie, you would go out a whole evening wi' him and never get a word out him. Unless maybe you'd to go on his bike. But I'd no' go. You'd not know where it would stop!"

"Nor him neither!"

"Ach, him! It's better to be daffing away but nae harm done. Like wi' Roddy. You'll be seeing plenty of Roddy, Jamesina?"

Jamesina drew herself up. "I do not, so! It's just the like o' Roddy MacCrimmon that frequents these Halls. And there's the way decent folk is against them."

"What was Roddy doing anyway?" said Isa, "I've aye found him a decent lad."

"He wasna doing anything wi' me" said Jamesina "but— my mother says——"

"Well, what at all does she say?"

"It's she does his washing" said Jamesina in a sinister voice, then blushed. The other girls cast down their eyes and giggled.

"She should try mucking a byre" said Isa, "then she'd no' be so pernickety. There's nothing wrong wi' the man, exceptin' he hasna a right lassie. If I wasna well settled——" she shrugged her shoulders and went over for her cup tea. Kate had been baking and had given her some extra nice queen cakes; she took good care to let the others know whose baking they were. Once she winked at Janet. Janet could do a day's work too, not like these trashy wee lassies in the village.

Jessie and Ella were working out another duet, a real nice one, but not too high. Nothing surer than they would have an encore. Maybe two. The visitors would sooner a love one, and in English. Jessie began humming over *The Rowan Tree*. Ella tried a top note, softly. "If once we get this Hall" said Jessie, "we could maybe think of a mixed choir. And we could try for the Mod. Do you no' think, Ella?"

"Aye" said Ella in a low voice, "and maybe a man to conduct. May gets terrible cross sometimes."

"A man could get worse cross" said Jessie.

"Aye, but I dinna get a thrill any out o' May getting cross. A man would be different. I wonder, does Roddy sing?"

"He hums to himself whiles if he comes in on a Saturday for a cup. I would say he had the music in him. Alasdair is a nice singer."

"Aye, he's a nice boy. And Angus had a lot of real bonnie English songs when he came back from the army. We could get a tenor line without any trouble at all! I'll be speaking about it when I start with the Forestry."

"Who's to be the new cleaner, Ella?" asked Anna Morrison.

Ella shook her head, "So long as it' no' me! I'm fed up wi' the wee ones forever in and out the lavatories and their mothers mumping at me. There's your own wee brother, Anna, and the mud he brings in with him! Let someone else do it."

"It'll need to be someone" said Jessie, "would you no' think to try it, Lizzie? It's good money and no more than maybe two hours' work in the day."

"There's the big cleaning once in the month forby that" said Ella, "but you can take your own time. It might suit you, Lizzie."

Lizzie shook her head. "You would get more unemployment money from the Burroo. If you'll ask for a whole-time job, they'll not stop it off you if you'll no' take the school. I like fine to be working in the summer season or an odd while else, but I wouldna like to work a' the year."

"Will the Burroo no' stop you after a while?"

"Ach, well, they're no' hard on us and they away at Halbost. I took a job from them a while in Oban."

"What was wrong wi' it?"

"Ach, I didna just like the folk; they went to the same church as myself right enough, but the lady was aye nagging at me. It's a great thing the unemployment money."

"Aye, and the fishermen are getting it now" said Anna.

"Soon they'll never be out at all!"

"Ach, you'll make away more fishing then you do off the unemployment" said Anna, "but it will be kind of handy all the same when the fishing is slack. Better you stay in than go out all week for maybe nothing but a few baskets at the end of it."

"Aye, there'll be a wheen cosy nights out of the unemployment pay!"

May Revie said suddenly, "When I was a lassie the same as you, Anna, I would ha' been black affronted if ony of my folk or ony man that I had any liking for had gone idle and taken money for it!"

"Ach," said Anna, "it's no' as if the money belonged to anyone, it's only the Government money!"

"Aye, but we're all of us paying taxes. Why would I pay for a lazy crowd that'll not do their right work?"

"I'm no' paying taxes" said Anna, and laughed, clear soprano laughter.

"You are, so! Every pack of cigarettes is mostly all duty and every time you go to the pictures at Halbost you are paying taxes. Dinna pretend to be ignorant, Anna Morrison!"

"Well, well" said Anna, "isn't it just as well then to be getting some of it back?"

May shrugged her shoulders. It was no use having a row. Anna was one of the best voices and although her folk were Wee Frees, she had not worried any about the concert in aid of the Hall; that would be with her being engaged to Colin—yes, and her father on the new Hall Committee; much good he'd be! But the talk had disturbed May. She was used to the way the lassies spoke about the lads, but now they were speaking in the same light way about money. But maybe it didna mean much either. They grew up to be good wives for all their nonsense. But some way it didna seem honest. Had this come with the war and money easier come by, but meaning less? She would need to speak to her father.

They went back to the song, going over it again for speed and expression. She would need to see could she get in some others in place of the F.P. crowd and the McCullochs, if they were truly set on going. After that they tried over a couple more psalms, just giving them a run through. It ,was getting dark a bit. Jessie went through to the room and brought back a Tilley and hooked it up. When they stopped, but before they were all at the talking again, May said, "There was one other thing I was thinking. Where will we get to practise? There was one or two of us thinking we should ask Mrs Snow to let us practise up at Tigh na Bheach? Seeing she's keen herself on the Hall. How would that be?"

"It's a long step over to the Bee House" said Sarah, "further than the school even."

"Aye, but it will be summer getting and it's no' so far for the Glen ones."

"But the Glen ones has bicycles."

"Maybe you could borrow one——"

"Catch me riding yon things! I'll trust my two legs. Could we no' go to your own house, May?"

"We're ower many. And I've ower many wee tables and that! And it's a bonnie piano up at Tigh na Bheach. What would Mrs Snow say to it, Isa?"

"Ach, she'd be pleased. She's lonesome a bittie. Maybe she'd join us for tea. She'll sing away to herself whiles."

"Does she now! I never thought she had the music in her."

"Ach, well, it's wee kind o' songs. Frenchy songs. It's mostly when Alice is back and they're at it together. But we'd need not to get upsetting Mr MacFarlan. He's kind o' crochety getting. Awful cross to her he is, whiles. And she's gey patient. I'd have the old bodach's head off if it was me."

"Is there anything in it between her and the Laird, Isa?" whispered Ella. May, who was showing Jessie a spelling mistake in the minute book, made to stop her, and then thought she would listen herself without seeming to. She had always been a wee bit frightened of cousin Kate and could never have asked her straight out.

"Well," said Isa, "I'd like to think it right enough, and her so decent. I'd like fine to see her up at the Castle, she'd have it scrubbed out in a week! And she's more clever than Mr Thompson for all he's above her on the Council. But they're neither o' them so young as they were."

"They say the old ones is the worst," said Ella, "if they're that way at all——"

"True enough," said Isa, "I mind of a cow I was working with, fifteen years old she was if she was a day——"

But here May felt she must stop it. "Well now," she said. "you write her a nice wee note, Jessie, seeing you are the Secretary."

"How will I begin?" said Jessie doubtfully.

"Ach, I'll show you. But put you it down in the minutes that we have decided to send it. And now, Robina and the rest of you, will you no' think it over? It's kind of silly to my mind saying you're to leave, after all the nice evenings we've had together."

Robina shook her head, "I could never-ever face my folks with this to tell them. No, no, we'll need to go."

"There'll be a terrible carry-on when this is known, all the same" said Euphemia, "I wouldna like to be you."

"Away you!" said Florag, "look at the visitors, doing every kind of thing on the Sabbath, playing their gramophones and going about in short trousers; but there's money at them and never a word of stopping them! And it's not always the church services that we ourselves have on the wireless on a Sunday afternoon and we up in our houses!"

"Aye, but—this that you're asking us to do, it would be flaunting. The same as Jezebel."

"Jezebel, is it! Was it no' David that danced and sang before the Ark of the Covenant? Are you telling me, Euphemia, you will never be coming to this Hall when we get it?"

"You'll no' get it" snapped Euphemia, "you'll not be let!" And she gathered up her coat and bag quick and went marching out, followed by Jamesina who gave a kind of rueful grin round as she left.

"Terrible like her mother" said Florag.

Robina and her friends gathered their books and coats too, not saying anything.

103

"I'm sorry, my dears" said May, "but maybe you will think better of this decision and if you do, you will aye be welcome back."

"I dinna know, I'm sure, Miss Revie" said Robina. She and Lizzie came from croft houses, Maggie's folk were at the fishing. They went out.

"What will I put in the minutes?" asked Jessie, worried.

"Just put that they resigned their membership" said May, "but it's a pity sure enough. We'll need to get in a few more. Would any of the Women's Rural crowd come? How about Minnie?"

"They like to be having their own songs" said Mrs MacMillan, and then, "do you think now they might come in wi' us over this concert? There's two-three good."

"So long as they dinna come as a choir" said Florag, "we could get Minnie singing *Mo Ghille Guanach*, she's real nice at that. But she mightna want."

"I think the best would be to speak to Miss Beaton. She and Sarah are in the Rural; and they'd have an idea how the rest felt. Ach, she's away. I wonder, how are the wee ones at Osnish. But I'll have a word with her. The Rural meets Wednesdays."

"If we could get maybe ten of them to join the choir," said May, "it's not as if they were all singers."

"Ach no!" said Florag, "Though they might be fancying themselves! They could come in with us over the concert right enough. But not to join the choir, not that crowd. They'd be interfering terrible. How about your sister, Christine?" she asked a rather silent tall girl, who worked in Jock's store, where he did all the talking.

"Aye, she might."

"How about Neil's Jessie?"

"No, no, she's going wi' Krooger's nephew; he wouldna want to help any."

"There's one o' my lassies at the hotel has a nice voice" said Mrs MacMillan, tying the scarf over her head, "but I'm no' sure how keen she would be to practise."

"Is there anyone else from the Glen, Janet, do you think?"

"Scarcely" said Janet, "and we will be getting into a row ourselves for staying most like. But I'll just say to my father that we are a moderating influence. He'll like that. Aye, he's no' the worst, is my father. But we'll need not to offend the kind of half-friendly ones. Ach, I like the feel of a nice psalm myself. There's a comfort in it whiles that you'll not get in a thing that's just a song. Though I like the songs forby."

"Aye, aye, there's room for both the two" said May, "and the Hall will be needing to be well conducted, that's sure, Janet." She went on, "is it true what I heard about Snash?" Janet nodded. "That's terrible, will someone not speak to the Inspector?"

"Someone will need to" said Janet, "but Snash will not make it easy. Indeed, I hope I'll no' need to be the one to speak."

"Mr MacTavish was over yesterday," said Sheila, "but Snash had his ears off almost; and wee Greta creeping about and snivelling and letting herself be put upon by Peigi and the rest. It's been going on for long enough. Too long. But you never like to interfere; I just hate to have folk interfering with myself, and they're aye doing it."

"Would your father not speak, Sheila?" May asked, frowning. She shook her head and half smiled. "But why at all not?"

"Well——" said Sheila, and then, "seeing we're among friends——" She looked round; most of the village ones were out of ear-shot. And the Glen ones knew. And you could trust May. "Well, it's this way, Miss Revie. We're a bittie over-stocked oursel's. With the subsidy and all. Indeed it's true of most of us. Your father will be over-stocked, Janet?"

"Yes," said Janet, "I suppose so. And the grazings will begin to show it one day or another."

"So there it is," said Sheila, "and there isn't one of us that would like to have attention drawn to him with the Grazing Committee or the Department, supposing Snash was to turn nasty. But you can hardly blame us, Miss Revie, and the subsidies so good."

"No" said May, "no, maybe not. Ach well, shall we have another practice here in a week's time? And will we all think of some good songs for the concert?"

"But we'll keep to Scots songs?" said Janet.

"We might have kind of classical English songs" said May, "*Where E'er You Walk*, that's bonnie."

"Aye, I'm just thinking of the old ones. If I could say to my father it was all Scots songs—well, he would be easier in his mind.

Ach, I'm not caring myself, but I'm terrible keen the Hall should have a good start."

"We'll never get some to think well of it however much we try to do things the way they want. You know that as well as me, Janet. Aye, they're just set against it and will be till they die. If a thing's no' godly it canna be good, according to them. But there's a few all the same we might win over. Aye, and more we could lose if we went the wrong way about it."

"That's so" said young Mrs Macrae, "there's some of us will have a hard enough fight to be allowed to approve ourselves. Hamish and me, we're right enough, but his folks is gey narrow. Well, we had a nice evening, I liked *An Aitchairachd Ard* extra well."

Everyone was going off now, calling goodnight, back to their homes through the spring darkness. And if we're not careful, thought May, there will be pressure yet put on the Glen ones, even on Janet, to stop them trying to help the Hall. And they'll give in, even Janet, because by and large the west is soft and they're not even that sure themselves that they could be right to do a thing that their own consciences approve, if once the Ministers and the Kirk Session tell them it's wrong. And our own Minister will need to be kept right, she thought, but never mind, my father will see to him. And after that, if once things could be cleared up about the lobsters——

Outside the McCullochs and Maggie had waited for Ella and Anna, for they went back the same way. "Did ye hear Miss Beaton laying off about us joggling?" said Jamesina.

"Ach," said Ella, "she'll ha' done some joggling in her time. Who hasna? Do you no' think Mistress Snow and the Laird——"

"Away, Ella!" said Euphemia, shocked, "they're gentry."

"And terrible old!" said Anna, laughing to herself.

"Aye, but she goes alone to the castle, and what at all would folk be doing else?"

"They could be listening to the wireless," said Euphemia doubtfully.

"It's awful nice in a car," said Anna, "and it right dark, and maybe six o' you, the way nothing canna happen."

"It'll happen right enough," said Ella, "but no' bad. Only maybe kind o' half bad."

"It'll no happen if you keep your skirt down."

"Aye, but the more you keep your skirt down, the more you get hands up under."

"Aye, but hands is no' right wicked," said Maggie anxiously.

"It would be terrible if it was wicked, and it happening so easy. But there's ne'er a thing about hands in the Book."

"In the Book there's only right good-going sin, the way it was in yon old times. It isna sin, this." They were off down the road now, still talking in low voices and looking round now and then, in case anyone should be listening.

But in the tea-room Jessie had finished writing up the minutes and was straightening the chairs and humming, not a Gaelic song, but an English one, or maybe American, there was no telling one from the other. "Did you get that from the wireless?" May asked. "Aye," said Jessie, "it's kind of cheery."

CHAPTER IX

TUESDAY: DISTRICT COUNCIL MEETING, MORNING SESSION

Isa was leaning into the car saying to Kate that she had another broody hen, should she put duck eggs under her? "We'll not have feeding for them all, surely?" asked Kate.

"Och, aye, why wouldn't we?" said Isa, and then, "will you be speaking about the new Hall at this meeting you're away to?"

"I expect so" said Kate, "We'll want to have an official recommendation. What were you hearing about it, Isa? Have folk been speaking of it much?"

"Speaking of it!" said Isa, "Hasn't it taken first place over everything! And will it be here, or will it be there."

"Where do you think they want it?"

"I'd say they mostly want it at the back of the Post Office, but Johnnie Crubach has his mind made up it will be on his ground. Do you know this, Mistress Snow, he was at me to ask would I speak to you about buying his hens after he has the ground sold. But dinna you do it! Not if they was the last hens in the world. Full of worms they are."

"I hope it isn't going to make trouble, Isa. We'll need to be sure of the site before we send in the next form."

"It'll make trouble sure enough, but what's about it? Certain ones are forever making trouble. Tell then to go to the diabhoil! Mrs MacLean will make trouble, for all she's on the Committee, with her being Johnnie Crubach's sister. Did ye no' know? She isna seeing him much the way she's Established and he's Wee Free —he changed over after the MacMillan lassie gi'ed him the chuck. But when it comes to a matter of money, then that's different again."

"They're a silly crowd, Isa!"

"Ach, they're silly right enough, they hanna enough work, so they must always be speaking; and one wanting to be better than another."

She laughed and slapped Isa on her broad, gay-overalled behind: "It's great you're not like that!"

"Ach, me! I'm kinna more contented than some. Well now, I'll set the ducks' eggs and if you happen to see Mr MacVicar in Halbost, just you be speaking to him kind of canny like about him giving us a Rhode Island cock in exchange for our fellow"— she pointed to where he was scratching by the scullery door— "and be sure now to be bragging him up plenty!"

"I'll do my best, Isa" said Kate and pushed the self-starter, no more certain than usual what effect this would have.

However, this time she started almost at once and down the road past the wishing well, giving it a hard look. If one ever got one's wish—except for Alice. And she away at school, getting further every term. This morning, at breakfast, her father had lost one of his note-books. Oh well, with any luck he'd have found it again before she was back.

Now she was passing the entrance to the Castle, a tangle of rhodies and hazel and another limb down from the ash. Yes, and surely that was the old Douglas gone at last! She could see the tip sticking up through some broken rhodie bushes. That must have been the storm when the telephone wires went. And how long was Sandy likely to leave the mess!

She turned north pass the Drum, with the Balnafearchar fields on the right. The Middle Park had come on well—it was new seed this year—and now they were rolling. The roller had left the young green in beautiful broad stripes like a lawn tablecloth. Donnie wasn't by the horse, he must be away still. Donnie would like the Village Hall well enough, but he would never have the courage to say so, let alone go there. Not while his father was alive. His father and his father's God. A queer boy, Donnie, good-looking, but he could never keep his eyes straight.

She was level with Norman's croft now. It was Norman's God too. A man's God. Norman came out to his house door and looked down across the field to the road. She waved to him, but he didn't wave back. No doubt his God was still offended at her. Well, if it only didn't interfere with the Hall——!

Most of the croft houses were the newer ones built with the grant, of poured cement with slate or asbestos roofs. A good many of them had cracked badly and were damper inside than the old ones. One or two had surface water off the hill piped into a cistern at the back, but most hadn't bothered. There would always be a woman in the family who would go to the well; it was away cheaper than putting in the water. And after all, thought Kate, there are worse jobs than fetching water, and I would sooner run the worst croft than work in a shop. She remembered the day she had been over at Janet's and met her coming back from the well with her pails dripping and the house lamb trotting after her bleating, and she singing at the top of her voice. Here was the croft now and Kate blew her horn; Janet straightened herself up in the potato patch which she and her father were planting and turned and waved. Young Mrs Macrae was standing at the foot of the brae that led up to their croft house. She had a blue scarf over her head and a brown paper parcel under her arm. Could she be wanting over to Halbost? Kate stopped to ask her, getting out of the car. She shook her head, "No, no, I was just waiting on Angus's lorry."

"Are you sending in a length of tweed?" said Kate, glancing at the parcel, "how is Hamish making out?"

Young Mrs Macrae went very red. "Ach, fine," she said, "fine, thank you." And she seemed to be squeezing the parcel under her oxter.

Oh dear, thought Kate, and felt herself blushing as she turned back to the car. I might have known it was black market! If only they'd let me explain to them. Because I see so well why they do it and I see how it's going to ruin the real tweed market. And then they'll howl!

She had happened to glance at her front tyres while she was out of the car. The right-hand one was almost down to the cord, and the spare, she knew, not much better. But it would surely take her into Halbost. She should have looked before she started. No doubt everyone else in Port Sonas knew she had a bad tyre!

The last of the narrow croft fields was past now and the road began to climb in earnest between the hills. There were light clouds on the top of T'each Mor, incoming from the Atlantic. The hills were dotted white with new lambs; the heart-piercing bleat drifting in through the open window of the car. A small Ford passed her going the other way: the District Officer from the Forestry Commission driving down to Port Sonas. She knew Roddy didn't like him much. The road to Kilmolue slunk off to the left, wriggling round a queer little hill, an old moraine perhaps, and out of sight. Would the Director be able to do anything about that schoolmistress and the books? He would have some of the members of the Education Committee on his top if he tried to move her, but still—— Perhaps she had better talk to Mr Stewart, she thought, as her own road began to turn east towards the pass.

Then suddenly the bumping began and she almost went into the side of the road. She got out, well knowing. Yes, it was that right front tyre. Thank goodness she had started in plenty of time. She took her hat off and put it on the seat, and then she blocked the back wheels, for there was too much of a slope. She got out the jack and the brace, unscrewed the spare from the side. It was warm in the sun; she took off her coat. The distant crying of the lambs came to her. It was after the jack was firmly under that the trouble began. First the hub cap stuck and nothing in the tool box to go under it. However, when she pulled out the cushion of the back seat and looked behind, she found one of the good horn-handled dinner knives. Alice no doubt! But it did the trick. Two of the nuts came out fairly easily, but the others stuck. She tugged at the brace and felt the strap of her slip give. But not the bolt.

She stood up and felt under her dress for the strap. If that damned nut wouldn't give—well she would just need to work away at it. She didn't want to be late at the meeting with the school cleaner to speak about. Mr MacFadyen would need to advertise. She had thought Ella was settled and here she was going off to Roddy! If it wasn't the summer visitors, it was the forestry now. Poor David, he was terribly down about it. She tried again, the thing must be rusted in. Perhaps a wee drop of oil. But there wasn't any.

And then she heard the lorry on the road behind and looked round. It would be Angus. She would get to the meeting all right! He drew up and got out. "Can I help you, Mistress Snow? Ach, aye, we'll soon have her fixed." His hand gripped on the brace, the muscles tightened on his neck and there, the nut moved. Then the other. "Oh, thank you!" said Kate, "I'll just jack her up a wee bit more."

"Not at all" said Angus, "you'll dirty yourself. Are you for a meeting? You should speak about this road."

"I always do" said Kate, "but they're terribly dear to mend, the roads."

"Aye, aye, things is dear these days. Would it be better, do you think, with the rationing off? There's some that's saying so."

"Certainly not—just look what happened to the sweeties! How is your lorry doing, is it paying for itself?"

"It would pay better if once we were to get the bridge. Do you think now that'll ever come?"

"It will be a while yet" said Kate, suddenly thinking how delightful it would be if some day she could announce that something had really been done! But then, they would know before she did! She looked over at the lorry, there was a reaper in it and one or two sacks, a packing case, and on the seat beside the driver, young Mrs Macrae's parcel. She looked away hastily. "Whose reaper is it?" she asked.

"That's the Tirnafeidh reaper" he said, "I'm taking her into Halbost, she's old getting and the steamer might give her a bad shaking up." He was tightening the nuts on the spare now. Then he knocked the hub cap home. "I'll just put the tyre in at the back here, it'll be handy for you. You'll mind and let them have it at Halbost before the meeting—or maybe I could save you the trouble, is it Kennedy's you go to? Ach, aye, I'll leave it in and they'll have it ready for you by the afternoon." He picked it up and put it on to the back of the lorry. "Will I speak to them about you needing a new tyre?"

"Oh, well," said Kate, "I've one ordered from Hughie, it wouldn't do to go past him."

Angus laughed; "It would not indeed and him so keen on the new Hall! I'll wake him up when I see him, for you're sorely needing another tyre." He gave the spare a kick, "I'll give her a wee pump up—no, I've my own pump; ach, you've a tyre gauge. Now isn't that great altogether!" He used it happily, then pumped. "Now go you on and if you have any trouble between here and Halbost, I'm no' very far behind you."

"This is kind, Angus," she said, starting the car. For indeed she didn't like driving without a spare and would have worried all the way. Now she needn't.

As far as the top of the pass it was all low gear running. A hen-harrier was standing on a post, slim and upright and heraldic; a mile or two further on there was a buzzard flapping square-winged, with something ragged in its claws. Then they were over the pass and dropping down to Kinlochbannag with the school and the hotel on the right and Kinlochbannag House on the left, the drive lined with splendid rhododendrons, deep scarlet and palest coral. Kate wondered if Miss Campbell's camellias were doing well this year, she must go and call some time. The hotel garage was standing empty. It looked as if Mr Thompson was away ahead of her. Likely enough, he always seemed to have plenty to do at Halbost!

From one stretch of road it was possible to see right down Loch Bannag to the Kyles and Sonas Point. Then the hills closed round them again and there was the long, beautiful, rather wearisome drive up Glen Lurg, green, green, feathers and fountains of birch, wild cherry, broom and again, again, puffs of green smoke against the heavy blue green of the pines, the wild birch scrambling from the roadside to the heights. The Torskadale track came in on the right and now for a few miles they were in sight of the sea, the blue glitter, and out beyond, the astonishing shapes and colours of the islands. There was occasional traffic on the road now and activity in the fields wherever the hills allowed a space for cultivation. Everywhere the braird was green and even, drills were being opened or closed. A fine haze of potato or cereal manure hung in the air. Here was a farmer sowing out, the delicate hay seed showering round him like a swarm of midges and his two hands swinging out right and left from the sowing sheet at his middle. Green was on the pastures too and the cows at it hard. Kate waved to an old friend who was repairing his stand for the Milk Marketing Board cans. She passed the Glenrig bus coming in, the driver gave her a friendly toot. Then she rounded the hill and came down into Halbost. Ten minutes yet before the meeting.

She glanced at her list. Yes, she could leave her father's boots to be mended—and fish—there should be some nice haddocks in now. A pity Matta wouldn't bother himself to get haddocks; he would sometimes try a line in summer with the visitors wanting fish, but never at this time. The salmon should be up soon; Sandy was beginning to grumble about poachers already and he would keep on at it for the next three months. She wondered if there were really any poaching or if it was all his imagination. Butter muslin for Isa. But she had better be getting along to the office.

She parked her car beside the monument and found Councillor Grant doing the same thing. As he got out of his car Kate saw he had a grievance again and sure enough he began on it at once, before they got to the steps of the office even. She couldn't quite follow it, but that was usually so with Mr Grant's grievances. It had something to do with the Agricultural Executive and drains. She nodded sympathetically and tucked her hair in under her hat.

Councillor Thompson was there talking to Mr MacFadyen, the Clerk, a young man with an over-tight collar. Mr Stewart the Continuing Free Minister was taking off his coat; he turned and came to shake hands with her and to tell her he had booked a table for the two of them at the Italian shop. Both of them much preferred fried fish and ice cream to the heavy lunch at the hotel where the rest of the Council could go unembarrassed by a woman or a Minister. Mr Stewart was thin and lively, with grey hair and black eyebrows and he spoke in an ordinary way, not like a Minister, unless it was the one word "God" and that floored him, the same as the rest. Mr Buchanan, Charlie Young and Sir Ian all came in and settled round the table. The Clerk distributed the expenses forms. Mr Buchanan felt in all his pockets and found he had not got the agenda or minutes. Others were found for him and it was fairly clear from his look of interest that he had not read them yet. Sir Ian looked at the clock, compared it accusingly with his own watch, coughed and settled himself down at the head of the table. The Clerk whispered to him and he intimated a written apology from the Rev. Murray McLennan and a verbal apology from Councillor MacDonald. Kate sat at the further end of the table on his left, from where she could see the museum. A generation or two back it had been the custom to leave curiosities to the Borough of Halbost. Some were local; stone axes, a bronze dagger, various pins and armlets, an amber necklace, some peculiar instruments of torture said to have been used on Papists and others, and the manuscripts of a forgotten poet of Halbost. But some were exotic; and there was one lovely ship model. There had been a time when Kate had wanted to organise out of this a small travelling exhibition for the country schools, but it had been firmly decided that this would be a waste of money, so nobody ever looked at it at all, except Mr MacFadyen's girl clerk who

114

dusted them and occasionally broke one of them slightly and had permanently borrowed a small Dresden figure.

It was Education to start off with, exemptions, school attendance, conveyances, the perennial difficulty in getting any contractor to go up to the head of Glenrig beyond the bridge to uplift the shepherd's children. School cleaners. "I didn't get the letter in time to put it on the agenda, Mrs Snow," said Mr MacFadyen, "but you will know about your own cleaner."

"Yes" said Kate, "I'm afraid you will have to advertise."

"Don't you know of anyone yourself, Mrs Snow?" said Sir Ian looking at her through horn-rimmed spectacles and frowning.

"If I did we'd have to fixed it locally!" she said. The old wretch, expecting her to know, he wouldn't have said it to any of the men! "But they're all busy with the tourists."

"We're hearing a lot too much about tourists" said Sir Ian. Councillor Grant agreed eagerly, but none of the others. They weren't going to speak against an industry that brought money into the place; certainly not Councillor Thompson with his hotel, nor Buchanan who had a milk round in Halbost and whose cousin owned the chief garage, nor Charlie Young who was in tweed.

"The cleaner at Alltsalach has asked for a rise" said the Clerk.

"And she ought to have it" said Mr Stewart, "she's a decent hard-working woman trying to bring up a young family."

"We don't want to create a precedent" said Sir Ian, who didn't like Ministers, least of all this one.

"It's difficult not to create a precedent in times of change" said Mr Stewart, "even for a body like our own."

Sir Ian suspected this remark; he wasn't sure what it meant, but it must be wrong. "If we give her a rise," he said, "what's to stop the rest of them?"

"I move that it be not granted" said Charlie Young, who was worried in case any rise might spread to the weavers. Mr Stewart moved for the increase.

"She's asking for an extra ten pounds, is she no'?" said Councillor Thompson, "Will we split the difference and call it five pounds?"

After some squabbling, this was agreed to and the Port Sonas vacancy to be advertised. School milk and meals were a sore subject too. But all that could be done over it all was to send up recommendations to the Education Committee. Kate wished, as always, that she was on that herself. She had a quite illogical feeling that somehow it should be a better committee than this one. She wondered if she would speak about the teacher at Kilmolue here. No, better not. It wasn't as if any of them cared much for books themselves or would be anything but amused at the happenings there.

Sir Ian looked at his watch and said abruptly that they had better adjourn for lunch. They all got up. He looked at Kate again. "I feel sure you could find a cleaner at Port Sonas, Mrs Snow, if you were to take a little trouble."

Kate couldn't stop herself from saying, "Did you ever have to find a school cleaner, Sir Ian?" and saying it in a rather shrill and aggressive voice, which was worse.

"Never needed to" said Sir Ian accusingly.

Councillor Thompson rolled over, "Ach, it's not easy at all, the cleaners, and Port Sonas so prosperous. I don't wonder Mistress Snow is having her difficulties. And how did you get on with the Village Hall Committee, Mistress Snow?"

"It wasn't bad at all" said Kate. "We got down to ways and means of collecting money and discussed the site. Will you manage to the next one on Saturday first?"

"I'm just not sure" he said, and then, "There's a section against it. Aye, aye, an influential section. I was speaking to one of them on the telephone and it is certain there will be a letter coming."

"You mustn't let yourself be influenced, Mr Thompson."

"No, no, they'll not put me against Village Halls. But the question is, Mistress Snow, is it timeous? It would never do to make half of the community enemies, would it now?"

"It's only a handful that are against the Hall and only the old ones."

"You wouldn't have us not give respect to age, Mistress Snow? And it would never do not to be democratic, but we'll see, we'll see. You heard about the Highland Panel Committee coming? Aye, well, I'll be over myself, but it's not them all, just a kind of wee group of them and nobody knows if the chairman's coming himself."

"That's Malcolm MacMillan, isn't it?"

"Aye, aye, and doing extra well for the Western Isles they say, but it stands to reason he'll not do as well for us."

"I don't think it necessarily stands to reason."

"Ach, well, he's nothing to gain over it the same as he has with his own crowd."

"But perhaps they made him chairman just because he doesn't think that way?"

"They might" said Councillor Thompson and gave a big rumbling laugh, "Ach, aye, they might!" He followed the others out.

Kate picked up her coat and turned to Mr Stewart. He laughed too, but differently. "Never you let yourself believe that everyone's on the same level in Scotland. There are a few honest ones, and Malcolm MacMillan is one of them. Come away now and tell me about your Village Hall."

Over lunch in the hotel, Grant was telling Sir Ian his grievance. He had bought a small estate at Glenrig and was farming it himself and he was convinced he knew more than any of his neighbours. Sir Ian didn't think so, but had an uneasy conviction that he should somehow be sustained. He had subscribed to the Party of which Sir Ian was one of the Vice-chairmen. They had a table to themselves. The others, plus the missing District Councillor, Donald Jimmy MacDonald, who had been held up with his new heifer calving—and he was not terrible keen on the education—came up to the Dining-room after their visit to the bar. They had the hotel's best, Scotch broth, mince with onions through it, boiled potatoes and a pudding just thick with currants. The link between Halbost and the landward parts was close. There was continual business done between them and everyone related to everyone else. None of them liked Sir Ian who had no finger at all in the tweed trade and didn't even go the usual ways about to make his home farm pay. But at least they hadn't the same suspicions about him that they had about one another. Nor yet the same kind of confidence and, in a way, affection. For every one of them would have stood by the other in, say, a tax case. They spoke of the markets, the bull sale, the subsidies and how best to circumvent the Forestry Commission without letting Sir Ian, who had dedicated part of his woodland and appeared to be on the side of the Commission, know what they were doing. But Charlie Young was trying to get the rest of them to back him for a scheme for a technical school for the County. So far he had not persuaded them that there was any money in it, though Buchanan was warming, but he knew Kate and the Ministers would back it. The other Minister on the District Council was from Muckle Isle, but he only came an odd time when there was some business connected with the islands, and who was to blame him, for it meant three days away? But when he wasn't there they were always kind of relieved, for Mr MacLennan was a crabbit wee man and quoted the scriptures at them. At least Mr Stewart, for all his queer ways, let them off that.

Meanwhile Mr Stewart and Kate were eating fried fresh haddock and chips in the Italian shop. She was telling him about the Village Hall, and the attitude of the Churches: "I was awfully disappointed in Mr Fergusson" she said, "I talked to him about it and he quite agreed it was a good thing. It shows a sad lack of courage on his part."

"That's maybe the commonest failing among my fellows" said Mr Stewart; "Yet he could well have been thinking of others. He wouldn't want to go outwith the approval of his Elders."

"But half of them approve anyway! They told me so."

"For good reasons? For your own reasons, Mrs Snow?"

"One can't always tell what people's reasons are."

"It might be that their Minister could tell better than you. Did you ever look at it that way? And he may have more thought than you for the weaker brethren."

"That's quibbling, Mr Stewart! Would you have preached for or against the Hall if it had been you?"

He hesitated, pushing the chips about with his fork: "You will know—won't you?—that I've run things myself along that line. Did you hear about my Club I had?"

She shook her head.

"Well, that was when I was at Toberglas. And there was nothing at all for the young men and boys and altogether too much drinking; so here, I cleared out a big room in the Manse. I bought a darts board and draughts and that and gramophone records. And I put in my own gramophone and the good classical records I had—the records I bought were songs mostly. I looked through my own books for anything they might like. And I got the young ones to come and to form their own committee for their own club."

"That was grand."

"Well, it went on well enough for a whiley. But there were some of the boys that had not much good feeling. I wasn't wanting to be always in and out, stopping them from doing things, but the time came when by the end of the evening there was always something broken, pages torn out of books and scattered around. As often as not they left me to sweep up their cigarette ends, for all I had asked their committee to see to that. And the next thing, didn't my Kirk Sessions come to me and say the boys were damaging the Manse and throwing an extra burden on the congregation! Well, I told the Kirk Sessions they should be ashamed when they had done nothing to help the boys: I spoke as one who knew better than themselves. And I spoke to the boys too and for a time they were better. But here, I began to notice that the ones from the decent families were not coming and in a while I was left with nothing but the rascals. Yet I thought it was my Christian duty to see could I help them. And I spent more of my time there than I should have and all the while defending them against the Kirk Sessions. But it was a struggle and me losing all the while, and none of them getting any better. And whenever I tried to check one of them it was always said that it was some-one else! And then one day when I went to let them in, there was a window broken and the darts board stolen and nobody willing to guess who had done it. That was the end, with me paying for the window and needing to acknowledge that the Kirk Sessions had the right of it."

"Did nobody ever help you with the boys?"

"Well, just at the very first, but they were the kind that seemed to scare the boys and they didn't like the free way I was wanting the boys to do it with their own committee."

"There you are then. They let you down as much as the boys did."

"Aren't we all letting one another down every way, Mrs Snow? They may have been in the right of it. I think of it often. Yet I doubt I would have been on your side over this Village Hall if it had been in my parish. Even if I had known it could never do all the good you are thinking."

"But, Mr Stewart, I know it isn't going to change the place

right away. I'm only hoping it will be—oh, the means of making a new pattern for the community, and most of all for the ones that are getting little out of the Churches. It's they that need it most."

"You know what that comes to? It's as much as to say that these ones must be given up by us, their shepherds. We must let them slip out of the flock because they don't like to be in it. You're never expecting me surely to accept that challenge and lie down under it?"

"I don't know what else you can do. You can't *make* them come to church. Well, you can more or less in a small place; but they won't get any good of it. Oh, I'm sorry; perhaps I shouldn't have said that to you"—embarrassment came over her. It was so easy to start speaking to Mr Stewart as though he weren't a Minister. Then you remembered suddenly.

"You should indeed. Most people don't take us seriously enough to say so. But if I were to believe it—oh well, well, I might as well give up the Ministry and then maybe I would make an honest fisherman!"

"Well, you're bound to want to try and get them into the Churches. But the fact remains that there are any amount of people, especially young ones, who only go there because their folks want them to. Or they find it is an easy way of meeting one another. Or they may like the singing. But it's nothing to do with Christianity or even a sense of fellowship; it won't stop them being dishonest, cruel, or malicious, or just unthinking to one another, will it? And it won't get them back to this Highland way of life we are always speaking about."

"Ah" said Mr Stewart, and pushed his plate away, "Now I've a question for you. This Highland way of life, and I think we know it when we see it, both the two of us: it's in the old folk, isn't it?"

She nodded, thinking of Norman and a half dozen more whom she knew between Halbost and Port Sonas.

"And aren't they all strict church-goers and in your own words getting something out of it?"

"I think I would agree," she said.

"They are not even in the Established Church, most of them. It's scarcely strict enough for the finest. It compromised. You know what I feel about that, Mrs Snow: the reason I am where I am with the Continuing Free Church. Part is in history and part is in practice. I don't want to be compromised with the State, even when it has a Government that's better aware of brotherhood than most. But you will find most of your best Highlanders of the old school in the narrowest Churches. Aye, in the Wee Frees and the Free Presbyterians even. It has them gripped into uprightness, so that they cannot be liars and dishonest in the ways we know, so that they see all men as children of the one Father, and because of that must be kindly and generous and believing good of others. Their word is their bond. They have values that are far away stronger than the money one. So that they are not tempted by money."

"And when the Church goes, that goes. And how can a Church stay alive when it's based on fear and hell-fire?"

"You don't believe in Hell, do you?"

"How can I?"

"By looking round the world, I would have thought, Mrs Snow. But it's true enough, that you can never make people believe by fear alone. Oh, I admit it's difficult. And most of it our own fault."

The girl brought their ices. Kate said "Are you sorry now you ran that boys' club?"

"No" he said, "never."

"Isn't that rather illogical of you? According to what you just said you should have stuck to the Church and—and this hell-fire of yours." She was suddenly finding herself angry; but either he hadn't felt it in her voice, or he was determined not to notice it.

He smiled and said, "Yes, that's just what it is. The human spirit is not a logical one. That's why I would be on your committee if I was at Port Sonas. It's why I am on this District Council and hope to get on to the County Council itself, for all it is a thing of the State. We can't learn without mistakes, they are the teaching of the Lord, bringing their own punishment when we go wrong."

"You mean the only good that club did was to teach you something?"

"It taught me a wee bit of humility. There's a thing we can never have enough of. And also that it's possible to go faster than folk are ready for; that's the key to democracy as well."

"Didn't it teach anyone else?" Her voice was still hard and belligerent.

"It will have taught the boys certain lessons. And also the congregation."

"That they could get by with it?"

"No, no, surely not that. There was a stirring of conscience."

"How big is Toberglas?"

"There would have been some two hundred souls in those times."

"And now?"

"Fewer, aye, fewer every year."

"Yes," said Kate, "and they'll be the young ones going off to the cities like they do everywhere. If you had been able to hold out with the club you might have been able to stop some of it. It's what we are going to try and do at Port Sonas, whatever opposition we get from the Churches."

"And if your way of keeping the young ones in the Highlands is to destroy the Highland way of life, what then?"

"I don't know" she said, "but I think that's going anyway. And we can't see into the future. Thank God, we can't see."

"Aye, that is one of His mercies."

It was the queerest thing, but Kate, who was very fond of Mr Stewart, suddenly felt that she wanted to hurt him. Wanted to use her tongue on him. Although he would be on her side over the Hall, and plenty of other things. They were mostly on the same side in the District Council, and would occasionally catch one another's eye and give a wee nod. What was it? Didn't they both believe enough of the same things to be deep-down friends? She finished her ice in silence, aware that he was watching her, afraid she might say something she knew she would regret later. She glanced at her watch: almost time for the afternoon meeting.

CHAPTER X

TUESDAY AFTERNOON:
DISTRICT COUNCIL MEETING

THERE WAS A GOOD deal on the agenda, including a letter from the Secretary of the Highland Panel. The meeting was to be on Port Sonas quay and afterwards in the Harbour Master's office. Councillor Thompson and the District Councillor, Mrs Snow, would be there. Probably nothing would come up which was within the competence of the District Council. There was one thing certain they would discuss, the hole in the harbour wall. "If there was a grant going, do you think the County Council might take over the harbour?" asked Kate.

Councillor Thompson could bring it up at the Road Board, said Sir Ian, "but I don't like all this taking over of harbours; we shall find ourselves landed with financial obligations."

"Aye, aye" said Mr MacDonald, "the rates is plenty high enough as it is."

"And if we take over Port Sonas, it will create a precedent."

"I doubt we'll not get the grant without we take it over" said Councillor Thompson "and there's other County Councils are doing it. Look at Argyll and Inverness and the great grants they're getting. We should be in on the same thing."

"All coming out of taxation" said Sir Ian.

"Aye, but all the more reason we should get some of it back" said Councillor Thompson, "we licensed victuallers know all about taxation. Now, if it's to be a grant, could we not put it forward from the District Council that Port Sonas harbour be taken over?"

"Is that a motion?" growled Sir Ian. Councillor Thompson looked round, counted his supporters, nodded. Kate seconded quickly. Mr Grant moved an amendment against, seconded by Mr MacDonald, but they and the chairman were the only ones voting for the amendment.

There was then a long discussion about the district steam-roller and the difficulty of getting spares. Then came the question of the name for the eight Council houses at the foot of Glenrig. "I understand," said Mr Grant the local Councillor, "that the new tenants want to call them—er—Sea View."

"Well, that's a nice enough name" said Mr Buchanan.

"Sounds to me like Margate" said Sir Ian, "Why the deuce do they want to call them that?"

"I understand" said Mr Grant, "it was the name they were given before they were built."

"Is there not a local Gaelic name?" asked Mr Stewart.

"Aye," said Mr MacDonald, "the land where they are is Ardnaslisneach, but maybe that's kind of hard to say for some; and Sea View sounds kind of modern and women-folk like that."

"I didn't think you could see the sea from the Glenrig houses" said Kate.

"Er—no," said Mr Grant rather uncomfortably.

"Neither you can!" said Mr MacDonald, leaning over towards her, "But you would have been able sure enough from the first site they had in mind, and that was how they put the name on to this one."

"Well, it seems to me sheer lunacy" said Sir Ian, "couldn't we give them a sensible name like, like——" he was lost for the moment.

But Councillor Thompson said, "Well, I think we should just let the locals decide, after all it's for them to live there."

The next item on the agenda was roads. Kate duly put in a plea. But there were many miles of roads and the District Council rates would only do a patch here and there. There was a question about fencing one of the old graveyards, and much discussion as to whose duty it was. Then the question of the Kinbeg 'phone box. Then came the Port Sonas Village Hall. Kate asked that the approval of the District Council should be communicated to the Education Committee.

"I suppose the Hall Committee, or whatever it is, are not going to call on us for financial assistance?" said Sir Ian, glaring at Kate.

"They have no intention of doing so" said Kate. But all the same she knew it would occur to Mr MacMillan, if not to the others, sooner or later. "We shall be raising funds ourselves." If the committee decided to ask for some money later, it wouldn't be her doing!

"Your fishermen coining money still?" asid Sir Ian disapprovingly.

"They've got plenty of bad years to make up for, Sir Ian" she said. Annoying as the fishermen were, he wasn't the man to be let criticise them.

"And they may have them again" said Mr Stewart quickly, before the Chairman could answer. "They need some encouragement, and they've done well for the country."

Sir Ian made a noise in his throat and turned to the next item on the agenda; the public convenience at Halbost. His eyebrows went up.

"Aye" said Donald Jimmie MacDonald, "it's time we broached the public convenience."

The whole of the District Council woke up. Here after all was an intrinsically amusing subject, made the more so by the presence of a woman and a Minister. Droll sayings formed themselves in the minds of Councillors Thompson and Young, which they whispered to one another. Kate stared at the Indian beads in the museum cupboard. Mr Buchanan, however, was thinking practically. The buses mostly waited up beside his cousin's garage. "Well, there's the site up by the market" he said, "if we make our recommendation I am mostly certain the Planning Officer will take it and it would be handy for the buses. There could be a wee shelter at the same time."

"But look," said Charlie Young, "supposing another bus company was to start, they might wait somewhere more central. There are other agents they might go to for spares." He didn't look directly at Mr Buchanan, but his intention was clear.

"It's possible, it's possible" said Mr Buchanan, "but it would be terrible queer if there couldn't be some agreement come to." That was no bad indication; for the moment Councillor Young let the subject drop.

The others took it up. The chairman was not much in favour. Besides, he wanted to get home in time for tea; he didn't like to have his meals disturbed. But Donald Jimmie was enthusiastic. "It will be a great place to pass the time" he said, "You'll often have half an hour before the bus."

"Could he no' get the opening hours changed?" whispered Councillor Thompson to Mr Buchanan, "he wouldn't need the other place to pass the time in then."

"I'm no' so sure of that" Mr Buchanan whispered, "you'll scarcely need the other without the one!"

"And if it was just to be painted a nice colour" said Donald Jimmie, "it would be an ornament to the place."

"And what would you say now would be a nice colour?" asked Charlie in the most serious way.

"Ach, well, a nice blue maybe."

"Would that not be a bittie cold?"

"Aye, but it would be mostly used in summer with the visitors coming."

"But we'll not be putting it up just for the visitors—unless we were thinking to make a charge?"

"Aye, but that would defeat its ends, which was kind of sanitary."

"Oh, it's his sanitary end he would be using there!" whispered Councillor Thompson.

But the chairman was getting annoyed with all this; "Have you made a motion, Mr MacDonald?" he asked. But at that Charlie Young wriggled his eyebrows and everyone giggled, except of course Mr MacFadyen, and Kate, who was not exactly shocked, but embarrassed, as any doctor would be, by such an anal reversion in adults.

Donald Jimmie himself was the most amused; "No' yet, no' yet, Sir Ian, but in the Lord's good time I may be doing just that if the County Council puts it through!"

"I think, Sir Ian" said Charlie gravely, "that this should go forward with the recommendation of the District Council."

"Is that agreed?" asked Sir Ian. "Very well, next item."

The next item was accounts, which were passed round. There was a fairly large one from the garage of which Mr Buchanan's cousin was owner. Mr Grant commented on it. A long look went between Charlie and Mr Buchanan. It passed. There was some discussion about the transfer of certain liabilities to National Health. They were all rather at a loss, except Mr MacFadyen, who knew exactly what he wanted and ended by getting it.

"You're on this National Health Committee' said Sir Ian accusingly to Mr Stewart, "or Board or whatever it is. Too much of that altogether."

"We find we can get a great deal done, Sir Ian, that was never done before." Mr Stewart spoke with the possibility of challenge in his voice. Kate prepared to back him if need be. But Mr MacFadyen diverted Sir Ian with a number of small cheques to sign.

"It's you that have the old poorhouse now, isn't it?" said Charlie Young, leaning over the table, "Did you ever get the chimneys fixed?"

"That was done in the first six months," said Mr Stewart.

"Well that's a blessing, sure enough. I was at them to have it done for years before it was taken over, but the County never had the money to spare. There's some decent old bodies in there and it was a shame the way it was. But you'll have the old difficulties over nurses?"

"Very nearly, in spite of what we have done for the staff rooms; you'll remember the state they were in, Mr Young?"

"Well enough I do! But the girls have no more notion to be nurses than to be school cleaners."

"They like your tweed mills better, Mr Young."

"Well," said Charlie, "I've done what I can for my folk and it's a cheery place and indeed the inspector was saying just that the last time he was by; music while you work and all. They wouldn't know themselves without the wireless and the loud-speakers."

"You'll be spoiling them for the Gaelic choirs, Charlie" said Mr MacDonald, who had been something of a singer in his day, and mostly always went to the concerts that the Halbost choir gave, and listened to them when they broadcast.

"Ach, that's finished, anyway, Donald Jimmie, and you know it. There'll be no Gaelic spoken in fifty years."

"Do you think so really?" said Kate, "isn't it rather a pity?"

"Ach well, maybe it's nice for some, but it doesn't do for a business world."

"But it's kind of handy" said Councillor Thompson "to be able to speak a wee word or so behind the other man's back. Indeed I've used it that way myself." He chuckled, "Oh, it's a great language for not being understood."

"The way I'm seeing it" said Donald Jimmie, "is that it was our fathers' language before us."

"But times have changed and you know that yourself, Donald Jimmie, and it wasn't our fathers that were asking for public conveniences."

"Maybe they were as well off without them."

But Sir Ian looked up, "Any other business, Mrs Snow and gentlemen? No? Well then the meeting's over." He got up.

"Vote of thanks to the chairman" said Charlie Young quickly and they all tapped on the table before gathering up their papers.

"How are you finding the District Nursing works out under the National Health scheme?" Kate asked Mr Stewart, "You know I'm not altogether happy about it. We used to have a local committee but now it's finished. It's all very well with Miss Beaton, who knows everyone, but suppose we got a new nurse, she would feel herself a wee bit lost; at least, that's the way it seems. Dr MacKillop isn't worrying, but then he never does. I'm afraid I am."

"I suppose it will all come straight in the end" said Mr Stewart, "but there's times I wish the head ones in London would admit there was a wee fault here and there instead of saying it was perfect." They went out together, discussing the Health Scheme and how it needed to be put right here and there, especially for the country districts with their special difficulties. They were friends again, on the same side. She couldn't think why she had felt so cross at lunch.

Sir Ian and Mr Grant both drove off. Councillor Thompson had to go and see his wholesalers. But the others went off to the hotel for tea; there was still an odd bit of drollery to get out of the matter of the public convenience. "We would need a special place for the Ministers" said Donald Jimmie, "in case they would be seeing too much of their congregations."

"They'll not be needing such places" said Mr Buchanan very seriously, "they're not made the same as the rest of us."

"Are you saying that?" said Donald Jimmie, and then realised that it was a joke and roared with laughter and slapped his thigh. "Here, did you hear yon set about the Minister that was getting married?" They laughed their way well all along the street and back in to the bar.

Kate picked up her fish and then went along to Kennedy's for the tyre. It was there and finished. "Angus said we were to be sure and have it ready for you" the girl said. After that she had a cup of tea with an old lady whom she usually saw when she was in Halbost, a far-off cousin on her grandmother's side and an excellent clarsach player. It was a relief to get away from the all-male atmosphere. They gossiped a little over their tea and short-bread and pancakes. Sir Ian was planning to sell one of his farms. And never knew what everyone else knew about what his tenant had been up to! "And how is Sandy these days?"

"Much as ever" said Kate, and grimaced slightly. "You should see the drive now and the mess everything's got into."

"And himself the same no doubt," said the old lady, "and the nice it used to be! Geraniums in the beds and all. Another pancake, my dear? You should take him in hand yourself, Katie."

"I've plenty on my plate without Sandy!" said Kate. "Do you know this, there's almost certain to be an epidemic of measles at Port Sonas and it'll take me as well as Dr MacKillop. They've been free of it for years now, so they're likely to go down badly."

"Is that so?" said her cousin. "Now isn't it the funniest thing, I'd Dr Macquoid in about my foot and he was telling me that there'd been a whole family down with them up Long Loan, in fact I've been sending them round jellies almost every day. Four wee ones he was saying, MacKinnon the name is——"

"MacKinnon?"

"Just that, and now that I've mind of it, haven't they relations up Glen Sonas?"

"Well now, that would be Janet and her father. But they might be related to the MacKinnons at Osnish who are the ones with the measles and their father's grandfather brother to Janet's grandfather. Ah well, I'll find out—— No, I couldn't eat another piece! It's beautiful shortbread, all the same."

"Och, I'm never without butter. There's plenty made around here and those that'll remember me among them."

"It's sugar that I find——"

"You should be a wee bit friendly with your grocer, Kate, the same as myself, and he'll not see you stuck. Isn't it democracy and all, the way they're forever telling us on the wireless?"

"Oh well—— But I'll need to be going."

"Tell Sandy we were speaking of him. His lugs should be burning!"

"I will if I see him. Are you one of his old flames?"

"Och, you'll be seeing him! He was too young for me. But I've danced with him. Aye, a bonny dancer he used to be. But he'd always rather the fishing."

But it was time for the road again. A mile out of Halbost she met a crofter's wife who had missed the bus, and took her to the Glenrig turn. Seeing it was one of the District Council, the woman asked her advice about a pension. Kate gave it; the thing seemed straightforward enough—if the woman had been speaking the truth anyway! The setting sun was in her eyes during much of the Glenlurg run. But it ended up behind a bank of clouds coming in from the west. Still the light lingered on, and here and there men were still working in their own fields. As she passed the end of the Torksadale track she thought, as always, if only the bridge was there I would be home in twenty minutes. She began to wonder if she would ever see it. Was there ever going to be ordinary, peacetime expenditure in the Highlands? Bridges and harbours and all that. Or would there always be some excuse? Defence . . . there can't be another war surely—if there is going to be everything is just silly. I can't stand another war, she thought violently, I'll kill myself—I can't stand everything happening again——

At the head of the loch the waters stretched silver and grey, washed over with palest mauve and purple. The lamps in the Kinlochbannag hotel were being carried through to the rooms. But it was still not dark when she dropped down from the pass towards the Glen and saw the lights in the croft houses stringing out ahead. It was so very beautiful that no criticism of it appeared to be valid. You forgot that the croft houses were cold nasty concrete, wringing wet if they'd half a chance, or else the old black houses, low and smoky with earth floors and maybe a flimsy tin-roofed bedroom built on. But there'd be a good tea on the table under the lighted lamp all the same, plenty butter and jam and fried eggs and if you went in there'd be a place and cup for you in no time, and the words of welcome, the voices. "*Where are the folk like the folk of the west?*" She almost caught herself humming it, as the car took the down gradient through the Glen, known curves and hollows. "*Here I would hie me and here I would rest.*" It would seem like that sure enough from Glasgow or anywhere. And the Revies stayed. Some of them. And she herself had stayed. How? How?

The road flattened out. She suddenly decided to stop at the schoolhouse and tell David the District Council would recommend the Village Hall of Port Sonas for the approval of the

Education Committee. Not that it meant anything, but David would like to hear.

She gave one glance at the Castle entrance. No light in the old Lodge. Probably it wasn't even habitable now. If Sandy had seen to it in time—— But he hadn't. Funny to think of him as a good dancer. He might have been, all the same. Might be yet.

It was dark enough now and seemed to have clouded over. She stopped at the school-house. As she walked up the garden path with the smell of wallflowers and jonquils coming at her sweet and strong, she felt the midges beginning to bite; there was a change of weather coming surely. She knocked and Miss MacTavish came to the door. "Ach, it's yourself, Mrs Snow, come away now, come away; David is through in the room and I have my kettle almost boiling." She swept her through. David and Roddy both got up from their chairs. She hesitated, it was the menfolk together again, maybe they would rather not—— But David was saying, "You'll have been at the meeting at Halbost, Kate, how did it go? Did the new Hall come up?"

"Yes, and was approved, so it will be before the Director and the Education Committee next thing. Have you any more Hall news?"

"Well, there's going to be a terrible strong opposition from the F.P.'s. And I think the Wee Frees are going to be near as bad when they've made up their minds the way their Minister wants."

"If only Norman and Pate Morrison stand firm!"

"If" said Roddy.

"I'm certain they will—Norman anyway! Don't you think so?"

"I wouldn't like to say" said Roddy, knocking his ash off into the fire, "It depends on—oh, plenty. Krooger's crowd will be shoving away at Mr Mackintosh—you'll know Krooger is an Elder? And my lot where I stay, they're dead against the Hall. But we'll do without them, Mistress Snow, if it comes to the bit."

"No, no, we'll not let them get us down" said David, and gave a nibble at his nails.

"Were they speaking about Ella at the meeting?"

"Yes, it's going to be advertised. But I don't know who we'll get, do you? Yet I'm sure there are plenty of girls here, even with Roddy taking them on at his nursery."

"It's the summer tourist trade spoils them" said David, shaking his head.

"They're just doing too well here, that's what it is" said Roddy, "even my lot in the nurseries, they don't break their backs working."

"It's with all the insurance and everything" said Kate, "there's no incentive for them to earn a bit more—only of course one oughtn't to say that, ought one?"

"Ach" said Roddy, "it would do them no harm needing to work a bit! And to have less of this overtime for this and that, and the devil of a row if they're asked to do anything different from what they think they ought to do. I'm doing plenty of overtime myself; and if we foresters were to charge it all up to the Commission——! But maybe we should" he went on, "aye, maybe we should. Maybe we would be more respected if we did."

"Ach, Roddy," said David, "I doubt you've got the thing wrong." He turned to Kate, "The District Officer was over this afternoon and Roddy had his plans set down on paper for a sawmill, and the District Officer wouldn't even look at them, and telling Roddy he shouldn't take it on himself to do such a thing."

"Is this true, Roddy, did he really say that?" said Kate, "Oh, that's bad! You know far more about it than he does."

"Thanks, Mrs Snow" said Roddy and grinned, "I believe I do." And that little dark stain on Roddy's tunic—was it possible that poor Roddy had been crying over it before she came? And men don't cry easily, not even West Highlanders.

"And that wasn't all" said David. "Roddy was wanting to try interplanting among the spruces, in the sheltered planting by Altnacoinne. He was wanting to try poplars among the soft wood."

"But that would be lovely."

"They'd not spoil the canopy" said Roddy, "And they would keep an even growth with the spruces. It's valuable timber. But—ach, he wouldn't hear of it." He lighted another cigarette. "He said I didn't know what I was speaking about. And I had thought it over plenty It's not been tried up here, but if the Commission aren't to try it, who is? Och well, at least I didn't tell him all the rest I had been planning—and I never will!"

"What else had you been planning, Roddy? I'm sure it was sensible. Do you know, David?" For Roddy was puffing away hard at his cigarette, not speaking.

"Well, he had plans for a kind of wee canteen at the nursery" said David, "and a plan for a Forestry football team—you could do that without him, Roddy! You don't need anyone's leave."

"It would be kind of funny if I did begin and he heard and stopped me! He'd tell me it was policy from the high-up ones."

"You've got a remedy there. You could ask one of them. They're sure to be around again one of these days; and most of them seem quite sensible."

"Ach, I would never have the cheek. Don't you be worrying about me, Mistress Snow. Maybe he was right. But I had my heart set on a wee saw-mill. It would be good for the place. Give employment: and a chance for some of the young fellows. Ach to hell! I'm sorry, Mistress Snow, it's no matter. But I had my heart set——" He stopped.

Miss MacTavish, David's sister, came in with a heaped tray and cheerful words. Roddy gulped his tea hot. Miss MacTavish cut into a freshly sticky and deliciously browned sponge sandwich. "Isn't it great to have the jam off the ration. Indeed we'll have everything we need soon. Take a good piece now, Mrs Snow, for you are doing plenty for all of us at Port Sonas and little thanks getting! Let me fill your cup now. You're eating nothing, Roddy, and you'll not get a cake the like of this from Mrs McCulloch—shop cakes for lodgers, isn't it now, Roddy?" He laughed at last and took a piece. "That's right, mo charaid. Was he telling you about the District Officer, Mrs Snow? Isn't it hard and him such a decent boy?"

"Is there anything I can do to help, Roddy?" asked Kate. She finished her cup, looking worriedly at him, as if he were a child. He shook his head. She thought of the next thing. "Is there anything more about Snash and the wee girl, David?"

"I got no further with Snash myself. But I don't like the looks of wee Greta, not at all. And it's making me suspicious of all the crofts. I wish the inspector would come some time they're not expecting him."

"I think I'll have to write to the inspector," said Kate, "but all the same it's the wrong way about. A man like Snash should be punished by the rest of the community. If they had their right feelings they would do it. Wouldn't you say so yourself?"

"That's the way it should be. If the community had the right feeling. But I wonder, has it? Well, we'll need to see. Are you for off, Roddy?"

"Aye," said Roddy and got up, "I've to be at my work in the morning. Goodnight Mrs Snow. Thank you for your hospitality, Davie." He went out, the brother and sister seeing him to the door.

Coming back David said, "Do you know this, Kate, when he came in poor Roddy was so terrible downhearted he was for resigning off the Hall Committee."

"We mustn't let him do that!"

"Well, I had a wee droppie of spirits in the press. And I talked him out of it. But I'm wondering if the Commission knows always the good service it's getting. And the better it might get with a spark of encouragement."

"We're all needing that maybe. How's Miss Gillies?"

"Not making things easy I can tell you! Any chance she has to speak against the Hall she'll take it and she's maybe doing more underhand than I know of. Do you know this, Kate, I've seen me dreaming she was dead and so grieved at my waking to know it was not true that I could scarcely take my porridge! Wasn't that a terrible thing and me a schoolmaster? But I can't complain to the Director on anything to do with school affairs, excepting that I hate the kind of twist that she'll try to give to everything, even the arithmetic!"

"It's difficult, David" said Kate, "and I don't see how we can get rid of her."

"Do you know what I'm thinking, Kate? In the old days I would just have gone to a witch and got her to make me a buidseachas."

"And melted it in the burn! Oh, yes, I'd have helped you! Well, I must go along, David."

"You'll not take another cup, Mrs Snow?" his sister said, "we've surely not heard all the news yet. Did you hear about Donnie Cameron, that's the latest, him getting engaged to his cousin in Glasgow while he was there over the week-end. They say the Glasgow Camerons are as godly as this lot. It's a thought, that!" She laughed.

"The news I'm expecting," said Kate, getting to her feet, "Is that there's another crop of cases of measles. It's time some of them realised measles was a dangerous disease."

"I'm thinking they'll know at Osnish" said David, "Dr MacKillop was telling me that the wee MacKinnon lassie has them on her gey bad."

"I wish he'd ever try—— Oh well, they're his patients. By the way, are they related to a family of MacKinnons at Halbost?"

"Yes, in Long Loan. They were over there at the week-end ten days ago."

"Ah, so that's the source of infection. It's as well to know. No, I'll not take another cup, thank you kindly."

David and his sister saw her to the door. Outside there was a soft fine drizzle of rain and the last midges biting wild through it.

CHAPTER XI

WEDNESDAY: WOMEN'S RURAL INSTITUTE

THE RAIN WAS ON now and looked like it would last. There were dollops of mud on the school floors, as Ella pointed out, and nothing extra for all the time and trouble it took her, and here, the Women's Rural crowd were coming and sure to bring in just as much with them! David explained, as he had done many times already, that her salary was to cover easy weeks and difficult weeks, and anyway she got extra for the Rural night. But she would lose nothing now by getting at him, so she grumbled away. At first he felt, as she meant him to, that it was some way his own fault. But then, suddenly, he couldn't stand a word more. She wasn't Miss Gillies after all! He stood and told her what kind of a cheek she had to be speaking to him this way, she, whose work was what anyone could do, and he who had trained himself with care and sweat for long years and knew history and arithmetic and geography; and had passed through Jordanhill with credits and was working for the good of the community! "And I'm not saying this to set myself up" he said, "but so that you should see yourself as you are!" And he gave Ella the severe look that he had practised but never managed to use on Miss Gillies. And not one cheep did Ella give, but scuttled off with her pail and scrubber.

"That's me getting into practice" said David, wiping over the blackboard himself, and then as he flicked out the duster, "but maybe I was not fair on her, the cratur', and if it had only been me like that with Miss Gillies or Snash!" The place looked decent now; he went out, leaving the doors unlocked.

Mrs MacLean and Minnie were the first to come. They had the prize and the raffles with them, tucked under their raincoats, which they hung on the children's pegs in the lobby. Mrs MacLean was cross; she had opened one of the new tins from Jock's store for the tea and it had a label on it great, but the stuff inside was nothing but crumbs and grease and a flavour you couldn't say was it one thing or another. Terrible what you would get in the tins! And now she had a nasty heart burn and a touch of wind. But Minnie was never cross; she was a big, heavy-built girl, but with a nice face and a smile would come across it; she dressed kind of carefully and she'd go to Halbost every once in a while and get a wave put in her hair. "So Donnie is to be married at last!" she said, and put a bunch of white rhododendrons she was carrying into a jam jar which she filled at the tap over the sink. Then she pulled the two benches out in front of the row of desks. Catch Ella doing that for them!

"It's a wonder his father thinks any woman godly enough to come to Balnafearchar" said Mrs MacLean.

"Oh, but this is his Glasgow cousin, she'll be godly. She'll no' let him stray."

"I wonder—was he straying?"

"Well, I heard it said."

"If they are not doing one thing they'll be doing another. If it's not women it is the drink. Men! We could do without them just great." She shoved the blackboard angrily out of the way.

Minnie didn't agree with her at all, but she answered soothingly: "Aye, aye, the men. It's queer how they come up for a holiday and their first idea is that they'll get whisky. You would say there was none in Glasgow! But it was time for Donnie to be married. He was no use the way he was."

The others began to come in now, first Mrs Fergusson, the Minister's wife, a nice enough woman but with an English voice, and her nose the wee-est bit crooked, not that this would be noticed in a Manse; and Jean from Molachy, Red Dougie's wife, a sonsy, nice woman, the kind that would be good to her man. They were talking about a pattern for knitted rompers, both having baby boys of the same age. After they had shed their coats they sat down near the middle. Mrs MacLean came and sat with them for a few minutes, whilst the others arrived. They all left raincoats to drip in the lobby and some changed their shoes as well. It was a pity the way the day had turned out.

"It is that" said Jean, "my Dougie was just wild with the way it's gone and his potatoes not in yet." She hunted in her bag, "See here's the pattern, it's real nice in blue."

"I can get the wool in the Assembly week" said Mrs Fergusson, "I'm looking forward ever so much to my week in Edinburgh.

I shall look in all the shop windows. That's all I can do on Mr Fergusson's salary," she added brightly, so that it shouldn't sound like a complaint.

"You'll go to the cinema and all?"

"I always go if there is any really *good* film. The film of the Royal Wedding now—that's what I call a nice film!"

"Yes," said Mrs MacLean, "the wedding group was real bonny. And that wee boy——"

"Ever so sweet and natural, wasn't he?" said Mrs Fergusson, "And I might see little Prince Charles this time. Oh, I always like the news. Or Shakespeare; I do like Mr Olivier."

"Ach, I saw him in the Henry one at Halbost" said Jean, "but I thought it was kind of stupid. No love. But they were saying the Hamlet one had some nice love in it."

"And will there be concerts in Edinburgh? And this New Look. But they say it's over now. Daft I call it, the way they're forever changing the fashion."

"Oh, I think fashions can be nice in the right place. I've a copy of Housewife——" Mrs Fergusson in turn fished in her bag. Several other members had women's papers with them. For a time they compared pictures and patterns. The funniest thing was the way the English had taken to the tartan, making it into every kind of thing that it was never intended for.

"We could make some wee kind of bags for the church sale in summer" said one of them. "We'll most of us have an odd bit of a kilt at home and that might go down well with the visitors."

"Yes, we'll need to be thinking of our sale" said Mrs MacLean, "And if there's to be a sale for the new Hall, that'll need to be earlier, or maybe later. We'll not need to spoil one another and I think maybe we should discuss it. Should we do that the next meeting of the Women's Guild, Mrs Fergusson?"

"Yes indeed. I shall be expecting the ladies of the Guild at the Manse next Tuesday again. There were some nice foreign mission photographs in the post today. Ever so interesting."

"We should start now to think about raffles" said Jean, "I'll make you some butter, that goes down great with the visitors."

"You know, dear, Mr Fergusson doesn't really approve of raffles."

"Ach, we'll not let on, will we?"

Mrs Fergusson laughed a little constrainedly.

138

"Well now, about the Guild" began Mrs MacLean, but then stopped. Two of the Wee Free members of the W.R.I. had just come in. "Well, we'll speak of it again" she said, "for I think it's time our own meeting was to begin. You'll do the judging, Mrs Fergusson?"

There were now a dozen parkins on the table, each with a folded slip of paper saying who had made them. The prize was a small blue vase, one of the pieces of prize, sale and raffle currency used in small communities, flotsam that comes in or goes out with the tide of summer visitors, but floats for a while on the local beaches. This vase, coming last from the Nursing Sale at Halbost, was neither useful nor beautiful, but as prestige currency had a certain value. And those who were called on to judge were bound to know that getting such things could give little pleasure, yet not getting them would give rise to much ill-feeling. Yet the non-Benthamite and non-Christian situation prevailed and Mrs Fergusson had to be its instrument.

She did this nervously, but with due regard to the shape, finish and texture of the parkins and knowing the eyes of the competitors were on her. It was likely that Jean from Molachy would have put in the best entry, having a light and skilled hand. Yet if she was to have the prize it might be said to be favouritism. With this in view, Mrs Fergusson drew in as many other opinions as possible, especially Miss Beaton who was not related to anyone else and didn't bake herself. Finally she made up what seemed to be the general mind, chose with a gasp and pointed. By the best of luck it was Minnie's parkin and she was generally popular and got a clap all round.

There were fourteen members present, not maybe a big turnout, but you couldn't expect the far-out ones to come on an evening like this. Still, there were the Macrae lasses from Osnish; they had been in for messages in the afternoon and had their tea with their granny. They were planning to be seen home by two of the Osnish boys. And it was nice enough to be seen home on a wet night, so long as it was not too cold. For there would be fewer folk about, and dry enough at the back of the big rock. Jeamus' sister Annabella had a fair walk from the Glen store, but she was not caring. She never even wiped the rain off her face. Then there were two of Krooger's crowd, Fiona and Mairi; one of them had some chewing gum she'd had in a parcel from cousins in America and she was passing it round; it was great stuff but you looked like a cow chewing away at it, and you had to laugh surely thinking of all those folk in America going at it the same way!

"Well, ladies," said Mrs MacLean, "Now we've had the judging, we'll just have the Minutes." And it was all she could do not to tell some of these lassies to have done with their giggling and sniggering and fashion pictures; they were none of them so extra when it came to the bit! She wished she'd brought her soda mints with her.

Minnie read out the Minutes. It had been Miss Campbell of Kinlochbannag showing them her photographs of Italy and an enjoyable evening had been had by all. "What was the name of yon town, Mrs MacLean? Florence? Ach yes, amn't I the stupid! We had a visitor last year called Miss Florence Patterson, her father was in sanitary fittings. It must be an awful nice town. I wish we could get one of the Arts and Crafts ladies over. I'm awful keen to learn this kind of wee lace edging they have on the blouses now. Awful nice and new."

"Och, you'll find it in one of the fashion books!"

"But then you'd need to study; I would rather the lady showing me, it's kind of cheery that. Or could we think of doing a wee play?"

"We'll do no play-acting" said Annabella firmly, but keeping on with her knitting. "We would need to draw the line at some kind of worldly things."

"Well, we could do a serious play" said Minnie.

"You would need to paint your face just the same in a serious play" said Annabella, unmoved. "And if the Rural is to keep its membership, there will not need to be harlotries the like of play-acting in it. Whatever the Parish Church thinks of them" she added, and began to count her stitches half aloud.

"Well, really!" said Mrs Fergusson.

"Ach, don't heed her, she's daft" whispered Jean.

Somebody suggested twenty questions. They went on for a while and Kitty Mor', the wife of Sandy the Coileach, came in, saying she'd had a wild job with the wee ones. They wouldn't stay in their beds and her sister had been late coming over. "It's time we had this Hall they're speaking on" she said, "And we'd no' have so far to go. They're saying it's to be at the back of the Post Office."

140

"And who is saying that?" asked Mrs MacLean dangerously.

"Ach, they're all saying it."

"Are they indeed! It will be a matter for the Committee."

"Well, Roddy was saying it was to be there," said Tina, who worked in the Forestry nursery.

"I'm afraid Mr MacCrimmon is not aware of the real nature of things at Port Sonas" said Mrs MacLean. And it suddenly came to her that there was no room for Roddy on the same committee as herself. Worse even than the schoolmaster, he was, and both of them pushing each other forward! She would speak to Mrs Snow about it. And how was it Mrs Snow wasn't coming to the Rural more? She was a member right enough; but she didn't come oftener than once a month at the most, and coming in late as often as not. A bad example to set the rest! She shook her head. "I think one of our members should favour us with a song" she said.

After a little whispering, Minnie sang *Count your Blessings*. It was one that went down well enough with the Wee Frees. There were no Free Presbyterians in the Rural. And then Miss Beaton brought up the question of the concert. But it was the wrong moment for Mrs MacLean. Bad enough to have Roddy Mac-Crimmon sticking his neck out about the site of the Hall, but if May Revie, who was not even on the Committee, was thinking she was to run a concert, and have the rest of Port Sonas trotting after her at her beck and call, and she to get all the credit—well, she'd made the greatest mistake of her life!

"The Village Hall Committee have very near decided there's to be a collection and sale for the Hall, and I was about to bring it to your notice myself, ladies. And we can't just go rushing this way and that after concerts that maybe won't come off at all. And I think you had better tell Miss Revie just that, Miss Beaton. And indeed I think there are some people at Port Sonas who will not like the idea of you having a concert."

"You're right" said Annabella, "and we should not be en-couraging any such thing. I'm not approving of concerts myself not at all, at all; and I'm not the only one. And I'm not approving of this Hall either."

"How are you saying that, Annabella" said Jean, who mostly shopped at the Glen store, "And your brother so keen to see it start!"

"Ah" said Annabella, "isn't that just it, and it's me that knows him so well."

Mrs MacLean was nursing her wrath. "I suppose Miss Revie was speaking of where the Hall is to be built, Miss Beaton?" she asked with a tightly polite smile.

But Miss Beaton hadn't noticed it and besides she was annoyed at the concert being turned down. "The best place for the Hall is by the Post Office" she said; "It will be handy for everyone, and I might be helping the Doctor or Mrs Snow with Red Cross classes there myself."

"I see you've your minds made up" said Mrs MacLean. And who would it be, she thought quickly; it will be this schoolmaster and this Roddy MacCrimmon and the two of them getting the ear of Mrs Snow. And I wouldn't be surprised if it wasn't with them being men, for she's not so old she mightn't be open to flattery by the men, and that forester's a right twister. It would serve them right if I was to go off the Committee in protest!

Meanwhile, tea was being passed round by Minnie and Kitty Mor' and the pennies collected. "I'm spited the way Mrs MacLean turned down the Concert" said Minnie to Miss Beaton, "the way I see it a concert would be just what's needed and it wouldn't spoil the Guild nor yet our own Church Sale. Wouldn't you say so, Mrs Fergusson?"

"Oh yes," said Mrs Fergusson "I'm quite sure if it was a nice concert Mr Fergusson would approve. I'm sure if we get the Village Hall and it is really well managed with a nice committee, and of course temperance—so long as the men don't get it into their hands——"

"Ah, men!" said Sarah and shook her head and smiled. She was awful used to Dr McKillop.

"You wouldn't give us a song yourself, Minnie?" asked Miss Beaton.

"Ach, what for no'?" said Minnie. "I've always stuck to the Rural, and my mother never getting on with the MacKeith crowd, but there's any amount of room now for the two boarding houses in Port Sonas, so I'll give you a song right enough."

It was time for the raffle now and discussion about the next competition. And should they ask for one of the instructresses? Two of the members washed up the cups at the sink, but joined in the discussion through the open door. The tickets were shaken up well and Fiona blindfolded and made to draw two of them. Katie Mor' got the jar of homemade chutney and Miss Beaton got the kettle-holder; she was thinking she would be able to send it on to her sister for the church sale at Ullapool.

After that the five members of the Wee Free congregation all left in a body, for it was the evening of the Prayer Meeting and a ten minutes' walk from the school to the church. There had been a lot of chopping and changing over this, for first the Prayer Meeting had been on a Thursday, the same evening as the Free Presbyterians, and then it went to a Wednesday, the way Thursday was early closing and it suited better for the Glen crowd that wanted both the shops and the Meeting. The Rural had thought to change to a Tuesday, but that was the day that suited Mrs Fergusson and the Guild, so it couldn't be that. Then it was to be a Friday. But that wouldn't do either, because of the Bible Study class, and if they put it back to a Thursday, that would be a deliberate affront to the Free Presbyterians, and although none of them belonged, you never knew what mightn't happen. But still and on, it was kind of awkward having it on a Wednesday, even with making it half an hour early to give the Wee Frees a chance, and maybe they would need to alter it again.

The Tilleys had been left ready in case the meeting went on late, and Minnie pumped one of them up. She said nothing to Mrs MacLean about having said she would sing at the concert. She was used enough from working with summer visitors to know there were times when you would need to hold your tongue. But Mrs MacLean had guessed—trust Minnie to show off her singing she thought. She would need to put her foot down; she would need to speak to Mistress Snow and show her the wrong turn things were taking.

The rain had taken off a bittie now and everyone wanting to go home before it got right dark. They sang a nice hymn to close the meeting and Minnie put the blue vase into her bag. It would decorate the East boarding house for the season before coming back into circulation.

CHAPTER XII

WEDNESDAY EVENING: AT THE BAR

IT WAS WARM IN at the Bar and they had the electric light on and all, though it wasn't near dark yet, and a cheery kind of glitter off the bottles and a right din of voices, and Humpy the barman, who was great at listening to anyone's stories and laughing just the thing. There were quite a few standing at the bar, and first they would have a beer and then they would have a whisky and then they would have a beer again, and so it would go. And you'd no need to watch your tongue for there was never a woman there.

This evening there was a good crowd and steam rising off them from the warmth on their wet things, and the smell with it, the smell of a man and his work: tar and net bark, raw wool, sawdust, earth, machine oil, cattle and horse dung, all the things that get rubbed into hands and hair and are sweated out in the crowded bar, with the beer going through them well. Some of them were in there mostly every night if it was only for a beer, but others came two or three times in the week and yet others only came on a Saturday, which was pay day for some and their evening in for the fishermen. Jacky, the crofter's son who had come back on leave by the Monday steamer, was there, and two or three of the young fellows with him: Alasdair and the Kettle and Tina's boy, Charlie. They were at one end of the bar and the older crowd at the other, Hughie the Digger, Archie the harbour master, Chuckie, Matta and his brother, Farquhar of Tirnafeidh and Postie. In the middle, young Jim, Archie's nephew, was speaking in a low voice with Malcie the joiner. The talk would be mixed Gaelic and English, and Humpy the barman, who was from Stornoway himself, used enough to orders in either. Big Jock from the store came in and started telling a set he had heard from the traveller who was around with brushes, about a wedding and the Minister hard of hearing, and everyone was laughing great. And then Hughie the Digger told one that turned on the words that make folk angry; like you should never call an Arran man Coinean mor, nor Raasay men saoithean. And this story was a long one, with plenty twists to it, but there was nobody in a hurry.

At the other end though the young men were talking about the Forestry and whether there would be some houses built for the Forestry workers. "Roddy was saying" said Alasdair, "that there might be some Swedish wooden houses coming. That would be great."

"Aye," said the Kettle, "we might be thinking of marrying if we had houses, but I've no notion of going into someone else's house."

"Ach, you're better to keep away from this marrying" said Alasdair, "you'll never be a free man again. I'd sooner my freedom."

"Aye well, it's nice enough the freedom, but there's times you can't get what you want. But if you're married——"

"Then maybe you'll not want it!"

"Ach, I wouldn't say. A nice wee wife that's good to a man, you'll need to go a long way to beat that."

"Are you thinking Minnie would be good to you right enough?" said Alasdair, teasing him. He coloured, for he didn't want to let on to the boys that he was serious—if once he had a house. He shook his head and grunted and finished off his beer. "And there's Kenny's Chrissie been good to the boys once too often" said Alasdair, "would that have been you now?"

"It would not" said the Kettle loudly, "I hanna been near the lassie hardly."

"Wasn't it you she was with in the ferry shelter? And she was heard squeaking great for a while."

"It wasn't me whoever it was" said the Kettle, "And indeed I'm not caring much for her at all."

"Well, she's been to the lawyers and I wonder who'll get the letter!"

"It's never me" said the Kettle still more violently. "Who was saying she'd been to the lawyer?"

"Ach, everyone knows, and some was saying the letter would be on one person and some on another. And I heard your name mentioned sure enough. Ach, don't look so spited, mo bhalach, she'll need to prove it."

145

But the Kettle was upset over it. If Minnie were to hear about it and maybe pick it up wrong—he called across to Humpy for another. The crofter's son, Jacky, laughed and said, "Well, it'll not be me anyway! But you would need to see the ones near our camp, letting on they're half-way to being Americans—dirty wee lassies, wanting nothing but the money, but awful clever, walking with a waggle on them so you would want to pinch the behinds of them all the while, and then before you would know, you would need to take them out to the pubs."

"Do they go into the bars down in England?"

"They do, so, and drinking like fishes!"

"Away! It's no' nice to have the women in with you, the stuff's scarce enough as it is."

"Do you know this," said Jacky, "they'll come in with you one on each side and the next thing they have you up the stairs with them. And here, it was me and my pal and these two lassies capering and their skirts up and nothing at all above the stockings!"

"Are you saying that?"

"Well, the way it looked to us they were out for sport and wanting the one thing and we thought we had it for them, both the two of us, but God save us, they'd to get every bit of money that we had on us first! Greedy as young stirks they were. And after that we werena so keen to go out with them. It's kind of sore on you when the lassies is only after your money. Poor wee Chrissie, she hasna made her fortune anyway."

"No' yet" said Alasdair, "but she mightna do so bad if the Aliment is proved on someone."

Mr MacMillan came in now and went round from one group to another, giving them encouragement and speaking to everyone. "And what were you boys at?" he said to the young ones, "was Jacky there telling you about the great life they have in the army?"

But none of them wanted to go on in front of Mr MacMillan with what Jacky had been speaking on, so Alasdair went back a bit to what they had been speaking on earlier. "He was saying there was nowhere much to pass the time here, and the bar not open all the while, and he was wondering when will we get this Village Hall?"

"My folks is against it terrible" said Jacky, "but they're

old-fashioned. They've forgot what it's like to be young. They're no' keen for me to be here, but they would sooner a bar than a Village Hall. It's more natural to them."

Mr MacMillan laughed. "Ach well, the two should get on together well enough." But he found himself getting a wee bit shaken. Supposing now the Hall was to come into competition with the hotel; that wouldn't do at all. No indeed. Maybe they had been over-hasty!

Red Dougie came in now, wet and cross, and asked for a glass. He needed to get something into him before he could speak. He nodded to Farquhar of Tirnafeidh and asked if he was sending stores into the sale at Halbost. Farquhar said he had four and had spoken to Angus for his lorry; had he any himself? Red Dougie held up two fingers and nodded, then downed his stuff. Baldy the baker came in and then Jackson of Achnahabhain in his black oilskin coat glistening with rain. Being kind of strict, he walked straight to the bar without turning his head to greet friend or acquaintance, and spoke low to Humpy, who brought him a whisky. Mostly he got a parcel sent over to him at home, but yesterday, with the rain coming on, he had finished it.

The warmth came to Red Dougie now, into his throat and stomach and blood and brain. He became determined to take action. He went up to Farquhar: "It's time we were to start a branch of the National Farmers' Union to get something done about Macbrayne's. Here's me waiting for my potato manure——" Farquhar listened and made noises of sympathy and general agreement. "Will you join then?" said Dougie, "and you can be the chairman and I'll be the secretary, and that way we will be able to send in complaints."

"Well" said Farquhar, "I'll need to consider it. There seems to be nae doing anything these days wi'out there's a committee started and subscriptions forby. And how are private enterprise and initiative to fare wi' that?"

"Aye, but this is for our own good" said Dougie, "it's private for the farmers right enough, and see what we'll gain by it—here's the papers. I rang up the secretary at Halbost the very day I didna get my potato manure and he put the things in the post. And you'll get insurance and every kind of a permit and I don't know what all else, for I hanna read them through right. Look you through them, John, and I will get speaking to

Jackson. There's five of us altogether and on top o' that we might get Fred Macfie from Balana in wi' us. I'm no' saying it will be yin of the biggest branches, but they'll need to take notice of us surely."

He went across to Jackson now and started to speak about the National Farmers' Union. Jackson had finished his glass and was standing there black and tall, waiting on his change. There was no saying what he might be thinking. He listened in silence; then he said, "I'm joining no godless association."

"But there's nothing godless about the National Farmers' Union!" said Dougie.

"Is there anything godly about it?" asked Jackson.

"Well, it's just the same as the rest of the farming, neither one thing nor the other. You'll not have a cow godly nor yet a tractor."

"There's only one kind of association that I will ever put my hand or my name to" said Jackson, "and you will not divert me from the straight path. And I can tell you this; it's no use you speaking of such vanities to Balnafearchar, for he will be heeding you as little as I am." And he picked up his change and walked out.

"Well, damn the like o' that!" said Dougie "for there's two out and I canna hardly suppose that the N.F.U. will say that three of us is enough to start a branch!"

Baldy, who had been listening, shook his head sympathetically, "Man, isn't it terrible altogether that! And they so holy the Bibles is wearing their bottoms out! But I'm feared you will need to wait a whiley before you can get started with the National Farmers' Union in Port Sonas. Well, what are you drinking, Dougie?"

"Well, I'll take a wee drop of the cratur', just for luck."

"You'll take a drop beer too?"

"Aye, I'll take a drop." So Baldy ordered two halfs and two half-pints.

Roddy came in and asked for a beer; he didn't touch spirits except on Saturdays or some special occasion, but Humpy welcomed him all the same, and so did Alasdair and the rest of the young fellows. Alasdair asked if there was any news of the new sawmill, but Roddy answered shortly, his face stiffening. He hadn't forgotten what the District Officer had said. Alasdair shut up quickly; he had guessed, and he liked Roddy. Someone began speaking again about the possibility of new houses. One of the Osnish crofters was building a new concrete and slated house with the grant.

"Easy enough for them" said Baldy, "no rates to be paid! And our own going up everywhere. We would need to speak to Kate about the rates."

"Better you should speak with Mr Thompson" said young Jim, overhearing, from across his shoulder, "It's him that's above her on the Council."

"Aye, but he doesna care for us at Port Sonas the same as her. So long as his hotel is doing well! You heard the way he's no' bothering himself about our water supply."

Three men came in together now, crofters all of them. They had been to the Wee Free prayer meeting which was just over and they needed a small refreshment to steady themselves for the Glen road, after all the prayers and the grand psalms there had been. After that the next to come was Angus in his blue overalls, straight from his lorry, for he had been taking her out late; he was his own master. He looked round a bit and then made for the younger crowd. Alasdair gave him a shout. "There's Angus, how are you the night? Any use of us biting your lug?"

"It's taking me all my time to bite my own" said Angus, and asked Humpy for a pint of draught.

"Were you over at Halbost again today?" asked Roddy.

"No, no, I wasna further than Kinlochbannag."

"You'll not have any word of my lobsters?" said Matta edging up to them. Angus shook his head. "Och, isn't that terrible! Someone is bound to know. But I'll find out some way, if it takes me all my days."

Angus swallowed his beer, "Ach, there's plenty more lobsters in it. You shouldna take it thon way, Matta."

"Should I no'? And me swithering what I should do next and asking myself where at all did they go and whether will the next box go the same way!"

"Sure it'll not" said Angus, "it was maybe some kind of foolishness that came over someone to take them, and it'll never happen again. You should look at the bright side! What'll you take, Matta?"

They had a half each. It affected Matta, who had already had as much as he needed, to such a tune that he began to weep about his loss on to Postie, who was related to him through his wife. Angus himself edged away between Roddy and Alasdair who were speaking about the houses still. Suddenly he said, "I heard some news from Kilmolue when I was up the Glen."

"What was that?" Roddy asked.

Angus began on it in a low voice, but in a while, when he began to feel the drink, loud enough for everyone in the bar to hear if they had a mind to. "You'll mind of the missionary at Kilmolue who was against the Hall, boys? Yon one that made the wee piper burn his pipes? Aye, and it's no' the first time he's been on to stop folks from doing some kind of cheery thing! They darena so much as whistle at Kilmolue! Well, it seems there was to be a mid-week service and all this holiness to happen again. And here didn't the congregation come pouring into the tin kirk like sheep and waited and waited, and the prayers starting up here and there but still no missionary. So a few of them went along to his house and they knocked, kind of scared in case he might be at the praying and it strong on him, and then louder, and at last they opened the door a crack and oh God, the words that were coming out of that holy place! For here the missionary had slipped on the stair and sprained his ankle and he was cursing and swearing like he might have been a Glasgow visitor! So they put him in to his bed. And do you know what was found just inside the door of the house? Aye, boys, do you know?" He looked round and they all shook their heads; most of them were listening to him now. "It was a buidseach" he said.

Charlie and the Kettle looked at one another; they had no idea what he meant. But it meant something to Jacky, only he wasn't quite sure what. But a thing you didn't need to be speaking about surely. Hastily he asked for another half. Alasdair wasn't too sure either; the word meant something away back into childhood; a fear and a superstition. Something a man who had been in the forces would try to forget with the rest of the Gaelic, having put away childish things. But it could be a thin waxen thing, white and terrible. Or it could be a tangle of knots, a thing you might mistake for a great wood spider, but it wouldn't be that at all. No. But Roddy knew well what was meant and his mind raced back to what had been in the back of his head about

Balana and the quiet man Fred Macfie, proud of not having anything to do with Kilmolue, and the set of pipes that he hadn't been able to guard. "Dhia gleidh sinn!" he said and gulped down his beer, "surely it's not true, that!" And all round there was a murmur of concern and aversion from the older men, and they with their glasses in their hands, standing around staring terrible at Angus.

"But that's not all" said Angus, "you know the other one that was so bitter against the Hall, Miss MacIntosh? Here, didn't she start vomiting and it's said, but, ach, they'll believe anything at all at Kilmolue, that there was pins coming up from her stomach into her mouth."

"And who," said Roddy, choosing his words carefully, "Who can they be accusing for this nonsense?"

Angus started to speak and then seemed to think better of it. He said to Roddy, "You'll maybe have as good an idea as myself."

"Superstition" said Roddy, "plain bloody Highland super-stition! You'd as well be seeing bloody fairies!" If once he could get swearing at the thing right it might stop being there and he might manage to prevent himself from believing, because in another minute he would be doing just that—here, even here in the bar under the electric light, and he knowing how to drive and repair tractors or lorries and having at his tongue tip the Latin names of a hundred conifers! "Bloody superstition!" he said again, half shouting it. But all round there was a nasty kind of hush.

"Mo thruaighe" whispered Lachie Macrae from Osnish, "a buidseachas. So near!"

At the further end of the bar Red Dougie, Farquhar, and the two Hughies were arguing and their loosened-up voices making a fine cheerful din, but outwith the door was dark and rain and whatever might be behind it, and gone, gone, all that should have protected those in the Bar. Humpy became aware of an urgent need in his customers. But Roddy was struggling still, "This Kilmolue crowd is so used to having the heavens open and the angels flapping themselves all round that they'll believe anything at all! And I'm not sorry to think of yon missionary with a sprained ankle and no more than he deserves; nor yet the schoolmistress after eating something that disagrees with her.

But to think of any kind of half-sensible man believing in—in yon things they were speaking about—och, it's plain ridiculous!" And he looked round for confirmation.

He got it from Alasdair, "Aye, ye're right, Roddy, so y'are. Man Angus, they've been kidding you on. Sure, you'll not believe this blether?"

"I'm not saying whether I believe or whether do I not!" said Angus rather loudly, "but there's one thing I'm telling you, I'll no' take my lorry down yon road to Kilmolue after night! Whether it's this or whether it's that, there's something no' right going on there."

"Isn't it as well it's not me taking the mails there!" said Postie, "and do you know this, I've heard Ian Ruadh speaking"—this was his fellow postman in Kinlochbannag, who drove a small mail van in and out of Kilmolue—"Aye, he was telling me there was the queerest shaped parcels going to yon place. Aye, and the smell off them, something tremendous!"

"That'll ha' been a bottle broken in the post!" said Roddy.

"It was not, so! They was, och, shaped wi' legs on them!" He began to see such a parcel in his mind's eye, as his hearers looked at him with half belief, and his imagination woke further. "And sounds coming from them itself! Och, the most outrageous groanings and squeakings. And the string that parcelled them up not right string at all!"

"Dhia seall oirnn" said one of the crofters backing away, "did he never complain, the honest poor soul, and him having the handling of them?"

"No, no," said Postie, "he wouldn't be doing the like o' that and him a Government servant the same as myself."

"Away you go, Postie!" said Alasdair, "there's not a word of truth you've been telling us!"

Postie gave him a look, shook his head and glanced towards the bar. Sure enough his glass was filled again and back in his hand. "You're ignorant, Alasdair; aye, aye, poor laddie, and you taken off to the wars so young. But it's the Post Office folk that are knowing great all that goes on and I've seen me needing to keep my mouth shut many and many a time. And the doleful telegrams and the terrible parcels and the wickedness of the postcards! You'd never credit the things that goes on in the world, Alasdair, and you so young!"

"Ach," said Alasdair, "this is the twentieth century, is it no'? And there y' are! Am I right, Roddy?"

"Aye, Alasdair, it's the twentieth century sure enough" said Roddy. But some way he didn't feel that this was enough. "I'll need maybe to have a wee talk to certain ones" he said half aloud.

"Keep you clear of it, Roddy my son" said Postie solemnly, "for it's wild the things that can happen and isn't the twentieth century nothing but the blink of an eyelid when it comes to eternity?"

"Ach" said the Kettle, disgustedly, "if it comes to eternity, I'm away home! What for are we speaking on eternity when we might be cheery!" He glanced at the clock. "Here's closing time coming on us and we speaking about eternity!" For there was not long left before time and the bell would start to ring and Humpy would be chasing them to drink up and be gone. So it was no wonder that the two men who came into the bar now were in a hurry and out of breath, although it was no distance to speak of from the Wee Free kirk to the bar. But Pate Morrison and Krooger being Elders had needed to stay behind a while after the service for a wee meeting of the Deacon's Court that had been called. And now they felt the need of a thing to settle them. But Pate was wishing he had the Whale with him instead of Krooger. However, he himself was the only one of the skippers at home and that was over the head of the Highland Panel.

Young Colin was seeing Anna home after the service and the same ploy with two of his ex-Service chums who had stayed in for the meeting. At certain times a man would sooner a lassie than a glass and indeed Pate could remember yon same time himself and he courting his own Annie. The stuff was cheaper in those days, but you had worse wages with the herring going dead cheap or needing to be dumped even. So it all worked out. He asked for a half and Humpy poured it, saying he had just the time to drink it in comfort before closing. Krooger had the same and joined in with the talk that was still going on between young Jim and Malcie. Shillings had come in on it too and they were discussing the contract for the new houses at Halbost and how at all it had gone to the ones it had gone to.

It was a kind of relief to the rest seeing Pate and Krooger and something to take your mind off what had been spoken on; more especially with them coming from the Deacon's Court and having spoken with Mr Mackintosh who was so strong for godliness and order.

"You'll have been considering the chimney stack on the Manse, Pate?" said Matta's brother, who had once for six months worked with a builder and thought he knew all about it. "Man, wasn't it a terrible bad piece of work yon, and not more than thirty years old hardly!"

"She will need to be done right enough" said Pate, "but I think she'll hold a while. There's a piece of sarking bad and the slates away on the wash-house. Krooger there will have a wee word to Malcie on his road home. He would get a wee allocation for that right enough and the Minister a great one at filling up the forms. Aye, aye, many's the form he would fill up and the truth in every line."

"Tell me this," said Roddy, and he was still feeling jangled and excited in his mind, "Was it the Village Hall you were speaking about? And if you were, what was Mackintosh saying about it? For he's my Minister the same as yours."

"Well" said Pate, "It's not easy. Aye, not easy at all! And indeed I'll not deny he was speaking about it and how we would not need to encourage any kind of backsliding by the young ones." He shook his head and finished off his glass.

"You'll need to stand up to him and you on the Hall Committee" said Roddy, "You and Norman between you. You'll not need to let him away with anything!"

"I'm no' just too sure of this Committee" said Pate, "Maybe we just hanna thought plenty."

"Man, you're never reneeging and you so keen and speaking away at the Committee!"

"Aye" said Angus, who had joined in, "And amn't I after hearing the great way you spoke for the Hall at your own Fishermen's meeting!"

"Ach well," said Pate, "I hanna exactly made my own mind up. But Norman has done just that, aye, and sent in his resignation in writing."

"Oh, poor Kate, the woman!" said Postie. "And her with her meeting and all."

Roddy was thinking the same thing; it had given him a shock. But he threw back his head and his dark eyes were fierce and fighting as he spoke, "Ach, to hell with the old ones, and the

154

crofters afraid of their shadows, every man of them! We'll need to go on without that crowd; there's plenty others more modern than Norman."

"He's a well-respected man is Norman" said Matta's brother.

"Aye, he's honest."

"Honest and god-fearing."

"Ach, to hell with god-fearing" said Roddy, "It's Minister-fearing he is. Worse than District Officers, the Ministers are, and that's saying plenty!"

But Pate Morrison gave him a look and turned his back. Too far altogether Roddy was going and the Village Hall had indeed been spoken about at the Deacon's Court. And it was not easy knowing what to do. Not easy at all and you could never be sure where a thing could end. And maybe you would be wisest to stick to the old ways, the ways that were proved by your forefathers. Aye, there was deep pondering to be done and himself not the man to be doing it. It was Ministers' work that. And why would Roddy be speaking against the Ministers, and he a newcomer almost to Port Sonas?

Humpy glanced at the clock. "It's time, gentlemen" he said, "Drink up now! No, Matta, I can't serve a drop more. Drink up gentlemen and be going." Mr MacMillan came through from the hotel and began shepherding the folk out. He closed one half of the door. Then he nodded to Humpy who set the alarm bell to ringing and the din of it went through even to the ones that were too far gone for a voice to be speaking to them plain. Wee Chuckie was crying quietly to himself, for hadn't Matta been speaking again about the lobsters and they still not found, the poor souls. Mr MacMillan edged him and Matta and Postie out together. The rest went out in groups still talking away. The cold air at the door shook them, it might give a new twist to the talk even, but the warmth remained in below. Red Dougie and Farquhar went off together, speaking about stirks. Another gust of rain came down and there was complaining at Mr MacMillan for turning them out into it. "Do you want me to lose my licence now?" he said "For you all know I've eyes on me terrible, and plenty that would be glad enough to do me a bad turn." But all the same some of them went round to the porch of the hotel itself and sheltered there a while and in the darkness there was a bottle passed and lifted a few times.

The crofters set off in two groups, one for up the Glen and one for Osnish. There was a kind of extra huddle about them and mostly Gaelic spoken. All along the dark road the stories whispered and trailed and whatever thing was started on it was ended in one way only, and they were stories of sorcery and the eye, and most of them not so long back. Before the war maybe. Yet if anything had happened in the last year or two it would scarcely be yet that one would speak of it openly.

Roddy got a grip of Angus and hurried him a bit past the young fellows. "This at Kilmolue" he said, "You're not believing it yourself, Angus?"

Angus said nothing for a moment; the cold wet gust had made him feel a wee bit dizzy. Roddy gave him a shaking, "Ach, pull yourself together, man, I'm wanting to know."

"Well then" said Angus "I wouldn't say I thought that whatever it was need be the cause of the other things happening. But sure enough there's some kind of thing that they saw there, and it like enough to what could be meant as a buidseach and whoever put it there will have meant harm to the missionary and the schoolteacher."

"Aye" said Roddy, "that's just about it. And maybe both of us have an idea who that could be. But we don't want any harm to come to the Village Hall by anything that might be said of one of the Committee."

"You're right enough there" said Angus, "even if they meant to do good, it's a thing that will need to be studied on."

"I'll need to see Davie" said Roddy thoughtfully" and we'll maybe study it out together. God, I wish he had thought to put a bewitchment on to Miss Gillies while he was at it!"

CHAPTER XIII

THURSDAY MORNING: AT THE STEAMER

With the weather the way it was there weren't so many down on the quay. But those that were about were keen and excited enough, for the Highland Panel folk would be on the steamer. Only one of the lobster boats was fishing. Matta and his brother were down in their boat cleaning the engine and waiting for the steamer to come in sight. And his cousins, who worked the third boat, the Tunnag, were redding up their creels. There would always be a few creels broken, and lucky if you didn't lose half of them in the season. The herring fishermen who had stayed in were there too. Pate was speaking low to Dunky, the elderly man whose rheumatism was indeed enough to keep him at home. Only he liked being at the fishing; he had been at it all his days; he was lost on shore. Colin and his ex-Service chums lounged around in their oilskins when the rain was on, but whenever there was a blink of sun, handsome in blue jerseys or white. Word had passed among them for a meeting of the Legion this very day that they were all ashore, but scarcely one of the old ones, and they so greedy! The thought of this put a bloom of satisfaction on Colin and Johnnie Neil and Lachie and the rest. Anna and her chums found means of going with messages to Jock's store, their red and green plastic raincoats making them bright as Woolworth flowers.

Andrew Revie came down and stood on the quay, his good boots not letting in the wet, his hat down over his eyes and his muffler up round his neck. Whenever Archie the harbour master came out of his office to putter around with his crates for the steamer, Andrew would stare at him ferociously.

Then Kate drove down and parked her car; she took her screw-top can into Jock's store for paraffin and asked for an Aladdin mantle. While Christine was looking for it in the back of the shop, she talked to Jock about the Village Hall. If there was a sale would he help? Ach, aye, he would help surely. He had thought at once of certain war-time groceries which were now on his hands, but they would make a fine big parcel for the sale. "I'm very glad you agree that we need a Hall" she said.

"Ach, well" he said, filling up the can, "as to that, no doubt there's two opinions. Aye, maybe more. But we'll see how the ball will roll." Christine found the mantle at last and Kate put it carefully into her shopping bag. It would be nice, she thought, if Port Sonas people would sometimes say what they meant.

Another gust of hard rain came down, sweeping out all sight of Torskadale point and then even the islands, sweeping away the girls into the store or the sweetie shop and the boys off after them. Andrew stood for a moment, then chose to realise it was a wee thing damp and made his way slowly to the Hotel. Kate beckoned him to come into the car, but he grinned and pointed his thumb over his shoulder and went on. She stuck her head out into the rain for a moment to see what it was and there was the Laird, his short fishing cape dripping like a wet roof all round him and a small suit-case in his hand. He climbed into the car beside her. "What on earth are you doing, Sandy?" she asked.

"It's the shooting tenants, Kate" he said, "they've been complaining these last three years about the larder. And here, I'd another letter last week. So I came over for brackets and screws." He held up the case. "But Jock hasn't them in."

"Why didn't you tell me, Sandy!" she said, "I'd have got them for you in Halbost. It would have been no trouble."

"Wouldn't it?" he said, in that queer surprised way that she always found, somehow, rather upsetting. "I planed the wood for the shelves" he added. "It's from that big cypress that fell across the drive two years back. The best of wood. Cupressus Torulosa. A specimen tree."

"I remember it" she said, "a beauty." She wondered if he was bound to let the shooting every year. She had noticed how it always coincided with a bad bout. The shooting had gone down badly too; he couldn't get much for it. The fishing was worth something, she supposed; and nice of him to keep a rod on the river for her. Did that take something off the price? Not much, but still——

The Laird had taken a small screwdriver out of his pocket

and was tightening up a screw on the dashboard clock—which had long ceased to go. "A most extraordinary thing," he said, "but you know that chap who drives the lorry?"

"Angus?"

"The same. Well, he asked me to join the local branch of the British Legion!"

"And did you?"

"Are you asking me seriously, Kate? If you are—obviously I said no."

"Why obviously?"

"Do you mean it doesn't strike you as—peculiar? I suppose it's with you being a woman and all that."

"All what?"

"Well, not being a man."

"I can't help it. Sandy, do stop doing things to my car with your cork-screw."

"Screwdriver, my dear. Now I've made you blush! But it's like this. I was through the first war and most of my friends went west. Passchendaele and thereabouts. I was too old for this war. They wouldn't take me. I'm too old for these young fellows. They had a different war. The word means something else altogether to them. See, Kate?"

"But there are men from the first war in the Legion."

"Granted, granted! I was so astonished that I stood there letting young Angus go through the whole rigmarole. Half the skippers were in the Navy in the first war, not to speak of old Andy at the Mission Hall! Oh, all the best people of Port Sonas. But they weren't my friends."

Kate said nothing. She was angry with him and sorry for him and did not think she could change him. He pressed at the door handle and got out of the car. The worst of the rain was passed. A blue gap opened for a moment in the clouds, then closed again. Andrew Revie came out on to the quay and so did some of the others. It had been observed that the Laird was in Kate's car. Indeed it was being spoken of already in the sweetie shop.

Now for a time it cleared. There was only the eager dripping of the rhones all round. The dampness that was still about settled on Kate's tweed coat without penetrating. It might be half an hour before the steamer came. She walked up behind Andrew Revie and spoke to him. He was so intent on his enemy that he turned round startled: "Guid sakes, it's yourself, Kate" he said. "I thocht—och, I thocht you might ha' been the polis!"

"Now what will you have been doing that you're in such dread, Andrew?" she said.

He laughed, "Ach it's no' me they should be after. But they are the same as the rain, on the just and the unjust. Aye, Aye. Ye've a worriet look on ye, Kate, is it this Highland Panel? Ach, you shouldna bother your head! They'll be here right enough and most like they are already settled in their own minds what they can do and what they canna."

"I'm not worrying much about that" Kate answered, "but I've had this letter sent over from Norman. I know you're not on the Committee, but you're a friend of his. What should we do?"

Andrew took the letter and hunted for his spectacles. While he read, Kate kicked at a half-loose stone. The letter had given her a shock. Ach, maybe just as well! But she had thought he was more generous, more deep-down kind. Could it have been what she and Janet had said about Snash and the Kirk Sessions that had put him against the Hall? She had forgiven him almost at once, but he——? She didn't know. Well, one thing was sure, she had written herself to Glasgow about the boarded-out children.

"Aye" said Andrew "Aye. He has made himself clear. Aye, verra clear." He folded up the letter.

"Did you know he was likely to do this?"

"I was hoping it wud pass him by. These Churches can be gey sore on a man. I had a notion sure enough that things werenie just richt wi' him, for a' he had been kinna weel disposed at the meeting."

"He seemed to be seeing it the right way at first. Oh hell, Andie, if he goes it'll put off a lot of the Wee Frees."

"I'd say so. Hae ye spoken to Pate Morrison there?"

"No, not yet. Perhaps after the Highland Panel meeting. If he's pleased with that, he'll be pleased with everything else too. Am I right there, Andie?"

"Aye, ye've a fair notion of it, Katie. It's a pity the way you hanna the backing of the whole community. Yon Krooger!"

"He came to the meeting, Andie. We might have convinced him. Wouldn't you think we might have?"

"Him, is it? No' him! As bad as Archie he is. A richt pair o' rascals the two o' them."

"After all he was proposed for the Committee and the only reason he gave for not coming on was that he was too busy."

"Dinna you be believin' the like o' Krooger. He'd come on quick enough if he wanted. It's all ower the head o' the bridge."

"But, Andy, that's years and years ahead at best."

"Aye, and so is Krooger thinking ahead. And he would want you discomfitted and out of regard with everyone and off the District Council itself before there'ld be ony word o' the bridge. He's safe enough with yon Thompson and him in the hotel at Kinlochbannag."

"Hard to believe, isn't it, that Highland people are so damned stupid and narrow and thinking of no one but themselves. Sometimes I wonder if the Highland way of life means anything at all now."

"Weel may you wonder, Katie, and whiles I'm wondering mysel' if it means onything at all but devilment and wickedness. Still and all, I married one o' them, and there's the proof of the pudden."

"Yes, Bessie MacKeith's a cousin of yours, Andie, and, here, I've been trying to get hold of her all the week about starting a Village Hall account with two signatures, but she's never there when I call."

"Bessie was saying to me that a wheen folk had been running to her with shillings and half-crowns and at her to put their names down in a wee book. But she wasna pleased the way she hadna been asked at the beginning would she or would she not be treasurer, and if she had a' been treasurer, there should ha' been a wee book issued to her."

"All that was over her not staying for the Committee meeting, and fine she knows it!"

"Och, that wouldn't stop her mumping! You'll maybe not keep her on the Committee. But you'll get as good fish as Bessie yet. This Highland Panel meeting shouldnie be in Archie's office anyhow" he added, suddenly changing over and scowling, "If we had the Hall now——!"

"You're just daft about Archie, Andrew" said Kate.

"Wait you now" said Andrew, "till I have him shown up in his richt colours. And I'll do it, if it's the last thing I do!"

Out of the corner of her eye, Kate saw May coming down and was pleased enough, for Andrew's face had darkened with anger and he looked more bristly. She was always worried in case his blood pressure was too high. But May would keep an eye on him. Now Janet came by on her bicycle and over to her auntie's shop. The silly woman had over-fed the puppy and here, it was sick, and she was sending messages all up the Glen to chase her off her work to see to it! A man might be daft enough, but not that way. And it was wearisome being at everyone's beck and call. There were times you would like a house of your own, even if it meant another man to look after. She felt cross and jangled. Maybe it was the weather. If something was just to happen now—something kind of nice for a choice, but anyway something to break up the rain and the low cloud blotting out Torskadale and settled down over the shoulders of T'each Mor as though it would never lift. She turned into the sweetie shop. Her auntie leant over the counter and began to speak about the Laird sitting all that while in Kate's car instead of going to the Hotel like his ordinar'.

Another cyclist came down the road and turned right on to the quay. It was Fred Macfie in his farm oilskins, black sou'wester and long black coat over Wellingtons. He went into the store to ask for a special size of battery that Jock was the only one to keep, and some knitting pins for his mother. When he came out, Roddy was just parking the Forestry lorry. He had an invoice for fertiliser for his nursery this time. Fred nodded to him and was going by, but Roddy gave him a shout from the cab of the lorry and came after him.

"A dirty day" said Fred.

"Aye, it's that" said Roddy. They walked a few yards together towards the edge of the quay and looked over into the south-west and the driving carry from beyond Eilean Everoch. "She should be in sight any time now" said Roddy, "it's a kind of miserable day for these Panel folk right enough." Fred said nothing. He didn't think this needed answering hardly. "You're no' that often in Port Sonas, Fred" said Roddy.

Fred assented, "I had business here," he said.

"Aye, there's always plenty on a farm" said Roddy. Fred didn't even answer but stood amiably enough waiting for the steamer to appear. "There's been talk around over the doings at

162

Kilmolue" he said, then more hurriedly, "but folk will be talking!"

"I know what you're at" said Fred, kind of scornfully, "but I didna think you were any friend to the Free Presbyterians, Roddy MacCrimmon."

It startled Roddy to be picked up so quickly. He had thought Fred would go round about it a while and himself with time to base his approach and his tackle. "It's not that at all" he said.

"Aye, but it is" said Fred, "either are you for or you are against. The same as wi' the Hall."

Roddy looked round and said in a very low voice, "You admit it then?"

Fred stared out over the water, not looking at Roddy, "What are you asking me do I admit?"

"The thing they are speaking about" said Roddy, "you know. Go on man, you know!"

"Name it" said Fred.

Quick fury came on Roddy, like a gannet diving into his middle. He was to be asked to put his tongue on that, was he! And Fred standing there like a great black fool of a clown, god knows what thoughts thinking! Trying to make him, Roddy MacCrimmon, believe in what he knew was ignorance and superstition, trying to make him think in the Gaelic! "Very well," he said, and his voice sang up and down with anger the way a Skye man's does, "You are not choosing to tell me anything, but I know, oh very well I know, and so does everyone. And it is not right, it is neither right nor fitting, for a man that's on the Port Sonas Village Hall Committee to be using sorceries and witchcraft! So now."

Beyond Eilean Everoch the plume of smoke was coming in sight. Fred Macfie stared at it. "You are making a great to do about very little, Roddy MacCrimmon: ach, very little indeed. And these ones at Kilmolue are easy frighted. They are like nothing in the world but sheep, and once there's a stumble from the big fellow, they will go whichever way they are herded. And forby that, someone will need to pay for the pipes."

"Are you telling me then, this that they saw, it is all—it is all imagination?" said Roddy, and some way he found this even more scaring than the other, to think that in the middle of the

163

twentieth century it would be possible to make grown men behave in this way!

"I am telling you nothing, Roddy MacCrimmon" said Fred, and now he was more abrupt, almost angry himself, "I was thinking you had a wee spark of sense! But if you are not wanting me on the Village Hall Committee, there is no need for me to stay, and I can write in my resignal as well as the next! And if you are not wanting help at Port Sonas, there is no need for you to take it then."

"What like of help?" asked Roddy, and his voice shook a little. "Ach, what kind of help were you meaning?" But Fred gave him a short hard look and walked away. "Dhia seall orm!" Roddy said half aloud. "How would I know——" He watched Fred's black back, a log up-ended, a tree walking away through the rain that was coming down again. He looked at his watch; just on eleven. He would have the time to slip up to the Bar for a quick one before the steamer came in. No! Why would he let any man scare him and anger him into spending good money, when he would need to save every bit, or he would never be able to get married in the way he wanted. Everything came rushing and bothering through his mind all at the once. And now the steamer was blotted out in a sudden drive of rain.

Kate called over to Janet to come and sit with her in the car till the rain was off again. "You'll know these Highland Panel folk yourself?" Janet asked, "is it true there is one of them a woman?"

"Yes, Mrs Mitchison from Carradale; she writes books."

"Wouldn't I like to write books! Next to teaching. What kind does she write?"

"I think they're historical novels, but I've never read them myself. I've read some of her articles in papers and I think she lives in a small kind of place something after this style."

"How does she know about the fishing?"

"I can't imagine, Janet!"

"Ach, well, it's fine to have a woman among the head ones, even if she mightn't know as much as the rest. It's kind of heartening."

"That's just what I think. I've half a mind to ask her to come over to the Bee House this evening. They'll be staying the night at the hotel, and going on by car on the morning. I would like to ask them all over only—well, it just depends on the mood my father's in. And he'd be sure to want to show them the teapots."

"Well and I'm sure they would like to see the teapots, why wouldn't they?"

"Well—it might be a bore for them. But I would like to have a talk with Mrs Mitchison if she seems at all friendly. I wish it wasn't such a bad day for them, but I suppose they're used to it. Janet, have you heard that Norman has resigned from the Committee?"

Janet fingered the knobs on the instrument board of the car in front of her, "I did hear" she said sadly, "Yes. There was speaking to my father."

"What does your father think, Janet?"

"Well, he is kind of disturbed. It seems they were speaking of the Hall at the Deacons' Court."

"Were they all against it, do you know? What about Pate Morrison?"

"Well, there was talk for a while, or so I heard, MacNab was saying there was no harm in the Hall, but Krooger was throwing in a word here and there to bamboozle the rest. And Norman had turned clean round. It's said he was speaking about the lasses— Alan was in last night late for a crack with my father and I was in and out the room and hearing it all. Norman! Plenty he knows about lasses! Aye, or my father either. All they know is they'll not take the blame for their own badness! Do you mind of my mother, Katie?" Kate nodded. She remembered a thin shadowy smile on a stooping woman and a shawl blown in the wind. "Well, it was when she was so ill—you know, Katie, she had a growth, and Dr MacKillop said to me that if she had gone to him sooner they might have operated. But father was saying all the time that she was not ill at all, she shouldn't be thinking about it, she looked as well as ever she was. I would say that was mostly because he was so feared to lose her. Every time she went down to the village, he was at her was she thinking to see the doctor, what did she want— he would get it for her! Ach, he would do everything for her in one way; everything but what was needed. I would say there wasn't a man that could put any kind of reasoning into his feelings about women."

"No" said Kate, "no. Maybe not."

"Doesn't it make you kind of sad," asked Janet, "living up at

Tigh na Bheach with no one but your father? After having your own home?"

"Well, you know how it was" said Kate, "it was after he—after the surgery was hit—I came up here with Alice, she was only four. And then our own house got a direct hit and everything was gone. I mean really everything; the pictures and china and the books and his chair and desk and the rocking horse in the nursery. And I just never had the heart to start again. Though maybe I would have been better to. I suppose in a way it's a waste—for a doctor——" It was her turn now to fiddle with the self-starter and the screen-wiper knobs, keeping back the tears which did no good.

"You could get married again" said Janet softly.

"No, my dear, I'm too old."

"But you could maybe marry someone that was not too young." Her heart was suddenly beating fast with excitement: would Katie speak?

"Well, nobody's asked me!" said Kate with a half laugh. Dear Janet, longing to pair everyone off! But Janet was thinking, so that's the way of it, he's never asked her—maybe if someone could just give him the word—ah, wouldn't it be grand to see Katie up at the Castle! But Kate went on: "What about yourself now?"

"Me, is it? Ach, I'm bound to come to it one of these days. But I'm not struck with any of the boys here. See, the rain's going off and here's the steamer almost in!"

Both looked out: there was Roddy going down to the quay. Kate, her hand on the door handle, pointed: "What about him?"

"Roddy's a decent lad" said Janet, "if it's him you mean. But it's the crowd you see him wi', Kenny's Chrissie and her chums, forever getting off to Halbost for the Saturday dances if there's any way at all! And he's taken a car full of them more than once."

"Oh well, there's safety in numbers." Kate got out of the car and looked round; the clouds were lifting and there might even be a blink of sun later, she thought.

"I'm no' saying he's at it often" said Janet anxiously, "ach, you mustn't think I would be speaking ill of him, for I'm certain sure he only goes with them because Mrs McCulloch is forever nagging at him and her two lasses as narrow as herself. But the way it is, I hardly know Roddy MacCrimmon."

They were walking down to the quay now and stood together a little behind the men. They could see several passengers on the steamer and five of them in a bunch together, one a woman with a dark handkerchief over her head and her hands deep in the pockets of a huge old leather coat.

"Will that be Mrs Mitchison?" asked Janet.

"I suppose so" said Kate, a little doubtfully.

Now the steamer was made fast and the fishermen all standing around not staring directly, but making remarks aside to one another. The Highland Panel group came down the gangway, looking about them, looking up at the sky to see if it was going to rain again in a minute. Pate Morrison was shaking hands hard with Mr Wood, the Chief Fishery Officer for Scotland, a big, square-shouldered, grey-haired man with an east coast voice and the east coast eyes that stay bright and blue when the face has aged round them. He introduced them to the others, Alec Anderson, Member of Parliament for Motherwell and Chairman of the group, a Caithness man, grey-haired too; Mrs Mitchison, short and solid in the leather coat, knitted stockings and heavy shoes; Colonel Henderson, small and quick and white-haired; and Miss Campbell, secretary to the group, refreshingly young and neat. All carried leather dispatch cases in various stages of dilapidation. Colonel Henderson had a string bag, which the discreetly gazing fishermen could see had in it, whatever else it might have, a bottle of milk and an open packet of oatcakes, and Mrs Mitchison had a more or less portable typewriter. Two of the sailors brought down a selection of suitcases and Mr MacMillan from the hotel introduced himself, picked up the lightest and called to one of the lads to bring the rest along to the hotel.

Meanwhile the unloading was going on. Roddy's fertilisers were being heaved out of the hold bag after bag. He had his lorry backed up close to them and was loading them up almost as quickly as they came. Red Dougy's fertilisers were there too and it seemed to Angus that he'd do best to put them on his lorry, and leave them over at Molachy. It might be weather for planting again in a day or two. There was a crate right enough for Bits, but the way it sounded, something must have got broken.

Hughie's spares were still not there. In the middle of the unloading a fair young man in an overcoat jumped off the boat on to the quay and came up to Andrew and May, who were watching the Highland Panel, Andrew scowling away at Archie who was just shaking hands with Mr Anderson. Andrew turned "Tam!" he said, "God a'michty, what are ye doing here!"

"I've got three days, father" he said and kissed May, "I thought I would just come through and see how you all were, and here, when I got on the boat, the first person I saw was the Chief Officer! Terrible nice to me he was too and we had a glass of beer together. But I felt kind of awkward coming down the gangway behind that crowd. How's Port Sonas, father? How's the choir, May? What like's the fishing here?"

"Well, begod, Tam" said Andrew, "you could ha' sent a telegram! What's for the dinner, May?"

"Ach, never mind, father! Tell me, did you ever have the meeting about a new Village Hall? You have? Well, it was time right enough." He looked round, "it doesn't change any, the wee place. Come on home, May, I'm not wanting to get mixed up with the Panel crowd."

"I'll stay for a wee while" said Andrew, "I've to keep my eye on yon Archie. Go you with May. Can you make a dumpling, May?"

"Away, father!" she said, linking her arm in her brother's, "I know as well as you what Tom likes."

By now the fishermen had been introduced to the Highland Panel and Kate had come forward and introduced herself as the District Councillor. She was so used to being snubbed by Sir Ian that it took her by surprise to find them all friendly, she might have been a man by the way they spoke to her! Colonel Henderson started telling her about the problem of herring transport and when she didn't immediately understand, drew her a diagram in pencil with arrows. She didn't dare to say she understood this even less, but trusted to picking it up later. Now they were all going off along the quay to look at the hole in the sea wall. Colonel Henderson was still explaining to Kate. Pate and Archie had Mr Anderson hemmed in. Mr Wood was telling Andrew what a fine young chap Tom was and how well he was doing in the Fishery Service, and Andrew was listening without a word and finding it terrible hard to keep from a daft kind of smile. The younger fishermen were eyeing Connie Campbell, but not addressing her, and Matta had isolated Mrs Mitchison to tell her about the lobsters.

Roddy drove away, but Angus, although he had loaded his lorry, was still there. He was watching the procession go trailing off to inspect the hole in the wall and the old jetty alongside what had once been Andrew's curing station. After a time they turned. The Panel were to have lunch at the hotel and the meeting after that. Mr Wood was now questioning Pate Morrison about the fishing. Mrs Mitchison climbed and jumped, rather heavily, into Matta's boat; it looked as if the lobster fishermen had got a good grip of her. Mr Anderson was looking through some home-made statistics which the fishermen had, comparing them with the official ones. Miss Campbell consulted her wrist watch and began to shepherd her flock.

Andrew was standing a little apart from the rest, and half wanting to go home, half intent on his enemy. If only he could have shown up Archie in front of the Panel. Wouldn't it be great that! All the times that the Harbour Master had bested him, or rather the times that he hadn't bested the Harbour Master, came back into his mind like the taste of stale whisky coming back into the mouth on the Sunday morning after a Saturday night. And he could take no pleasure in what Mr Wood had been saying about Tom. Angus approached him casually, "A dirty day, Mr Revie."

"Aye" said Andrew, "and plenty of dirty folk in it."

"Ach, well" said Angus "maybe we're all of us kind of half dirty if it comes to that." He looked down at the boats and added, "There's Matta still taking it sore over his lobsters. There's any amount more lobsters in it! The whole o' the coast is lousy wi' lobsters, and him still distracted over the loss of a handful."

"They lobsters o' Matta's was stolen" said Andrew, "and it was a dirty trick and a shame on us a' and if I could catch the bugger that did it—but I've a strong notion who it was; a verra strong notion." He nodded his head and spat over the edge of the quay.

"And who would you say it was?" said Angus "for the notion I have myself is that the whole thing was just a kind o' caper by some o' the young fellows."

"Not at all" said Andrew, "de'il a one of the young ones. It was yon old bugger of a Harbour Master and him disguising them up in yon office as a crate of jelly jars!"

"I think maybe I could give you news of them" said Angus, and he swung himself on the heel of one foot.

"Could ye indeed!" said Andrew eagerly, "did ye see him at it, man?"

"It's no' that at all" said Angus, "and I'm wanting to tell you, Mr Revie, but I'd no' like it to go any further——"

"If ye saw Archie or Jim at it, we'll need to send for the polis" said Andrew, bristling.

"It wasna them at all, Mr Revie" said Angus and now his voice had dropped to a kind of urgent whisper. "But I ken who it was——"

Andrew looked at him, up and down, scowling, and then he stamped his foot, "If it wasna them" he said, "you needna be telling me." And he turned his back and was off home.

CHAPTER XIV

THURSDAY AFTERNOON:
HIGHLAND PANEL MEETING

KATE HAD ASKED RODDY to come to the Highland Panel meeting to represent the Forestry Commission, who would naturally be interested in improvements for Port Sonas harbour, from which they might well be shipping timber, and he had promised to come. He was bound to now. If he did not go, there would be questions. Once, a few years back, felling an old and twisted pine, it had come sideways and he had not jumped in time. All the rest of that day he had gone about in a daze, not realising how his head was still oozing blood. Could it be like blood that was coming out of him now? Or only—courage and confidence. He kept on putting his hand into his pocket to feel was the letter still there. If the McCullochs were to get at it— and he knew they'd take a read at any letter of his if they'd to get the chance—well then, it would be all up. So long as he kept it to himself, there was a chance of getting round it somehow. The hard corners of the envelope were already beginning to bend and get sticky with fingering. "Our client informs us that you are the father . . . medical certificate . . . what steps you are proposing to take . . . admit paternity . . . our client . . ." Our client— up against yon tree. But he had never—— It hadn't—couldn't have—not that way! And his savings. When he'd not done one thing or another he'd wanted. When he'd not even let his mother know for months about his rise in case he'd need to feel he should be sending her more. And all because he'd wanted to get married, to be able to say to the right lassie—but not to the like of Chrissie! And if once she'd to get her fingers on it and these lawyers helping her, making out it was his fault, he'd done her wrong, and they never-ever asking what was the truth of the matter! But he'd pay her sooner than marry, that was one thing certain.

He walked along from his wee office, keeping by the edge of the quay, his hand in his pocket over the letter. Could one answer it? Get time that way. Time for a plan. How did one write to lawyers? Who would know? Who would help? Davie? Would he have the education right to answer the lawyers? You'd need to know what to say or they'd twist it on you. For a hundred yards he walked unseeing, between the puddled road on his right and the high tide of mucky lapping sea water on his left, and all that was in him a hatred of all lawyers. Two young ex-Service fishermen, Crookie and Johnnie Feetie, going the same way, spoke to him, but he did not wake out of his hate.

"What's eating Roddy?" said Crookie to young Jim, Archie's nephew. Jim winked. "You're telling me!" he said, and then gave a jazzy wriggle to his hips and hummed "It's that thing, boys, it's that thing!" The others were laughing great at that. Jim was as good as the pictures.

It was Andrew Revie who came up to Roddy and spoke to him, making him take notice. "Watch you Archie when it comes to the meeting!" he said, "Aye, and Jim. We'll see if they blench, the two of them, when there is word of lobsters!" It all seemed daft to Roddy. Why couldn't they leave the lobsters be? There was mostly plenty to worry about, without lobsters. "I'll get the law on to them yet" said Andrew.

The law. The law. Roddy saw the law whizzing away there, like a circular saw, and whatever got on to the sliding table dragged up to it and ripped through. Inside himself he knew he was screaming like ripped wood. "There'll not be much spoken about lobsters, Mr Revie" he said, and suddenly added "And God knows there's worse things that folk can do to one another."

Andrew stared at him and started to say something, then shook his head. "Ach well, we'll away to the meeting" he grumbled, half to himself. "The bad ones will be there right enough." A car went by them—Councillor Thompson on his way to the meeting. Then the Fishery Group, with Kate, who was talking to Mrs Mitchison. Andrew shook his head: "It's a maist extraordinar' thing, the way there's women everywhere. And nae waur than the men, for a' that."

When they got to the Harbour Master's office, they saw that most of the rest were there. The Panel crowd were warming hands and bottoms at the stove. Mr Anderson was talking to Councillor Thompson and the fishermen were all at Mr Wood. Mrs Mitchison was standing rather behind, perhaps feeling awkward, though there had been plenty of these Fishery Group meetings all round the coast. She was beginning to edge towards Kate when the thing began to shape itself into a meeting. The harbour master had provided an inky little table and two glasses of water. Mr Anderson, the chairman, sat himself down behind it, Miss Campbell with her notebook on his right and Colonel Henderson beyond her, Mrs Mitchison and Mr Wood on his left.

Councillor Thompson was in the middle of the front bench, Pate on one side and Dunky on the other; the rest of the fishermen crowded behind. Kate looked round when Roddy came in, and he sat down behind her. There were a few others whose interests might be affected, twenty-five or so altogether. Mr Anderson leaned forward, smiled, and began on his chairman's remarks about the functions of the Highland Panel as an advisory body and how they could help the fishermen. He had an easy kind of Caithness voice and spoke as though he might be meaning most of it. But he had been a schoolteacher earlier on, so maybe he was used to doing just that. He introduced the other members of the Panel. When he said with a wee jocose kind of thing in his voice that Mrs Mitchison was a ring-netter from Carradale, didn't Pate let out with what he mostly always said when the ringers were mentioned! But it was only half aloud and no harm done.

Roddy was trying to listen, trying to concentrate on something other than his own problem. But his mind and eyes were jumping instead of listening. He noticed that the rest of the Panel had heard this often before. Colonel Henderson shut his eyes; Mr Wood beamed at the fishermen; Mrs Mitchison kept looking about, tugging her kilt down over her knees, or biting her pencil.

Led by Councillor Thompson, everyone applauded when the chairman finished. Then Mr Wood got up and began to talk to the fishermen about loans and grants. They listened keenly, especially Colin and his friends. It was then suggested that they should have a few words from the local Councillor. This was Mr Thompson's opportunity and, indeed, there would be the elections soon enough, and it might be that someone would have the cheek to stand against him. He spoke about the hole in the wall, and was eloquent about the worth of this God-fearing little fishing community. The Panel nodded sympathetically. Kate supposed they were well used to it, but suddenly noticed that Mrs Mitchison had seen something less pleasing than Councillor Thompson. She looked round and found, somewhat to her

173

surprise, that Mr Mackintosh had come in, looking every inch a Wee Free minister. If it had been any of those ones coming, she would have expected Mr Fergusson. What did the Wee Frees think they were up to?

A general discussion followed about the status of the pier, whose ownership was lost in mists of obscurity and argument, about seine netters, about fish transport and about grants and loans. Pate began about the foreign trawlers coming and taking the fish from under the noses of the rightful fishermen. Mrs Mitchison asked him just when the last illegal trawler had been down. "When?" he said, "I canna mind just on when, but it was a short enough while back." He appealed to the rest: och, yes, the trawlers! Something should be done about it, sure. And here was this bloody woman not believing a bloody word he said and just how you would know a ringer would act!

Colin and Johnnie Feetie asked more about the grants and about how they stood as ex-Servicemen. Mr Wood explained it again and indeed there seemed to be no catch in it and the Government doing everything almost except give them the boats! Colin began figuring it out: there would be £100 maybe coming with Anna, and if once she'd to give it to him in his hand and not get spending it on sheets and towels and that——

Then there was talk about the price of nets and gear. Worse than it looked, even, and that was bad enough. In the old days every man of the crew might put in a net, but he'd need to think twice now. And sisal rope lasting half the time of manila and how couldn't the Government make yon black fellows in Manila give us the right rope? What was governments for if they couldna do the like of that?

Now Matta got to his feet and out came the story of the lobsters. There was clicking of tongues and exclamations of sympathy, though by now all had heard of it. But this was due to a new audience. Andrew, just behind his enemy, leant forward, almost breathing down his neck in his eagerness for the thing he wanted to happen. But Archie appeared perfectly calm and so did Jim. If they were but to say a word, how he would follow it up! But nothing came. The Panel made kindly noises, spoke about the marketing of lobsters, but made no attempt to be detectives.

All this time Crookie could not take his eyes off Connie Campbell, and her putting down everything in a wee kind of book. Halfway through the discussion he made as if to speak to someone on the far side and had then stood edging along the wall until he could get a glimpse of the wee book, and here it wasn't words at all she was writing, but kind of marks, and her fingers flying and not a hair out of place on her head! Wonderful, that.

And now an old man got to his feet—old Sanntach from Larach, and what was he doing at this meeting? He coughed and gathered his words. "Seeing the head ones are here" he said, "could something not be done for the croft road? It is just the same way it is for a hundred years and worse in it every winter."

"Sit you down!" shouted Mr MacMillan from the hotel. "We are here about the harbour and not about your roads!"

The Panel, however, listened. After all, they were there to get the feel of everything that needed done in the Highlands. Colonel Henderson said it should go to the Transport Group. "Probably a Department of Agriculture road" said Mr Anderson. "Make a note of it, Connie, please."

"Well if that truslach is to be made a note of" said Mr MacMillan, "the Panel should know about the water. Maybe they'd be interested in my sample——" He put his hand into his pocket and lugged out a muddy-looking medicine bottle—"and this is what they'll be drinking tonight."

"Och, they'll have better stuff than that" said one of the fishermen. Wonderful, thought Kate, how you never got a gathering of Highlanders without some joke about whisky. It must be a very deep fixation. Too little breast feeding possibly— they'd been put on to the bottle—— But Mr Thompson had turned round and was saying to Mr MacMillan that the County Council had not forgotten the water scheme—it was all the fault of the Edinburgh crowd, and maybe next year——

"Well, if the water is not in order, how about the bridge?" said Roddy suddenly. Several hands got at him to pull him down, for he was speaking with an anger and soreness which was out of all proportion. He persisted. "If there was this bridge across to Torskadale then more folk would be using the harbour and more right to have money spent on it! Some of the Torskadale men might go in for the fishing, and it's only sense, the bridge!" Here Kate and Andrew managed to stop him. Mr Anderson asked if he was representing Torskadale.

"No," he said, "I'm from the Forestry Commission, but when a thing's plain sense I can see it as well as the next. And the bridge is not getting a fair deal!"

Colonel Henderson had taken out a map and pushed it across to the others. "Thank you" said Mr Anderson, "we will make a note of it. What is your opinion, Councillor Thompson?"

"Aye well," said the Councillor, "it will be a good wee whilie before there's any talk of the bridge."

"Not with you at the Kinlochbannag Hotel" said one of the fishermen, half aloud.

Krooger, who was in at the back, said "The ferry is always found very serviceable." Again there was sniggering and half-heard remarks from the fishermen. The Chairman called them to order and asked if there was anything more to be said about the harbour. Roddy had dropped back in his seat, sweating; what at all had made him speak? It was daft, his judgment was going, oozing away . . .

Along the benches one or another looked round at his neighbour and whispered. Archie, the harbour master, who had already spoken, said the Panel must bear in mind that maybe there would be larger steamers and then the steamer berth would need seeing to—indeed, the fenders were half done and unless he himself was authorised to see to repairs—— Mr Anderson, seeing through this with the ease of long practice, said he was sure that the Forestry Commission would send down a couple of butts of good Scotch if they were approached: nothing like the native timber for fenders.

Councillor Thompson belched but did not speak again. There were a few questions from the Panel members. Colonel Henderson asked about fish transport; unsatisfied on this, he remarked that it should all be done as an Army operation.

Then from the back up rose Mr Mackintosh. He had the curiously Semitic look of the well-fed and under-exercised black Highlander, thick hair and lips, a smile that went outward but meant nothing. As he spoke the vowels rippled and doubled, so that every word singing up and down took on a special and need-less significance. He spoke of the great obligation that Port Sonas was under when it should be visited by so important a body as the Highland Panel, and of the conservation of the best moral and religious traditions of the Highlands. Pate and Dunkie turned round in their seats, delighted at this display from their Minister,

176

but Mr Thompson, who preferred speaking to listening, was annoyed and kept his back firmly turned. So was Andrew annoyed, and fidgeted and whispered to Kate. Nothing had come out to the detriment of Archie and it seemed to him that Archie had won again. Roddy was just not listening at all. Nor were the Panel best pleased. Mrs Mitchison scribbled a note and passed it round. Mr Wood grinned and the Chairman's urbanity became slightly strained.

At last Mr Mackintosh sat down, well pleased with himself. He had emphasised at good length the need for hard work and thrift such as had been the wont of the righteous, and for the detaining of the young people not only in the Highlands, which was undoubtedly the function of the Panel, but in the ways of their fathers. It had long been in his mind to speak so if ever there should be a chance of seeing the Highland Panel and lo, the Almighty had led them into his hand.

"Thank you, Mr—ah?—Mackintosh" said the Chairman, about to close the meeting. Pate and Krooger and some of the rest were feeling greatly edified to think what fine folk they were and if only the young ones would grow up like them. And here didn't Mrs Mitchison get to her feet, and Kate could see she was an angry woman, and say "Of course we all agree that the young people should stay in the Highlands, but they'll not stay unless we do something to encourage them. I hope you have got a Village Hall here?"

There was a moment's stillness as the rings spread by the dropped brick made contact with the minds of the audience. Kate took a breath—it was up to her now—but Mr Mackintosh rose again, his smile as sticky as black treacle: "There has been talk of such a thing, but the morals of the young people must be protected, and we cannot countenance any occasion for sin."

"Are you opposed to village halls?" said Mrs Mitchison, and the touch of Edinburgh that had softened her voice earlier had given place to a cold English accent.

"The Free Church is not opposed in principle to village halls," said Mr Mackintosh, "so long as they are used rightly. We do not, for example, object to their use for the singing of serious songs."

"Dancing reels to the pipes is part of the Highland way of life," said Mrs Mitchison. "Would you object to that in a village hall?"

"I would most certainly do so" said Mr Mackintosh, but Mr

Anderson had risen to his feet, looked round him as though nothing at all were happening, and remarked "As we have heard all that the meeting has to tell us about the Port Sonas fisheries and harbour, the meeting is now adjourned. Thank you all very much."

Everyone stood up. Councillor Thompson bethought himself and proposed a hearty vote of thanks to the Highland Panel. Clapping and stamping, the meeting decanted itself out of the Harbour Master's office and rapidly re-formed into groups just outside.

The rain was off, the sun shining and the puddles beginning to steam. Kate went across to the Panel. Mrs Mitchison was swearing like a medical student. She turned round to Kate. "Sorry" she said, "I'm allergic to Ministers."

"You see" said Kate, "we have just formed a Village Hall committee and we are having a good deal of difficulty."

"Hell's bells" said Mrs Mitchison, "did I put my foot in it?"

"Hard," said Kate. "You wouldn't come over this evening to my house and have supper, perhaps?"

Mrs Mitchison spoke across to the Chairman "Alec, will Connie be safe with you boys if I'm out for supper? Oh, Alec, why did you shut me up? I wanted to kill him."

"I just thought you might, lassie" said Alec Anderson.

Outside, the Wee Frees had sorted themselves out round their pastor. All except Roddy. For a moment there had been something else to take his mind off himself, but now it had all come down on him again, no longer with quite the same jag of anger, but with a horrible blackness, a fog, spreading over his whole life, nothing left untouched by it. If only it was opening time he would go to the hotel, yes, in working hours, against all the rules he had made for himself. But it wasn't. Pate Morrison tapped him on the shoulder. "Roddy MacRimmon, we should take ourselves out of this Village Hall committee, both the two of us, before we are leading ourselves and the young crowd into the Pit."

"Away you go, Pate," said Roddy. "There's nothing changed from what it was and weren't we all agreed, and the rest of the fishermen as well?"

"I hadna thought it out right" said Pate, and grabbed at Colin. "Now" he said, "now you, Colin, you're one of the young

178

crowd, and I'm asking you straight out, are you for sin or are you against it?"

Colin wriggled a bit away from his future father-in-law. "Ach, nobody's for sin."

"If you were to get taking my Anna to this Village Hall——"

"It'll not be for a good while yet," said Colin, and then, hastily, "but maybe you are in the right and the time not ripe for it."

"See now," said Pate triumphantly, "even the young ones are taking nothing to do with it."

"Is this all over the head of what happened at the meeting?" Roddy asked.

"Aye" said Pate, "and wasn't it just like a bloody ring-netter to be driving us to sin?"

As Kate came out, Councillor Thompson rolled up to her. "I have been speaking to some of the folk here, Mrs Snow, and I am just afraid, aye well, it's clear enough that they are not unanimous for the Village Hall—indeed they are kind of half unanimous against it."

"But you mustn't take this too seriously," said Kate. "It's nothing at all, but the Wee Free Minister getting upset——"

"Ah, but it's more than that. There is my good friend Mr MacMillan from the hotel and he is thinking it would maybe not be for the best in the place."

"Nonsense—he's chairman of the committee."

"Ah yes, yes, but it's easy done, getting into a committee, and a namely man doesn't like to refuse and most of all with yourself asking him. No, there's none of us can refuse the ladies!"

"Do you mean to say he is resigning?"

"Well, I wouldn't just say, but I'm doing that myself, Mrs Snow, and the same for my friend, Mr MacLean, and I should advise you to let the thing be for a while. What's a year or two or ten years itself? They've been two hundred years without a village hall and it will do them no harm to wait a whilie longer."

"If we did that every time, nothing would get done," said Kate, trying to keep calm, but beginning to feel a rise in her voice.

"And all the better, maybe," agreed Councillor Thompson. "Isn't it the things we don't do that upsets folk away less than the things we do do? It's what I'm forever saying on the County

Council. So my advice is to dissolve your committee and just let things be for a whilie."

"I wonder if you realise how much work I have put into it already, Mr Thompson?" She had half turned away now, staring past him.

"Ach, you shouldn't work yourself so hard, not at all. It's little thanks any of us gets."

"I see. Well—I'll think it over, Mr Thompson." She walked away quickly, stumbling a little. Now that the rain had cleared the sea was brilliant blue, tender green on the shore, a dazzle of wallflowers in Archie's garden. It swam under her eyes and she almost knocked into Miss Beaton on her bicycle.

"I'm going up to Osnish, Mrs Snow" she said. "The doctor was there earlier and the wee MacKinnon's are real bad with the measles."

"You'll let me know if there's anything I can do?"

"Surely" said Miss Beaton, and spun away with her black bag into the sunshine.

CHAPTER XV

THURSDAY EVENING:
MEETING OF THE BRITISH LEGION

THE PORT SONAS BRANCH of the British Legion was apt
to come and go, depending on how the fishing was, who was the
Secretary and what other attractions there were. It was mostly
the young fellows. The veterans of the first war were not all so
keen, and that maybe was with most of them being Masons. But
Jeamus had quarrelled with the Masons some time away back,
and all over the head of him being caught on the river by George
the Keeper and him saying to George that as a Brother he would
surely let him away. But here, George was having none of it, and
Jeamus was sure enough taken to the Court and fined almost the
price of a good salmon, and where was your brotherhood in the
like of that? So Jeamus was in the Legion, and so were Coories and
Sandy, but both of them were out tonight with the Silver Bird.
There were two or three more of the older fishermen members
and when they did come they talked down the young ones. But
all were away fishing this Thursday.

The meeting was called for six, in the Mission Hall. Andy
Smith, who had refused utterly and on principle to become a
Mason, was a member of the Legion and, indeed, it was the best
way he could escape from his wife. She had not been over-anxious
for him to join, but for once he had turned and defied her.
Nor would he tell her what went on at the meetings; he himself
knew that there was no occasion for sin as he saw it; she could
think what she liked, and if at times one of the boys were to forget
himself in the language, well, weren't they all comrades? Even
these young ones who were only in the patrol boats in the near
waters and knew nothing of Givenchy and the dead men working
down into the mud and the last bit of a kilt draggling away after
them. Ypres. Vimy Ridge. Before he was saved and married to
Bella MacConnachie.

One of the older fishermen was Chairman, but tonight he was out and Colin MacLean was Vice-Chairman. He came in with his chums and he was telling them about the carry on he'd had with Pate Morrison. "Silly old bastard, speaking away there about sin" he said. "Sin, him! But I'd need to ca' canny and me going with Anna."

"It's your own Minister" said Johnnie Neil, who was Established.

"Ach, the Ministers! They'd need to do a job o' work the same as the rest of us. Then they could talk. I never heed what they say."

"Did ye hear the set about the Minister that had two cats? Well, see you, this Minister——" but one of the others dug him in the ribs, because Andy had come in.

Angus was secretary; it had been a good idea having him, for he could speak to folk going round in his lorry. He had brought Jeamus and Hamish MacRae down with him from the glen, but none of the others. One or two of the crofters were ex-Service, but none of them had bothered themselves to join. There was no one from the farming community. They had all been exempt.

Then Alasdair came in with the account books. "Roddy's no coming. He gave me the books."

"That's queer, now" said Angus, "I was speaking to him this morning and he said then he was coming."

"He seemed kind of upset" said Alasdair. "Maybe it's over yon district officer. A pure bugger, the man. He's my boss, is Roddy, but I'd stick up for him any day. He's fair and he'll let you speak. It's the higher-up ones that need their arses kicked."

"Aye, that's so" said the Kettle.

They worked their way easily through the minutes and the treasurer's report. There were one or two letters from headquarters; some branches would be doing plenty. "It's kind of a pity there's no grievances here we could write in over" said one of the boys.

"Aye, you get mostly everything out of the Health and Insurance and that. It would be great if we hadna got it and then we complained and we did get it."

"Well, we hanna got houses" said the Kettle.

"Ah, it's yourself wanting a house, mo bhalach! And then there'll be another good lad lost!"

"Ach, it's no' for that——"

"Isn't it, now? Sure, you want a house! It's no' nice to be taking a lassie in under the bushes!"

"Ah, wasn't poor Chrissie saying——"

But Colin, noticing that Andy was beginning to look uneasy, called them to order. "Well, boys, what do you say we write in asking for homes for ex-Service men?"

"Aye, fine." "Great, that!" "Who will we write to?"

"We'd need sure enough to write to Councillor Thompson."

"Ach, Jocky Thompson, he's no bloody use, him! Besides, he'd know it was just ourselves. Better we write to headquarters and they write to the County Council. Will we do it, boys?" Everyone agreed and there was much discussion as to what was to go into the letter.

After that Alasdair leaned over to Angus and asked "Did you ever see the Laird about him joining?"

"I saw him right enough," said Angus, "but he's not joining."

"How?"

"Ach well—he's maybe no' seeing it the same way as oursel's——"

"I could ha' told you that," said Jeamus and gave a wee croaking laugh. Tomorrow night there would be a salmon less in the Laird's river.

"Bloody toff!" said Alasdair, "setting up to be better than the rest of us!" The others mostly agreed and there was some growling and calling of names. But Angus was wondering uncomfortably how much they themselves wanted to have the Laird in at the meetings. Wouldn't he be worse than old Andy Smith or the skippers? In a way it had been hardly honest asking him and all they wanted was his subscription for the New Year party and that. And you'd need to be half honest in the Legion. But how could he speak about honesty, him? Yes, by God, how could he speak of it!

"There's those that'll no' join," said Hamish MacRae, "my own cousin's the same. But they say the Laird's queer getting. The old ones gets yon way when they hanna a woman."

"Well, he could ask Kate, could he no'? She'd come quick enough——"

"Maybe that's just what she's done!"

"Now, boys!" said old Andy, "we shouldna be speaking scandal in the Legion and least of all over our District Councillor."

"Aye, you're right there," said Colin MacLean, "she's working hard for us, the woman. And indeed, I know this—if it was herself an ex-Service man, she'd join fast enough. And I canna say fairer than that."

"I'll no' need to put it in the minute book, will I?" said Angus. "This about the Laird."

"Ach no" said Colin, "there's some things that looks well in the minutes, aye, so there is; but there's other things that'll just spoil a minute book."

But Crookie was looking at the clock. He got up. "Me and Lachie will need to go."

"How?" said Colin. "We have to speak about the new Hall yet."

"Ach well," said Crookie, "maybe it's best if we go, seeing we couldna give you our vote, the way we're placed both the two of us."

"Ach, it's the prayer meeting!" said Colin. "It was out o' my mind clean. Sure, you needna go, Lachie?"

He shook his head. "My folk would be at me wild if I reneeged. They dinna like me being in the Legion even. And I'd not hear the last of it if I stayed on over the prayer meeting."

"Well, well," said Colin, "my own crowd's bad enough, but the F.P.'s willn't leave a man to brush his teeth without it's in the Book." He shook his head. "Now, boys, you've mostly all heard we may be getting a Village Hall. Were some of you at the meeting? I was there myself."

There was silence. Suddenly Andy said "I was there, boys."

"So you were, sure enough" said Colin. "I hadna minded." He looked uncomfortable.

"Well, boys," said Andy, "if you were wanting to vote on it, I'll just abstain and we'll say nae more."

"That's the lad, Andy" said one of the other young ones, and slapped him hard on the back, so that he felt oddly happy.

"Well" said Colin, "the way I look at it we need this Hall, and you mostly all heard the arguments, one way and another. What do you say?" As usual nobody spoke for a minute, then half a dozen spoke together. It was clear enough that the young ones were all for it.

Colin and Angus whispered together and then Alasdair. Then Colin said "It looks to us it's our unanimous desire for a Hall, not counting Andy, and we all know how he's placed. Here, we can say he went out."

Hamish MacCrae got up. "I'd as soon you'd not say it was unanimous, Colin, with me known to be here. I'd like a Hall well enough and so would my wife, but you know fine the way things are up the glen and I'd never-ever hear the last o't."

"Aye," said Jeamus, "there's terrible saints up the glen! We'd need to gae awful canny the way the wind is setting these few days back. Maybe we'll need to bide awhile till the water's settled." Colin bit his pencil; he was thinking of Pate—and Anna.

Jeamus watched. He was sure enough on the side of the Hall and wouldn't it spite the Hotel—for all he was on the committee now, but he'd not stay there long!—and big Jock and that crowd. Masons, every one of them and he'd like fine to see them downed, them and their aprons! It gave him a kind of wicked thrill to be thinking the words even, and he taking them so serious at one time. Kate, the woman, she'd never know how it was he was on her side. Andy was no Mason, had said—he chuckled over it to himself as he always did.

Johnnie Feetie suggested they should write a second letter to headquarters. He liked the grand thought of these letters being sent off and received. But Angus said he was writing one letter only, and it would be bother enough. Then it was suggested that there should be a deputation. That was a popular idea. Deputations and petitions, well, there was more to them than letters. You would be able to speak about them for years maybe after they were past. It was decided that the office bearers of the Legion should go on a deputation to Councillor Thompson, maybe at the week-end when Angus would be taking the lorry into Kinlochbannag on his Saturday run anyway. Then someone said "What about the District Councillor. Will the deputation not see Mistress Snow?"

"Why not?" said Colin. "What do you say, boys? Will we go tonight?"

"Maybe we should get Roddy," said Alasdair. "He's good at the speaking."

"Well, see can you find him" said Colin, "and we'll go over at the back of nine. She'll have had her supper." The meeting broke up, pleased with itself. As soon as they were out of the Mission Hall, some of them started in to sing Army songs.

CHAPTER XVI

THURSDAY EVENING:
FREE PRESBYTERIAN PRAYER MEETING

THE OLD MAN SANNTACH, and that was a name meant badly enough too, but so long since it had been given to him that he never thought about it at all now, took his tea with some cousins he had at Port Sonas, another old man and his sister living in the Back Road, a row of two-roomed stone cottages behind Jock's shop. The old ones were kind of used to it, but you would never get a young couple to live in the Back Road. It was mostly the Gaelic that was spoken there, where you would scarcely hear it round the harbour. The rents were low—only a shilling or two a week, but you couldn't look for repairs out of that. The old age pensions hardly allowed for it either, but maybe the house would do for a whilie longer.

The old brother and sister used to get the unsold papers from Janet's auntie's shop, and papered them across the cracks. If there was a picture in them that was not at all a godly picture, then they would paste it upside down. But there were some nice enough pictures of babies and cats and royalty, and they kept the plaster lying back on the walls. There was a strong smell in the kitchen, but if they had opened the window it would have hurt the geranium on the sill and it was thriving great. Sanntach duly admired it and, having asked a blessing, they sat in to their tea. All were going on to the Free Presbyterian prayer meeting.

For a time there was talk about the Highland Panel, and the old cousins admiring the boldness of Sanntach in speaking of the Larach road. "But I thought it was agreed, the road, between the Board and yourselves" said the cousin.

"That was so, in a way, Tearlach, but the Board said we were to do part of the work on it ourselves."

"Well, it is mostly that way for the croft roads, and yourselves the only ones to profit by it."

"All very well and good, but the most of the young men are gone, and why should I be working on the road at my time of life?"

"Well, there will be some who could, surely."

"That was well enough in the old days, Tearlach, but now the Government should do these things for us." Sanntach took a deep sup of tea, sweet and thick, rumbling warmly down. It was a lawful consolation for the righteous—there was no sin in tea.

Meanwhile in one home or another preparations were being made for the prayer meeting. Black mantles were taken down from the pegs, boots cleaned, collars and ties adjusted. With the evening clearing up, quite a few walked in from Larach and Osnish. Cameron of Balnafearcha and Jackson of Achnahabhain met one another in the road, nodded, spoke briefly of farm matters: Jackson asked could he send over for the seeder, he was ready to drill in his turnips: Cameron assented without comment, as befitted a prayer night. Young Donnie was with his father, a heavy, rather handsome redhead, expressionless. Jackson shook hands with him solemnly. It would not be seemly to speak of such a thing as an engagement, but congratulation was understood.

Thoughts and footsteps were now turned towards the tabernacle. Other inhabitants of Port Sonas drifted or hurried by them as weed or fishes crossing the path of a determined fleet. Strangers were seen—the Highland Panel ones, but nothing was allowed to distract the flow of anticipation.

There were a few family groups: Lachie and Crookie walked sheepishly behind their families. Lachie had been saved when he was sixteen years old and had been lapsing ever since. After two years in the Navy he no longer believed in God even, let alone in all that he was called on to believe. He was deep ashamed of that week he had been saved; any time now that he did a wrong thing he felt he was paying out the boy he had been at the time. And yet, all the same, it was sore on him to do wrong things and he scarcely could manage it unless he was away from Port Sonas and with the drink in him. But there were wrong things to be done at home that were not counted. His folk were crofters from Osnish. When he was home on the Saturday, his father might tell him to drown some of the collie pups, and that in spite of the tears of

188

his wee sister. The crofters thought nothing of it, but he, having seen burned men drowning in an oily sea, knew that there was a wickedness about a deliberate drowning. If Colin MacLean was to get a boat and he would be engineer, they might do better than the old ones. They would work harder and drink less. They would be on their own, nobody telling them what to do and what not to do. And then there might be a chance to get clear of all this snarl he was in.

The group stepped aside as the bus came in from Kinlochbannag. This was the end of its run from Halbost, and it was half empty. But it was observed that a man got out from it who was not one of themselves, but wore a soft hat like a Minister's and carried a despatch case. Then one of the crofters recognised him and whispered. In a short while everyone knew that it was the new gentleman from the Department. He would doubtless be round in the morning and there were a few thoughts of what should maybe be set in a certain light before he was there to see.

Miss Gillies walked alone. She preferred it so. It was her duty to maintain discipline and inculcate morals into a class of forty children and little help from those above, whose duty in turn was to aid her. Yet the Lord had mightily strengthened her hand. She knew that she was feared.

Behind her, some of the young ones were straggling out. Robina was in distress and darkness of mind; her eyes were red. Every now and then she gave a sniffle and her hanky was crumpled tight in her hand. It was the thought of the Village Hall and of her own uncertainty. For, although she had testified, yet it had been kind of half-hearted; and within herself—oh she had heeded the temptings of Satan! She had thought maybe there was no harm in it. Indeed, she had *wanted* the Hall. She had felt a terrible movement in herself of wanting it. Wanting maybe to be with the rest of the choir, even although they were not saved. She had felt herself to be questioning the wisdom of her elders. The ones that knew best. Or did they? She was that disturbed she never-ever looked the same way as one of the boys even.

Wee Lizzie was looking an odd time at Donnie, though, and so was her chum she was walking with, Jackson's niece from Achnahabhain, a clever wee girl, extra good at baking. "I

189

wonder what like Donnie's cousin he's engaged to is?" she said.

"He doesn't look awful cheery" said Lizzie.

"No" said the other "I wouldn't like to be the one Donnie is marrying. He was over at my uncle an odd time and I was speaking with him. He liked my scones, but och, he was forever bragging his motor bike—and, well, I don't think some way he's awful kind."

"I wonder" said Lizzie, "has Donnie made a public profession?"

"I dinna think," said her chum, "we would have heard, surely, and he's young enough. Some folks put it off. Och, Lizzie, my uncle's terrible set on me being adopted to the Lord, but I'm kind of scared."

"Aye, you'd need to be right sure. But it's terrible all the same to be a sinner. Supposing the bus was to run over you?" The two girls moved a bittie closer and hurried up the path towards the door.

The tin tabernacle swallowed them all and Port Sonas was both relieved and irritated. The last old man, Willie the Tank, came hirpling and hurrying, speaking to himself, for he was queer-getting. You'd not like to meet him in the street. But he was quiet enough within the tabernacle.

Mr Munro was mainly troubled in the Lord over two things. One was the Roman Catholic Church, forever assailing the realm of Scotland, and the other was the Port Sonas Village Hall. After much wrestling and after speaking on the telephone with a brother in the Lord in the town of Halbost, he had come to the conclusion that Village Halls were part of a Papist plot. Had they not, in the Village Hall of Glenrig, held a party with a tree idolatrously decorated at the Romish festival time called Christmas? The enemy was determined and powerful. Last year there had been a known Papist staying at the Castle on the pretext that he was an old friend of the Laird, and had not Mistress Snow been at the Castle and that alone, with what carnality of purpose he would not even dare to think, and might not the seeds of this attack against the godly have been there implanted? All came swingingly into his mind, the way of a revelation.

By the evening of the prayer meeting he had it all, with the Lord's help, clear in his mind. He would lay it before the Lord and the congregation, and power would be added unto him. And indeed it was so and his words had arrows in them to convict the lapses of some who might have hankered after the temptations and devices of Satan. Robina and Lizzie wept. True enough, they had testified against the Hall at the Choir meeting, but without sufficient conviction of righteousness, almost with shame, forgetting the precious and notable privilege that was theirs in being Free Presbyterians. Horror was on them and on all to think that the Hall was a trap laid by the Romish power before their innocent feet. That Thursday night, strong things were spoken there in Port Sonas against Rome, the mother of harlots and the abomination of the whole earth. Well were the godly warned that the time-serving politicians, yea, even their own Member of Parliament, had been duped by the snarling Pope into defending the Vatican against Communism. And what was this Communism? Was it not a rod for the chastisement of sinners? Was it not in the Lord's hand, where, having served its purpose by the destruction of the Romish power, it too would be broken into fragments? Yet, if the politicians and worldly men could be so deceived by the howlings and ravings of the Pope, why not themselves? And let them take heed on this matter of the Village Hall!

So with great and mighty striving did Mr Munro lead in the prayers, and edifying groans came from one part or another of the tabernacle. One after another of the men rose mightily to his feet and was moved to prayer. There was no weakening of the main matter with either psalms or reading from the Book, although the words of the Prophets were at the back of all tongues, those same prophets having in their time had muckle wrestlings with the city of Jerusalem, fully as sinful in her day as even Port Sonas, fully as rat-riddled with backslidings and idolatries of all kinds, although so many of the temptations which are now common, such as the cinema in Halbost, were not known in Jerusalem.

There was praying from a certain one that the wrath of the Lord might be lifted from the community of Osnish. This was an uncle of the wee MacKinnons and they near to death and all that comes after for those that are not adopted to the Lord. And the working of sin is manifest even in young children, as Miss Gillies knew. But it seemed to others that the wrath on Osnish must needs be justified and Fearchar MacKinnon should not be seeking to turn it.

Nor did Mr Munro give much countenance to this. While others were praying away at their own fashion of words, his mind was still on Romish plots and Village Halls and all the other sins that might lead therefrom and had most assuredly led thereto! Sin and ignorance and the wiles of Satan, pressing all about us, against which we should wage continual warfare, strong in the armour of Christian principle. And now a sanctifying leaven was at work on souls. Miss Gillies felt herself strengthened in her work for the Lord. From henceforth, she thought, there shall be no arithmetic period in which the true light shall not be made manifest. Sanntach and the cousins were also visibly strengthened. Standing upright to pray they felt themselves as rocks, firm in the adoption of the Lord, part of God's people. Themselves would be raised up and others would be cast down. Aye, there would be a wailing and gnashing of teeth. Willie the Tank had now stopped muttering, since thon same words were flowing and sailing into his outward ear.

Donnie Cameron stood near his father: he did not want to hear too much: not about sin. He shut in his thought tight, but then it was going back to Glasgow and his betrothed cousin. Once you were married it was not sin any longer. It was sanctified. It could be every night, orderly and without fear of what might be said. What would she be like? Would she laugh yon daft way——? He pulled himself up. Sin. Sin. His back was turned on sin. We are all lost, we are desperately wicked. But we can be saved. He thought of his own wickedness, his deceitful heart, and groaned slightly. His father, hearing, was glad but made no movement. And this offer that is made to me, thought Donnie, this offer of atonement. Christ's blood offered gratis; deal generously with your soul while the low prices last, it will repay you, oh in eternal life! He would turn from wickedness, he would sell his motor bike, he would cease altogether from carnality. Now, now was the time, the appointed time—he groaned again as the leaven worked in him like a terrible great godly dose of castor oil.

But it was Robina on whom grace acted first, Robina who apprehended most sharply her fallen state, who clutched quickest at salvation. Robina with tears streaming down her face, her soul convulsed in spiritual leapings until lo, she reached into the light and knew the blood of Jesus spread as balm on wounds, knew for one moment which yet had in it all eternity, that her will was wholly given up to good, so that sin could no longer touch her. She stayed in that moment of knowledge for a short temporal time. When she looked round again, convicted, sentenced, pardoned and freed, the tears were still wet on her cheeks. She saw her parents, approving, understanding, near to her, aye, sharing her tears, her father's tears noble on his bearded cheeks, sharing her joy, sharing her salvation. She saw Mr Munro transfigured, shining as an angel. Had he not shown her the way? Wonderful now it was, to be free of sin. To be no longer afraid of Satan, since at last you had found the way to master him. And who would want a Village Hall when she had Jesus?

Lachie looked on; he had a sick feeling around his stomach and the back of his throat. Why did folk do this? And feel afterwards the way he himself was feeling ever since. Oh, poor lassie. But Robina's chums were beyond all edified. And a wee thing scared. Robina would be different now. Thinking of different things.

Mrs Campbell whispered to her friend "This is a great sign surely to the Lord's people, that we are to be strong and diligent over this matter of a Village Hall."

"It is, so," said her friend, "for wasn't Robina MacDonald one that might have backslid. And now she is a partaker in the grace of adoption!" They nodded their heads together.

"Amen, amen" said Mrs Campbell "and this will be a rod for the chastisement of Mistress Snow and the godless Established Church that would countenance such blasphemies. There will be no breach in the walls of Zion!"

So also thought the most of the congregation and great was their faith that a sign had been shown. Aye, blood-bought and blood-marked by the Redeemer. Eyes of approbation were on Robina and after the service hand-shakes and murmurs.

She felt herself dazed still; the remembrance of the moment of sinlessness was with her, sustaining her, and yet it was vanishing from her, diving away with the speed of the gannet that drops.

"I had a thought that the spirit was working with you, Donnie" said his father as they walked back to Balnafearchar.

"Aye, so it was" said Donnie, "so it was. But some way it didna come right." And he himself was a sinner yet, a sinner with a motor bike.

CHAPTER XVII

THURSDAY EVENING: AT THE BEE HOUSE

KATE, WITH A PENCILLED list of her original committee, was explaining her difficulties about the Village Hall to Mrs Mitchison. Her father had at last left them, after discussing his collections most of supper time, while Mrs Mitchison sat rather glumly, rolling bread pills and wishing she hadn't come. Kate had finally said: "Now father, we must talk business" and, after waffling round for a bit with a tea pot in each hand, he had finally retired. Kate poured out coffee, put the shortbread within reach and got a bottle of madeira out of the cupboard. Things began to liven up. "How I like madeira and how I hate whisky, and how I always get given whisky!" said Mrs Mitchison. "Now, let's see your list. Councillor Thompson and his friend off. Well, that's all right, isn't it? He seemed pretty damn stupid to me."

"He carried weight."

"Fifteen stone it looked like! But you'll be much better yourself. Norman MacDonald?"

"Wee Free. Such a dear, though."

"These bloody churches. Was that his Minister?"

"Yes, and that little fracas with him unstuck our other Wee Free, Pate Morrison. He was the skipper who talked about foreign trawlers."

"Oh dear, I'm afraid I jumped on him rather. But all fishermen are always putting the blame for bad fishings on to other fishermen, and we do want a little accuracy. Fred Macfie?"

"He just sent me a formal letter, I've no idea why he resigned. Then there's Mrs MacMillan, who's chairman of the W.R.I. She came to see me after your meeting, explained how I was being led astray by 'the wrong people' in the committee, let fall a lot of dark hints, and resigned. It's a pity because she's one of the few people in Port Sonas who can read a book."

"What sort of books?" asked Mrs Mitchison, with all an author's hope that they might be her own.

"Oh, travel—light biography—whatever the County sends in the book-box. I think she's really jealous of some of the others, but of course she can't say right out. Well then, I went to see Bessie MacKeith, who's supposed to be treasurer and she resigned because, she said, folk were bothering her to give her money and she should have been given a wee book."

"She doesn't sound keen. Perhaps you're as well to be rid of her. I see you've a query after Mr MacMillan."

"Yes, I think he's doubtful. He's the Hotel keeper, you know."

"Oh yes, we met him. I suppose he thinks it might spoil his trade. Who's David?"

"He's the schoolmaster, David MacTavish."

"I expect you're sure of him. Our schoolmaster at Carradale's been awfully good with the Village Hall there."

"Well, I'm very fond of David, but I think he's getting worried. People will be at him. He can't stand up to them as he should. Roddy's the forester. He's all right, only he annoys people. He's an incomer, a Sgitheanach."

"I like Skye people. You know, the Forestry Commission might do a bit more over Village Halls. But you're in a bit of a mess. I say, I'm awfully sorry I put my foot in it."

"I don't think the committee would have survived anyhow. It hadn't got enough corporate life to stand up against the pressure from outside. Another cup of coffee?"

"Yes, I'd love one." Mrs Mitchison fished in her bag for a rather dirty lump of sugar. "I always take an odd lump from the House of Commons. No, it's only ink on it. You think committees have a corporate life?"

"Well, any group of people with a common purpose——" But here there was a knock and the door opened. Kate jumped up. "David! Roddy! Oh, do come in. This is Mrs Mitchison from the Highland Panel. We were just talking about the Village Hall."

Roddy looked embarrassed. "Och, we'll not be bothering you now——"

"No, come in, do! David, you know your way to the kitchen, put on the kettle and we'll have some more coffee. Madeira, Roddy? No, come on, doctor's orders!"

He took it with a kind of thankfulness. It would put off for a while the speaking with her that he must have. That he would find so hard. David had talked him into coming round. She might be able to advise him what way to answer the lawyers. But the other thing. What would a lady think? Would she despise him? If she did, well, well—at least he was damned if he would serve on her committee!

David too, coming back from the kitchen, was glad of his drink. It had been a wretched evening and every kind of worry going through him, for if this was proved against Roddy, wrong as it might be, what would be thought? What would be said of his friends and of the committee on which he sat? Yet it might be the lawyers could be bested by someone else from their kind of world, and Kate was the only one. Yet how could they get round to speak of it? Meanwhile the bad moment was put off and, indeed, it was an interest to him, meeting one of the Head Ones.

Over the fresh coffee there was more talk of the Village Hall, Mrs Mitchison asking questions, getting the hang of it, David shaking his head over the new resignations. Then Isa came in: "Mistress Snow, there's a deputation to speak with you. Will I tell them you're busy?"

"Oh, what fun" said Mrs Mitchison, "that's just like home! Do have them in!" But Isa glared at her: the woman should have more sense.

"I expect I'd better see them," said Kate, "what kind of a deputation is it, Isa?"

"Ach, nothing at all! A trooslach of young fellows. Colin and Angus, and that Alasdair, giving me great cheek, all of them!" She tossed her head.

"But what are they a deputation from?"

"They were saying it was the British Legion, but you can't believe a word they say, that crowd. You shouldn't be bothering yourself with them."

"I think I'd better, all the same, Isa. Sometimes the young ones have more sense than the old ones." She got up. "So long as it's not against the Hall!"

As she went out, David said gloomily "That's just what it will be. There's hardly one now that's not against the Hall, the way everything's come on the wrong foot. And indeed, we might do better to think no more of it for a while."

"Don't you think you may have got the wrong people on to the committee for a start, Mr MacTavish?" said Mrs Mitchison.

"It could be" said David. "Aye, there's the list." She had it in her hand. "And some kind of reason for every one of them!"

She looked it through. "Except Fred Macfie."

Roddy, who had finished his glass, laughed suddenly: "You'd not believe it if I told you why he resigned." He looked at her with a kind of challenge.

"You'd be surprised how many things I can believe" said Mrs Mitchison.

"Well, I'll tell you then! He was practising sorceries, on Free Presbyterians, and that's a thing we can't have on a Village Hall committee!"

"Away you go, Roddy!" protested the schoolmaster, "she'll think you're daft."

But Mrs Mitchison was listening with much interest. "On Free Presbyterians, did you say? What a splendid thing! I wish I could do that. Oh goodness, you aren't Free Presbyterians, either of you?"

The schoolmaster shook his head. Roddy laughed. "Me? Nae fears. I'm kind of half a Wee Free, but that's no' much. Can you believe it, then?"

"Easily" said Mrs Mitchison. "Did it work?"

"The buidseach, is it? The way it sounds, it worked well enough." He began to tell about it. David dropped his head into his hands, ashamed and unhappy.

When Kate came back, she was obviously pleased. "Do you know this!" she said. "It was a deputation from the British Legion and all for getting the Hall. I said to them that they should put one of themselves on to the Hall Committee."

"That'll put us up to four!" said David wryly, "just about a quorum."

"We've got to make a new start" said Kate, and then, "I wish I knew why Fred Macfie resigned."

"I'm just after telling Mistress Mitchison" said Roddy. He was excited, a little scared, but some way longing for the next thing to be said. "She believes it right enough. Aye, she does, so, Davie!"

Mrs Mitchison looked up from the pencil she was chewing. "I think it's like this," she said. "Kilmolue must have been the church of Saint Molue—you know, one of the Columban saints, he left his pastoral staff in Lismore. Well then, Kilmolue was taken over by the Free Presbyterians. They probably let the old church go to ruins." David murmured yes, remembering the old walls, falling to nettles and bracken, at the back of Kilmolue school. "I thought as much. You see, they brought it on themselves. And then this chap, Macfie—Mac an-t-Sith could it be? —or is he a son of the Faas, the Pharoah-folk?—well, anyway, he comes from Balana. That's the township of Ana and Ana was the White Goddess, the Goddess of life, the fertility Goddess who was there before Saint Molue even. Her man would be bound to be against Free Presbyterians, the people of death, wouldn't he?"

"I don't know what you're talking about" said Kate flatly.

"I kind of half know" said David, "it is said—but ach, it's just a tale!—that Fred was putting some kind of sorcery onto the schoolmistress and the preacher at Kilmolue."

"How very odd" said Kate, "but why should he resign? A wee spark more in your glass, Roddy? It's doing you good."

"Thank you indeed," said Roddy, holding the glass out. "Well, it was my doing, for I was thinking he could get the Hall committee a bad name. But maybe I was wrong."

"Of course you were wrong, Roddy—why, the whole thing's nonsense. We can't have people resigning over something we can't possibly believe in."

"But he admitted it" said Roddy.

"Grand chap!" said Mrs Mitchison. "What did he do to them?"

"There was talk" said Roddy, picking his words, "of the preacher spraining his ankle and the schoolmistress vomiting pins."

"Gosh, I wonder if he can always pull it off! We could use him on the Highland Panel. Or does it only work on Free Presbyterians? Anyway, wouldn't he be an awfully useful committee member? Couldn't you get him to work it here?"

As she said this a terrible nasty thought and longing went through David and he recognised that he had admitted for a moment—oh for a moment only!—that it could be true, and he had seen the face of Miss Gillies in the back of his wish. "The thing is nonsense, oh it couldn't be more so! But if it is believed at all"—he cast a glance at Mrs Mitchison: *did* she believe it, or could it be she was laughing at them?—"well then, maybe we'd best not have him on the committee."

"No, Davie, we can't let ourselves be bullied," said Kate "and if Roddy spoke to him about this in the first place, then Roddy must ask him to withdraw his resignal."

"He will only do that," said Roddy deliberately, staring at her, "if we ask him for his help. Do we do that?"

"Do you mean he believes in it himself?" Roddy nodded. "I don't see that we can have anything to do with—witchcraft."

"There was the way I thought myself" said Roddy, "but maybe —och, it'll be better if I am resigning too!"

"Don't be silly," said Kate. "What do you think, Mrs Mitchison?"

"Write and say there has been a misunderstanding and you don't accept his resignation. And do—oh do!—find out just how he did it. Just how he thought he did it, anyway. Find out if anything else happens at Balana."

"Angus was saying——" said Roddy, and checked himself. Better she'd not know too much. It was enough and plenty the woman *did* know. She was speaking away still about this White Goddess.

"It's a bit awkward," said Kate, "I wonder if I ought. Suppose it is some kind of witchcraft. After all, I'm a doctor."

"Good doctors use an awful lot of suggestion and so on, don't they? Almost witchcraft. And after all, that crowd are the enemies of your Hall."

"That was what *he* said" Roddy muttered into his glass. "Are you for or are you against."

Kate got to her feet, walked over to the window, stared out at T'each Mor but got nothing from it, came back and leaned against the mantelpiece, kicking in a half-burnt log that was falling away from the fire. David wondered if she had heard anything of the Osnish children; one of them was said to be right bad. And nothing done yet over Snash——

Then Andrew Revie came in, followed by his son. "Ach, you've company, Katie," he said, half crossly, so that everyone else got up to go. Kate settled them all again; there was plenty of coffee. David had signalled Roddy to come away, but now, the way things were going, Roddy wanted to stay, to see it out, to overlay his own pain, yes, he would take just a wee spark more of the drink, it was giving him back his courage. He'd write a sharp letter back to the lawyers, saying he'd not pay for another man's dirty get, aye and tell them whose it might be! That would teach her, a right hoor she was, you'd know it in her laugh and the way she'd walk showing off her behind, so you'd be bound to follow, a right wee hoor. Aye, you'd know it when you caught up with her at the back of a dyke and she'd go soft straight away, where a right lassie would stay hard and proud and quivering like a tree with the axe on her, god, if he could get a right lassie he would treat her a different way, he would do great things for her, oh a lassie that would want him to do great things and not this one wee thing only!

Meanwhile the rest were speaking about the common purpose that holds together a committee or any other body. Mrs Mitchison and Kate were speaking about a book that they had both read but none of the others had, a book called *The Meaning of Treason*, written by an Englishwoman, and both of them were saying that it was a book that could only have been written by an English person or, perhaps more accurately, an utterly Anglified person, since it took for granted that the English point of view was not only morally right, but right in the same way that a sum of arithmetic is right. "She writes as if there was only one kind of loyalty, and there are a dozen!" said Mrs Mitchison. "There's family and class and job, as well as nation—and church."

"Yes, there's church right enough" said David gloomily. Kate was thinking of Mr Stewart. What would *he* say about having Fred back on the committee?

"And then there's political loyalty" Mrs Mitchison went on, screwing up her face as she thought about it. "Have any of you here got political affiliations?"

Nobody spoke. It was a daft, awkward thing for her to say, and kind of like a schoolteacher. You didn't want to speak simply to please someone, but—Tom Revie looked up and grinned. "I voted Labour, Mrs Mitchison, but you'll know for yourself that a Fishery Officer can take no active part in politics, whatever he'd like." She nodded. "But here we've a kind of a job loyalty, we're Government servants. And, forby that, there's the fishing industry itself, and you'll get the fishermen trying to do every kind of thing in the way of getting advantages for themselves. You'll not be able to please everybody. You'll need to try and be just."

"I know," said Mrs Mitchison, "and fishermen are always ready to blame everyone but themselves if something goes wrong! But I've met a fair few fishery officers on this Highland Panel job and they're a great lot of men. Mr Wood is typical; I'd trust him through and through. It's seeing things in terms of service: always trying to help the fishing industry but seeing a bit beyond the immediate fuss that the fishermen happen to·be making. Well, there's your job loyalty: I'd be awfully surprised to find a fishery officer taking a bribe."

Tom laughed, instead of being embarrassed or affronted, the way a pure West Coast man might have been. "Nobody does themselves any good, taking presents, not in the long run. And it would be letting down the Service."

"Aye, that's so," said Roddy suddenly, for he had minded on a certain time, a while back, when he had been offered an obligement in return for some timber. And nobody would have known, the way it might have been worked. And he had not taken it. But if he had that money now—God! Maybe he'd have spent it by now, all the same.

"You see," Mrs Mitchison went on, "a community can't work, I don't care what size it is, village or nation or world, unless people can be reasonably honest."

"Like having clean parts in an engine," said Tom.

"Trusting one another" said Kate.

"Exactly. Well, it's the same with a committee. You've got to have trust, that's the glue that keeps you together. Or maybe the oil that keeps your engine running sweet and smooth."

Tom nodded. "And a common purpose," said Kate.

"Yes; I suppose that's what loyalty is—the two things together; and, some way, because of one another. Now, I'd trust you, Mrs Snow, because we've got a common purpose——"

"Have we?" said Kate, smiling a little.

"Oh yes! The welfare of rural communities and all that. Besides, women are mostly honest with one another."

"You'd not think that from the movies!" said Tom.

"Oh, the movies. To hell with the bloody movies. Of course if Mrs Snow and I were both after Clark Gable——! But we aren't. We'd trust one another. I wonder why."

"I was a doctor," said Kate, "the Hippocratic oath and all that."

"Of course! But what about the others? Mr MacTavish, you're a schoolmaster, aren't you? Well that's another kind of person with a common purpose for good—*l'union des clercs*, loyalty to truth, I suppose—at least he ought to have. He does if it isn't all eaten up with—oh, I don't know, what do you call your occupational disease, Mr MacTavish?"

"Complacency?" suggested David and blushed a little.

"Yes! Not getting contradicted." Mrs Mitchison nibbled her pencil: it looked suddenly as if she had started thinking off on her own, away from the rest of them, perhaps about schoolmasters who had not had much loyalty to truth or any other purpose common with her own.

Kate went after her. "Roddy here is the forester. He's loyal to the Forestry Commission—which doesn't always deserve it." She thought suddenly how wrong it was to let the District Officer hurt that loyalty.

"Too right it doesn't! But I know, I've got forestry friends. They've got to see a certain distance ahead too, and not for their own gain. And I rather think they're apt to have a feeling for natural beauty. That might come into it too." She trailed off again on her own thoughts, then jerked herself back: "What had the rest of your committee in the way of loyalties?"

"They were mostly out for themselves," said Kate slowly. David nodded. "Except for those that had a counter-loyalty which was stronger. The Wee Frees. They'd have called it a common good. A higher good, too."

"After all, that's just like a national traitor who has a different cause. Joyce and Amery. Or Allen May and little Fuchs."

"I suppose so. They wouldn't admit it was betrayal."

"Of course not. Nor would John Knox have admitted that he was trying to betray Scotland to the Protestant English. Nor does a good Presbyterian admit it about him today! I think, though, that one has some kind of sympathy with anyone who has a common cause. Even if it's a Church with all it's horrible narrowness. Even John Knox."

Andrew Revie, who had been busy trying to get his pipe to draw, suddenly lifted his head and asked: "And if it was thae Communists?"

"Certainly," said Mrs Mitchison, "though perhaps they're an extreme case. Them and the Catholics. But one could trust a good Communist or a good Catholic on anything not to do with their particular vision of ends."

"Wouldn't everything be part of it, though?" asked Kate.

"That's the snag, of course. But I'd sooner them than the person who just doesn't care. Who doesn't have a vision. That lot—they're just raw material."

"For what?"

"Oh—Dr Buchman. Something mucky. I don't know. I'm afraid I've talked the hell of a lot. Look, who else could you trust on your committee? Who's got any kind of decent loyalty?"

"Well," said David, "the fishermen have that in a way—to one another."

"And why it's strong" said Tom Revie, "is because of the danger. They'd need to be loyal. They'd need to be able to trust one another. Not over a wee thing of buying and selling, mind you, but with the storm broken on you and the engine stalled. Even a modern boat might have a breakdown. I've known it."

"Aye," said his father, "and me. But it was maybe a stronger hold when the fishermen were dead poor, most o' them, and kinna apart from the rest. D'you no' think, Katie?"

Kate nodded: "But why, now, would I trust you and Tom? —apart from the blood relation, that doesn't just always work out that way!"

"Ah'm f'ae th' ither coast" said Andrew, with a sudden accenting of his speech.

"Nonsense, Andy" said Kate, "that's nothing to do with it But I've an idea you've dealt honestly most of your days—except maybe with the lasses once in a while!" Andy chuckled. "It's come to be a habit. And you're gey kindly."

"There was my undoing wi' the lasses!" said Andrew.

She considered him. "I've known you thrawn as an old cow. That I have, Andy! But you've the experience that honesty and decency are the only way for folk living together, in the long run. It's in the family by this time; none of us would care to let the rest down. But that about the East coast—ach! You know yourself there's full as many crooks in Aberdeen as in the whole of the west and they'll not do it with the same grace!"

Mrs Mitchison laughed: "I'm from the east myself, though I'm living among the western crooks. Did you read Alastair Alpin MacGregor's book?"

"A terrible book that!" said David, "a wicked book."

"But kind of half true, don't you think? Isn't the point that there are as many unsocial types in the Highlands as anywhere else, not more, but they shock us for two reasons. First because a good many of them are such charmers and they aren't ashamed of being dishonest, in fact they make it into a lovely story and are proud of it—so it might even have some social value—and second because there's been all this ballyhoo about the Highland way of life and not betraying Prince Charlie and we think it's there still. But the Highland way of life hasn't stood against the money values of today, rotten as they are."

"Wasn't I saying just that" said the schoolmaster, "after the committee meeting! But Mr MacGregor was as bad as the rest, saying what he did and after the kindness that he will surely have had."

"Oh, granted. If I was writing a book about the Highlands, I'd try and make people mixed, the way they are. My own crowd at Carradale were dirty enough, when they put me out of the County Council in May. But I see why they did it."

"Why did they, then?"

"Oh, by and large, I was a witch, a stranger. I did things out of pattern. I upset people. I wore the wrong kind of hat. Let's not talk about it."

"Yes," said Kate, "one's got to go slow about changing the pattern. Even when one's got something new and good to give. Like a Village Hall. I was thinking, Andy, if we're to go on with it, you'd better come on the committee."

"Take you May," said Andrew, "she'd like it fine and she's a good wee streak o' the East in her, the lassie. For a' you say, Kate! She and Florag was speaking of concerts and that. Florag would be a better treasurer than her mother. She'd two years at Fort William."

"In the Grammar School? Yes, I suppose education is another thing that makes for loyalty. You'll learn to see a bittie beyond yourself, into history."

"Sometimes!" said Tom. "But I've known some gey bad ones that were educated, Aunt Kate, and so have you. They'd need the thought of service to bring out the good in the education." David murmured agreement.

"Well," said Kate, "there's one thing I must tell you; the

deputation from the Legion was asking could they have a representative on the committee, so I told them they'd better choose one of themselves, and there and then they chose Angus. How will he be for loyalty and that?"

"He's a decent lad," said Roddy, "and his army record good enough. Wasn't there some kind of a medal he had?"

"That's just fine then. I think we'll need to co-opt at our next meeting. I'll call it for Saturday, at the school, David."

"You're sure you're going on?" David looked worried. "Well, maybe it's the right thing. But would we be in order to co-opt?"

"I'm just not sure," said Kate, "but as we've no constitution written, I can't see how we wouldn't do it."

Mrs Mitchison laughed. "You've been bitten by the west coast bug yourself, Mrs Snow! But God, so have I. It's the only way to survive. Look, tell me before I go, what about the White Goddess man? Where's his common loyalty? Are you getting him back?"

"I suppose he wants what you call a change of pattern, and he seems to want the same change as we do. Though he goes a funny way to get it. I'll write to him tonight. You know, the queer thing is, he's almost the only one of the Village Hall committee that's not in some other kind of organisation as well. The place is full of them and all pulling away at the folk that are in them."

"Well," said Mrs Mitchison, "even if they seem a bit daft, they're the hell of a lot better than communities where people don't belong to things. It's those kind of—of *dry* places with no social glue—where people get swept off their feet by silly newspaper cruelties and panics and that. I bet people here don't believe what they read in the papers."

Andrew chuckled. "They'd not believe if it was the Angel Gabriel telling them wi' the feathers sprooting oot his rump! Aye, aye, an unbelieving generation. And maybe the better o't. But they'll be gey and sure about their ain wee crowd."

Mrs Mitchison got up. "I must go back to my crowd now— we usually talk over our meetings in the evening. Thanks a lot, Mrs Snow. If I can do anything to give your Village Hall a hand, I'll do it."

All shook hands and said goodbye, then settled back to talk

her over. "These women" said Andrew, and shook his head, knocking his pipe out against the fender, "near saying she'd favour the Communists!"

"She didn't, Andy" said Kate. Or had she?

"She was usin' words she shouldna ha' used, onyway!" he answered.

But all the same, thought Roddy, she gave the Minister a right doing. It'll show him up for the whited double-speaking hypocrite he is—if there's any that doesn't know it. And he'd get to know, the Minister would—if this letter came to be spoken of—and everything coming to be spoken of in time! How could you speak of freedom in a village, and everything known and the Ministers ready to pounce and get you down! Good and well if you were Andrew Revie's age and all your sins past and nothing to worry you. You could snap your fingers at the Ministers or anyone at all. Once you'd lived it, your life was your own. And suddenly Roddy found himself wishing, wishing desperate, that he was old and respected, with all this over.

Now David was speaking to Kate about the boarded-out children, and he was wondering, should he write to anyone and if so who would it be and how would he make sure his own name would be kept out of it? "I wrote," said Kate, "it's a matter for the boarding-out authority. If the Children's Officer is any use, Snash will never have any more boarded with him."

"And that'll be difficult too," said David, "for he'll never make a living out of the croft alone, for it's nothing much, and he has Peigi and the rest of the wee ones."

"He could make as much, taking in tourists, if he'd do out the room the Glasgow kiddies have—if they *do* have it—and his wife would bestir herself to work."

"But there's no water."

"And wee Greta was carrying it in the pails! Och, David, does Snash deserve that much pitying? It's a bad look-out for crofting when they need to make their money this way."

"I wonder will he think it was me spoke of it" said David.

"Anyone who likes can tell him it was me," said Kate, "he wouldn't vote for me anyway if there was anything in the shape of a man standing, even if it was straight out the gaol!"

Just then Mr MacFarlan came in and looked with disapprobation at his late wife's nephew. "I thought you said you were talking business, Kate" he remarked. "And Isa has let my fire go out."

Andrew got up: "Aye, aye, we were speaking of the Village Hall. Either myself or May's to be on the committee. But I'll need to be going."

"You should have let me know, Kate," said Mr MacFarlan. "I would have been glad to join you in a cup of coffee. Which I see is now cold. The next time perhaps, you will be more thoughtful."

Kate looked away, stopping herself from answering. David gave her a glance of warm sympathy. But it was Tom who said "We were just speaking of your collections, Mr MacFarlan. Have you found anything new?"

Mr MacFarlan glanced at him suspiciously. So few of his wife's relations took any genuine interest—"As it turns out, I have made some interesting additions. Most interesting. To those who appreciate such things. My daughter, unfortunately, finds herself too occupied. The District Council takes first place in her affections."

"Perhaps you'd show me, sir," said Tom and steered him out of the room.

"So the District Council has first place in your affections, Katie!" said Andrew, "is it Sir Ian that's after you? Och, the dirty old devil!"

"You know what my father's like, Andy," said Kate, "that was sweet of Tom."

"Aye, he's a decent kinna boy. He'd not see anyone stuck. Well, I'm for home, Katie, and he can come when he's clear. But I'm needing to think of some other way to deal with yon villain, Archie, and him getting off so licht with the Highland Panel!"

She saw him to the door. And now, thought Roddy, now, oh, it is not to be faced. He got half up. David got him by the arm. "Misneach" he whispered, "misneach, a bhalaich," and then to Kate. "We've a thing we are needing to consult you on, Mistress Snow." She knew by the formal address that it was something serious, and stilled herself to listen. Did the other woman, this Mrs Mitchison, find herself having to look after people, listen to them, think out ways for them? Perhaps. David was saying "My friend, Roddy here, has had a letter, a lawyer's letter, and we are wanting to consult you on the way it should be answered. But I must tell you, before you read it, that it is not true. Not true at all." He held it out to her. She wondered if it could be from the District Officer, then saw the heading from the firm of Halbost solicitors. Reading it gave her an odd kind of physical shock; she felt her heart-beat quickening, and a slight tremor coming to her hands, which she controlled. It was as thought she had suddenly seen Roddy stripped: stripped and handsome.

She looked up. Roddy was frozen. They were both frozen. They were afraid of what she was going to say. How often she'd seen this in the consulting room. She found herself putting on the consulting room manner, buttoning an invisible white coat, drawing invisible rubber gloves on to her wrists, isolating herself sufficiently to give reassurance. "You say this is not true?" she said. David nodded. Roddy seemed unable even to do this. "There must, however, have been some reason which made her give your name to the solicitors." Which girl was it, she wondered, this Christina, oh, now she had it, Kenny's Chrissie! Well, well. Roddy was not answering. "We must get the facts, you know" she said.

"Speak then, speak, a charaid!" said David.

"She was after my savings," said Roddy, low, scraping the heel of his shoe along the floor. "She knew I had money saved."

"I see," said Kate, "that could be her reason. But I suppose you had something to do with her?" He nodded. "Well, you'd better tell me just what happened. No, sit down, Roddy. Tell me in your own words." No answer. It might have been at the surgery, in old days . . . how long have you had this pain . . . ? "Well, Roddy, what did you do? Did you—did you ever go to bed with her?"

"I have never been to bed with a lassie in my life," said Roddy, truthfully and puzzled. The nearest had been yon lassie in the lodgings he'd been in when he was ganger and she'd come in when he was smoking in bed and started off by giving him the edge of her tongue and then he'd got her talked round. . . .

Kate crossed one foot over the other. "Well, what did you do?"

"But I'm after telling you, Mistress Snow. I didn't do it at all!"

"There must have been something."

He looked down. Now he saw right what she meant. But how could one be speaking of it? To another woman. But there she was waiting. And she could get angry and then, no help. Maybe if he let on to himself that he was not speaking to her at all. Only to himself. "We were up against a tree—odd times. But—but she never had her skirt up. Not for me."

"So it couldn't have been you."

"No. No it couldn't. There was one time she might have been going a bit further. But some boys came along."

"Have you any notion of who she might have gone further with?"

"I was hearing she—och, Mistress Snow, how can I be speaking of it to you—you a lady?"

"Never mind," said Kate, "doctors hear plenty worse things. Doubtless she'll have lifted her skirt for someone."

"Aye. And she hadn't always what she should on under. It might have been Jim. Though you canna believe him, what he says. Or one or two of the Glen boys. There was young Lachie."

"He's a Free Presbyterian, isn't he?"

"Ach, she didn't stick to the one church! And the Free Presbyterians are the same made as ourselves." He seemed to sense a kind of silence from Kate. "Ach, have I said what I shouldna?"

"Not at all, Roddy, it's all right. I'm just thinking what to do."

"And then—there's Donnie. He's in that same church."

"Donnie Cameron? I didn't think he was seen much with the girls."

"You're right enough there. He's not seen. Not the way I've been seen myself and many another from Robbie Burns down! But if he can get one of them away on his bike——"

David suddenly said: "I know for a fact that she was out with Donnie Cameron on the back of his bike before he was away to Glasgow. My sister was telling me."

"Then that's who it'll be!" said Roddy. "For he'd not let her away with less than she'd got if once he'd to get her well up one of the croft roads, maybe. Aye, that's his game right enough. And the Balnafearchar crowd so holy and so against the Hall!"

Kate and David looked at one another across him, a quick glance and then shame. For if the holy ones could be dis-comfited—— But it was wrong, wrong. It was no honest thought, that. This was another thing altogether they should be thinking on. "He's a red-head, Donnie" said Kate, half to herself, looking at Roddy's black Highland looks, dark eyes, fine bones. "You should say that you would be willing to submit to a blood test." Not that there was any correlation between hair colour and blood groups. But it might do for a beginning. He looked blank. "We'll write a letter." She went over to the desk. Poor little Chrissie, wanting to do her best for the child she's going to bear. And we are thwarting her. Her lawyers will tell her that a blood test has been suggested. I think that will frighten her off. "Anyhow, Roddy, it looks to me as if this was a try-on by her lawyers. If you don't accept, there's a Court case, and if she is known to have gone with others, it won't be proved against you. See?"

"But I'd have my name in Court——"

"So, it appears, would a number of respectable citizens of Port Sonas. Don't get into a panic. That's what the lawyers are counting on. They want to frighten you. It's no use trying to keep it dark. People will talk anyway."

"If my District Officer gets to know——"

"You've denied it, haven't you? That's good enough for him. Oh Roddy, you silly gowk, behave as if you're innocent. More especially if you are!" She poured him out another glass. The state he was in hadn't let the alcohol take its full effect. He gulped on it. She began to write. The other two watched her. There was a framed photograph on the desk; it must be her man, thought Roddy, he looks—different from ourselves. She scratched out a line, put in another. It was like writing a prescription. She almost said, take this to the chemist.

"Didn't I tell you she was the boy for this" murmured David to his friend.

"There" she said, "now you write this out tonight and send it back to the lawyers. Keep the copy, but don't let it lie about."

"Nae fears," said Roddy, folding it and putting it into his pocket book, "and—and I must thank you—I never thought— och, if you knew the easy I feel about it now!" They backed out, David too, full of gratitude for her cleverness. It was dark now, all colour gone from the golden azaleas, only a thick pale sweetness brushing against them. And great to see the stars above them, now that a man could lift his head again!

Kate collected the coffee cups on to the tray, tipping the cigarette ends and ashes—why will they never use ash-trays?— into the fire. Better write to Fred now. But what was his loyalty?

This White Goddess idea, was there anything in it? If so it meant he was loyal to an older church, an older pattern than the present and maybe more like the future, the same way grandmother and grand-daughter can be friends sometimes, across an unsympathetic generation. But that must be all nonsense, mustn't it? This odd woman, Mrs Mitchison, sitting and talking and biting her nails, not what you'd expect from a Government committee. Perhaps she'd get one of her books out of the County Library.

She held the decanter up. Yes, they'd pretty well got through it. Just as well perhaps, or Roddy mightn't have spoken. Queer, how good it made you feel, to be asked to help, and to have the knowledge to do it. Exercise of power? No, hardly. But the same thing that made you a doctor.

And after the White Goddess? Well, then it was the church. Up to a short time ago, Scots people had an overriding fierce loyalty to their church. To the presbyterian, revolutionary church of John Knox. Binding because it was revolutionary. Because it had seemed to free them—yes, *had* freed them—from one thing. But only to thirl them to another. And now, in the last few years, the loyalty had broken down. Through the fault of the church. That was no longer revolutionary, but static. Did that always happen? She gave a quick, scary, mind-glance at Russia, was it happening there? She didn't know.

But, once this loyalty is destroyed, people are left in a bad moral position. Why bother to be decent if you have no loyalty? She sat down and pulled the writing pad towards her, unscrewed her fountain pen. She looked up, met the eyes of the photograph, nodded and smiled to it. "Dear Mr Macfie" she wrote: "I received your letter today. But——"

Someone was knocking, who on earth could it be? "Come in" she said, turning her head. "Why, Angus!"

He edged his way in and stood on one foot. "I was waiting till the others would be gone, Mistress Snow," he said.

"Waiting outside?"

"It was the great smell altogether coming off yon yellow bushes," he said.

"Well, well, and what did you want to see me about?" He didn't answer. He has the poise of someone who should be wearing a kilt, she thought. "Can I help you at all?" she went on.

Suddenly he said: "It is with me coming on to the Hall Committee."

"I hope you aren't thinking of resigning!" said Kate.

"Och no! No. It is—it is about the lobsters."

"The lobsters?" said Kate, "the lobsters, did you say? Don't tell me the lobsters are sending a representative too!" He looked away and his foot tapped. This ill-timed frivolity, thought Kate, oh dear, oh dear, one ought never to make the wee-est joke without ringing a bell first! "Yes, Angus, I'm listening. The lobsters?"

"It was a few young fellows," said Angus and he was staring at the wall over her head as though he were trying to make a hole in it. "And there was a bet on. Whether would it be dared. And there was one older man was with us. And it will not be repeated. Indeed it was not meant at all—that way they took it."

"I see," said Kate, "it was just devilment." He made a gulping noise of assent and stood silent. You could sum up the Highland way of life, she thought, if you were unkind, in four words: devilment, obligement, refreshment, buggerment.

"And I could not come on to the Hall Committee" said Angus, "with that not said." He looked at her now, a look difficult to read.

"You've made a lot of trouble for a lot of people, Angus," she said, "and a loss to poor Matta and his brothers."

"I was thinking," said Angus, "that I could maybe write Matta an anonymous letter and put in the money"—she saw he had something crumpled in his hand, two or three pound notes it looked like.

"Yes, you could do that," she said.

"But how would I write an anonymous letter? It's kind of difficult to know how to begin. I was thinking maybe you could help me, Mistress Snow."

For a moment Kate couldn't think what to answer. Asking her how to write anonymous letters! But it was with a good intention and indeed the practical way of doing the thing.

"You don't need to write a letter" she said, "just print in capitals 'For the lobsters.' Perhaps you should say 'sorry.'"

"Indeed I could say just that!" said Angus, "in the big letters. And on plain paper."

Silently Kate handed him a sheet of paper and a cheap envelope. "You can't very well register it," she said, "and you'd better not leave it at his house."

"Och, it'll do fine in the post box" he said, "it'll not vanish between there and Matta! We're mostly honest folk in Port Sonas."

"Yes, yes, quite," said Kate breathlessly. "We're holding our next committee meeting on Saturday first in the school room." They shook hands and she let him out, managing not to start laughing till the door was shut. "Poor Andrew!" she said aloud, "oh poor Andie! It wasn't Archie after all!" and stuffed her hanky in her mouth in case her father might be still about. Then, still bubbling with occasional laughter, sat down again to finish her letter to Fred Macfie.

CHAPTER XVIII

FRIDAY MORNING: GRAZING COMMITTEE

Norman was long on his knees that morning, but what kind of petition he was putting up was not known to his elderly sister, as she went about the house, blowing up the fire for the morning kettle and sweeping away odd tags and ends of wool from below the loom. It might be, she thought, over this godless Hall, or it might be over the Grazing Committee. She took a couple of pails and went to the spring at the back. It was a clear morning and the early potatoes beginning to show well; his Arran Pilots were as far on as anyone's, praise be! So long as the maincrops did no worse. She came back to the house slowly, with the full pails, but he was still on his knees. Well, well, he was a holy man, her brother. There were old potatoes in by the press; she sat down and began to peel them, as she had done morning after morning for as far back as she could mind, and put the peelings into a pot for the hens. The whole room was faintly full of the sting and scent of the peat smoke; going out was always soft on the eyes and coming back you would rub them a moment before you were used with it. The great loom blocked half the light, but you did not need to use much for the potato peeling. It would have been different altogether had you had occasion to read.

When Norman read the morning's chapter aloud, he sat in the hard chair by the window, having laid the well-budded musk pot gently on to the floor. She had the tea infused and as he closed the Book she set the cup sugared beside him. "Will you be working at the loom?" she asked. They were speaking in the Gaelic, as always to one another.

"Later" he said, "later, Mhairead. There is the Grazing Committee."

"We need not trouble ourselves," she said, "we are not over-stocked."

He supped his tea with a piece of her scone, buttered with their own butter. "You will be remembering Snash and the Glasgow children," he said.

"I am, Tormod."

"It is borne in upon me that I must speak over this to the gentlemen from the Department."

"Snash is our neighbour, Tormod."

"The children also are our neighbours whom we must love, and they are without help unless the Lord help them through his servants."

"It could be that Snash will mend his ways."

"It could be, Mhairead. But I was wrestling long in prayer over this matter and it is on me now that there is only the one way."

"I understand, Tormod" she said, "and may the blessing be with you." She laid her hand for a moment over the roll of tweed, its end still on the loom, waiting for the weaver's hand. "It is a beautiful piece, this" she said, "there is a warmth in it."

"It is all in the first setting up," he said, "It is in the deep red it is." He stood beside her for a moment. "There was this deep red in the piece I was weaving in the winter of the hard frost. Have you mind of that piece, Mhairead? It seemed to be putting warmth into the room."

Janet, cleaning out the hen house, watched her father walking away off the croft towards the meeting of the Grazing Committee. She knew they were slightly overstocked, but not so badly as some. If only someone would speak about Snash! But they would be so busy bringing up their grievances to the gentleman from the Department, that they would have no thought for the children. And besides—well, if only Norman would not be speaking against the Hall! For the rest followed him, and her father was uneasy, for all there'd been letters from both the boys, in answer to her own of the week-end, saying it was a great thing that there was to be a Village Hall at Port Sonas. If only she could have been doing more, herself, to help Katie over the Hall. Katie who was always doing so much, who was thinking and working for others and never for herself! Katie who might get tired of the stupidity and ingratitude of Port Sonas—and who would blame her—and go away back to the south, to be a right doctor again. And desolate would that day be for Janet, oh cold the year without her friend! If there could anyway be an anchor found for Katie.

One of the hens was laying out, most likely in the scrub oak and old ferns beyond the field. But the chances were she was clocking and then in a while she would come back with a dozen wee ones, so nice they were, the bonny wee chicks, and stronger, some way, than the ones you'd set yourself and fussed over. And terrible pleasing for the hen, poor soul, to be doing it all for herself! Janet wheeled the barrow with the hen's dirt down to the wee garden she had made in the lee of the house. She would dig it in where the broad beans were to go. There was a seed-bed ready under the wall for her lettuces. Her father thought nothing of them, but they were great for the boys' tea when they came home. She had packets of annuals too and the chrysanthemum cuttings from the Bee House. How glad she'd be to show the garden to Katie when it was all to rights!

She'd need to clean the early potato drills before she'd start on the garden, all the same. Where had she put the hoe now? But first to set the table for her father's dinner when he got back. There was a stew in the pot: it would do. She'd not need to do out the earth closet today, that was one thing. It was her worst job and every other woman would say the same. If once they could get the water in! But none of the men would bother terrible much about that, unless it would be young Hamish MacRae. There were certain things always left to the women. But if they had the water, then maybe they'd need to take in the summer visitors and that wasn't always so good. Turning your home upside down for a woman from the town and then maybe not to be pleasing her at the end of it!

She laid hands on the hoe and went out to the potato drills. After half an hour or so, she heard her own name cried from the road, looked up and saw young Mrs MacRae. She laid the hoe down, glad of the break, and crossed the brairding oat field to the edge of the road. "What is it?" she asked quickly, for Mrs MacRae was troubled looking.

"Do you know what Angus is after telling me when he passed?" said Mrs MacRae. "It is about the wee MacKinnons at Osnish. The little lassie is dead of the measles and they say her wee brother will not be long following her. Och, isn't it terrible, Janet?"

"Terrible indeed" said Janet. For a moment she stood there, her eyes swimming, thinking of her cousins. Then anger came to her help: "and all for a pure stupidity of their mother, letting them come to the treat!"

"And how many others will catch the thing!"

"Aye, how many! And they were living and happy this day last week. And it was not even as though the treat had been a pleasure to them, the way they were. Och, poor woman, poor woman. She will be repenting sore on this."

"To have borne the wee ones and then—can it be the Lord's will, Janet? It makes you feared to have a bairn, even."

"It is said that everything is the Lord's will." She jabbed her hoe two or three times into the earth. "I can scarcely believe it. I think that is the kind of thought the men have made to punish the women with. To save themselves from taking trouble!" The two young women stood there, staring at one another. Mrs MacRae nodded suddenly and went back to her croft. Janet walked slowly up towards the potatoes again. Katie would be angry at this. If only Katie was more thought of, more able to get folk, for their own good, to do the right thing. And suddenly it became apparent to her how this was to be done. And once Katie was at the Castle, things would fall into their right pattern and she would be well and truly anchored to Port Sonas, aye, and it was the thing she wanted—surely—— If she, Janet, could once have the courage to act! To give courage to others. For that only was needed. And then, by marriage with a good woman, the Laird would be cured of his wee failing. For it was always so. Had she not read that in the wee books in her auntie's shop? A good woman is all that is needed, and surely Katie was that!

The committee had walked across the common grazing of the Glen and were now standing on the turf dyke. Underfoot there was continuous stirring of leaf and flower, heather and milkwort and sedge, thin fern and blaeberry tufts, young spikes of orchis and asphodel, peat-lovers elbowing out the decent grass and leaving only the deer-grass, bright green but tougher and almost less edible than rushes. The wiry stems of bog myrtle sprang again after the boots had passed. The sphagnum moss, pressed down and oozing, rose again. The gentleman from the Department, whose name was Edward Drummond, observed the state of the grazing, spoke about drainage, took notes and watched the committee.

He had been over at Larach in the early morning, discussing the matter of the road; he had noticed how the land was going out of cultivation and wondered whether there would be anyone at all living there by the time the road was finished. That road, however, was a departmental decision already arrived at. In his view the piped water supply at Osnish should take priority. Coming back through Osnish he had seen the little black crowd, heard weeping, spoken to the doctor. But road and water supply had gone through the In and Out trays in St Andrew's House, at the appropriate pace. It would quicken things, he thought, if the County Council would give a shove. But they, doubtless, were after showier game.

Alan was turning over in his head this matter of drainage and who was to pay. He asked a quesion or two, considered, whispered to his neighbour. Edward Drummond had recently been transferred from an Inverness district. The day before he had spoken about this transfer to a friend of his in the Glasgow Corporation Offices. This friend had recognised the name of the place and had told him of a letter which had just been received about the ill-treatment of boarded-out children. Now Edward Drummond, looking round at the faces of the crofters, anyone of which could have gone into an official Highland propaganda film, wondered which was the one. In his old district he had seen good treatment and bad; he was not prepared to be surprised at anything.

It had not been altogether easy to get a count of the sheep. How many of them, he wondered, are overstocked. The grazing was not in very good condition considering the mild weather and the time of year. Draining, of course, would help, but highly unlikely that they would all agree to it and one or two could hold up the rest—not legally, but just that nobody would want to do anything against the others. Re-seeding was the answer, but what a hope! There'd need to be a change of heart worse than John Knox before you'd get that on a common grazing. Most of the calves were sturdy enough, but little growth on the yearlings, compared with what it might have been. No doubt they'd qualify for subsidy, but—— Had they any notion, now, of a different breed of bull for next year?

There was much talk and some reminiscences of the Oban or Fort William sales: pleasing memories of good prices and the glass that had sealed the bargain: male laughter discreetly suppressed. And what would the gentleman from the Department be writing down in his wee book, now? Hamish MacRae began asking about a septic tank. It seemed he was thinking to pipe the water in himself, but this other thing was beyond him. It was with him having a young wife. Snash muttered something half aloud about the women and their ways. His neighbour tittered into his beard. Edward Drummond suggested that they should take a walk across, towards T'each Mor. It was all very well to be slightly overstocked, but if the rest of the grazing was no better than this—— Yes, they had good boots and clothes and maybe a wireless set in the house and a couple of decent chairs, and tins of pilchards and plums and condensed milk for the winter, but there were times he wished the hill-sheep subsidy could be taken off. That would mean a row, though; the big hill-sheep men would get questions asked in Parliament. He stuck his stick into a black patch, wondering how deep the peat went. The committee were stringing out now. He wondered if some of them intended to do a little sheep driving.

Now he was walking with two or three. And now with one. An oldish man, clearing his throat for a remark. About sheep? No. No indeed. "I do not like to be speaking evil of my neighbours, sir" began Norman, "but it is the children." Edward Drummond listened. At the end he passed his tobacco pouch over to Norman for a fill and noticed that the old man's hands were trembling.

"You are perfectly right to tell me" he said, and then: "Rest assured, something will be done." And if he thinks that Glasgow's retribution is really the long hand of the Department of Agriculture, well then, he will be all the more impressed. Even if he finds out later that it was Glasgow—and who would have written about it?—the first impression, of an all-powerful Government, would still remain. Loyalty to St Andrew's House glowed softly. This would be a good beginning in his new district.

This was a fine old boy, too: Norman MacDonald, wasn't he? He offered his lighter and both puffed away. Here was a ridge of bracken. Better ground, no doubt, if you could once get the bracken out of it. They walked across to the next point. He would have to consider what was to be done about the overstocking. And so the morning wore on.

Janet came hurrying back from her errand and jumped off her bicycle at the path up to the croft, hoping that her father would not be back yet from the Grazing Committee. He was there at the door, however, and in a good mood. He had even taken the stew out of the oven on to the table and put on the kettle for their tea.

"You'll be glad of this well enough" he said, "though Dhia knows how will it work out. But Norman was speaking to the gentleman from the Department over Snash and the wee ones. And it is said that there will be action taken."

"Oh," said Janet, "isn't that great now, father! For indeed it made me ashamed every time I was passing them. Oh, I had hoped it would be said!"

"Well, well" said her father, "you have your wish. And were you writing to the boys?" He pointed the stump of his pipe at the ink-bottle and pad of paper.

"I was writing" she said shortly, and cut the loaf, held against her for firmness, and busied herself getting out the butter and sugar from the press.

CHAPTER XIX

FRIDAY EVENING: BIBLE STUDY CLASS

Florag, Christine and Minnie were walking over together to the Bible Study Class at the Manse, three bonny, sonsy girls of them, and nobody to tell by the clothes they had on that they weren't summer visitors and all. Florag suited the red and it was a red suit she had on; the other two had the long coats over flowered dresses. They were speaking about the concert there was to be for the Village Hall: "There'll be some against it," said Christine.

"Do you know this?" said Florag, "there'll be more against it than for it at Port Sonas, the way things have gone this last week. But who's to say how they'll be in a year's time when they're used to it?"

"Maybe your auntie will go back on," said Minnie.

"Och, what's about her! She should never have been put. They've not the same interest, the old ones. But why at all did Mrs MacLean go off, Minnie?"

"She was kind of cross," said Minnie equably, "you know the way she is. She doesna like me to be singing with yourself, Florag, the way she's all for the Rural and thinking we should be against the Choir! Ach, they're daft, the old ones."

"I mind the carry-on my folk would be at about your own, over the boarding houses, och, a wild carry-on altogether, and us not speaking to one another at the school—d'you mind of that, Minnie?—but now there's any amount of visitors for the two of us, so there's peace made."

"And thanks be for that, or where would our duet be? I think we should try for the Mod, Florag. Would you not write for the papers?"

"Aye," said Christine, "do that, Florag! It would be great. Do you think our folk would be raising any objections?"

"What's about it?" said Florag, "it's easy enough getting jobs in the towns if they try to be nasty on us. I was asking about it at Halbost and you'd get a job at £5 easy. Keep you that in mind and you'll not have to do one thing the old ones say to you."

"Aye, but—you'd not want to go against your folks," said Christine.

"That's right enough," said Florag, "but if once they'd to get it in their heads that you could get free of them if you wanted, then they'll not dare go against you. So mind you of that, lasses, when it comes to the Hall!"

"Would you say," said Christine, "that this Hall is—is someway important—like, maybe—och, I don't know—like things seemed like in the War?"

"Just the same," said Florag, "for it's meant for the good of every one of us, the way they said the War was."

"If once folk would see it yon way!" said Minnie, and began to hum their duet, Una Chil Bhan under her breath.

Jean from Molachy caught them up on her bicycle, jumped off and wheeled it beside them. "I thought I'd be bound to miss the Class," she said, "the men came late back. It's aye the same wi' the spring work. Never through and fit to eat the lug off the teapot when they come in."

"D'you like the class, Jean?" said Florag.

"Och aye, I like thinking about yon old times and the folk some way like oursel's, making a living and whiles getting into a terrible snarl, the same we could do. Poor Jepthah, the man! but he shouldna have made yon kind of promise."

"You'll see things as bad in the Sunday papers," said Florag.

"Och, one canna believe all one sees. But I'd be gey spited to miss the class. Mr Fergusson is terrible good, having it. There's plenty Ministers wouldna bother."

"It'll be Mistress Fergusson the day," said Minnie, "for Mr Fergusson was called away the morn early; his mother was taken ill."

"Och, och, the man! Poor Mistress Fergusson will be in a taking. We'll need to gae easy and no' be asking her ower hard questions. And here, I'd one marked."

There were most of the others waiting for them at the Manse gate, Tina and Charlie, Isa, Ella and the Kettle, who gave the appearance of surprise at seeing Minnie. You'd say she was the last person he was wanting to see. However it so turned out that he was sitting next her at the Class, and here, he had forgotten his Bible, so he was needing to look over hers.

Mrs Fergusson was in a twitter. She was not keen to be taking the Class at the best of times, and her husband had gone off in a tearing hurry when he got the wire. And if that wasn't enough, Mrs MacLean of the Rural had come early to explain just why she had resigned from the Village Hall committee and just what wrong hands it was getting into—would not Mr Fergusson, who might have some influence, speak about it to Mrs Snow? So when Mrs Fergusson met the rest of the Class she felt herself anything but well prepared for Bible teaching. Even after she had said a little prayer to herself, she still felt a dreadful uncertainty as to whether she was fit for it. The chairs, however, were arranged as usual in the study of the Manse, along the bookshelf and below the photographs and the view of the Lake of Lucerne, where Mr and Mrs Fergusson had spent a Protestant honeymoon.

They filed in, feeling themselves affected even by the smell of the room, a holy and respectable smell with plenty of furniture polish in it. Florag had asked herself, odd times, why at all she came to the class, and the answer some way was in the smell, for it kind of steadied you into a thought that was clearly better than any day to day thought, since it was not about money nor yet boys, but about the strange ways of God, which were never what one had thought at the first and which must be puzzled over till the brain fair buzzed, and the Manse smell became part of the puzzling. Most of them had come on into the class from the Sabbath School, but they almost all dropped out after a while: it was kind of dull, compared with what ordinary young folks might want to be doing. There were one or two others who came an odd time, but were not at the class this evening.

Mrs Fergusson put her husband's notes on the desk beside her, wishing she were cleverer at reading his handwriting. If only nothing difficult would happen! All opened their Bibles. For a time the study took on the feeling of a schoolroom. Once or twice Minnie giggled a little and then blushed, but the Kettle kept a straight face. Mrs Fergusson thought it best to take no notice.

They had made their way through Chronicles, and oh, Mrs Fergusson was glad she had not been called upon to preside when certain chapters were read. These dreadful kings, such an example! Now they had come to Ezra III, the building of the

224

Temple. She had practised saying "Zerubbabel the son of Shealtiel" and managed it quite nicely. They found Tyre and Sidon on the wall map. Charlie said there was a fine cedar of Lebanon in the policies of Kinlochbannag House. They came on to the end of the chapter with the builders laying the foundations and the brass band standing by, trumpets and cymbals. "It's a wonder to me they had nae drums," said Jean suddenly, "you'd make a drum easy with skins, and see the beasts they brought with them to Jerusalem! Drums and trumpets, that would be away nice than yon cymbals, wouldn't it now, Mistress Fergusson?"

"I believe" said Mrs Fergusson with a little gasp, "that I heard Mr Fergusson saying one day that drums would be heathen in those days!"

"It's as well they're not now," said Florag, "there's nothing so cheery as a good pipe band with the drums. But it's a nice ending to the chapter, isn't it now, the old men crying for joy! *So that the people could not discern the noise of the shout of joy from the noise of the weeping of the people.* That's well put." They all agreed. It was nice, that, it was a thing you could see in your mind. The old folk that had been speaking on this for a great while back and never thought to see it in their lives. And now it was come. And suddenly Florag was thinking if once it could be this way with the Village Hall! But it would scarcely do to be saying that, not with the way the most of the ancient men of Port Sonas were! And yet, some way, the thought stayed with her.

They went on for a bit to the Persians. Mr Fergusson had left a passage marked in the History of Greece he had got as a school prize. It was bound in tree calf and Mrs Fergusson felt just a teeny bit proud, reading it aloud. The Bible Class listened. But there were not many questions, since everyone was a wee bit sorry for Mrs Fergusson and not wanting to bother her, let alone that they had no great respect for the answers she might have. After a time she glanced at the clock: "Well, we seem to be over very early today, don't we? I wonder what we should——"

"We'll just sing some nice hymns, Mrs Fergusson," said Florag firmly. Minnie agreed. She liked to be singing the hymns and it drew out the time nicely. Mrs MacLean looked disapproving; she was now half wishing she had not resigned from the Hall committee. But if that Roddy MacRimmon and that David

MacTavish were to be allowed their own way—— The way she had intended it to go, Mrs Snow would have begged her not to resign, would have said that the forester's nonsense was no longer to be taken seriously, would have chosen to understand that there was only one place for the site. Instead it had all gone wrong. But she had her position to keep up. If it was to be known in Port Sonas that she had resigned, then it was also to be known that there was good and sufficient reason. They would be sorry in the end that they had not treated her right.

They sang *Fight the Good Fight* and *Souls of Men*. It was nice to have the two men's voices in with theirs. Florag was thinking now of a mixed choir. If May was to start that and get in the Kettle, then Minnie would come to them whatever the Rural crowd said. But could May manage to conduct a mixed choir? Well, there'd be nothing like trying. It would be great getting to practice in the Bee House.

Now Jean was condoling with Mrs Fergusson: "And him needing to go off so quick! Isn't it bad enough for any of us, but worse for the like of yourselves."

"Yes, indeed, Mr Fergusson always has so much to do!" his wife said. "And all the arrangements for the Sabbath, oh dear, it was almost too much for him. But at last he managed to get Mr Stewart from Alltsalach to take the services. You'll like him, I'm sure. And then, wasn't it fortunate, really almost providential? —he found that the Hotel brake was going into Halbost with the Highland Panel, so he managed to beg a seat with them."

"Well, well, there will have been some great conversations between Mr Fergusson and them!"

"Oh, I quite envy them all! He would be able to put the right point of view before them about so many things, dear. Do you know, I was quite horrified to find that Mr Mackintosh had actually gone to the meeting. Most pushing. We would not have dreamt."

"Ach, the Wee Frees!" said Jean. "They're up to anything. But I was hearing Mr Mackintosh was none too pleased with the way he was spoken to."

"Dear me! If only Mr Fergusson had been there."

"Mr Mackintosh was speaking against the new Hall, they're saying."

"What a pity. Oh yes, that's what Mr Fergusson says, such a

226

pity. We shall have to support the Hall, Jean—so long as it is in the right hands, of course," she added hurriedly, for Mrs MacLean might have been listening. "How glad I am that Mr Fergusson will have had an opportunity for speaking to the Panel. You see how our crosses turn out to be blessings! And Mr Fergusson's mother is over 80. I had almost felt that some of us should have paid an informal call on the Panel. Just to bid them welcome."

Isa said: "There was one of the Panel ones having supper with Mistress Snow last night." Everyone else stopped talking and waited for what she'd say. "It was the woman body. But Mistress Snow was telling me she was one of the head ones. They say she has written books."

"There was one of hers in the County book-box once," said Mrs MacLean, "but all about folk in some country you'd never heard of and names you'd not get your tongue round. A senseless kind of book."

"I like a book about ordinar' folk" said Jean, "the kind you could meet if you went to Dunoon."

"It might have been a *good* book" said Mrs Fergusson anxiously. Good books were sometimes difficult. Especially theology.

"It didna look to be a good book" said Mrs MacLean definitely. "But what kind of a woman was she, Isa?"

"She seemed daft to me," said Isa. "But it did Mistress Snow good, some way, having her in, so maybe she wasna sae bad."

"Poor Mrs Snow, she must be very lonely sometimes," said Mrs Fergusson. "But she could always come over to the Manse."

"It's aye hard on a woman when the man's dead," said Jean. "There's nothing at all takes the place o' that. It would be terrible nice if she was to marry again. Is there no' a chance up at the Castle, Isa?"

"I dinna think," said Isa, "but still and all, it's wonderful the way things happen."

"I was hearing" said Mrs MacLean, "that Archie was speaking to Malcie about the Highland Panel crowd, saying they should have some new timbers for the fenders on the quay, and Malcie was thinking he could work up a good wee contract."

"It would need to go through the County Council, yon."

"Mistress Snow might speak for him. You'll see the way he'll be strong for the Hall now and thinking he'll get her on his side!"

"Malcie—him!" said Jean, "d'you know this, I was wanting a wee porch for myself and he'd not look at it under £20, the villain! Better they should get the Forestry timber. Surely to goodness Roddy MacRimmon could give them all they need."

Mrs MacLean reddened. "I'd sooner trust myself to Malcie than to yon man. Setting himself up as though he'd been born in Port Sonas! But maybe he'll be brought low. Aye, maybe!"

"How?" asked Jean softly. Mrs Fergusson had her back to them, putting away the hymn-books. The two young men were standing rather apart, saying nothing.

"Well, I was hearing, I was hearing mind you, that Postie had a letter for that Roddy MacRimmon from Halbost and on the back of it the name of the lawyers in a wee kind of seal. And you'll have heard that Kenny's Chrissie was at the lawyer's——"

"Och, och, isn't he the wicked man!" said Jean, "and he could have been courting a decent lassie!"

Isa said: "That's a daft-like story to make out of a bit letter and isn't it like Postie! It could have been over the new Forestry houses." She pulled Minnie over by the arm. "When will the Forestry houses be, Minnie?"

"I'm sure I've no notion at all," said Minnie elaborately, her head in the air.

"Have you nò'? I was hearing they're to be great houses altogether, with bathrooms and all."

"They're to have three bedrooms," said Florag.

"Aye, ye'd need that afore you're done" said Isa.

Minnie broke away, blushing, and walked out, followed by 'Tina. After a decent moment's delay, Charlie and the Kettle followed.

"You shouldna look at poor Minnie as though she was a quey, Isa!" said Florag, half laughing.

"Och, I'm meaning nae harm" said Isa, "you can see fine she's no bulled yet!"

Mrs Fergusson saw them to the door. It was a lovely evening, so still that you could hear a petal suddenly drop off one of the white tulips. Mrs MacLean was complimenting Mrs Fergusson on the Manse rhodies and Mrs Fergusson was answering that the garden was a great burden on Mr Fergusson and such a pity a man with his brain could not devote his whole time to learning, and Jean, observing the poor state of the Manse cabbages, had made up her mind to ask Dougie could they not send over a load of dung, and Dougie would do it surely, for wasn't he awful kind, the best you'd want, once you knew the way to take no notice of his tongue—and then Mrs MacLean stiffened, and her voice went hard, for hadn't she seen Roddy MacRimmon walking down towards the quay—aye, or it might be the Bar!—and who was with him but yon Fred Macfie from Balana and what devilment at all would the two of them be up to now!

CHAPTER XX

SATURDAY MORNING: AT THE BEE HOUSE

KATE HESITATED OVER her fruit bottles. Should she open a jar of black currants for Mr Stewart? Or raspberries? Yes, there was any amount of cream. Cream and eggs. Spring cabbage. Herring—for the boats were back. You'd never get a herring except at the week-end and that only if one of the fishermen remembered. You could never actually buy herring at Port Sonas, but this morning there had been a paper of herrings left at the gate, perhaps by the Whale. She split and boned them and laid them ready on the dish of oatmeal. Nothing better than fresh herring! The fishing was still patchy and mostly further out, but these were no spent herring; no, they were fat and good, so that they would fry themselves in a matter of minutes after Mr Stewart came.

Or would he rather a pudding? No! She would make meringues. The war had been over long enough for one to think of meringues. It was a still, sunny day, the kind that comes so often after a storm, and without a wind she'd have a cool oven, just right for them. So long as her father didn't then think there should be meringues every day. . . . She began to break the eggs. Isa had been shocked that she hadn't had a hen killed, with a Minister coming to take his dinner. But Mr Stewart had the sense to appreciate a herring. He'd be taking his tea at the Manse with Mrs Fergusson and only coming back in time for a cup of coffee in the late evening. And madeira? Or was he temperance? She just couldn't remember, but if he was he'd doubtless take it seriously! It was nice having him to stay all the same. Her nephew Tom would likely be over in the evening too; they'd have a great crack, among them.

She took the bowl with her to the seat outside the kitchen window, and while she whisked up the whites of the fresh eggs, she began to think about the Village Hall committee meeting that evening. David was worrying about it, of course. It was possible that Mr MacMillan from the Hotel would not come. Probable even. If he were to go off they'd need to get another chairman. Andrew? Or was he right, that the one to go on should be May? Well, now would be the time.

Then she began to wonder about the measles cases. Dr MacKillop had been worried enough himself and out there most of the night. Pneumonia following measles, a common enough thing—even nowadays. She half wished he had called her in all the same. Not that she could have done anything more. No doubt it was a simple death, from obvious causes. Brought it on themselves: like most patients. Poor bloody fools. She caught herself staring at a hole in the dyke beyond the azaleas. Yes, no doubt of it, a wren's nest! There she goes—and my eyes caught on her before my brain took her in.

She looked down at the bowl. The texture was coming right now. We shall never get out of the habit of scrimping sugar, she thought, or shall we? Will everything be forgotten? No, not everything. And when all sorts of tins are easy to buy again, shall we cease to value this basic feminine occupation of skilled food-providing?—make women feel again that this capacity of theirs is unwanted, so that British cooking will again go down to the depths of devaluation. No, she thought, reaching her hand in to test her oven, nobody's ever going to be able to tin meringues!

She could leave them in for a good while now: till after twelve anyway. Meanwhile she went back to the sitting room and began to look through a pile of copies of the B.M.J. and the Lancet. She seemed to remember an article about the use of convalescent serum in measles. But there had been enough contacts to bring all the children in the place down, let alone the younger MacKinnons. Well, they'd need to look out for what would happen next week. After a time she became absorbed in the articles. A lot of interesting work going on nowadays. Still turning it over in her mind, she went back to the kitchen.

And now to whip the cream. Lovely stuff! She sat on the edge of the kitchen table, near her oven, and began to hum to herself, something dating from student days in Glasgow. It had come into her mind with her thinking along the lines of her own job. When the knock came on the kitchen door, she jumped, for it was none too decorous a song. She hadn't even remembered it for years. "Come in" she said, a little guiltily. But David MacTavish was not paying any attention to any tune she might have been humming. "I thought I'd best come straight and see you" he said.

"What's wrong now?" she asked, a little wearily. Couldn't things ever go straight?

"Well—that's just what I'm not sure." He stood beside the kitchen table for a moment, picking up a spoon, balancing it across the sugar tin and then hastily putting it back. "It's this. Kate, did you write to Fred Macfie?"

"Certainly. I'm Secretary after all! But I didn't get an answer.'

"I heard from one of the boys he was over last night. That would be after he got your letter. And seen with Roddy."

"One can't blow one's nose in Port Sonas without everyone knowing! But that's all right then."

"That's just what I'm wondering. Kate, Miss Gillies went down with the measles. Last night."

"Did she indeed! That'll be a relief for you, Davie!"

"Yes, but——"

Kate stopped whipping the cream, put down the bowl, slid off the table and stared at him. "You aren't suggesting, Davie——"

"She could have got it at the school treat, off the wee Mac-Kinnons, couldn't she?" he asked, eagerly.

A week, thought Kate. Normal incubation period, ten to fourteen days. Of course the children might have been infectious a day or two before. But equally Miss Gillies wouldn't have admitted to anything until she was really ill. And none of the children getting it. She had warned David to be on the look-out next week. Could she think of any cases of an seven-day incubation period? He was staring at her now, she could see his fingers gripping hard on the edge of the table. "Of course," she said, "just what might have been expected."

He seemed to relax. "Aye, it'll be that, sure enough. Poor woman. But I'll not deny it's a kind of weight off me. I've rung up the Director and he'll send me out a relief teacher. So— she'll just have taken it the ordinary way."

Kate nodded. And then suddenly got a warning look from the kitchen clock. "Oh, my meringues!" she stooped quick to the oven and pulled them out. They were just browning a little, but nothing to spoil, only a shade of old gold. She edged them off their tin and on to the wire tray. David watched her, fascinated. He would need to tell his sister when he got home. "They'll just have time to cool" she said. It was ten minutes past twelve. Mr Stewart would be a while yet; his bus was not due in till one o'clock. And then there was another knock on the kitchen door: Roddy, straight from work, mud and bits of bark on his boots and breeches. "I knocked on the room door," he said, "and then I heard you speaking. You'll not mind me as I am, Mistress Snow? I came straight over. I—I was needing to see you. And Davie forby."

"About Fred Macfie?" said Kate, taking a shot. She put on the water for the potatoes, which Isa had peeled ready for her.

Roddy nodded. "You knew then?"

"No, I guessed. What happened? He came over last night? Why didn't he answer my letter?"

"It was the way I said," Roddy answered. "He wanted us to ask him for his help. Most of all me, because it was me told him to resign from the committee."

"And did you?"

"You wanted him back on, Mistress Snow, you were saying so! What else could I do?"

"Did he mean—*that* kind of help? Are you sure, Roddy? He might have meant—oh—keeping the Hall accounts, running a jumble sale——"

Roddy gulped. "He meant only the one thing. He was gey quiet about it. But he was making certain that I myself knew what he meant. That I was to put my agreement upon what he might do to the folk that are against the Hall."

"There are rather a lot against the Hall" said Kate. "He can't go putting enchantments on half Port Sonas!"

"It was—the Free Presbyterians mostly. Because of yon wee piper. Och, you'll not know about that. But he had his reasons. And then, when I had agreed to it, he went off laughing on his bike, with the Lord knows what hellment in his pockets. But he had them full, I could see that——"

"Full of *what*, Roddy? Do pull yourself together!" She was fighting now to keep up an attitude of decent scepticism, with Roddy gone right over and David almost as bad.

Roddy said something in Gaelic to David, using two or three words whose meaning she had no notion of. Then he seemed to be

233

trying to compose himself. "I could not say at all" he said, "there are times it is better not to be looking."

"As far as I can make out, Roddy" said Kate, rather coldly, "you are trying to tell me that Fred Macfie went off with a pocket full of charms to make the round of the patients! Don't you see it's fantastic?"

Roddy brushed the sleeve of his tunic over his face: he was sweating. A small leaf stuck on his nose. He put up his hand and dabbed at it, ineffectively. "Late in the evening I saw Mr Sinclair."

"The policeman?"

"Just himself. I was wanting him to keep a bit eye on my wood store. He told me that Donnie Cameron had come charging down the Alltnacoinne side road on his motor bike and had dented the wing of Angus' lorry——— Och, nothing much at all and nobody hurt, but Angus had reported it. And Kenny's Chrissie was on the back of the bike."

"That probably lets you out, Roddy. Really it's providential."

"You may call it providence, Mistress Snow, but it's a queer kind of providence altogether, and mind you of this. Donnie's father was strong against the Hall and they are Free Presbyterians, every one of them. They will be in shame over this. Shame and confusion."

"Look, I don't believe for one moment that Donnie Cameron running into Angus' lorry had anything at all to do with Fred Macfie."

"Nor that Miss Gillies and her illness has to do with him?" said David.

"Is the woman ill?" said Roddy. "A Dhia nan gras! It is Fred."

"It is a coincidence" said Kate. And then: "If you believe this, you two, it means—oh, it means a hole in the wall of sanity we've built through the last thousand years—against the sea of super- stition and ignorance, yes, and cruelty before its done! If you start believing it you'll start being afraid of Fred and so will other people and next thing you'll be burning him! Aren't there enough people in the world believing horrible crazy things with- out you two———" Her voice died down.

"Yon other lady, her from the Highland Panel, she had no trouble at all in believing" said Roddy.

"She doesn't live here. She doesn't have to face the consequences. Listen: nothing has happened so far that mightn't have happened quite easily by accident."

"The schoolmistress at Kilmolue?"

"I shan't believe she vomited pins till I've seen them. It's all rumour and panic. You've a duty not to believe, David."

"Och, Kate, the thing is too strong for me! And if only *she* believes it—a buidseachas—she'll likely ask for a transfer to another school!"

Kate began to laugh: "Now, there *is* a reason! Poor Miss Gillies! Measles is a nasty thing for an adult. By the way, David, do you happen to know if Miss Gillies has been in Halbost lately?'

He shook his head: "No, no, she'll not go in any godless bus if she can get a Service at home!"

"I see." Kate smiled. So that source of infection was ruled out. However, the woman was bound to have got it *some* normal way. She looked at the two men. "Now, David and Roddy; you mustn't ever believe in witchcraft inside yourselves. Understand? Not in this house."

"Not in this house." Roddy repeated it, as though it were a calming thing to say. He looked round at the sunny kitchen, the scrubbed table with the food on it, bright eggs and cream, the rainbow skin of the fresh herrings clothed with wholesome oatmeal, the sweet smell, the pot boiling on the clean enamelled stove. He would have a kitchen like this one day for his own lassie, where all would be clean and sweet and without sorcery. Again he wiped his hand over his face. Saturday and his shirt a week worn, grimy at the cuffs, with resin and impacted dirt. Perhaps it was none of it true, Fred was having him on. God, if he'd let himself be had on! And this with Donnie, it would let him out. He had hardly thought of it that way. They would not bring a Court case. The District Officer would never need to know.

Kate picked up two half meringues, crisp and sweet outside, meltingly, warmly sticky within, shook a big blob of cream onto each and gave them to the two men. "I must tidy myself up before Mr Stewart comes," she said. "I'll be over early for the Committee meeting. Now, go along, both of you."

"And sin no more" said David with a small smile, and nibbled

235

the edge of his meringue: "Gosh, Katie, this is great stuff you've been making!"

Kate went energetically about the kitchen when they had left, then out to the garden for a mixed bowl of flowers, narcissus, tulips and wallflowers. A pity Alice had gone back to school before the parrot tulips were out. And so few days before the wind would wreck them. Winds always came to break the blossoms. One mustn't worry.

Her father, she noticed, was talking to Malcie. It would be about the greenhouse he was planning. What fun for Malcie! Still, he might come down on the right side over the Village Hall. Then she saw Mr Stewart at the gate, his little black case in his hand.

It was not easy to do much talking until after lunch. And the first thing he would ask about was the Hall. Should she or shouldn't she mention this—this survival of pagan belief? She spoke, first, about the County book-box and the schoolmistress at Kilmolue. Essentially it was an administrative question. Miss MacIntosh had tampered with the machine of which she was part: that would bring its own response. "But has she the backing of her own community in the matter?" asked Mr Stewart.

"I'm afraid so," Kate answered; "But——" she was going to tell him the sequel now.

He had picked it up in another way, though. "Of course, it opens the whole question of censorship. Is she perhaps right in the sense that we have a moral duty to protect 'the immature mind? We teach children to read and think we have done right by them. And give little heed to how they are using their new power!"

"I'm sure the County book-box had nothing anyone in their senses could object to!"

"Aye, aye, that's so. Oh, I've nothing against the County Library. There are books I'd not want to read myself, but others would like to well enough. But this woman was narrow and she'd see it wrong. Yet I'm certain you wouldn't let young people read everything, Mrs Snow?"

"If they've been decently brought up they'll prefer something worth while. But they've got to eat their peck of dirt." She thought of Alice and her awful comics that she used to get at the paper shop and share with Isa! But she'd grow out of them.

"If we could count on decent bringing up, there would be no problem. We all know that." He spoke a little sharply. "But with our knowledge that the family can no longer be trusted to protect its own members, there is a duty on us to do it for them."

"Not by censorship," said Kate firmly. "If once you start that you may find yourself anywhere." No, perhaps, after all, she wouldn't tell him any more, not until she had made up her own mind. Instead she began to ask about a plan they were both keen on—a hostel run by the Education Authority for the boarded-out children. Mr Stewart asked about the Glen children—she had told him about little Greta on Tuesday. "My letter was quite definite," she said.

He nodded. "Aye, it would be so! You let us all know what's in your mind, Mrs Snow."

"Do I?" She smiled a little.

"There's nobody else who talks to me as you do. And you will have written to Glasgow the same way. No doubt the lightning will come down on this Snash of yours!"

"Someone has to make up their minds that a thing needs done. If they don't, there's no Highlander that won't stay balanced on one toe, hoping that a dilemma will vanish of its own free will! Instead of getting worse, as they mostly do."

"Would you say we were worse than most at facing things?"

She hesitated for a moment, then answered flatly: "Yes."

He nodded: "Maybe that's what the churches are for. To give people—backbone. And that's why they need to be extra strict in the like of the Highlands."

"Maybe. But somehow, I like bones best in their proper place: inside. Your's that you fasten onto people from the outside—they're just a bit too like my old mother's stay-bones!"

Had that shocked him a wee bit? She wondered. He said nothing for a moment, but walked over to the window and stared out. Abruptly he said "Are you coming over to the morning service tomorrow?"

"I expect so," said Kate; she would not have in the ordinary way, but it would be only courteous for him. And then: "Will you have anything for me?"

"I'll try," he said, "God helping me, I'll try."

He looked at his watch then. It was time he went over to the Manse. Mrs Fergusson would be expecting him for his tea and he

237

would not like to hurt her feelings. But she would scarcely have made meringues for him!

Kate was intending to sow carrots. Alice loved young raw carrots, couldn't wait to wash them! Fun to prepare already for the long summer holidays. She was lining out her rows and humming the same students' song when the Laird pushed open the garden gate. He heard her and side-stepped the house, which might contain her father and did contain his collections. Incredible how tidy Kate kept her garden. It was remarkable, really remarkable, the weeds that were growing in his own. Rare ones, even.

She looked round, pulled off her gardening gloves and reached up a hand: "Hullo, Sandy! Who'd have thought of seeing you here. Lord, I'm as stiff as a board!" He pulled her on to her feet, but rather gingerly, a certain distance kept. "A cup of tea?" she said. And shall I let him have that extra meringue I was keeping for father's supper? I will.

"No," he said. "I'd as soon not. Kate, do you want to marry me?"

"Sandy dear!" she said. "No. Oh no! I think we're better as we are. Don't you?"

"Well, thank God for that" he said. "I agree with you entirely. Yes, just as we are. There are a few salmon up, by the way."

"What made you ask me?" she said.

"Well, you might have wanted something of the kind. To reform me. God knows. Women seem to like that kind of thing."

"I don't think you're reformable, Sandy," she said, "not now. And I mightn't like you so well as a reformed character."

"Or you might have wanted to put the Castle in order."

"God forbid!" she said, and laughed first a little and then a great deal. "But what put it into your head all of a sudden, Sandy?"

He coughed and looked away over her head. "It was brought to my notice," he said.

"Goodness," said Kate, "did you have a deputation?"

"Almost," he said, and then: "Read that, Kate: you'll maybe know the hand."

She took the letter. Her eyebrows went up and very slowly she began to blush. At last she folded it up and gave it back to him. "She meant well, Sandy," she said.

"She?" said the Laird.

"Well—I'm pretty sure I know who it is. And why she did it. Oh dear! They do things for the best, bless them. You must have felt awful, getting this, Sandy!"

"Awful? No. But a bit inadequate. I remember you well enough when you were a girl. A crazy young whelp of a medical. I didn't want to make love to you even then, Kate."

"We always thought you were a bit high-hat with us, Sandy."

"We? You and your cousin? Yes, you were tough, the two of you. Times I'd thought I'd like to have the skelping of you, Kate. But not now. How about a day on the river?"

"That would be fine. Was there enough water to get them up?"

"Hardly what you'd call a right spate. But still there'll be a few. If they're not all poached."

"I wonder if there are really any poachers, Sandy." They were going up to the house now, and both conspiratorially lowered their voices.

"There's not a man in Port Sonas that isn't a poacher. But some are discreet. Nobody minds a salmon going if it's for someone's tea. But I object to supplying the Halbost hotels at black market prices which I don't get! Or your friend Councillor Thompson at Kinlochbannag."

"Do you really think it's like that, Sandy? Come into the kitchen! We'll have a cup. My feeling is it's mostly talk."

"Talk never left scales on the bank. How's your Hall going, Kate? So-so, eh? Ah, to the devil with them all! Dirty hoodies!"

"We must be patient, Sandy——"

"And let the like of them walk over us? Not on your life, Kate. We'll die fighting and be buried without benefit of clergy."

She made the tea and brought it over to where he leant against the dresser, then stooped to the low shelf where she had the meringue hidden between two soup plates. He stroked the back of her neck with the tips of his fingers, his rough nails catching in her hair: "You ought to have a string of pearls, Kate," he said. "There should be my mother's put away somewhere. But God knows what the cousins would say! Sure you don't want to get married, Kate?"

She stood up, smiled and shook her head. "Wouldn't it have you scared out of your wits, my dear, if I'd said yes? Now, eat up your nice meringue. I couldn't have made it better if I'd had the run of the Castle kitchen, Sandy!"

He nodded. "I believe that. Though maybe it wouldn't be the reason anyone would ask you to marry them, Kate." He sipped the tea, but without great enthusiasm. "Old George was telling me there's great scandal going around about one of your friends, Kate."

"I'm not surprised. Which one?"

"The forester. They say he's going about getting girls into trouble——"

"Only one, surely?"

"George thought it was a brace of them. But he exaggerates."

"It's not true, anyway."

"Pity. He's a good-looking young fellow. How d'you know?"

"He told me."

"Believe him?"

"As a matter of fact—yes."

"Well, well, you'd know. He's on your committee, isn't he? The hoodies'll be at anyone of you that's got any kind of weakness. In their black coats." He quoted at her:

> "The grim Geneva Ministers
> With anxious smile drew near,
> As you have seen the ravens flock
> About the dying deer."

"But they never got him!" said Kate. "Not Montrose. Not really. And they'll not get me. Nor my friends. It's worrying about Roddy all the same. I wonder how it got round." But then, above them, they heard a chair pushed back and steps. "You'd better escape Sandy!" she said. "When shall I come over and get your twenty-pounder?"

"Whenever you like, my dear" said the Laird, "whenever you like," and gave her a dry little peck on the cheek and slipped out, quickly and quietly as one of his own poachers. Kate switched on Isa's wireless and put the cups into the sink. Her cheek remained aware of the two thin lips, her nostrils of the smell of smoke and whisky, a tinkerish sort of smell. She took out the big mixing bowl and began to weigh flour into it. This was definitely going to be one of her cooking week-ends.

"I thought I heard voices," said Mr MacFarlan, looking

round, "but I suppose it was only that machine. Has Mr Stewart left?"

"Yes, he had to go over to the Manse. He will be coming back later on after the Hall committee meeting."

"Another committee! Really, Kate, you appear to think of nothing else."

"I'm thinking of some beautiful scones, father," she said, rinsed her hands in cold water, and began to rub in the fat. "Jock let me have some sultanas."

"Was there a meringue left after lunch?" said Mr MacFarlan.

"No, father, I'm afraid not."

"You might have thought to make one or two over" he said. "Your mother always did so."

She did not answer, but went on rapidly rubbing and lifting and dropping. If one is good towards some people, it is dreadfully easy to be bad towards others. Which should save one from the sin of spiritual pride. Her father turned and went out again. Oh damn, she was being nasty! His poor shoulders drooping. It can't be helped. Five minutes at least by the clock for rubbing in. She switched the wireless off. Dear Sandy! Perhaps after all Janet had done no harm. But if anyone had seen the kiss! She began to hum: "Gin a body meet a body, Gaeing to the well, Gin a body kiss a body, Need a body tell?" Yes, of course, it was the first thing they'd do! And there was Roddy back again in her kitchen. . . . "Well, Roddy" she said. "I hear it's all over Port Sonas now. How was that?"

"I've no idea at all. Unless it was Chrissie herself. But I'd scarcely believe—— You heard, then?"

"Yes, I heard." She took her hands out of the bowl and flicked the flour off them.

"Mrs McCulloch has given me notice to quit. In case I would be corrupting her lassies. Never will I set foot in the church again!"

"It's a wonder she hadn't heard about Donnie."

"Maybe she had, but she'd sooner believe it was me. We were not getting on too good."

"Where will you get lodgings?"

"I don't know at all. There's nowhere much."

"She can't turn you out at a moment's notice."

"Aye, but I was that angry I said I would go at once!"

241

"Oh Roddy, isn't that like you! You'd better come here for the week-end. You can have Alice's room."

"That's terrible kind of you. But willn't it—I mean, there's your own good name to be thinking of."

"I've got Mr Stewart from Alltnasalach staying."

"But he's a Minister. They're different."

"Really? I thought they managed to procreate. Or are you suggesting that all Minister's wives——" Her foot tapped with impatience and irritation.

Roddy looked down and blushed. "I'm sorry" he said.

"Well then, go and pack. You can leave most of your things at the office and just bring a wee case here."

"It would be great to move out on her straight!" said Roddy. "I will then. But how about the committee? Willn't it be bad for that?"

"Remember you're innocent, Roddy," she said, "*if* you are."

"Aye, so I am" he said in a sort of surprised voice. "Well then—I'll just be back." And at least, she thought, as he went out again, it's taken his mind off the buidseachas. And it will be nice to have him in Alice's room. A kind of son—I'd better clear two or three drawers. She's sure to have left her usual muddle!

CHAPTER XXI

SATURDAY EVENING: VILLAGE HALL COMMITTEE

For once, thought David, everything was working out just the thing. He leant nearer into the wee looking-glass and put a shed into his hair. He shook his head at the young man who was reflected and addressed him with great seriousness: "Oh what a tangled web we weave, When once we practice to deceive!" The young man in the reflection looked seriously back at him, pursing his lips. But we do weave, thought David, and at the end maybe something to show for it, and the tangles all smoothed out and forgotten.

For he had asked his sister to ask Janet in to tea. And his sister, thinking he was making his mind up at last, and approving of his choice, had consented happily and made four separate plates of baking. But it was so that Janet would be there when it came to the co-option and he would say so with the greatest surprise in the world, and wouldn't Kate be terrible pleased and forget she had ever been angry with him, and if Janet came on that would mean they had a kind of footing again with the Free Church, not that a woman altogether counted, but still her father was as much respected as Norman. And if she was asked sudden to come on, as she would be after a co-option, then, because she loved Kate she would surely come and not think too much of what the rest could be thinking—and so it would all work out.

He came downstairs. There was an unusually delicious and appetising smell. "What's for the tea, Silis?" he asked, and looked in the pan. There were salmon cutlets frying, rich pink and deep brown. He raised his eyebrows. "Where got you them?"

"Wasn't it Sandy the Coileach brought me a cut over" his sister said, "and I could hardly refuse it and him speaking so nice and saying you were doing great work for the new Hall, David."

"It will be one of the Laird's salmon" said David.

"It will" said his sister.

"We'll not need to tell Kate what we had for our tea" he said.

"No, that we'll not" she agreed, and shook the pan.

The rest of the Village Hall committee were getting themselves ready for the evening. Angus brought in his lorry, had a long and careful look at the back axle, decided it was all right, and then cleaned his plugs. It was great to have this other thing off his mind. And indeed it would do no harm to go steady for a while. He could maybe see a bittie less of Krooger's nephew and that crowd, in fact he'd need to now he was on this committee. If there was a Hall, now, there'd be things to do there in an evening which could take your mind off the kind of ploy he'd been apt to find himself on. If they were thinking to have a sale, the way he'd heard, he could maybe make something for a raffle. He went home for his tea and a right wash.

Fred Macfie cycled in from Balana, whistling. He was pleased with the way things were going. The piper had come over to Balana at the back of midnight, grieving, grieving for his lost pipes. In time there would be a lament made over that. And a great hole in the power of the missionary. A hole you could see the blood running out. And he would do everything to help this Port Sonas crowd that the missionary had spoken against. Roddy MacRimmon had asked for his help and it was a warm, nice, neighbourly thing to be asked. And it was great that he knew how to help, the same way he knew in the war how to use a rifle and kill Germans. He had been a sniper and off on his own more than once. He had liked that. He liked, now, still to be wearing his battledress or part of it.

It was observed by several people that Roddy had gone to the Bee House with a suitcase and now he was walking over to the school with Kate. Well, well, they wondered what would the Laird say if he knew that she was taking the like of Roddy into her house! But the Minister from Alltsalach? Ah, he wouldn't understand at all, the man. There was, however, another whisper. Maybe it wasn't Roddy at all. There was this that Sinclair and Angus were saying and, though you'd not believe a policeman, it was kind of suspicious, and memories were going back some four months and thoughts of Donny Cameron's motor-bike up a back road by itself and bye and bye Donny coming out of the bracken and a while after Chrissie, and it would not have been the sacred music he would have been after teaching her! It will be surprising if this can be kept from the Glasgow cousin. Aye, aye, there will be no very pleasant evening at Balnafearchar and Sin coming so near! What will Donnie be saying to his father now? The one thing that nobody was doing was asking any questions of Kenny's Chrissie. It might be the measles themselves on her, with the distance folks were keeping. And would she get the sack from the Forestry after this? Well, well, she'd not do for the school cleaning anyway!

Over at the schoolroom, Kate went to the table and began arranging her papers. Roddy was telling David about the gossip and poor David was frowning and fidgeting. After all, everything had not worked out! Then Angus came in, scrubbed and brushed. All greeted him. "What about Mr MacMillan?" said Kate.

"I'm mostly sure he'll not be," said Angus, "he was saying so to me when I was unloading his cases. He's not exactly resigned, but he wants to ca' canny and maybe not be chairman."

"Well then, we'll need to appoint a new chairman. Will you do it, David?"

"I second" said Roddy quickly. David hunched his shoulders and walked over to the table and as he did so, Fred came in, took the bicycle clips off his trousers and sat down at the back.

"Come along up," said Kate. "We're just a small company now, Mr Macfie. I'm pleased that you're with us. We'll need all the help we can get." She saw Roddy gulp and shift a tiny bit along the desk he was sitting on as Fred came up. Angus fidgeted too. Fred looked less like a magician than you would think possible. He couldn't, she thought, have taken the smallest rabbit out of the largest hat. "Well, at least we're a quorum!" she said cheerfully.

"This'll not need to be too formal" said David, "and me not accustomed to be in the Chair. But I think I'd be right in asking Mrs Snow to read the minutes."

She opened the jotter and read them. Angus, who had not been there, listened to them conscientiously and moved that they be adopted. Kate thought she wouldn't tell him he was out of order and none of the others noticed. David asked for correspondence and she read the letters from the Director and from the Council for Social Service. They were, of course, encouraging and helpful, but held out no hope of any building being permitted for some years. "But we shall have to spend two or three years collecting money anyhow" she said, "so perhaps by the time we're ready, they'll be. In fact we shall have plenty to do."

"Two years, maybe, or three" said David, and suddenly she wondered if she would still be in Port Sonas. Not south somewhere, using her skill?

"We could get the site fixed on and maybe bought" said Roddy.

"We could maybe do a bit to the foundations ourselves" said Angus. "Some of the young crowd from the Legion could help and I'd give the lend of my lorry."

Would she find some place to live in the south which was honest and orderly, sane and civilised, with the reasonable kindliness of the English? A place where her responsibilities would be merely professional. If that was what she really wanted. But was it? One didn't live in Port Sonas without forming attachments, she thought, looking at her committee. And had Matta got the letter yet? Maddening, crazy attachments. But then, anything which binds you is maddening; you want to fly and find you are rooted. And love your roots. They were full of plans now for putting in voluntary work on the Hall site. But would anything come of it? "We'll need to appoint a new treasurer," she said. "What about you, Angus?"

But David said "That could be one of the co-opted members. Or someone from an organisation. We'll need to ask them all. After all, there's none of the fishermen now."

"Colin was saying" said Angus, "that you should maybe wait a wee while to write to them, until the storm has blown past. There will be second thoughts over the Hall, aye and third. It would be no' such great, terrible surprise if Pate were to come back, for he liked being on the Committee and getting to speak."

"Well, will you give me the word when to write? Maybe I'd better wait a while for the Rural?"

"You could write when Mrs MacLean is visiting her married sister in Barrhead" said David.

"Well then, there's the Choir."

"They could send May" said David, "indeed I'm half certain they would."

"Or Florag. I think we might co-opt one of the two."

"Well," said Angus, "I was speaking to Florag—oh, kind of jocose!—but I'm mostly sure she'd be treasurer. Would we not just co-opt her?"

"Is that unanimous? Fine, then. And that would leave May for the Choir to put on. Who else?"

"I'd say Alasdair. He's a decent young fellow" said Roddy.

"That would be great" said Angus, "and then, if Colin MacRae were to come on from the Fishermen, then there'd be three of the ex-Service boys for a start. You're not thinking to ask the Masons, Mrs Snow?"

"I don't officially know they exist! But I think we should ask Mr Fergusson's Kirk Sessions."

"So long as he doesn't get on himself. That would spoil our committee right away. Maybe it would be Baldy: that could be worse. Will we all agree to Alasdair then?" Everyone nodded.

"He's maybe too busy now," said David, "but later, in the back-end after he's his potatoes lifted, I think we should ask Red Dougie from Molachy."

Fred looked up: "He was speaking to me about a branch of the Farmer's Union. But the rest spoiled it."

"Who?"

"The Free Presbyterians" said Fred. He had taken two or three grains of oats out of the bottom of his pocket and was chewing them. And would he also, thought Kate, put sorceries on to his opponents in the N.F.U.? Yes, yes, nothing was too improbable. He had half pulled something else out of his pocket along with the corn. What on earth was it? Could it be binder twine wrapped round—what? He shoved it back with a negligent elbow. She found her heart pounding in the oddest way.

"We should try and have someone from the Glen in place of Norman" said David.

"Do we need a crofter?" said Roddy. "They're more bother than they're worth."

"Well, maybe not one of the crofters himself" said David, "but——"

"I wish we could have Janet MacKinnon" said Kate, falling feet first into his trap.

"Now isn't that a coincidence!" said David. "Here's Janet

taking tea with my sister. What do you say? Will we co-opt her right away and ask her to come through?''

"Moved from the Chair" said Kate. "I don't know that it's just quite in order to have her in, but still if it's unanimous——"

"Go you over and get her, David," said Roddy. "It'll give us a bit lift to have another one in." David went out.

"This is getting more like your sort of committee, Roddy" said Kate.

"My sort?"

"Do you remember speaking of it last Sunday and the need to get things run by the young ones, not the old women and the respectable?"

"Did I say that?" said Roddy. "Well, I've let you down right enough as far as the respectable goes!"

"Away, Roddy!" said Angus, "it's only a few that are speaking against you."

"Who were doing that?" asked Fred.

Roddy gave him a quick uncomfortable look. "Oh, you can't be believing anything!" he said. But had Fred meant——

David came back into the schoolroom with Janet. "Well, here's our first co-opted member!"

She was looking extra nice, thought Kate, with her hair smooth and glossy as a blackbird's wing over her head, but curly a bit at the edges, and her cheeks warm and red with the life-blood in her. She fitted herself into a desk, smoothing the cotton dress down over her thighs and knees. "I'll do my best" she said. "I suppose it will be mostly raising money at the first?"

"That's so," said David, "and keeping the Glen ones from listening too much to Mr Mackintosh."

"That will be the hardest" she said gravely, "but I will try." Her eyes were on Kate, who realised, with a start, just what she would be wondering. The dear silly idiot! Let her wonder. Not a sign would she get from either Sandy or herself and that would teach her not to write anonymous letters! Apart from which, it was nice to have her on the Committee.

"I think we might go ahead over the site" said Kate. "We'll need to get Planning Permission. Then we'll ask for a feu."

"The Laird'll not be hard on us—if it's the right site we get—will he?" asked Roddy.

"I don't think so," said Kate primly. "Possibly the committee

248

should approach him and ask his views." Suddenly Janet began to blush right down to her neck. Not a very practised wrongdoer! Roddy was watching her sideways. "Miss Campbell of Kinlochbannag might take an active interest," Kate went on. "That would have its influence with some. The main thing is to pull the community over to us."

"I agree with you there" said David, "and that's about all for now. Read you the letters, Janet." He handed them across.

"Oh, by the way," said Kate, "when it comes to getting a feu and drawing up titles, we should get a firm of lawyers——"

"No!" said Roddy.

"They only do what they're told, you know! Like a collie dog. And of course if you happen to be the stray black sheep, you get nipped." She rested her chin on her two hands, elbows on the table, and observed her committee.

"Well—so long as it's not yon ones at Halbost" said Roddy. "I canna like to think of their names even."

Davie looked up: "Did you hear this? Matta is saying he knows now who took the lobsters and he's in great trim with it altogether."

"He knows——?" said Kate. Angus was completely still, under control.

"Well, there's what he's saying. But if you ask me, he knows no more than he ever did. But some way he's got it into his head that it was some young fellows out for devilment and he's saying now he'll pay no heed to anything but just carry on with the lobster fishing and let bygones be bygones. That's sense, right enough."

"Maybe that was the advice he got from the Highland Panel crowd" said Angus.

"More than likely," agreed Kate. "They'd sense. By the way, Roddy, are you going to find a couple of good butts for the fenders on the pier?"

"Archie hasna' asked me" said Roddy, "but maybe the District Councillor could do it!"

"I tell you what I'll do" said Kate. "I'll write up to the Glasgow headquarters. That'll short-circuit your District Officer." He nodded. And at the same time, she thought, I can put in a good word for Roddy. You never know when it mightn't help.

Janet gave back the letters: "That's interesting, David. It

means—oh, we are being thought of and considered by the Head Ones. That's something, indeed. And maybe we will get our Hall."

"Nothing surer," said David. "And now, ladies and gentlemen, that concludes the business." He got up. Fred Macfie rose heavily and mumbled "Vote of thanks to the chairman." "Hear, hear" said Kate and the others tapped on their desks. Janet slipped out from her desk, easily as a cat. Roddy moved over towards her.

"Well, I must be going," said Janet, "it's a long step up the Glen."

"But haven't you your bike?" said David anxiously.

"Oh well, Sheila borrowed it and here, it punctured on her, and it's not mended yet."

"Come back with me and I'll run you over in the car" said Kate.

At the same time Roddy said: "I'll see you over to the Glen, Janet." She gave him a quick glance from under her dark brows like a moment's look of blue sky from between thunder clouds. "That is," said Roddy, "if you'll not mind after all that's been said about me." And he bit his lip and looked away towards David.

Janet winked at Kate, the way neither of the two men would see it. "I'd not dream of bothering you for the car, Katie dear. It's not dark yet and Roddy will walk back with me a piece." She had an oilskin hood for her hair, but instead of putting it on, she let it hang by the strings. "Seeing we're both on the Committee now," she added, and then she said "I was telling Silis just now there was a man over at Snash. He came in a wee black car with a Glasgow number and he had a case in his hand, the same a County Councillor might have. So we were all of us hoping it was about the children. Ach well, we'll know by church time."

"Well, isn't that great," said David. "They've not been slow, those boys."

"Sheila was saying she'd maybe manage to take in the wee Greta lassie—they are kind of wanting to make it up to her. That is if Snash would not be making a row."

"And if he does?" said Kate.

"Ach, we'd manage it some way, one or another of us. We've the Grazing Committee past too—and it's been an extra nice committee."

Janet turned to go. Roddy held the schoolroom door open for her and went out, carefully at a certain distance. "Oidhche mhath" he called over his shoulder.

"Oidhche mhath." "Oidhche mhath agus beannachd leibh."

"Well, well" said David softly, "Roddy's getting his nerve back. But I hope my sister will not be seeing it, after all her hopes!"

Angus was reading again the letter on headed notepaper from the Council of Social Service. It was great to see the phrasing of such a letter and to savour the long words of it. He shook his head appreciatively and laid it down again. "Well, I must be away over" he said. "Goodnight all."

Fred Macfie stooped for his bicycle clips. "You'll say, Mistress Snow and Mr MacTavish, if there is any more I could be doing any time to help you?" He scratched his head. "If you'd a sale we'd send in a dozen of eggs or a hen itself from Balana."

"Thank you kindly, Fred" said Kate, "we'll bear that in mind. But for the moment I think we should be persuading folk, gently. I'll send you a card about the next meeting."

He went out. Kate, who was writing up the minutes in the jotter, turned to David. "He means to help, surely you can see, just ordinarily. The way I said."

David said: "Did you not hear him ask Roddy who had been miscalling him? He had Roddy scared."

"Roddy and you—you scare too easily. There's nothing to it!"

"Do you know what Miss Beaton said, Kate? She was in seeing to Miss Gillies and Miss Gillies said to her she was going to ask for a transfer to a more godly place. She'd a nasty fever on her, I know that, but maybe that makes folks speak the truth—would you say that, Kate?"

"It would take several degrees of fever to affect the West Coast much!" said Kate, "but she might mean it. Oh yes, she might well mean it."

"That would be great" said David.

"You might get Fred to tackle the school cleaner while he's about it" said Kate. "I suppose you haven't heard of anyone?"

"You're laughing at me, Kate."

"If I wasn't," said Kate, "I might be believing."

"And that would be bad?"

"Yes," said Kate, "that would be bad." He stood silently,

scratching in his hair, reflecting. She finished writing, screwed up her pen and slipped the letters into a large envelope, which she put inside the jotter. "I'm glad Roddy's seeing Janet back, all the same," she said. "I wonder, what will they do."

"I wouldn't put it past him," said David, "to try slipping an arm round her." He looked out of the window. "Aye, it's dusk getting. But that wouldn't be till they were well past the houses. And then, if that's allowed—ach, he's had the devil of a bad time between the District Officer and the unco' guid and yon bad wee cratur Chrissie."

"Janet'll not need to let on to her father who it was saw her back."

"Trust Janet!"

"Ah well, they're in the same church and that might be a kind of help."

"You're an awful match-maker, Katie!"

"Well, it would be just what I'd like, Davie—if you're out of the running yourself! For then Janet would stay here and I think she'd have a good chance of being happy. I'd miss her terribly if she went. You know, she might just go and marry a visitor: so as to get away from the place. But here's me talking about marrying and all because two folk are walking up the Glen together and most likely never dreaming of such a thing."

"Aye, they'll have been speaking about the Hall. Until they're up out of the village, anyway. Poor Roddy, it's a lesson he's had."

"No one's the worse of a lesson. I've learnt plenty this last week. And doubtless it'll go on. I wonder if I dare ask Roddy how he got on when he comes back to us! Not if Mr Stewart is there."

"Ach, no, not before a Minister you couldn't, Kate. Poor Roddy, he'd be terrible affronted!"

"Poor Roddy, is it? Poor Ministers that we all treat as though they weren't human beings at all! If once we could start treating the Ministers like ordinary decent folk, we'd get help out of the churches instead of the harm they mostly do."

David looked round nervously: "That's a terrible thing to say, Kate—even if it's true and maybe it is. You've no notion of the difficulties I'm in with Religious Instruction! But—I was always feeling we'd need to put up with the way the churches are because without them—well, without them we'd be nothing but atheists."

"With horns and tails, remember, Davie! You know there are a few folk that contrive to be good without the fear of hell fire at their tails. But maybe we'll not manage to treat the Ministers right till they stop wanting to be treated as something special. I wonder which side of the fence Mr Fergusson's going to decide to fall off!"

"It'll be mostly his congregation are on the side of the Hall. And after all, it's for the congregation to tell the Kirk Sessions and the Kirk Sessions to tell the Minister. There was what John Knox meant."

"Yes, if it worked out like that. But it's like all democratic systems, it only works so long as the people are interested, and of course it leaves out the women." She had started drawing again on the cover of the minute book.

"Aye well, but the opinions of the women are carrying great weight with the men. I'd say Mr Fergusson would hardly dare go against us. And some way, Kate, och, I've the feeling this'll be a great committee we have now!"

"We've all of us got some kind of loyalty" said Kate, "and some kind of trust in one another. That ought to make us together more able to achieve something than we could ever do separately."

"Surely!" said David.

"Though I've had my wicked thoughts" said Kate, "that the best committee's a committee of one!" She had drawn a cynical-looking fish on the jotter; it had better have some seaweed.

"I know," said David, "and for a while it's great, but a committee of one's a wee bit apt to—to kind of lose touch—and if it's just to falter for a moment, then it's done. The same as Hitler was."

"How nice you are, David!" She looked up quickly and saw him back away a step, embarrassed, running his hands through his hair. "No, all I mean is, you're quite right. I hope no psychiatrist ever gets hold of this minute book!"

"How would he, Kate? It's our own minute book it is—everyone will know it now. Will I give you a lend of my red pencil?"

"No indeed, you shouldn't be encouraging me! Well, I must be getting back. But we're no further with all we were speaking on last Saturday. Would this Village Hall be for or against the Highland way of life?"

"And is that way of life a real thing any longer?"

"No, we've not thought about that. Or at least we've not decided. Nor how a Village Hall can become a gathering point of all that's good and vital in a community. And that without getting into the hands of the over-respectable."

"And whether should we try for a cinema——"

"No" said Kate, her hand on the minute book, "we haven't got down to any of the real problems yet. But we're going to!"